Mystical Richard Returns:
The Homecoming

Book 2

By Larry Cashman

Mystical Richard Returns: The Homecoming by Larry Cashman
Copyright © 2021. All rights reserved.

Published by Pen It! Publications, LLC in the U.S.A.
812-371-4128 www.penitpublications.com

ISBN: 978-1-954868-33-5
Cover Design by Donna Cook
Edited by Dina Husseini

Dedication

To Lynne, thank you for being part of my life and for your patience while I worked on this.

Special thanks to my sister, Janet Johnson for helping with the proofreading.

And a special thank you to Pen It! Publications. They made this all possible.

Table of Contents

1

Richard Returns

Monday, January 19, 2004

Matt knew he had to make the dreaded phone call to Mr. Turco.

He called and it went to his voicemail. "Mr. Turco, this is Matt White and unfortunately the end of our last performance did not go as smoothly as we hoped it would. I'm calling to apologize. Last Saturday's show was...well, I--- I don't know what happened to be honest, and I wish I could take it back, but I can't. Would it be possible to call me back at your earliest convenience? Thank you."

Around 11:00 AM, the phone rang. "Hello?" Matt said.

"Matt, this is Steve Turco. I'm not in the office today but I got your message."

"Mr. Turco?"

"Where do I begin, Matt? It was a disaster and I wasn't too sure that I was going to hear from you again. Two people called. They weren't too happy with what they saw."

"I understand," Matt said, with agitation in his voice.

"I'm not done."

"Sorry."

"As I was saying, that's not acceptable, however, another person called. Richard. Isn't there a Richard that works with you?"

"Yes, but he left, I have no way of getting in touch with him."

"Richard explained what went wrong, and he asked and pleaded with me not to hold this against you."

"Okay."

"I see no other way of doing this, except adhering to Richard's wishes."

"Which means?"

"On January 31st there won't be a show."

"That can be arranged," Matt smiled.

"This will give me some time to run an ad in the paper explaining something about malfunctions. However, Steve with a firmed tone, said, "On February 14th, you'll be back, but you have to clean up your act."

"If I don't?" Matt asked.

"You had better, if you want to work in this theater again."

"I will...Thank you for returning my call."

Matt hung up the phone and thought maybe this is fixable. He had 25 days to get in touch with Richard, but how? He remembered a note Richard left for him.

If you need me just think to yourself that you do, and I'll be in touch. Matt whispered to himself, Richard, I need to talk to you, now."

A FedEx truck pulled up in front of the house. US mail does not operate on Martin Luther King Day but FedEx does, Matt thought. The driver came up the front stairs and Matt opened the front door.

The driver said, "I have a package for Mr. White."

"That's me; do you need me to sign for it?"

As Matt was about to look up, the driver was already gone. He went to the kitchen to cut open the package and tore the paper off in a hurry. There was a note on top. Matt opened the package- inside was the journal Richard kept. There was another note on the cover.

Matt, I want to apologize for the embarrassment I caused you, again. I called Mr. Turco to make things right, hopefully. In the meantime, you should contact your friend Al, he'd love to work with you. Just use some of the money, under the bed, and get Mr. Firmani a new suit. He needs one. I understand that Mr. Turco told you to skip the next performance. That should give you and Al a few weeks to get together. Just go through the journal and start from the beginning. You'll notice that only the first trick is described. Once you've done that, the second one will be in the book. It would be a good time to stash this note, now. Sarah is on her way in, tell her you signed for a package, for Mr. Mooney, across the street.

Matt looked on the sofa and there was a package addressed to Mr. Michael Mooney.

Sarah walked into the living room and asked, "Matt, did I hear you talking to someone?"

Matt answered, "Yes, a FedEx driver asked if I could sign for a package for Mr. Mooney."

"Oh OK, I'm going to the other room to read if you want to join me."

"Sure, I'll be there in a minute." Matt pulled the note from behind his back and looked at it.

See, I told you she was coming.

Matt walked to where Sarah sat, "I called Mr. Turco. I told him Richard left."

"Did he sound happy?"

"Does Mr. Turco ever sound happy?"

"I get it. What will you do now?"

"I decided to call Al to see if he wants to take Richard's place."

"Really? Al can do that stuff? Could he replace Richard?"

"Honey, nobody can do what Richard does."

"You're right, Matt. I guess you know what's best for you."

"I hope so."

Tuesday, January 20th

Matt walked in the door around four fifteen and went right to the phone and called Al Firmani. It went right to Al's voicemail. Matt left this for a message: "Al, this is Matt, could you please give me a call when you get in?"

At ten minutes after five, the phone rang it was Al and he said, "Hey Matt this is Al. How are you?"

Matt answered, "Doing okay Al. Listen, I have some news here."

Al asked, "What's going on?"

Richard took off and then I got a letter from him in the mail. He recommended I ask you to help me with the shows. What do you think Al? Do you want to work with me in the theater?

Al answered, "Matt, I'd love to do that but I can't do what Richard did."

Matt responded, "Al do not worry; I have it covered for the both of us and you can learn as we move along. The good news is we're

3

going to JCPenney tomorrow after work and I'm buying you a new suit. I'll see you tomorrow, OK?"

Al answered, "OK."

Seven Months Later: Saturday, August 28th

It was a little more than seven months since Richard left the note on Matt's kitchen table. A couple of changes took place since that time. The first one was that Matt hired an old friend Al Firmani to take Richard's place. More importantly on June 7th Matt and Sarah became parents to a 9 lb. 9 oz. boy, they named Thomas.

Matt asked Sarah, "Honey, are you sure you'll be okay tonight by yourself?"

Sarah answered, "Of course I'll be fine and I will not be alone. Thomas is here with me."

Matt said, "Okay, I'm going to head out. I told Al I will pick him up around five so we can go over some things." Matt headed out the door and drove to Al's house.

Al came outside and got into Matt's van. Al said, "Hey Matt, another big night for us.

Matt replied, "Yes, and I don't mind telling you I'm getting nervous again. Al, it's not you. I managed to pick up a lot from Richard and I wish I could've picked up some self-confidence."

Al replied, "Matt, I'll give it my best, and try not to let you down."

Matt pulled the van into the parking garage and said, "Al, that's all I'm looking for."

They made their way into the theater and headed for the front row. Once inside, they were seated and Matt said to Al, "Remember we ask for a volunteer and we have them come up and look the piano over. The good part is when we have them sit and play a couple of songs. I'm sure the audience will like it. Now, if you can give me a few minutes I just want to rest my eyes."

Just then they heard a voice coming from behind them and Matt heard the person behind them ask, "When are you two lads going to spice things up a bit?"

Matt and Al both turned in the seats and Matt thought the voice sounded familiar. When they turned around, they did not see anyone.

Then they heard the voice again, "You should be looking up front," and Richard was standing on the stage right in front of them.

Al whispered, "Isn't that Mr. Jenkins?"

Matt answered, "I hope so and if it is, he'll be welcomed back."

Al replied, "Of course!" Richard said, "Al Firmani front and center please; I have a request for you. Do you know the Dunkin' Donuts at the end of the corner?"

"That's almost three and a half miles from here," Al replied.

"I know this," Richard said, "And, that's why I have arranged to have a car out front for you. Please, I need you to go outside and get to your destination. We need four large coffees brought back here. Here is a fifty-dollar bill and we'll be waiting. Thank you, Al."

Richard waited until Al was out of earshot and then sat down next to Matt. He asked Matt, "How have you been?"

Matt said to Richard, "Look, I know there was a mistake made. I never said everything would go off without a hitch. I never expected that from you." Richard tried to say something. "Please, I'm not done. I hope you're not going to take off again if something doesn't go right. Mistakes happen and we'll get past them. Now, I'm finished. Oh, and by the way, the great news for me, and Sarah is our son Thomas was born on June 7th."

Richard put his hands out and said, "Congratulations! I trust mother and son are doing well. I know they are."

Matt looked at his watch and said, "I hope Al makes it back on time."

Richard responded with, "Of course he will and if he doesn't, I would love to fill in."

Matt smiled and asked, "Do you mean that?"

Richard answered back, "You bet I do but stick with Al for tonight and I'll watch in the background like before. I can see Al coming back in now; I'll just go check the piano." Richard went over to the piano. He ran his fingers along with the keys and then he brushed his fingers in the other direction. He called out to Matt, "I got this covered."

The show got underway and Matt and Al were performing at their best. The time got to be about 8:40 and Matt made the announcement, "Ladies and gentlemen, we have time for one more."

Al got a couple of assistants to help move the piano out to the center stage. Matt called out to the audience, "We need a volunteer to come up and I'm looking for someone that has never played the piano before. Please, this will only work if you meet that criteria."

A woman who looked to be in her mid-30s raised her hand and stood up. She said, "I'll do it."

Matt replied, "Very good, please come on up here."

Once on the stage, Matt extended his hand and said, "Hello, my name is Matt and this is my assistant Al. Your name is?"

The girl put out her hand and said, "Nice to meet you, I'm Maureen McGuiness." Matt said, "Maureen the way this works is you'll sit at the piano and you're going to play a couple of songs. First, I want you to inspect the piano and look for any recording devices. Al will lift the lid and you'll see there is no tape recorder under there. It will be all you."

Maureen looked around and underneath the piano. Al lifted the lid and she checked under there as well. She stated, "I don't see a tape recorder."

Matt replied, "Then please have a seat and we'll begin." Maureen sat on the bench and Matt put his hands on her shoulders and said, "Play 'Saturday in the Park' by Chicago." Maureen started playing and the audience started cheering. She played two other songs after that.

Maureen sat on the bench when she was done and said, "Thank you, Mr. White, that was fun."

Matt said to Maureen, "Please stay where you are while I say goodnight to the audience." Matt called out to the audience one more time, "Ladies and gentlemen that concludes our show for tonight. My name is Matt White and this is Al Firmani. We hope everyone had a good time and please drive safely." Matt turned to Maureen and said, "Just to show my appreciation for your efforts I want to give you a couple of free passes for another show. Let me give you a hint too. Wait a few weeks and you'll see a new act."

Maureen put her hand out and said, "Thank you very much," and she walked off the stage and left the theater.

Richard came out from behind the curtain and said, "I want to say bravo to both of you."

Al looked over and said, "Thank you Mr. Jenkins; that means a lot coming from you."

2

The Diner

Richard asked, "Would you two gents care to finish the night off at the diner? It's my treat."

Al spoke up and said, "Jeannie is waiting for me but thank you for asking."

Matt answered, "Mr. Jenkins I would be honored to be your guest at the diner."

Richard replied, "Good, you can drive."

The two of them made their way over to the diner and sat in their usual booth. Matt started the conversation, "Richard I am very happy to see you; however, I have to tell you I was taken back that you left me without warning."

Richard replied, "That's understandable Matt, and I thought I let you down."

"We had many great shows together and the last one did not go so well. You did not fail me you did not let me down. Now, I have two questions for you. Are you back to stay and do you want a comfortable bed to sleep in tonight?"

Richard answered right away, "Yes, and yes."

Matt continued, "Your room is just like you left it. We did not change anything in anticipation of your return. You're back and I know Sarah will be happy to see you. Come home with me and you'll have your old room back."

Richard responded with, "Thank you, Matt, and please let's go back to the living arrangements as before. I will take care of all the cleaning and cooking. The good news is I have more to add to the journal."

Matt asked, "Are you ready to head out? I am beat and I am ready for bed."

Richard stood up and said, "After you Mr. White."

Sunday morning Matt came downstairs around six twenty and Richard was sitting at the table with his newspaper in front of him and his coffee. Matt greeted Richard first, "Good morning Richard. You know all the times I made coffee in the morning I've never been able to get it to smell like the coffee you brewed."

Richard replied, "Good morning Mr. White; thank you for the compliment and I am so glad you didn't cancel the newspaper."

Richard asked, "Can I fix you some eggs and toast for breakfast?"

"I'd love an omelet but eggs are on the shopping list for today."

"Has that ever stopped me before?"

Matt answered, "You're right; I forgot. Sarah will be getting up soon or whenever Thomas is hungry."

Richard offered, "That'll be an additional eighteen minutes from now. I can't wait to see the little guy. Did you know he's going to be a doctor?"

Matt answered, "No, I didn't know that but I suppose you can tell me in what field."

"Of course, I can, Thomas is going to be a vascular surgeon. He'll also get straight A marks when he goes to Harvard Medical School."

"WOW! You're setting the bar quite high for him, aren't you?"

"No, I don't think so. I am just telling you what's going to happen."

Just then a door clicked upstairs and Matt looked at the time. Eighteen minutes had passed on the dot. Matt went to the bottom of the stairs and called to Sarah, "Honey, would you like an omelet for breakfast?"

Sarah answered, "I'd love that but I don't feel like cooking now."

Matt replied, "You don't have to."

The kitchen door swung open and Richard said, "Hello Mrs. White. It's been a long time."

Sarah replied, "It certainly has and we missed you." Sarah hugged Richard and said, "It's great to see you."

Richard added, "Thank you, it's nice to be back and now please let me fix you two a hot breakfast." Richard went back to the kitchen and went straight away to the cooking. He couldn't help but notice how untidy the place was. Richard thought to himself how could the house get like this in seven months?

Richard emerged from the kitchen with two hot plates of food and brought them to the dining table.

He said, "Please sit and eat."

Matt and Sarah had their breakfast and Sarah commented, "I forgot how good your cooking tastes. When you were here you spoiled us with all the good meals."

Richard replied, "I was very happy to do it. After all, your husband gave me a nice home to stay in and he introduced me to some of his friends. If it wasn't for Matt, I'd still be sleeping in the back of the theater."

Sarah said, "Don't say that; it's not true."

"Thank you for the encouraging words Sarah and I believe you need to tend to Thomas now."

Right when Richard said that coming from the baby monitor were the wake-up cries from Thomas. Sarah said, "I'll be back in a couple of minutes. Sounds like someone is hungry."

Fifteen Minutes Later

Sarah brought Thomas downstairs and said, "Richard I have someone I want you to meet. This is our son Thomas and he's almost three months."

Richard looked at him and said, "It's a pleasure to meet you, Thomas. Are you being good for your mother, I hope? I think I found something that belongs to you." Richard reached behind his back and into view came the cutest brown bear. It made Thomas curl up a smile.

Sarah said, "WOW! I never saw him smile before."

Richard replied, "Well, I'm sure he'll be doing it a lot more now."

Matt added, "I'm sure of it. Now, if we can only get him to sleep through the night."

Richard offered, "That's not a big deal. We can take care of that right now. Thomas, it was a pleasure to meet you, however, my coffee is calling me."

Richard finished his third coffee which was no major feat for him. Matt asked Richard, "Would you care to take a ride to Albertson's later?"

Richard answered, "Let me know when you're ready."

Sarah asked, "Honey, do you have my list?"

"Yes, I do and I promise not to mess it up."

Matt asked Richard, "Are you ready to go?"

Richard answered, "Yes I am."

Once in the store, Matt said, "Sarah gave me a small list of things we need."

Richard replied, "Of course, I already have those up here." Richard pointed to his temple.

On the ride back from Albertson's Richard asked Matt, "So, is Mr. Firmani working out for you?"

Matt answered, "I like the fact Al was willing to get in there and help, but there's something about him. Al doesn't have the personality for this. He's so serious all the time; he needs to loosen up a little. Al doesn't have the finesse that we had as a team."

Richard offered, "Perhaps we can come to an arrangement that should remedy the situation."

Matt asked, "Arrangement, what kind of arrangement?"

Richard explained, "OK, I can fix it so Mr. Firmani gets a nice promotion at his work. With his promotion comes a lot more money and unfortunately longer days. Believe me, after one week of this new position Al will be begging to get out of this."

Matt asked, "Do you think this will work? Wait a minute, this means I'll be going solo again."

Richard added, "I know it will work and I could use some part-time work." Matt responded, "Mr. Jenkins, you are making my day."

Richard added, "Glad to hear it and you can expect a phone call from Mr. Firmani this Friday evening."

Friday, September 3rd

Friday evening came around and it was just like Richard predicted. The phone rang and Sarah answered the call.

"Hello?"

"Hello, this is Al. May I speak to Matt please?"

Sarah replied, "Hello Al, this is Sarah. Let me go find him. I'm sure he's in here somewhere."

Matt came to the phone and said, "Hey Al, how are you?"

Al answered back, "Matt I have good news and bad news. I got a promotion at work and with that came a hefty raise but more responsibility and more hours."

Matt replied, "There's nothing wrong with that; everyone can use a little more money."

"Oh sure, I can use the extra income Matt but I'm only one week into this and I am exhausted. I have a question for you. Matt, I am sorry to ask this, but would you be able to get a replacement for me?"

Matt replied, "Al, I understand, and thank you for working with me the past seven months. You were a great help and you were there when I needed you. I couldn't have done it without you."

Matt put the phone down and said, "Yes" to himself, and then he went looking for Richard.

Richard was upstairs taking care of the dusting. Matt found him in the spare bedroom and Richard asked, "Did Mr. Firmani just give notice over the phone?"

Matt answered, "Yes, he did and it was just like you called it."

"OK, so let's pick up where we left off beginning Saturday the 11th. I'm certain we can do that performance over again and this time there'll be no complications."

Matt asked, "You mean that trick with the giant saw blade coming at me?"

Richard responded, "Precisely! I took the liberty of hiring a couple of assistants. It looks more professional."

"That'll cut into the profits."

"Not exactly, I'll be taking care of their compensation."

"Okay, as long as you don't mind doing that."

3

The Next Show

Eight Days Later: Saturday, September 11th

Saturday morning Matt came downstairs around 6:30 and Richard was in his usual spot drinking his coffee with his newspaper in front of him. Matt greeted Richard, "Good morning Richard, how are you?"

Richard answered, "Just splendid Matt, and good morning to you."

"I find I'm getting used to rising this early every morning including weekends. I don't get the luxury of sleeping later."

Richard replied, "Mr. White, welcome to the world of getting older. It catches up with everybody."

Later That Afternoon

Sarah was sitting in the living room with her feet up on the loveseat. She had the latest Sue Grafton novel 'R is for Ricochet'. She knew she had to take advantage of Thomas being down for his naps because these didn't last long sometimes less than thirty minutes.

Matt walked into the living room and asked, "Is he...?"

Sarah pointed to the baby monitor and put a finger up to her lips signaling Matt not to make any loud movements. Matt nodded and said, "Relax, we'll talk later."

Matt went to the kitchen and poured himself a coffee. That was one of the benefits Richards provided when he lived there. There was always freshly brewed coffee. Sarah came into the kitchen behind Matt and put her arms around him and said, "Hey you!"

Matt asked, "How's your book?"

Sarah answered, "It's good; I'll get back to it later."

Matt replied, "Earlier, I wanted to suggest to you it would be nice to get together with the Gilhoolys. We can have them over some night. I have the show tonight if you want to give Karen a call."

Sarah replied, "Sounds like a plan. I'll call Karen later on."

Later On, Around Five-Forty

Matt and Richard headed out to the theater. They took their seats in the front row and Richard said, "I have it worked out so tonight's performance will go perfectly smooth. There's no need to worry about any glitches."

They started their show right at 7:30 on the dot. Matt and Richard performed their regular illusions flawlessly. It was 8:40 and Matt made an announcement, "Ladies and gentlemen, we have time for one more."

Richard had the monitor above come on and said to the audience, "Please look at the screen above you; this is a film clip of David Copperfield performing his death saw trick. Tonight, we are going to put on our version and we hope you enjoy it."

The curtain closed and the stagehands worked diligently moving the props in place.

Matt came out to the center to address the audience, "Ladies and gentlemen a lot of magicians follow the steps of David Copperfield and continue to reinvent this trick. It's among the most famous tricks in the history of magic and illusion. Copperfield was able to make the audience believe that he was sawing himself in half. Until this very day despite the number of versions of tricks, this trick has never been surpassed. We'll begin at the end of this video."

Matt was brought over to a flat table and he laid down on his stomach. Two assistants strapped him down on the table but they did not cover his torso like was done in the Copperfield version. The buzz saw hung above Matt lowering slowly by a few feet every twenty seconds. Matt was struggling to free himself of the wrist restraints but had no luck. The saw dropped again and now was only ten inches above him. The saw lowered itself and was almost in contact with Matt's back. The audience was in a low murmur. The saw lowered again and simultaneously one of the assistants ran over to the table to free Matt of the restraints. Off to the right, the audience could see Matt walking out to the center of the stage. Applause and laughter were coming from the audience at the same time.

Richard said to Matt, "I'm glad to see you're okay."

Matt replied, "I'm fine but I'm going to need a new jacket." Matt took his coat off to show Richard and the audience there with fray marks and rips on the back of his jacket.

Richard responded, "I know the name of a good tailor."

"Let's say goodnight," Matt said to the audience, "Ladies and gentlemen that concludes our performance for tonight. My name is Matt White and this is my good friend and partner Richard Jenkins. If you like what you saw, please tell your friends. Have a good night and please drive safely."

Matt then looked at Richard and said, "Well Mr. Jenkins, looks like we pulled it off again."

Richard offered, "Of course we did and we had a great time doing it."

The audience filed out and Matt asked, "Are we ready to head out Mr. Jenkins?"

"Lead the way, Mr. White."

Sunday Morning, September 12th

Matt came downstairs on Sunday morning around six-thirty. Richard was sitting in the corner enjoying his coffee reading his paper. Richard greeted Matt first, "Good morning Matt, how are you?"

Matt answered, "OK, and good morning to you Richard. I thought last night's performance made up for what happened back in January."

Richard added, "I agree with you and if I'm not mistaken the boss is on her way downstairs."

Matt replied, "WOW! Usually, I can hear the doorknob unlatching but not this time."

"That's because you didn't close it all the way so there was no click." Richard stood up and took out a bottle of grapefruit juice from the fridge.

17

Matt asked, "How did you know which juice to grab?"

Richard answered, "I think by now you should know I have 99% of the answers."

Sarah came downstairs wearing her robe and entered the kitchen. She said, "Good morning honey. How was your show last night?" and she leaned in to kiss Matt.

Matt responded, "The show was great."

Next Sarah said, "Good morning Richard," and before Sarah could say anything about it, Richard handed her a glass of grapefruit juice. "Thank you, Richard."

Richard offered, "You're welcome and if you'll excuse me, I need to start on the laundry."

Sarah put down her glass and said to Matt, "I called Karen Gilhooly last night and I invited them over next Saturday for Chinese food. At first, I thought I would offer them home cooking but Richard makes me look sick in that department. I figure by us getting takeout he won't get the feeling of us treating him like he's a servant here. I don't know about you but I do not think of him in that way."

Matt added, "That's great honey about the Gilhoolys coming over and I don't think of Richard as a house servant either. I think he knows that."

A few seconds later sounds were coming from the baby monitor. Matt said, "Honey allow me; you work hard enough around here."

Matt hustled up to the bedroom expecting to lift Thomas out of the crib and Richard was holding him. Thomas had a big smile going. Richard said to Matt, "He's just letting us know he's awake and hungry," and he handed Thomas off to Matt.

Matt said, "Thank you, hey I just noticed Thomas wasn't crying when you were holding him."

"That's because he felt safe. I know it sounds hard to believe but an infant can sense if the person holding them is nervous. I came up here to retrieve the linens when I heard Thomas wake up. It's time for me to get back to it." Richard went in the hallway and there was a laundry basket floating about three feet off the floor following him. There were already sheets in the basket and Richard turned around and grabbed the basket and said, "Here we go."

Matt brought Thomas downstairs intending to grab a bottle for him. Sarah met Matt at the doorway to the kitchen and handed him the bottle. "Here you go," Sarah offered.

Matt was sitting in the wing chair while feeding Thomas. Thomas' eyes closed as he finished his bottle. Sarah looked on and commented, "Like father, like son. I need to remember to have my camera ready for next time."

Sarah very carefully took Thomas out of Matt's arms and said, "I'll put him down and be right back

."Matt stretched his arms and legs out as much as he could. He was not keen on sitting still for fifteen minutes. Sarah came back downstairs and said to Matt, "I have a few things on a shopping list. Do you mind going before it gets too crowded?"

Matt answered, "Of course not, I'll just check with Richard to see if he wants to tag along. He usually does."

Eight-Twenty-Five

Richard and Matt left for Albertson's and on the way, Matt said to Richard, "You probably already know this. Sarah invited some friends for next Saturday."

Richard commented, "Ah yes the Gilhoolys. I hope they're getting along alright and while we're here, are we getting food for Saturday night?"

Matt answered, "No, I thought we could get takeout Chinese to give you a night off from cooking. Oh, and you will be eating with us."

Richard added, "Very well Mr. White, as you wish."

Matt pushed the carriage around the corner and he realized what was happening with the groceries. Every time Matt pushed the carriage into the next aisle more groceries were added into the carriage.

Matt said to Richard, "Now I see how you finish the shopping so fast. I've only seen you put one thing in the carriage so far and that was in the first aisle. Every time we get to a new aisle, items are magically added to the carriage."

Richard offered, "This is true and Matt believe me I make sure there's no one else that can see the carriage. I don't want to bring any unnecessary attention to us. You see I grew accustomed to getting rides over here from Gary and I didn't want to tie him up too long. He was nice enough to donate his time."

Matt responded, "I guess that sounds reasonable. Let's get this stuff home."

Richard offered, "Just a minute, would you mind bringing the carriage through? I'd like to get Sarah a scratch ticket."

They loaded the bags in the car and Richard handed Matt the ticket and said, "You should give this to Sarah. It shows you're thinking of her."

Matt replied, "Flowers are the answer to that. I'm tired; I don't feel like going back in."

Richard added, "Just give her the carnations then," and Richard pointed to the floral bouquet sticking out of the top of one of the bags. "Matt, you give her the flowers and I'll give her the lottery ticket."

They were back at the house by nine twenty-five and Matt carried in the groceries. He didn't see Sarah. After everything was put away, Matt crept upstairs trying not to make a sound. Sarah was reading in bed with her legs up. She put her index finger over her lips indicating for Matt not to make any noise.

Matt just waved and mouthed the words, "I'll be downstairs."

Matt went back downstairs and Richard was pouring a coffee. Richard asked, "Care for a pick me up?"

Matt answered, "Sure!" Richard and Matt sat at the table together drinking coffee.

Sarah came downstairs a little before 11:00 and the flowers were already in a vase on the table. She noticed the flowers and asked, "Are those for me? What's the occasion?"

Matt answered, "The occasion is I love you; oh, and by the way, Richard bought you a scratch ticket."

Sarah smiled and said, "Thank you, Richard." Sarah reached in the cabinet in the bowl with the loose change for a quarter. She stood against the counter working on her ticket and started getting excited. "Matt, Matt, I think I have something here. Please double-check me."

Matt looked at the ticket and said, "Whoa honey, you won $5,000. It's time for a celebration." Matt called, "Richard, Sarah won on the ticket."

Richard replied, "Excellent!" He already knew she was going to win. "Matt, I only buy winning tickets. How are we going to celebrate? I know, we can get pizza and salad from Maggiano's."

Matt asked, "What do you think honey?"

Sarah answered, "Oh, I'm good with that. Matt, can you look at this again?" Sarah handed Matt the ticket.

Matt looked at Sarah's ticket and asked, "What am I looking for?"

Sarah answered, "Honey I swear I looked at the ticket before I started scratching and it said WIN $5,000. Now, it says WIN up to $15,000."

Matt responded with, "OK, I believe you. Wait, is that part of the ticket a hologram?"

Sarah fired back, "No, I don't think so; look at it again."

Richard overheard Matt asking about the hologram that's when he knew it was time to change something. Matt had the ticket in his hand and he said, "Honey, here it is right here in the corner and it also says WIN EITHER OR. That's why the first time you saw $5,000."

Sarah asked Matt, "Do you want to go with me to the store so I can show them my ticket?"

Matt thought for a minute and answered, "I will, but I think we need to pick up a claim form at the store when it's that big of a prize. I have a thought; I'll stop at the store and pick it up on the way to DiMaggio's"

Sarah smiled and replied, "Sounds good to me. I can't wait to see what EITHER OR on the ticket means."

Later That Day: Around Five O'clock

Matt announced, "I'm leaving for Maggiano's to get our dinner. Richard, would you like to come for the ride?"

Richard answered, "Love to, let me get my jacket."

The two of them got in Matt's van and Matt said, "I just have to stop at the market and pick up a claim form for Sarah."

Richard asked, "Don't you think a bottle of red wine like a nice Merlot would be in order?"

Matt answered, "That's a great idea."

"I know and that's why I mentioned it."

From Albertson's, they headed over to Maggiano's and were back at the house a little before six. The three of them were eating their dinner and Sarah mentioned to Richard, "Richard, thank you for the scratch ticket. I haven't bought a scratch ticket in years and I never had any luck with them."

Richard replied, "You're welcome Sarah. I picked out that ticket for you thinking a winner would brighten your day."

Sarah replied, "It sure did. Tomorrow, I'm back to work after extended maternity leave. I have to drop Thomas off at daycare in the morning."

Monday Morning, September 13th

Matt came downstairs around six twenty-five to get coffee. Richard was sitting at the table with his newspaper in front of him. Matt greeted Richard, "Good morning Richard, how are you?"

Richard answered, "Just splendid Matt. I understand Sarah is bringing Thomas to daycare today for the first time."

Matt was leaning against the counter and sipping his coffee. He nodded to Richard in agreement and then rinsed his coffee cup. Matt then said, "I hope she's okay with it. I already told Sarah a couple of times she did not have to go back to work if she doesn't want to."

Richard added, "Matt, I'm sure Sarah wants to feel productive and like she's contributing."

Matt responded with, "Perhaps, I have to go. I should be back by four fifteen."

Richard replied, "Have a good day Mr. White." Matt walked out of the front door and left for work.

The front door closed and Sarah was coming down the stairs. Sarah made her way to the kitchen and Richard greeted her in a quiet voice, "Good morning Sarah and good morning Thomas."

Richard handed Sarah a heated-up bottle to give to Thomas. Richard asked at the same time, "May I have the honors?", and he reached out to hold Thomas.

Sarah answered, "OK, but don't be surprised if he starts screaming because he doesn't know you."

Richard put his arms out to hold Thomas and proceeded to feed him his bottle. Thomas did not even let out a whimper. Sarah looked on and could see how content her son was in Richard's arms.

Sarah asked, "Could you hold him a few minutes longer? I want to get his travel bag ready."

Richard replied, "Of course!"

Sarah went into Thomas's room, grabbed the bag and she noticed it felt heavy. She opened it up and saw the bag was already packed. Sarah brought it downstairs and left it at the bottom of the landing.

Meanwhile, Richard was in the kitchen cradling Thomas. Sarah asked, "How are you doing?"

Richard answered, "Just fine, the little guy is almost done with his breakfast."

Sarah added, "I'll take him so I can burp him."

Richard fired back, "Nonsense, please you need to get breakfast in you and it's waiting on the table. Please go sit before it gets cold."

Sarah looked at the table and there was a plate for her with eggs, toast, and a slice of melon. She went back into the kitchen and said, "I just need to get some juice."

Richard made a motion with his head signaling her to look on the table. There was the beverage of choice waiting for her and today it was grapefruit.

About Twenty-Five Minutes Later

Richard followed Sarah out to the car while toting the travel bag out for her. She closed the door and said, "I'm off."

Richard replied, "Have a great day Sarah and let's hope Thomas enjoys the daycare."

That line was just something for Richard to say. Richard had another plan in mind for daycare. He never believed in daycare facilities for the mere fact that these facilities were run by an individual or two that had to monitor ten to twelve infants. How could a child feel safe there or for that matter how an adult can spend enough time with any of the babies.

Richard went back into the house and spent about two hours cleaning. He decided it was time for coffee and he set his cup down on the dining room table and pulled his journal out of the drawer. Richard thought to himself it was up to him to add to the journal knowing Matt was too busy to contribute.

He opened the book and with a wave of his hand eight more pages filled in. Richard was satisfied after looking over his work and knew that would keep them busy for a while. He put the journal back in the drawer and returned his coffee mug to the kitchen. Richard continued with the cleaning.

Later That Day, Around Four-Fifteen

Matt came home from work and went into the house. He called for Richard, "Hello Richard, are you here?"

Richard was sitting in one of the wing chairs with a book on his lap. He answered, "Hello Matt, how was your day at work?"

Matt answered, "Stressful and that's because most of the eighth-graders are last year's seventh graders and we had to spend the entire class reviewing some of last year's material. This is stuff they should have remembered."

Richard responded, "I have the solution that will fix this."

Matt asked, "Really, and what would that be?"

Richard answered, "Let me come to your school and talk to your students. I will dazzle them with some great card tricks."

Matt looked at Richard with a puzzled look and asked, "You think by showing my students some card tricks will expand their IQ?"

Richard added, "No, but I'll be putting a spell on the whole lot while I have their attention. What time do you want me there?"

Matt responded with, "Is eight-thirty too early?"

Richard answered, "Not at all seeing as I'm up every day by 4:10. Now, if you'll excuse me, I need to get dinner started. I hope you're in the mood for pork chops tonight."

Matt replied, "I'm so hungry I could eat a horse."

Richard commented, "You skipped lunch again, didn't you?"

"Yes, but it wasn't my intention; it's just that I got caught up with reading the curriculum. I kept drifting off while I was thinking about our next show. I should have been thinking about Sarah starting her day by having to bring Thomas to the daycare."

Richard added, "I'm sure Sarah is doing enough worrying about that on her own. There is no need for you to fret over it too. Oh, can you take out the breadcrumbs please?"

It was six-fifteen and Sarah walked in with Thomas.

"Hello Matt, Richard," she said.

Matt replied, "Hey honey, how was your day?" Matt kissed Sarah *hello*.

Richard stepped in and asked, "Hello Sarah, how was your first day back at work?"

Sarah answered, "Hello Richard, it was good to be back. I'll be back in a couple of minutes."

Sarah put Thomas in the baby carrier and put him on the table so Matt could keep an eye on him. Matt immediately took over his meager parenting skills and started making funny faces at Thomas.

Richard caught a glimpse of this and asked, "What are you doing?"

Matt answered, "Just trying to keep Thomas entertained."

Richard added, "There are better ways than that; here put the salad and bowls on the table. Then come back and watch and learn."

Back in the kitchen, Matt saw a small stuffed bear dancing in front of Thomas.

His eyes were glued to the bear and Matt commented, "Sorry, I can't zap a bear out of Thomas's room when I want to."

Richard replied, "Here, it's your turn to move the bear around while I finish the salad."

Sarah put Thomas in the bassinet and the three of them sat down for dinner. Matt asked Sarah, "Overall how was your day?"

Sarah answered, "I like being back at work, taking care of the claims. I've only been back one day but I wish something could be done about the daycare for Thomas."

Matt asked, "What's wrong with the daycare?"

Sarah answered, "It's not that there is something wrong with it. What bothers me is having to leave over an hour earlier than usual to get to work at a reasonable time."

Richard was sitting there listening and added, "Sarah, may I offer a possible solution?"

Sarah answered, "I'm all ears."

Richard continued, "Okay, you finish out the week with the daycare facility. You're going to drop Thomas off and Matt will pick him up on his way home. Starting Monday, you'll be going to work except for dropping off Thomas. Thomas will not have to be moved out of his environment."

Sarah asked, "Who'll be watching Thomas?"

Richard answered, "Yours truly and if you're looking for the feminine touch..." and, Richard pointed to the phone.

The phone rang and Sarah said, "Excuse me please."

Matt asked Richard, "What's going on?"

Richard answered, "Just a little problem solving and I believe this will work out so everyone's happy."

Sarah was on the phone in the living room yakking it up with Denise. Denise told her she was laid off from a job but still had her job at the card store.

Sarah asked Denise, "So, what are you going to do now?"

Denise answered, "I'm not in any hurry to get back to work. It's so hard to find the right job. I was going to help my sister Eileen with her four-year-old but she decided not to take the job at Liberty Mutual."

Sarah replied, "I have an idea that will use up your time if you're interested and I will pay you."

Denise asked, "What's that?"

Sarah replied with another question, "How are you at babysitting when there's a three-month-old involved?"

Denise answered, "I can do that. I have plenty of experience from watching my nephew although it was almost four years ago."

Sarah replied, "I'm sure you'll do fine. Richard is here during the day if you need help with anything. So, what do you think?"

Denise answered, "Would it be alright if I come to meet Thomas first? I mean, no offense but I'm not keen on watching a colicky baby."

Sarah continued, "Sure, do you want to come over one night this week or Sunday afternoon?"

Denise answered, "Sunday works for me."

Sarah said goodbye to Denise and came in the dining room and said, "I think my dilemma is solved and before I forget, Matt thank you for packing up Thomas' bag this morning."

Sarah kissed Matt on the cheek. Matt smiled and said, "Normally, I would say you're welcome but I have no idea what you're talking about."

Sarah said, "Hmmm, if you didn't do it and I didn't pack it up." Matt pointed to the kitchen door without saying a word.

The kitchen door opened and Richard explained, "Just trying to help; I hope you don't mind."

4

Richard Visits the School

Matt came downstairs at six-twenty to grab a coffee and start his day. Richard was sitting at the kitchen table in the corner with the newspaper folded in front of him. Matt greeted Richard, "Good morning Richard. How are you?"

Richard answered, "Doing okay here, and good morning to you too."

Matt took a sip of his coffee and asked Richard, "Did you mean what you said about coming to my school and talking to my students?"

"Matthew, I'll be there if you'll have me. I already have a plan for the class. Did you say eight-thirty?"

"Yes, I did. How are you going to get to school?"

"Matt, I am still capable of walking."

"Okay, I have to go. I'll see you around eight-thirty."

Matt got in his car and headed off to work. Right as Matt was leaving Sarah came downstairs carrying Thomas. Richard greeted the two of them, "Good morning Sarah, good morning Master Thomas."

Sarah replied, "Good morning Richard. Can you help me for ten minutes?"

"Of course." Richard took Thomas from Sarah and gave him his bottle.

Sarah ran back upstairs and finished getting ready for work. She came back down fifteen minutes later. Richard had Thomas' bag all packed and ready to go.

He said to Sarah, "Here, you take Thomas and I'll follow you out to the car with his bag."

29

Sarah responded, "Thank you, Richard. You're a big help. I'll see you around six-thirty."

One Hour Later: Around Eight O'clock

Richard headed out the door a few minutes after eight. He walked two blocks. Richard looked to the left and then to the right. Once he was satisfied, he would not be seen he let himself vanish and he showed up a block away from Matt's school. Richard had never been to Matt's school before.

He had the foresight to make sure he appeared behind the school out of sight. Richard went into the front door and up the first staircase on the left. Matt's classroom was the first one on the left. Richard looked at his watch and it was only eight-twenty. With ten minutes to spare he knocked on the classroom door.

Matt opened the door and said, "Hey, you made it."

Richard replied, "Yes, I did. So, where are these future Rhodes Scholars?"

"Well, you're ten minutes early. My first class is at eight thirty-five. Now, that you're here, you can tell me what you're going to do."

"Yes, I can, but I'm not going to. Do not worry. You will not be disappointed with the results." A few seconds later a very loud school bell rang and Richard asked, "Does that happen every morning?"

"Yes, and it happens every three hours. That was the warning bell to let students know it's eight-thirty."

Richard replied, "That is loud and an eye-opener. Okay, before we start, how many students are there? How many of them are having trouble?"

"There's seventeen and four of them need more help than the others."

Richard replied, "Okay, got it."

The classroom door opened and two of the students walked in followed by three more.

Matt said, "Good morning." The remaining twelve students were inside and seated by eight-thirty.

Matt addressed the class and said, "Boys and girls, I want to introduce you to a very good friend of mine. This is Richard Jenkins. He's going to talk to you for a few minutes."

Matt said to Richard, "They're all yours." Matt then walked to the back of the room and took a seat at one of the empty desks.

Richard stood in the center of the room and said, "Okay, I'd like to have everyone's attention if I may. I'm here to explain to you how important it is for you to pay attention to what is going on around you. I am here to show you what can happen when you're not alert. Okay, for example, it just so happens I have a deck of playing cards in my pocket."

Matt called out from the back, "Wow! That's unusual. Sorry, go ahead."

Richard continued, "Okay, hopefully, there'll be no more interruptions. Excuse me, your name is Jason, correct?"

The student nodded and said, "Yes."

Richard continued, "Jason, can you please take these cards, examine them, and make sure they're all here."

Jason took the cards from Richard. He fanned through the cards and counted them. Jason said, "They look normal to me."

Richard said, "Excellent. Now, Jason, when you fanned through them did you notice any two of the same? By that, I mean two of the same cards."

Jason answered, "I didn't see any two cards that were the same."

Richard replied, "I think maybe you should look again."

Jason opened the cards a second time. His jaw dropped. The left half of the cards were all the king of hearts. The right half changed to the ace of spades except for the last two cards. The last two cards changed to the two jokers.

Jason yelled out, "WOW! How did you do that?"

Richard answered, "I hope you're paying attention. I want you to look at the cards again."

Jason opened the cards a third time. And once more he was stunned. Two of the cards were the king of hearts. Six of the cards changed to the eight of clubs. Four of the cards changed to the nine of diamonds. Eight of the cards were the jack of spades. Six of the cards changed to the five of hearts. Four of the cards were the jack of clubs. Eight of the cards changed to the queen of diamonds. Six of the cards changed into the ten of spades. Four of the cards were the three of hearts. Two of the cards changed to the seven of clubs. Two of the cards changed into the five of diamonds and the two jokers remained the same.

At this time, another student moved her desk closer to Jason.

Richard asked, "Okay, Ashley, are you paying attention? Do you know if Jason was watching close enough?"

Ashley answered, "I am watching you close but I cannot figure out how you did that,"

Richard replied, "You're not supposed to because then it wouldn't be a mystery and then there goes the magic. Let me show you this. This one is good."

Richard took out another deck of cards.

He said, "Ashley, it's your job to check through the cards and then give them a good mix."

Ashley looked through the cards and then gave them a good shuffle.

Richard continued, "Ashley, please count out the top thirty cards and put them face down on your desk. That leaves twenty-two cards that we do not need."

Richard then scooped up the pile of thirty cards. He dealt the first fifteen cards and put them face down in front of Ashley. He took the remaining fifteen cards and laid them out in front of himself.

Richard spoke up and said, "Please pick one of the fifteen cards and do not reveal it to me. Just whisper it in Jason's ear. Let me know when you're ready."

Ashley leaned toward Jason and whispered her selection in his ear. She said, "I'm ready."

Richard said, "Very well. He picked up the fifteen cards that were laid out on the desk. He then laid them out again on the desk. Richard then asked Ashley, "Is your card here?"

Ashley stared at the laid-out cards. She spoke up and said, "It's gone."

Richard said, "Hmmm strange. Perhaps you should look in the pile in front of you." Ashley turned the other pile over and her card was there.

Ashley said, "Whoa! That was cool. Is there any chance you'll tell me how you did that?" If not, you have to show us another card trick."

Richard replied, "Actually, there is no chance I'll show you how I did that. As for me showing you another trick, that is up to Mr. White."

Matt was watching in the back the whole time. He heard Ashley give the ultimatum and said, "That's fine by me."

Richard continued and said, "Okay Ashley and Jason please turn your chairs around. I want another student to help." Richard pulled a different deck of cards out of his pocket. He pointed at Louis and said, "Louis please look at these cards and make sure they're all different like a normal deck."

Louis looked through the cards and counted them. He said to Richard, "They look like an ordinary deck of cards to me."

Richard said, "Thank you." He took the cards and split them in half. Richard told Louis, "Take three cards off each pile and put them to the side. Now, fan through one of the piles."

Louis opened the cards up and looked at them. He raised his eyebrows and then gave Richard the thumbs up and he said, "WOW! That's awesome." Louis turned the cards over. The cards changed into a set of Arithmetic Cards.

Richard looked at the clock and realized he had been there for fifty minutes. He said to the class, "I hope you like what you saw. If Mr. White will allow it; I will come back in a few weeks. Please pay attention in school. It will help you so much. Thank you, everyone, for bearing with me. I have to go."

The students clapped for Richard as he waved bye. Matt went up to the front of the class and said, "I hope you enjoyed that. Now, the bad news is tomorrow we're back to the regular Math. I'll see what I can do about getting Mr. Jenkins back in four weeks."

Later That Day: Around Four-Twenty

Matt walked into the house and yelled, "Richard, I'm home."

Richard came out of the kitchen and said, "Hello Matt. I trust the rest of your day went well."

Matt replied, "Yes, it did. Thank you for coming today. The students enjoyed it."

"Oh, anytime Mr. White. I'm glad I was able to help."

5

A Visit from the Gilhoolys

Saturday, September 18th

Matt was sitting at the dining room table organizing some things for school. Sarah walked by with a book under her arm and waved to Matt. She showed him her Sue Grafton novel.

Sarah whispered, "He's asleep."

Matt quietly replied, "Good, sit down and put your feet up. You may want to close your eyes a little bit. Remember, the Gilhoolys are coming over tonight."

Sarah replied, "Yes, I know. We still getting Chinese takeout?"

Matt answered, "That sounds like the easiest thing."

Seven O'clock That Evening.

The Gilhoolys pulled in the driveway at seven. Sarah looked out the window and said, "They're here."

Matt replied, "I know, everybody on their best behavior. I just thought of something. I hope I have a beer to offer Jim if he wants it."

Richard overheard Matt and said, "We're all set in that area."

Sarah opened the front door and Jim and Karen walked in. Sarah greeted them, "Welcome, it's been a while since we've seen you two."

Karen replied, "Yes, it has. How are you?"

Sarah answered, "I'm doing well, as you can see, I have plenty of help here. You remember my husband Matt."

Matt put his hand out to greet them and he said, "Welcome to our home. He asked Jim, "Can I offer you a beer?"

Jim answered, "You don't have to ask me twice."

Matt asked Jim, "What kind of beer do you like? Oh, I should check to see what we have first." Jim answered, "I'm not fussy but my two favorites are Bud and Michelob."

Matt responded, "Got it, I'll be right back." He went into the kitchen and opened the refrigerator. There were five bottles of Bud and six bottles of Michelob Ultra.

Matt handed Jim a beer and Jim said, "Karen told me Sarah mentioned something about getting Chinese food."

Matt said, "Yes, that's the plan. You care to take a ride with me?"

Jim responded with, "Sure, and the rest of this will be for later," and he handed Matt back the bottle of Michelob.

Jim and Matt went outside and Jim offered, "Matt, please let me drive us. It took me a few days of car shopping to find something with legroom."

Matt replied, "Sure!"

The two of them got in Jim's car and backed out of the driveway.

Jim asked, "Where to?"

"China Star, it's on Milwaukee Ave."

Jim replied, "I know where that is." They went in to pick up the food and Jim said, "Here Matt, let me get this."

Matt added, "Jim, no that's alright I got this. Besides, we invited you. I know technically Sarah invited you but it was my idea. If you want, you can treat the next time."

Jim replied, "OK Matt, I'll remember you said that."

They got back in Jim's car and Jim asked Matt, "Are you still doing your shows at the theater?"

"Yes, I am and it's going quite well. Although, there was a rocky moment back in January."

Jim asked, "What do you mean?"

"The last act in the show didn't go quite as planned and there was a mishap where my assistant got injured. The audience saw the whole thing. Richard was so devastated he felt responsible for everything that happened. He felt so bad for what happened that he took off for a while. Richard left me a note of how bad he felt over the incident. But Jim, please not a word about this when we get back to the house. It's a sensitive subject with Richard."

Jim responded with, "I understand, and don't worry I will not utter a word."

Jim pulled back into Matt's driveway and Matt said, "Jim, there's one thing I have to tell you. If it wasn't for Richard, my show would've ended a long time ago." The five of them sat at the table eating and Sarah was looking around and Matt asked, "What's wrong honey?"

Sarah replied, "I don't see any egg rolls."

Richard spoke up and said, "Oh excuse me, I think they were left on the kitchen table. Let me get them." Richard went to the kitchen and removed a small plate, looked around, waved his hand quickly and five egg rolls appeared on the plate. He went back to the dining room and said, "Here we are."

Sarah said, "Thank you, Richard."

Richard replied, "Of course, before I sit down, does anybody need anything? Ah yes, Mr. Gilhooly let me get you another cold brew." Richard went back to the kitchen and grabbed another Michelob for Jim. He noticed a note stapled to the bag apologizing for the missing egg rolls.

The note said: *With our apologies due to the shortage of ingredients needed for the egg rolls you were charged $4.00 less.*

Richard ripped the note off the bag and crumpled it up. He went back into the dining room and handed Jim his beer. Richard sat down at the end of the table. His plate was filled with an assortment of food thanks to Sarah.

Sarah looked at Richard and commented, "I hope you don't mind and besides, you're always waiting on us. This way if your stomach is full you won't mind performing for us later." Richard reached down picked up the beef teriyaki.

"Sarah you know I love performing these card tricks especially in front of a small audience. A small audience always gets a better view of what's going on."

Sarah replied, "Great! Can you show us something I haven't seen yet?"

Richard answered, "I don't see why not. Sarah, please reach behind you and on the hutch, there should be a deck of playing cards."

Sarah took the deck and said, "Here they are. Oh wait, the box feels empty." Sarah opened the box and it was empty.

Richard added, "In that event, I'll get a fresh pack out of my room and he waved his hand up slightly."

Sarah was about to put the box back and she could feel the box getting heavier. She looked at Richard and he just winked at her. Sarah smiled back at Richard and put the deck on the table.

Richard finished eating and said, "Okay folks, let me just clear the table here."

Karen Gilhooly spoke up and said, "Please let us help especially if you're providing entertainment. Karen and Sarah started clearing the table.

When the girls left the room, Jim asked Richard, "How did you learn how to do these card tricks?"

Richard answered, "I taught myself this craft and perfected it on my own with a lot of practice. I don't mind telling you this I always try to leave my cards set up for the next trick. For example, give me a number from two through fifty-one."

Jim responded with, "Sixteen."

Richard continued, "Okay count down in the deck to the sixteenth card. I believe that should be the seven of diamonds."

Jim quickly counted the cards out any discovered Richard was correct.

Jim said, "I'm impressed."

Matt cut in and said, "That's nothing, he's just getting started. These are just warm-up exercises for him."

With that, Richard said, "If you two gents will excuse me, I'll be back in a few minutes. I'd like to brew some more coffee."

Richard stood up and he used his thought transfer process to Matt. He sent a message saying: "Don't worry we're going to see something tonight that even you haven't seen yet."

They will not remember this.

The girls came back in the dining room and Richard was not far behind them. Richard said, "Please sit and I can show you a card trick where everyone is involved. Karen could you please deal five cards to everyone except for me. I'm going to hand each one of you a piece of paper. Okay, next everyone please look at your cards and Matt we'll start with you.

38

"Here is a pen please write down the five cards in your hand and then hand the pen to Jim so he may do the same. Now, everyone should have their cards written down. The next thing to do is to put your cards face down in front of you and cover them you're your left hand. I'm going to count to three one…two…three. Matt, we'll start with you. Look at your cards and look at your paper."

Matt opened up his hand and he was stunned.

He asked, "How can this happen? You never touched our cards." The cards in Matt's hand were all different than what he wrote down.

Richard explained, "I didn't touch anyone's cards because I was not supposed to."

Jim and Karen looked at their cards and they both looked at each other in disbelief.

Karen chimed in and said, "I pretty much know the answer. Richard, can you show us how you did that?"

Richard answered, "I cannot do that and I believe it's always better to keep people guessing. If I was to show you my secret behind this you would want to know all my secrets. But I tell you what I can do and I'll be right back." Richard went into his room and came out with two decks of cards. He offered, "Okay, Karen, I want to teach you how to do this. You may take these cards home with you. Please cut the deck in half and I need to see the bottom card of your cut."

Karen reached over and removed the top half and revealed the nine of clubs to everyone. Richard put his hand out and asked, "May I hold that card for a second? Karen, next look at the top card off the bottom pile but do not let me see it. Once you're satisfied, put the card back where it was."

Karen looked at her card taking note and it was the jack of clubs. She put it back on top of the bottom pile.

Richard continued, "Next, we'll just put the top pile back on."

Karen was sitting there patiently and asked, "Next?"

Richard continued, "I just need to squeeze the deck together and with my index finger I will tap on the top twice." He tapped on the deck twice and instructed Karen, "Please look at the top card."

Karen flipped over the card and it was the jack of clubs.

She said, "WOW! You made the card move from the middle to the top of the deck."

Richard replied, "Yes, and that's what you'll do if you follow me into the kitchen, I'll explain how it works."

Karen said, "Great."

Richard went into the kitchen and Karen followed right behind him.

Richard handed Karen a different deck of cards explained to her about the key card.

"When we were in the dining room, you witnessed the jack of clubs at the top of the pile. That's where it was from the start. If you look at this deck, you'll see the top card is the ace of spades. Every other card is the same and the key cards are cut just a little narrower than the rest. This enables the deck to be cut this way so the key card will always be on top of the bottom pile. It's a very easy trick to do and it's all set up for you."

Karen replied, "Thank you. I'll show some of my co-workers this on Monday."

Richard shot back, "You're welcome and I believe the others are getting antsy in the other room and may want to see more."

That said, Richard and Karen went back into the dining room. Karen said to Jim, "This is good. Richard explained to me how this works. I'm going to show some people at work on Monday."

Richard announced, "I can do one better if you people want to see it."

Jim spoke up and said, "Sure! As long as our host doesn't need us out of here."

Matt responded, "No, you're good."

Richard replied, "Great. With this one, I shall require the assistance of Mr. Gilhooly."

Jim asked, "What can I do?"

Richard continued, "Okay, take these cards and fan through them. You'll notice they're in sequential order. I need you to check to ensure they're all here."

Jim fanned through the cards and was satisfied.

He said, "Looks like they're all here."

Richard continued, "Splendid! Please think of any card you want from the deck." With that, Richard motioned to Matt, "Paper and pen please." Matt slid the paper and pen in front of Jim. Richard continued again, "Now Jim, please write down the card you thought of and then turn the paper over so no one can see your selection."

Jim wrote his choice on the paper, turned it over as instructed, and asked, "Now what?"

Richard continued with, "Now, hold the cards between your thumb and your index finger. I'm going to count to three. One...two...three. Now Jim, please check your cards to see if your card is there."

Jim looked at the cards and noticed his card wasn't in the deck. Jim said, "It's not here. I wrote down the queen of hearts and it's gone."

"Wonderful! That means it worked," Richard remarked.

Jim asked, "Where did my card go? I don't understand."

Richard answered, "Jim, to find your card you need to ask your wife to look in her purse."

Karen spoke up and said, "Wait a second. I didn't take anyone's card and to prove it; I'll open my bag." Karen opened her purse, reached inside and lo and behold there was Jim's card. She spouted, "Son of a... how did this get in here?"

Richard chimed in and asked, "Isn't magic wonderful? However, I have to bid you all a good night. Jim and Karen, it was a pleasure seeing you again. Matt, Sarah, I'll see you in the morning."

The four of them said goodnight to Richard. Jim asked Karen, "What do you say? Should we get going?"

Karen answered, "I'm ready when you are. Sarah, Matt, Jim and I are going to cut out. Thank you for the food and please tell Richard we said thanks for the entertainment."

Sarah replied, "We will. Thank you for coming. It was a pleasure seeing you guys." Jim helped Karen with her jacket and then put his on. Karen reached in her right pocket and felt a playing card. She pulled the card out and it was the queen of hearts from earlier. She showed it to Jim and he smiled. Karen turned the card over and the words 'Thank you" were on it.

She slipped it back in her pocket. The two of them went out of the front door and the card was no longer in Karen's pocket.

41

6

Denise's Interview

Matt came downstairs at six-thirty to grab a coffee before Thomas woke up. Richard was sitting in the corner of the kitchen reading his paper.

Matt said quietly, "Good morning Richard."

Richard lowered the paper a little; made eye contact with Matt and nodded. Next, Richard pushed a piece of paper from the corner of the table so Matt could see it.

The note read: *Don't worry Thomas will be on his best behavior.*

Matt put the note down and said, "I hope this works out. I just want Sarah to be happy."

Later On: Around One O'clock

Denise's car pulled into the driveway and Sarah heard the car door open. Sarah said, "She's here, please everybody on their best behavior."

Sarah opened the door and said, "Good afternoon Denise, come in."

Denise walked in and said, "Hey Sarah, it's been a while. How have you been?"

Sarah answered, "Very tired, I took extra time off for my maternity leave. My work was very understanding and they let me have twelve weeks off. I've only been back five days and I have to leave earlier every morning to drop Thomas off at daycare. I'm not saying anything against the daycare business but I wish I could eliminate that and get someone to watch Thomas here."

Denise replied, "I understand and I'm sure it does a number on you. My sister went through the same thing with her son. I have a couple of questions."

Sarah responded with, "Sure, ask away."

"When do you want me to start and how early do you need me in the morning?"

Sarah answered, "I know it's short notice but I'd like you to start tomorrow and can you be here at six forty-five? Matt is usually home around 4:00. I know that's a nine-hour day and we'll compensate you for it"

Denise answered, "Sure, when do I get to meet Thomas?"

Right after Denise asked that sounds were coming from the baby monitor. Sarah answered, "It will be in a couple of minutes. I'll be right back." Sarah went upstairs and returned with Thomas in her arms. "Denise, this is Thomas."

Denise responded, "Hello Thomas, do you mind if I watch you during the week?"

Richard was patiently watching in the background. He walked towards the kitchen and before he got to the swinging door, he rubbed his temple on the left side, and with that Thomas stopped crying.

Denise said, "I think he likes me."

Sarah asked, "Do you want to give him his bottle?"

Denise answered, "Sure!"

She put her hands out to cradle Thomas and Sarah handed Denise his bottle. Thomas was being held and fed by Denise. He looked very content in her arms. The bottle was emptied and Denise eased the bottle away slowly.

Denise smiled and said, "I'll be here tomorrow."

Sarah responded with, "Thank you, Denise I can't begin to tell you how much of a relief this is. Okay, we're getting lunch for ourselves and of course, we want you to stay."

Denise said, "OK thank you, I don't have to be anywhere. Do you want me to put Thomas back upstairs in his crib?"

Sarah answered, "Thank you. That'll be great.

Meanwhile, Richard was in the kitchen preparing lunch for the four of them. About ten minutes later, Richard brought out a tray of cold cut sandwiches to the dining room table.

Matt came into the living room and said, "Lunch is ready and on the table. Denise, do you like iced tea? If not, we have some bottles of spring water and diet Pepsi."

Denise answered, "Iced tea will be great. Thank you, Matt."

The four of them sat at the dining room table eating lunch and making chit chat. Richard was sitting at one end with a coffee in front of him. Matt asked him, "You're not eating?"

Richard answered, "I'm not hungry right now, maybe later. He then stood up and asked, "Can I get anyone anything else?"

The three of them answered, "No, we're good, thank you."

Richard replied, "Very well then if you'll excuse me, I need to check on something."

With that, Richard left the table taking some of the dirty plates with him and went to the kitchen.

Matt walked in after him and asked, "Do you think this is going to work out with Denise? I am only asking because you seem to know everything."

Richard responded with, "Matthew, I have two things to say to you. One is yes it will work out with Denise and number two you're correct; I do know everything. Now, if you'll excuse me, I'd like to visit my journal and make sure it's up to date."

Sarah and Denise were still in the dining room talking away. After Richard was done looking at his journal, he went into the dining room and asked, "Can I get you, ladies, anything?"

Sarah answered, "I think we're good for now. Richard, please wait a second. Do you mind showing Denise and me a card trick?"

Richard answered, "Sarah, you know I love performing card tricks." He walked over to the hutch and reached for the playing cards. Richard handed Denise the cards and asked her, "Will you please examine the cards to make sure they're all here?"

Denise took the cards, she fanned through them and said, "They look okay to me."

Richard continued, "That's great! Next, please think of any card in the deck and write it on this paper and do not show me your pick."

Richard reached for the cards and started shuffling them.

He was giving the cards a good mix and Denise asked him, "Is this a trick deck of cards or something?"

Richard answered, "That you'll have to see for yourself," and he placed the cards on the table in front of Denise.

Denise turned the cards over and they all changed to the jack of diamonds. She looked at Sarah and turned the paper over. She wrote the jack of diamonds on her paper as a pick.

Denise's eyes opened wide and she asked Richard, "How did you do that?"

Richard answered, "I'll tell you what I tell everyone else. This is something I call magic. It's something I know how to do and I enjoy doing it. If you're not in a hurry to go, I can show you another one."

Denise offered, "OK, go ahead."

Richard continued, "Very well, here we can use the same cards again. Please look at the cards first."

Denise picked up the cards from before and the first thing she discovered was the cards were back to a normal state. She fanned through the cards and was satisfied with the deck.

Richard continued, "Now, take the deck and pick out any one card for yourself. Again, do not show me the card." Denise picked up the deck a second time and removed the ten of hearts. "Next, take that card and put it in your handbag."

Denise took the card as instructed and put it in her bag.

She asked, "Now what?"

Richard answered, "Here's the good part." He took the cards, tapped them on the table, and continued, "Please look in your bag for your card." Denise reached in her bag, pulled out the card, and looked at it.

Richard asked, "Is this your card?"

Denise answered, "No, it's not."

Richard asked, "Can you tell me the card? Wait, do not tell me. Just draw cards from the top of the deck and stop when you get to the seventh one and turn it over."

Denise started drawing the cards from the top and she got to the seventh one and turned it over. It was the ten of hearts.

She looked at Sarah and said, "That's amazing."

Sarah said, "Oh yeah, I've seen quite a few of them. Richard is very good at what he does."

Denise looked at her watch and it was almost 1:30. She said, "Sarah, I should get going. I need to get some things at Albertson's."

Sarah replied, "OK, but we didn't discuss a salary for you."

Denise added, "That's okay. I'll call you when I get home."

Matt and Sarah walked Denise to the front door and they said their goodbyes. Sarah said to Matt, "She's going to call me when she gets back to her house. What do you think I should offer her for a salary?"

Matt stood there and thought for a minute, "This is going to be tax-free money for her. I was thinking $400 a week and tell her lunch will be provided. After all, the daycare is $450 a week but we can claim that on our taxes. When she calls back you can ask her if she has a figure in mind."

Sarah offered, "OK, I'll do that."

Ninety Minutes Later

It was three-fifteen, the phone rang and Sarah answered it. It was Denise as expected. Denise said on the other end, "Hello Sarah, it's me, Denise. I told you I'd call you when I got home."

Sarah replied, "We were just talking about you and now I have to ask you, "How much do you want for doing this?"

Denise answered, "I thought about it on the ride to Albertson's and I think $400 a week is fair."

Sarah replied, "You got it and Matt said we're providing you lunch. Just bring your lunch on Monday and give Richard a list of the things you like. We'll make sure we have it here for the rest of the week."

Denise added, "OK great! I'll see you tomorrow."

7

Denise's New Job

Monday Morning, September 20th

Matt came downstairs at six twenty-five and poured himself a coffee. Richard was sitting at the kitchen table with his newspaper in front of him. Matt greeted Richard, "Good morning Richard."

"Good morning Matt. I believe this is Denise's first day of watching Thomas."

"Yes, it is. I hope all goes well."

"Matt, believe me, there is nothing to worry about. Sarah's friend Denise is a good fit for this position."

"I hope you're right about that. I have to go. See you around four-fifteen."

Richard replied, "You have a good day, Mr. White."

Matt backed his car out of the driveway and saw Denise's car coming up the street. He waved to Denise but she did not see him.

Denise pulled in the driveway around six forty-five. She got out of the car and headed up the front stairs.

Richard opened the door and greeted her, "Good morning Miss Bennet. How are you?"

Denise answered, "I'm doing well Mr. Jenkins. How about you?"

Richard answered, "Just splendid. I have fresh coffee brewed. Please help yourself," and he pointed to some clean coffee mugs on the counter.

"Thank you, Richard." Denise reached for one of the mugs and poured her coffee.

"Please have a seat and relax while you can. Sarah should be downstairs in a few minutes so drink your coffee while it's hot.

The bedroom door opened upstairs and Sarah came down with Thomas. Richard looked at Denise and said, "Looks like you're going to work."

Denise smiled, opened the refrigerator, and took out a bottle for Thomas. She said to Richard, "I need to warm this up."

Richard put his hand out for the bottle and took it from Denise. He handed it back to her after five seconds and said, "You should be all set."

Denise was holding the bottle and could tell something strange was going on. She thought to herself, 'I hope I didn't make a mistake accepting this job.'

Sarah walked into the kitchen holding Thomas. She said, "Good morning Denise. Thank you so much for doing this."

Denise answered, "Oh, I'm glad I can help. Now, do you want me to wait 'til you get home or...?"

Sarah answered, "Oh no, Matt usually gets home by four-fifteen and he will relieve you. Here is my cell phone number if you need to get a hold of me. Richard is here all day if you need help with anything."

Denise replied, "Okay, thanks. I'm sure we'll be just fine. Be careful about going out to your car. It's very windy out."

"Okay, I'm off, so good luck, and thank you again for doing this. Bye."

At five minutes after seven, Sarah left the house. Denise sat in one of the wingchairs feeding Thomas. Richard walked into the living room and laid a towel on her shoulder. Denise looked up and said, "Thank you, Richard."

Richard nodded and said quietly, "Be back in ten minutes."

He went into the kitchen and started a fresh pot of coffee; Richard also heated a couple of pastries. Ten minutes later he returned to the living room with a tray with two fresh coffees and two raspberry turnovers.

Denise stood up and carried Thomas upstairs and laid him in the crib. She made her way back downstairs and Richard was waiting in the other chair.

He said, "Please sit, you have a two-and-a-half-hour break for yourself. Now would be as good a time as any to have a chat. Let's call it a briefing."

"A briefing about what," asked Denise.

Richard replied, "Okay here goes, Matt knows I have special talents or capabilities whatever you want to refer them as. Denise, I have special powers where I can make things happen. I can do things all others wish they can do. I think it is best I tell you this seeing as you're going to be here during the week. Please, do not feel as if I'm trying to scare you. That is not my intention at all. However, I do not wish this to be public knowledge. It doesn't have to be and I'm hoping you'll keep it to yourself. Can you give me your word on that?"

Denise answered, "I promise, you have my word and I'll keep it to myself."

Richard went on, "The other day you were on the phone with Sarah and you were talking about starting this job. During the conversation, Sarah brought up to you how lunch would be provided. I was not in the same room when Sarah was on the phone with you."

Denise sat there trying to absorb everything Richard was telling her. She asked, "How do I know that Sarah or Matt did not tell you about our phone conversation?"

"I knew you were going to ask that. I tell you what. Let's put it to the test right now. Think of something and I will tell you what you were thinking of."

Denise replied, "Okay, go ahead."

"You were just thinking you wished you brought your Stephen King book with you today. I believe it's titled 'From a Buick 8.'"

Denise looked down at the floor for a second and then looked back at Richard.

She said, "That's right! You did it."

"Of course, and here's the good news. Your book is laying on the seat of your car."

Denise stood up and asked, "You mind if I go check?"

"Go ahead. Thomas is not due to wake up for almost two hours."

Denise walked out to her car as fast as she could. She opened the back door and there was her book just like Richard said. Denise picked up the book and brought it in the house.

She said to Richard, "I could have sworn I left this on my coffee table."

"Well, you have it here now to read during your free time. If you'll excuse me, I'm going to get another brew. Would you care for another cup?"

"Thank you, Richard, that'll be nice."

Richard went into the kitchen and poured two coffees. He returned and Denise was sitting in the wing chair with her book opened. "Here you go." Richard placed a coffee on the end table next to Denise and the baby monitor.

Denise said, "Thank you. I can relax for a few minutes. It's nice now. Thomas is sleeping peacefully."

Richard replied, "Yes, and according to his schedule he's not due to wake for another ninety minutes."

"I'll be ready for him."

Later That Day: Around Four-Ten

Matt walked in the front door and said, "Hello Richard, Denise I'm home." He went straight to the living room and Denise was holding Thomas.

Denise looked at Matt and smiled, and said, "He just fell back to sleep."

Matt sat in the chair next to Denise and asked, "Did you have any problems?"

Denise answered, "Not at all, he was good as gold."

Matt replied, "If you don't mind, can you put him back in the crib, and then you'll be off the clock."

Denise whispered, "Sure." She brought Thomas upstairs and laid him down in his crib. Denise came back downstairs and said to Matt, "Okay, I'll see you tomorrow morning. Have Sarah call me."

Matt countered with, "Will do and just a second, Sarah told me you were going to write a list of what foods you like so we can pick them up for you."

Denise did an about-face, pulled a small piece of paper from her bag and said, "It appears Richard already took care of it. I didn't know he was so talented."

Matt replied, "He's something, alright. I'll have Sarah call you tonight." Matt went to the dining room and saw Richard's journal on the table. Matt turned around and Richard was coming out of his room.

Richard said, "Hello Matt, I trust your day went well. Before you ask, the journal has been there a few hours but not for Denise to see. She wouldn't be able to see it even if she entered the dining room. I have it there so you can give it some attention."

"Okay, I'll look at it later, I promise."

With that, Richard went into the utility room and moved the clothes from the washer to the dryer.

Matt followed him and asked, "Do you think Denise was okay with being here?"

"Of course, she was okay with it. She needed employment and at the same time, Sarah wanted to get back to the insurance company. This is a win-win situation for both of them. She told you herself he was good as gold. I was here all day so I can attest to that."

"I just want this to work out for Sarah."

"Then, there is nothing to worry about. Think of this as one of our performances. So far, there's been only one incident where something has gone wrong. I admitted before I made the wrong decision. In this case, you and Sarah have nothing to worry about."

Matt replied, "Thank you for the reassurance. Is there anything I can do to help with dinner?"

"I'll take care of dinner. You can bring the two baskets to the top of the stairs and then I can start on dinner."

Matt grabbed one laundry basket and brought it up. He returned for the second one. Matt was coming downstairs and he heard the front door open. It was not quite five-thirty and Sarah walked in.

Matt greeted Sarah first, "Hello honey," and he kissed her. "Denise wants you to call her when you get a chance."

Sarah replied, "I can do that now." She went into the living room and called Denise. Sarah was thinking on the way to the phone, 'I hope nothing went wrong on her first day.'

Denise answered, "Hello?"

Sarah answered, "Hey Denise, it's Sarah. Matt told me to give you a call."

"Yeah Sarah, I just wanted to tell you that Thomas and I got along just fine. He was no trouble at all and thank you for giving me this opportunity."

Sarah asked, "Denise, are you kidding me? You are a godsend coming into our lives now."

Denise replied, "One more thing, what's going on with Richard at your house?"

"What do you mean?"

"I'm not going to say he scares me or anything like that. It's just that he knows everything."

Sarah replied, "That's Richard alright, a man of extreme intelligence and many talents."

"Okay, I'm going to let you go so I can get something ready for dinner, I'll see you in the morning."

"Bye Denise, see you in the morning."

Sarah put down the phone and went upstairs to check on Thomas and change into some more comfy clothes. Thomas was still sleeping. Sarah came back downstairs intending to get to the bottom of what Denise and Richard had discussed. Sarah asked, "Richard, may I have a word with you?"

Richard answered, "Of course Sarah. What can I help you with?"

"Well, I just got off the phone with Denise and she told me that you know everything."

Richard responded, "She is correct. I merely anticipated her meal schedule and it won't be necessary to make a special trip to the market."

"That's all you told her?"

"Yes, but not in those exact words. However, she asked me how I knew what she likes to eat for lunch and I told her I can read minds."

"Oh no!"

Richard replied, "Sarah please, she's not going to remember what I said. Otherwise, she would have mentioned it to you."

"I hope you're right about that. I don't want Denise to be nervous when she's in the house."

Richard replied, "Then you have nothing to worry about. The good news is dinner will be ready in less than fifteen minutes. I won't object if you volunteer to set the table."

"I can do that." Sarah reached in the cabinet and removed three plates. She next took three sets of silverware from the drawer. Twelve minutes later, the three of them were sitting down to dinner.

At the table, Matt spoke up and said, "Well, so far there are no complaints from Denise and that's a good thing."

Sarah replied, "It sure is. I just hope she doesn't have any problems."

Richard cut in and said, "Excuse me, Mrs. White, I am very confident there'll be no issues. I would not tell you this if I did not believe it wholeheartedly."

Sarah responded, "Thank you. Richard."

The Next Day: Tuesday, September 21st

Matt came downstairs at six-twenty for his coffee. Richard had his paper opened and was sitting at the kitchen table. Richard looked up from the paper and said, "Good morning Matt. How are you?"

Matt answered, "Tired, I definitely could have slept longer."

Richard offered, "Sorry to hear that Matt. You'll feel better a few minutes after you have your coffee."

"I hope you're right." Matt finished his coffee and said, "I'm off and I'll see you around four-fifteen."

Richard replied, "Have a good day Mr. White."

Matt got in his car and backed out of the driveway and he saw Denise's car waiting to pull in. He got to the end of the street and felt a burst of energy. Matt thought to himself, 'Of course Richard was right. That was no surprise.'

Denise pulled in and went to the front door. Richard opened the door and said, "Good morning Miss Bennet. How are you?"

Denise answered, "Good morning Richard. I am doing well, thank you."

"Please help yourself to a coffee. Sarah will be downstairs with Thomas in less than ten minutes."

Denise poured herself a coffee and said, "Thank you." She put down her bag and sat at the kitchen table. She looked at Richard and said, "I hope today goes nice and smooth like yesterday."

Richard let out a sigh and replied, "Miss Bennett you have nothing to worry about. Every day will be smooth sailing here. I give you my word on that and here comes Sarah now."

8

The Show Goes On

Sarah was sitting in the wingchair reading her latest Sue Grafton novel. Matt walked into the living room and asked, "How long has he been asleep?"

Sarah answered, "I put him down at twelve-thirty, so a couple of hours. He should be waking up soon."

"Well, you relax here. I'll get him when he wakes up. You deserve a break."

Sarah smiled and said, "Thank you, honey."

Matt replied, "You don't have to thank me for wanting to take an active part in taking care of our son. Besides, Richard and I will be heading out to the theater a little after six."

At two-forty sounds were coming from the monitor. Matt stood up and said, "That's my cue, I'll be right back."

Matt hustled up the stairs, went to Thomas' room, and removed him from the crib. He came back down to the kitchen to get a bottle.

Richard was standing near the counter and said, "I believe you'll be needing this." He handed Matt a warmed-up bottle and a small towel for his shoulder.

Matt replied, "Thank you, Richard. Once again you anticipated my needs."

"Of course, Matthew, we're here to help each other."

Three Hours Later

A little after six o'clock Matt and Richard headed off to the theater. They took their seats in the front row and Richard said, "Matt, we should go over our big act now. I believe you told me you never saw this being performed. Please, join me up on stage."

Matt stepped up on the stage and asked Richard, "Okay, what can you tell me?"

"Okay, as we've done in the past, we get a volunteer up on stage. The volunteer is getting in the truck with you. We'll have the volunteer take a walk around the truck first. I'll slide myself under the truck up near the front wheels. You put the truck in first gear and when the truck moves forward you should feel the front end go up slightly. Do not worry. I know what to do to make this look believable and prevent myself from harm. Also, whatever you do once the vehicle starts moving keep going until the rear axle has crossed over me."

Matt asked, "So, you think this will work?"

"Of course, it will and the audience will love it. There will also be a monitor above playing the version that was televised. You'll see, our version will be so much better."

It got to be seven-ten and the crowd started coming in. The show got underway and Matt and Richard performed their acts flawlessly.

The time was eight-forty and Matt called out, "Ladies and gentlemen we have time for one more and we'll be needing a volunteer. Before I select a volunteer, could everyone please look at the monitor above me? Here, you'll see a version of our next illusion. Please watch this and I think you'll like ours better." The video stopped and Matt asked, "Now, can I have a volunteer? Please rest assured you'll not get injured in any way."

A bunch of hands went up and Matt looked out at the crowd. He picked someone from the seventh row.

Matt said, "Please sir, come on up." The volunteer came up on stage. Matt put his hand out and asked, "What is your name sir?"

The volunteer put his hand out and said, "Tom, Tom Hennessey. It's nice to meet you."

"It's good to meet you as well Tom. Now, if I get you to look over this big truck here. As you can see, aside from being a replica of a vintage moving truck, there's nothing unusual about this."

Tom walked around the vehicle and looked it over. He opened the driver's side door, stuck his head in, and poked around. Tom was satisfied and closed the door.

He said to Matt, "It looks okay to me."

Matt replied, "That's great. Thank you, Tom. Next, my partner, Richard is going to lie down in front of the truck." Richard took off his jacket and laid on the floor under the truck less than twelve inches from the front wheel. "Okay, Tom, you get in the passenger side. Are you ready, Richard?"

Richard answered, "Ready as I'll ever be."

"Good, here we go."

Matt put the truck in first gear as Richard instructed. The truck moved slowly and when it got to Richard it went up in the air a couple of inches and then came back down. The vehicle moved forward a little more and once again it went up in the air just a few inches and then came back down a second time.

Matt looked at Tom and said, "Now, let's check on Richard." As Matt stepped out of the truck, he could see Richard sitting up brushing his shirt off. Richard stood up and Matt said, "I'm glad to see you're okay."

Richard responded and asked, "Why wouldn't I be? It would have been better if the tires weren't so filthy."

Matt added, "Well, that's something we need to work on. Okay, Tom as you can see, Richard is okay. What do you think?"

Tom answered, "I don't see how he's okay with us going over him with the truck."

Richard added, "Tom, it's nice to meet you. This is something I call magic and I enjoy doing it with my friend Matt. Please wait up here Tom while we say goodnight to the audience."

Matt called out to the audience, "Ladies and gentlemen, this concludes our show for tonight. Please if you liked what you saw, tell your friends and relatives. My name is Matt White and this is my partner and good friend Richard Jenkins. Please have a good night and drive safely." Matt next said to Tom, "I'd like to give you a couple of free show tickets for helping us out tonight."

Tom put his hand out and said, "Thank you, Mr. White. I enjoyed the show. Would you mind if I make a suggestion?"

Matt answered, "By all means, go for it."

Tom offered, "Okay when you bring a volunteer up here for an act like this don't have them get in the truck with you. I could not see what was happening outside the truck."

Richard spoke up and said, "Tom has a very good point there. Tom, before we go, give me just a minute."

Richard went backstage for less than two minutes and returned. He said to Tom, "Check out the monitor above." The monitor was playing a short clip of Matt driving the truck. Tom could see the vehicle going up slightly over Richard's body and flattening him. Richard said, "That is what you missed."

Tom responded, "Thank you, Mr. Jenkins. Mr. Jenkins, are you okay?"

Richard answered, "Of course I am. I made a promise to Mr. White a long time ago that neither one of us will ever sustain an injury during our performances. So far, we've held to that."

Tom added, "Well, I had a good time, and thanks for showing me what I missed. I'll tell my friends. Goodnight." Tom Hennessey left the stage and walked up the main aisle.

Matt looked at Richard and asked, "Well, Mr. Jenkins, are you ready?"

"Yes, I am and I wouldn't mind skipping our trip to the diner up the street tonight. I need to get in my bed."

Matt replied, "That's fine by me. Let's go." Matt and Richard left the theater and headed home.

9

Thinking About Vacation

Matt came downstairs at six twenty-five to get his coffee. Richard was sitting in the corner of the kitchen reading his paper.

Matt greeted Richard first, "Good morning, Richard."

Richard countered, "Good morning Matt. It looks like it's going to be a beautiful day."

Matt took a break from sipping his coffee and said, "I agree with you there. Do you wish to join me on the food shopping errand later?"

Richard answered, "Of course, I do. There is a list started on the refrigerator and I'm sure Sarah will want to add to it."

Sarah came downstairs a little before seven-thirty. "Good morning honey." Matt kissed her on the cheek and asked, "Are you ready for breakfast?"

Sarah answered, "I'd love that but I have to take care of Thomas. I'm sure he'll be stirring soon."

Richard cut in and said, "Please, Sarah take a seat at the table. Matt and I have this covered. How about some scrambled eggs and wheat toast?"

Sarah smiled and answered, "Richard, you spoil me."

Around eight-thirty Matt and Richard headed out to Albertson's. Once in the store, they made their way through the aisles loading up various groceries. They went through the checkout and unloaded the carriage.

On the way home, Richard said, "Matthew, I had an idea the other day and I was hoping I could run it by you."

"Sure, what do you have?"

"I was thinking we should plan a small vacation, a getaway if you want to call it that."

"Okay, but to where?"

"I was thinking Las Vegas. We don't have to stay that long, maybe four nights. It would be just enough time to take in some of the magic shows. Some of the shows are very good. I think it has a lot to do with the presentation. After watching some of the shows you'll have more of a respect for what we go through and I'm sure you'll appreciate me more."

"Richard, I know with you by my side our shows cannot be matched. The problem is now I don't think it would be fair to leave Sarah alone with Thomas."

Richard replied, "I agree one hundred percent and that is why she would be coming with us. Thomas will be a few months older and I bet we can get Denise to take care of him."

"You think Sarah's going to be okay with leaving Thomas for the week?"

Richard answered, "We can sweeten the pot with Sarah and tell her to invite Sean and his wife along. You know she enjoys seeing her brother. Promise me you'll think about it."

Matt responded with, "Okay, I like the idea but I still want to run it by Sarah. Of course, I won't have to ask for any days off if we wait until school vacation in February or April. We'll talk more about this later."

Matt pulled into the driveway. The two of them brought the groceries inside. Sarah was upstairs rocking Thomas back to sleep. Richard asked, "Is Sarah upstairs?"

Matt answered, "I believe she is."

"Good!" Richard waved his hand back and forth and all the groceries were put away including the items for the freezer in the basement.

Later On: Around Four-Forty-Five

Richard had dinner in the oven and it was set to be ready at five-thirty. Matt walked into the kitchen and asked Richard, "Is there anything I can do to help?"

Richard answered, "Matt, your timing is impeccable. Please set the table and grab some salad bowls."

"You got it," came from Matt.

At five-thirty Sarah came downstairs and Richard said, "You're just in time. Dinner will be ready in three minutes and I hope you're hungry."

Sarah replied, "I am always hungry. Let me just wash my hands."

A few minutes later the three of them were sitting at the table. Matt spoke up and said, "Honey, Richard has come up with this great idea for a vacation."

Sarah looked up and asked, "Really, what's the big idea?"

Matt answered, "Okay, we were thinking we could go to Las Vegas next year. We can even invite Sean and Katelin to come along. It will give us a chance to see some of the magic shows out there. Sarah, I think you'll agree we can all use a break."

Sarah responded, "That sounds nice, but are you forgetting something?"

"Such as?"

"Are we supposed to bring Thomas with us?"

Matt answered, "No, we won't have to. By the time we go on this trip, Thomas will be more accustomed to Denise. You told me she works part-time at the card store. We give her enough notice to ask for five nights off and I'll reimburse her for her lost wages."

Sarah asked, "How could she refuse that and when did you want to do this?"

Matt answered, "How about during the April school break of next year? That's six months away and it leaves us with plenty of time to plan."

Sarah added, "Okay, I'll look to see if I can get that time off."

The Next Day: Monday, September 27th

Denise pulled in the driveway at six-forty and Richard opened the door for her. Denise went up the front stairs and Richard greeted her, "Good morning Miss Bennett. How are you?"

Denise answered, "Good morning Richard. I'm doing well. Thank you for asking."

Richard continued, "As always please help yourself to the coffee. Sarah should be down shortly."

Five Minutes Later

Sarah came downstairs with Thomas in her arms. Sarah said, "Good morning Denise. Thomas is ready for his breakfast. Do you mind?"

"Of course not." Denise opened the refrigerator and as she looked inside, she saw Richard off to the right holding out a bottle for her. She took it and said, "Thank you."

Richard replied, "You're welcome."

Sarah cut in and said, "Okay Denise, I'm leaving and Matt should be back by four-fifteen." Sarah said goodbye to Richard and kissed Thomas goodbye.

Denise walked over to one of the wingchairs and sat down with Thomas. Richard asked Denise, "Do you mind if I grab a fresh coffee and join you?"

Denise answered, "Not at all, please sit."

Richard walked over holding his coffee and settled himself in the chair. He took a sip of his coffee and said, "I trust you had a good weekend."

Denise replied, "Yes, it was nice and quiet."

Richard continued, "That's good. Look, I'm just going to come out and ask. I was talking to Mr. White yesterday. Matt and Sarah want to plan a vacation for next April. Sarah intends to ask if you could care for Thomas for the six days. Of course, you will be well compensated for your efforts. I understand you still retain part-time employment at the card shop. We will cover any wages you'll not be earning that week. Please just think it over."

Denise responded, "I don't see any reason why I can't. You said this is going to be for next April. That's seven months away. I can give Mr. White the thumbs up when he gets home."

"Thank you, Miss Bennet. This will be greatly appreciated."

Matt walked in and called inside, "Hello, I'm home. Denise? Richard?"

Richard emerged from the kitchen and raised a finger to his lips. He whispered, "Denise is in the living room with Thomas. He'll be drifting off any second now."

Matt replied, "Okay, I'll just run upstairs and get changed. Be right back."

Richard made his way to the living room and Denise whispered, "He's out." She was holding Thomas who looked like the perfect little angel in her arms. Denise was being cautious not to wake him.

Five Minutes Later

Matt came downstairs and waved to Denise without making any noise. Denise stood, smiled, and brought Thomas upstairs to put him down. She came back downstairs and asked Matt, "Can we talk for a minute before I head out?"

Matt answered, "Sure, what's up?"

"Mr. Jenkins told me you wanted to plan a vacation for next April. I'd be more than happy to take care of Thomas while you're gone. Just let me know as soon as you have the dates figured out. This way I can give my boss at the card shop plenty of notice."

Matt replied, "Thank you very much, Denise. I'll get the dates for you soon and I'll give Sarah the good news."

Five-Forty-Five

Sarah walked into the house and called in, "Matt, I'm home."

Matt was sitting at the dining room table and he got up to greet Sarah with a kiss. He asked, "How was your day?"

Sarah answered, "Don't ask. So many things went wrong and Paula called in sick to boot. I need some good news. Do you have any?"

"I do have good news. Richard took the initiative and asked Denise if she could watch Thomas for us so we can go on vacation.

Denise spoke to me and told me she'd be more than happy to take care of Thomas. She told me to get her the dates soon so she could give her work notice."

"WOW! Matt, that is great news. I've never been to Las Vegas. I bet it's going to be so much fun."

Matt replied, "I'm sure it will be. There's a lot to do out there aside from the gambling."

A little before six-fifteen the three of them sat down to dinner. Sarah spoke up and said, "Richard, two things, first is dinner is delicious as always. The second is thank you for talking to Denise today about our trip."

Richard responded with, "Of course Mrs. White, you do not have to say thank you for that. I know you two are due for a much-needed vacation."

Sarah replied, "You mean the three of us."

Tuesday Morning: September 28th

Tuesday morning came around and Richard was sitting at the kitchen table with his paper and coffee beside him. Matt came downstairs to grab his coffee and start his day.

He greeted Richard first, "Good morning Richard. How are you?"

Richard answered, "Just splendid Matt. How are you?"

Matt replied, "Okay, I am still enjoying the feeling from yesterday from the good news we received from Denise."

Richard responded with, "Ah yes, it's Denise to the rescue again."

With that, Matt said goodbye to Richard and headed off to work. Denise's car was waiting to pull in the driveway as Matt was backing out. Richard opened the door for her and said, "Good morning Miss Bennett," as she walked up the stairs. "I just brewed fresh coffee and as always help yourself."

Denise replied, "Thank you Mr. Jenkins, and good morning to you." She put her bag down and fixed her coffee. "It's very windy out this morning. I would hate to be working outside."

Richard responded, "Fall is with us now."

Two Minutes Later

The bedroom door upstairs closed and Sarah made her way down the stairs. She got to the bottom and saw Denise holding a coffee.

Sarah said, "Good morning Denise, be right back."

Sarah turned around and went back to retrieve Thomas. She came back down and Denise was waiting with open arms. Sarah was all dressed for work and she said, "I have to get one more thing."

She came back down and said to Denise, "I'm sorry, I have to head out a few minutes early today and before I forget, thank you, thank you."

"For?"

Sarah answered, "For taking care of Thomas and agreeing to watch him on our vacation."

Denise replied, "Oh, that's not a problem at all as long as Matt gets me the dates."

10

Sherry LaPointe

Eleven Days Later: Saturday, October 9ᵗʰ

It was another show night coming for Matt and Richard. Richard prepped the coffee a few minutes earlier than he usually had. Matt came downstairs around six-thirty to get his coffee. He spotted Richard at the table without the newspaper in front of him.

Matt greeted Richard first, "Good morning Richard. Where is your newsworthy companion?"

Richard replied, "Good morning Matt. I already read that front to back. I thought I would take the extra few minutes to get a head start on our journal here."

Matt asked, "You mean you're adding to it?"

"Yes, that's right."

Matt saw the book in the corner and asked, "Do you mind if I have a peek?"

Richard answered, "Of course not, go right ahead."

Matt opened the book to about the half-way point and he saw Richard's handwriting going in the book. Richard was not holding a pen or any kind of writing utensil. The handwriting stopped by itself under Richard's command of course.

Richard said, "The journal should now be up to date. Our performance for tonight is already listed here. There'll be more to go in later, so much more."

Six-thirty That Evening.

Matt and Richard headed out to the theater at six-thirty on the dot. They sat in the front row and discussed their upcoming performance.

Richard asked Matt, "Do you feel confident about tonight?"

Matt answered, "Of course, why wouldn't I?"

"I want to make sure. Tonight, we're doing the same show from two weeks ago and then we're on to new acts."

Around seven o'clock the crowd filed in. Matt peeked from behind the curtain. He turned, looked at Richard. "I think it's going to be a full house."

Richard replied, "Of course, it is. Matthew, we have the best show not only in the city but in the state. Within time, our show will be number one in the country."

The show got underway and Matt performed some of his acts solo. Then Richard joined him for some of the bigger ones. Everything was moving along like a well-oiled machine.

It got to be eight-forty and Matt called out, "Ladies and gentlemen, we have time for one more. We'll be needing the services of a volunteer for this one. Before I select a volunteer, could everyone please look at the monitor above me? The monitor is going to play a version of our next trick. Please watch this and I think you'll like our version better."

The video stopped after three and a half minutes.

Matt asked, "Now, can we have a volunteer. Please remember you'll not be harmed in any way."

A bunch of hands went up and Matt looked at the willing participants. He picked someone from the twelfth row.

Matt said, "Please miss, come on up." Matt put his hand out and asked, "What is your name?"

The volunteer put her hand out and said, "Sherry, Sherry LaPointe."

Matt replied, "It's a pleasure to meet you, Sherry. Now, if I can get you to look at this truck here. As you can see, aside from being a replica of a vintage moving truck, there's nothing unusual about this vehicle."

Sherry walked around the truck and looked it over. She opened the driver's side door, poked her head in, and looked around.

Sherry said to Matt, "It looks good to me."

Matt replied, "Awesome! Thank you, Sherry. Next, my partner, Richard will lie down in front of the truck." Richard took off his jacket and laid down on the floor just ahead of the front tires. Matt continued, "Okay Sherry, you get in on the passenger side. I'm driving." Matt asked, "Richard, are you ready?"

Richard answered, "Ready as I'll ever be."

"Good, here we go." Matt put the truck in low gear.

The truck moved forward slowly and when it got to Richard it went up in the air a few inches and then came back down. The vehicle rolled forward a little more and once again it went up in the air a few inches and came back down.

Matt said to Sherry, "Now, we just need to check on Richard." As Matt opened the door, he could see Richard brushing his shirt off. Richard stood up and Matt said, "I'm glad you're okay."

Richard fired back at him, "Why wouldn't I be? It would have been better if the tires weren't so filthy."

Matt added, "Well, that's something we can work on. Sherry, as you can see Richard is okay. What did you think of that?"

Sherry answered, "We just drove over your partner and he's okay. I don't see how that was possible."

Richard cut in and offered, "Sherry, this is something I call magic and I enjoy doing it with my friend Matt. Please wait up here Sherry while we say goodnight to the audience."

Matt called out to the audience, "Ladies and gentlemen, this concludes our show for tonight. Please, if you like what you saw tell your friends and relatives. My name is Matt White. This is my partner and good friend Richard Jenkins. Please have a good night and drive safely." Matt, next looked at Sherry and said, "I'd like to give you a couple of free passes for helping out tonight."

Sherry put her hand out and said, "Thank you, Mr. White. I thought the show was very good and I enjoyed it." Sherry then asked, "Mr. Jenkins, are you okay?"

Richard answered, "Of course, I am. I pledged Mr. White a long time ago that neither one of us will ever sustain an injury while performing. So far, we're holding to that."

Sherry offered, "Well, I had a good time and I'll tell all my friends. Goodnight. Sherry went down the stairs off the stage and walked up the main aisle.

Matt looked at Richard and asked, "Are you ready?"

"Yes, I am and I don't mind skipping the diner tonight."

"That's fine by me, let's go." Matt and Richard left the theater and headed home.

Sunday, October 10th

Matt headed downstairs around six-twenty. He barely made it halfway and he heard Thomas stirring. Matt made an about-face and went into Thomas's room. He scooped his son from the crib and started his journey downstairs a second time. Matt made his way to the kitchen to get a bottle for Thomas. Richard was sitting in the corner at the table and pointed in the direction of the counter.

He said softly, "All warmed up."

Matt countered, "Thank you, and good morning, Richard. I'm trying to let Sarah sleep in."

Matt was feeding Thomas without sitting and Richard offered, "Good, she'll have an additional fourteen minutes, and then she'll be down here."

Fourteen Minutes Later

Sarah made her way downstairs just as Richard predicted. She made her way into the kitchen and said, "Good morning Richard. It looks like Matt beat me to the punch. I feel so out of place without holding Thomas first thing in the morning."

Richard responded with, "It was Matthew's intention for you to get some extra needed rest. How unfortunate that it was limited."

Sarah offered, "I'm just used to getting up early so it's hard to just stay sleeping. Now, it's time to search out my husband." Sarah went into the living room and Matt was sitting in one of the wingchairs with Thomas. Thomas finished his bottle and was sleeping in his father's arms. Sarah waved to Matt without making a peep.

Matt smiled and said, "I'm going to bring him back up."

Sarah nodded, grabbed her notepad off the end table, and started a shopping list. She wrote down about fifteen items and handed the list to Matt.

"Here, take this and if you can think of anything else, we need, go for it. Please pick up things for Denise for the week. I'm sure Richard knows what she likes for her lunches."

Matt replied, "Okay, will do. Let me go see if my partner in crime wants to come for the ride." Matt went into the kitchen and asked Richard, "Do you want to come with me for an Albertson's run? I'll be ready in less than twenty minutes."

Richard answered, "You know I do. I'll be ready when you are."

Twenty Minutes Later

Matt and Richard headed off to Albertson's for their shopping. Once inside they made their way through the aisles filling the carriage.

Matt started the conversation, "Richard, I have a couple of questions."

Richard offered, "Fire away, no wait. Yes, I already planned our next show. Secondly, Denise is quite comfortable watching Thomas. Remember, she used to watch her nephew for her sister. Denise would have let Sarah know by now if she didn't feel at ease. Matt, if there was any doubt in my mind that this woman was not capable, I would have spoken up a couple of weeks ago. I knew Sarah was itching to get back to work. That was why I initiated those phone calls."

"Thank you for that Richard. That puts mine and will put Sarah's mind at ease. Wait, a minute. What do you mean you initiated those phone calls?"

"You're welcome and do you think Denise called Sarah on her own? I made that happen and it worked out for the best. How about we go over our next show when we get home."

Matt replied, "That works for me. Let's get this stuff home." They loaded the bags in the car and headed back to the house.

Matt walked in the door around four-twenty. He called in, "Richard, Denise, I'm home."

Richard emerged from the kitchen and greeted Matt, "Hello Matt, I trust you had a good day. Denise is upstairs changing Thomas. After she gets him back to sleep, we can go over our next show seeing as we didn't discuss it Sunday."

Fifteen Minutes Later

Denise came downstairs and saw Matt. She said, "Hello Matt, Thomas is sleeping. Before I forget, I think the monitor needs new batteries. I didn't know if you had any new ones or where you kept them."

Matt replied, "Okay, thanks we keep new batteries in this drawer. In the future, Denise please do not hesitate to ask Richard. He knows everything about our house. I'll replace these in a minute. So, I'll see you tomorrow."

Denise left and Richard said to Matt, "Good, she's gone. We can discuss this before Sarah gets home. Are you ready?"

Matt answered, "Yes, but I want to take care of the monitor before I forget."

"The baby monitor does not require new batteries. Look at the monitor. It's not designed to work like that."

"Like what?"

"The device should not be laying down as it is now. Just stand it up and then we're done." Immediately faint noises were heard coming from the speaker. "I think Denise accidentally knocked it over getting out of the chair."

Matt said, "Once again, you got it right. Let's go into the dining room."

Richard and Matt sat at the table and Richard opened the journal.

"This illusion is a good one and it involves both of us. I got this idea seeing Greg Frewin performing this at the Tropicana in Las Vegas. We start by having a box on stage in the shape of an old-fashioned coffin. You get inside and there will be a small explosion on the stage just enough for a distraction.

"The way Mr. Frewin does this is the explosion goes off and he's gone from the coffin. Now, he's located at the back of the theater standing on one of the tables. The way we'll do this is I will appear on the table with the lights on me and then snap my fingers. You appear in my place. I know the audience will love it. They'll be clapping and we're not done."

"Not done? You mean there's more?"

"Yes, after you appear, you're going to say to the audience, 'Ladies and gentlemen, please look upfront. Then you point in the direction of the stage and I am standing in front of the audience. I'll hold both my arms out with my palms facing up. I then rise to the stage. This is what we talked about the other day. Okay Matt, are you with me?"

"I love it. Do you think it will work?"

Richard answered, "Of course it will, and please don't ask me that every time we go out to perform. Now, if you'll excuse me, I need to get dinner started."

With that, Richard stood up and made his way to the kitchen. Matt noticed he left his journal there. He sat for a minute and noticed everything Richard just explained to him was in the book. Matt remembered when Richard opened the book in front of him there were very few words on the page.

Matt stood up and grabbed the journal to put it away. He called out to Richard, "I'm heading upstairs to wash up. I'll put your book in the hutch." Matt felt the book vanish from his hand and it was back in the drawer.

Five-Forty

Sarah walked in and yelled, "Hello Matt, I'm home."

Matt greeted Sarah with a kiss and asked, "How was your day honey?"

Sarah answered, "Long as usual. How is Thomas doing?"

"He's upstairs sleeping and should be waking soon. Denise put him up there right before she left."

"Good, that gives me a couple of minutes to get changed." She went upstairs, changed into some sweats, and as soon as she stepped out of her room, she heard Thomas crying. Sarah said, "Coming honey."

Sarah went into Thomas' room, scooped him out of the crib, and asked, "How's my little angel today? I know you're hungry. Let's get you a clean diaper first and then go downstairs. Five minutes later the two were on their way into the kitchen for a bottle.

By six-forty-five Sarah had Thomas fed and the three of them sat down to dinner. Sarah said to Matt and Richard, "Sorry for the delay, someone was hungry."

Matt spoke up and said, "We understand honey. I have good news."

Sarah asked, "What good news?"

Matt answered, "Richard and I sat down, planned our next show and it's going to be something you've never seen before."

Sarah replied, "Okay, I hope there's not going to be any knives or sawblades coming at you. I'm not thrilled with you being lowered upside down in a tank of water either."

Richard cut in and said, "Excuse me, Sarah, I have to get this in there. Matt is my friend, your husband, and the father of your son. I wouldn't dream of letting anything bad happen to him."

Sarah asked Richard, "Richard, with all due respect are you telling me you always have control of the situation?"

Richard answered, "I know I have full control of our show. I am capable of controlling everything that happens to us." With that, Richard waved his hand and pointed at the empty chair. The chair went up in the air about fifteen inches, turned all the way around, and then fell back to the floor. Richard asked, "Did you see that?"

Sarah answered, "Okay, you sort of made your point."

'Richard asked, "What do you mean sort of?"

Sarah answered, "I want to see something and I will be convinced if I pick what I want to see. I want to look out the window and see my van roll forward in the driveway. The driver's door is to open and close just once."

Richard responded, "As you wish. Please look at your request being done outside."

Sarah looked out the window and just as she requested there was her van going forward. The van rolled forward twenty feet and then stopped. The driver's side door opened all the way and then closed. The garage door opened and the van went inside and then the garage door came back down.

Richard looked at Sarah and said, "I hope you don't mind but I think your van will be better off in the garage."

Sarah replied, "That's fine in the garage. I have to say you do have control."

Richard added, "That's exactly what I've been telling you, Mrs. White."

The Next Morning: Wednesday, October 13th

Matt came downstairs around six-fifteen and went directly to the coffee. Richard was sitting in his usual spot with his newspaper. Matt greeted Richard first. "Good morning, Richard. How are you?"

Richard answered, "Just splendid and good morning to you as well Matt."

Matt took a few more sips of his coffee and poured the last half-inch of coffee in the sink. He looked at Richard and said, "I have to go and I'll see you around four-fifteen."

Richard replied, "Have a good day Mr. White."

Matt got in his car and backed out of the driveway. He caught sight of Denise's car coming up the street. Matt and Denise waved at each other as they passed. Denise pulled in the driveway at six-forty. Richard opened the front door as Denise walked up the front stairs.

Richard greeted Denise, "Good morning Miss Bennett."

Denise responded with, "Good morning Richard. How are you?"

Richard answered with his usual response, "Just splendid Denise; please help yourself to coffee. Sarah should be down shortly."

Seven Minutes Later

Sarah came downstairs and she was not holding Thomas. Sarah said, "Good morning Denise. Thomas is still sleeping. Do you mind getting him when he wakes up?"

Denise answered, "Good morning, and not at all."

Sarah continued, "Denise, Matt told me to tell you there's another show coming up on the twenty-third if you want to go. He said you can have two tickets for you and Tom."

Denise responded with, "Okay, I'll call Tom tonight and tell him. It will be nice to do something other than going to the movies."

Sarah added, 'They're supposed to have new material for the show. I told Matt I don't care to see him involved in anything dangerous. I tell you what, you and Tom go to the show and then let me know if it's safe to go to the next one."

Denise asked, "What do you mean safe?"

Sarah answered, "I say safe because I don't consider Matt getting put in a tank of water or having a buzz saw come at him a good thing to watch. That makes me too nervous. Well, I have to go. I'll see you tomorrow."

Denise added, "Okay, bye. Have a good day."

Ten Days Later: Saturday, October 23rd

Saturday morning bright and early Matt came downstairs to get coffee and start his day. Richard was sitting at the table with the newspaper folded in front of him.

Matt said, "Good morning Richard. What's the matter? Does nothing interest you in today's news?"

Richard answered, "Oh no, that's not it at all. I was just thinking about something. Good morning by the way."

"Thinking about?" Matt asked.

"What else, our upcoming vacation. I know it's six months away but I'm looking forward to it. We all deserve this vacation."

Matt replied, "You can say that again. I forgot to ask. What about props for tonight's show?"

"I knew you'd be concerned about that and it's already taken care of. All that's required now is we get there about forty-five minutes early to go over our final act."

Five-Forty-five That Evening.

Sarah was sitting in the room reading her Sue Grafton book while Thomas was napping. Matt said, "Okay honey we're heading out now."

Sarah responded. "Oh Matt, I forgot to tell you Denise should be at the show tonight."

"Oh good, we'll see her there. We should be back by ten-thirty."

Matt and Richard left and headed for the theater. They took their usual seats in the front row.

Matt said to Richard, "I don't mind telling you this time I'm nervous."

Richard asked, "Why?"

"I've never been shot out of anything never mind a wooden coffin."

Richard explained, "First of all, relax. I have it covered and you're not getting shot out of anything. You'll be in the box briefly, but that's as far as it goes. You can tell the audience to stay focused on the wooden coffin. I think it would be best if we just refer to it as a wooden box. You'll go and lay down in the box. There will be a small and I do mean small explosion on the stage. This is only for setting a distraction. Once the explosion goes off is when I make my move."

"You make your move?"

Richard answered, "Yes, you'll appear standing on one of the tables after I snap my fingers."

Matt asked, "Is that it?"

Richard again answered, "No, there's a little more. This is what happens next. You're going to say to the audience, 'Ladies and gentlemen, please look upfront' while you're pointing in the direction of the stage and I'm standing in front of the audience. I'll hold both my arms out with my palms facing up. I then float up to the stage. We talked about this the other day. Are you with me?"

Matt answered, "Okay, I got it."

The crowd made their way in. Matt heard the crowd coming in and he said to Richard, "We need to make ourselves scarce."

Matt and Richard got out of their seats and went backstage. The show started promptly at seven-thirty. The two of them performed their acts flawlessly. Matt performed one of his illusions with Richard watching from behind the curtain.

79

Richard walked out and rejoined Matt on the stage. Matt said to the audience, "Ladies and gentlemen, this is my show partner and good friend Richard Jenkins. I am going to leave him alone with you for a few minutes."

Richard said, "Thank you, Mr. White." He continued, "Ladies and gentlemen I appreciate the opportunity to share with you what I like to do. Now, I have that question, "A lot of magicians ask, who wants to volunteer?"

Ten people raised their hands from the front section. Richard picked a man looking to be in his twenties.

He said, "Please come on up sir."

The volunteer walked up on the stage and Richard asked, "Your name is?"

The volunteer answered, "Glenn, Glenn Sparks."

Richard replied, "It's nice to meet you, Glenn. There's no need to be nervous and I hope you like card tricks. I have in my pocket two new decks of Bicycle playing cards." Richard handed Glenn the decks of cards and he continued, "Glenn would you please hold the cards out so the camera can see they're still wrapped in plastic."

Glenn held the cards high in the air. Richard said, "Glenn, there is a cameraman right behind you." Richard signaled for the cameraman to move in closer. Richard continued, "Glenn please unwrap both decks of cards and put one of them on the table behind you." Glenn unwrapped both decks and put them on the table as instructed. Richard continued, "Now, Glenn, I want you to fan through the cards and look at them. They should be in their original order."

Glenn examined the cards and said, "You're right. All the cards are in order like a new deck."

Richard continued, "Okay Glenn, please give the cards a good shuffle."

Glenn took the cards and shuffled them for twenty seconds. Richard said, "Glenn when you're done, please fan the cards open and let the cameraman see them." Glenn fanned the cards open and held them in front of the camera.

Richard said, "That's great. Now, if you'll just hand me the cards so I can check your shuffling results." Glenn hands the cards back to Richard. Richard looked at the cards and said, "We're not getting anything accomplished unless you get these cards shuffled. Richard fanned the cards open and held them out to the cameraman. The cards were back in an order resembling a new deck.

Richard continued, "Glenn let me shuffle the cards for us, please. After I mix these up, I'm going to teach you how to do your card trick." He shuffled the cards up a few times and Richard said, "That should do it. Glenn I'm going to hold the deck of cards with the faces down in the palm of my hand. I want you to think of any card. When I say NOW. I want you to tell me the card you're thinking of. Okay?"

Glenn answered, "Got it."

Richard waited three seconds and said, "NOW." He pointed at Glenn.

Glenn spoke up and said, "I was thinking of the king of spades."

Richard continued, "Please turn over the card in the deck."

Glenn turned the card over and it was the king of spades. Richard continued, "Glenn, please think of another card and it cannot be your previous choice. I'm just going to slip the king in my pocket. One...two...three...NOW"

Richard pointed at Glenn a second time. Glenn sounded out, "That time I was thinking of the ace of diamonds."

Richard continued, "Okay Glenn, one more time please turn over the top card."

Glenn turned the card over and it was the ace of diamonds. He asked Richard, "Is this the card trick you're going to teach me?"

Richard answered, "Yes, it is and not to worry Glenn. You can do this."

Just as Richard finished speaking a member from the audience stood up and asked, "How do we know that Glenn doesn't have the top few cards memorized? I mean it seems pretty convenient that he predicted the top card twice."

Richard explained, "Sir, I assure you or can I call you Charles? This is on the up and up. Remember, I shuffled the cards last. Please, let me show you." Richard walked off the stage and motioned for the cameraman to follow. The cameraman was close behind as they walked over to where Charles was standing. Richard was standing in the aisle with the same cards in his palm. He said to Charles, "Please think of a card and when I saw NOW, I want you to tell me the card you're thinking of."

Richard continued, "One...two...three...NOW!"

Charles replied, "I was thinking of the queen of hearts."

Richard responded with, "Charles, please look at the top card." Charles turned over the top card in Richard's hand. It was the queen of hearts. Charles asked, "How did you do that?"

Richard answered, "I can't tell you that. You have a better chance of winning the lottery. By the way, that won't be happening either. Thank you for your help Charles but I left Glenn up there and I need to return to him."

Richard walked back on the stage and said, "Glenn thank you for your patience. These cards are for you." Richard slipped the cards back in the box and handed them to Glenn.

Glenn took the cards from Richard and said, "Thank you, Mr. Jenkins."

Richard also shook Glenn's hand and said, "Thank you for your help. Please have a good night." Richard's shaking hands with Glenn was Richard's way of transferring the power that would allow Glenn to do this card trick. Glenn's new skill would be short-lived. Richard kept that little bit of information to himself.

Glenn left the stage and returned to his seat. Richard made the announcement, "Thank you, ladies and gentlemen. I think it's time we bring Mr. White back out here."

The audience started clapping and Matt waved to the audience as he walked to center stage. Matt put his hands up and said, "Please give a big hand for my friend Richard." The audience continued with the clapping and Matt put up his hands again, "Ladies and gentlemen, we have enough time for one more. I call this one the quick shoot."

The curtains closed behind them while the stagehands worked diligently to set the props in place. Matt addressed the audience again, Ladies and gentlemen, please look at the monitor above me. Here, you'll see Greg Frewin performing the trick we're about to attempt. I am not saying we can outdo or even match Mr. Frewin's performance. I don't think anyone can perform like Greg Frewin. However, we do like to add a little something to our version. We'll begin at the end of the video."

The video ran for six minutes and the curtain reopened. Matt said to the audience, "Ladies and gentlemen please keep your eyes on the wooden box up here." Matt pointed to the box and then was escorted up a few steps by two beautiful assistants. When he got to the top, he stepped into the wooden box that was in the shape of an old-fashioned coffin. Matt laid down in the box. There was some dramatic music playing and then a small explosion on stage. Smoke engulfed the area where the box was located.

There was more music and the audience heard, "Hey." Matt was standing on a table at the back of the theater with the spotlight on him. Matt hollered out, "Everyone, look upfront." Matt pointed in the direction of the stage and then climbed down from the table. Richard was standing upfront with his palms up. He then rose slowly up in the air until he was standing on the stage. Matt jogged down the main aisle and joined Richard on the stage. He made his final announcement to the audience, "Ladies and gentlemen, "That concludes our show for tonight. Please, if you like what you saw, tell your friends. My name is Matt White and this is my partner and good friend Richard Jenkins. Please drive safely and have a good night."

Matt said to Richard, "Well Mr. Jenkins looks like we pulled it off again."

Richard replied, "Yes, Matthew, I agree tonight's show was a success. Here's a thought, let's stop at the diner for a coffee. I'll even let you treat."

"That's so nice of you Richard. Let's go." The two of them left the theater and stopped in the diner for a coffee. Once they were in their usual booth, Matt said to Richard, "I hope you don't mind if we don't stay too long. I'm not too keen on leaving Sarah alone."

Richard replied, "I understand Matthew. What if we stay here for just fifteen minutes? Sarah is doing just fine right now. You have my word on that. While we're here, I want to tell you I have something planned for the next show. This is not a borrowed trick that we add something to. This is original and it will be all us, well actually all me. We can discuss it more in detail during our food shopping excursion."

Richard took his last sip of coffee and said, "I'm ready when you are."

Matt said, "That makes two of us."
Matt finished his coffee and they left the diner and headed home.

11

A Little Warmer

Sunday morning Matt came downstairs at six forty-five to get his coffee and start his day. Matt saw Richard sitting in the corner and he said, "Good morning Richard."

Richard replied, "Good morning Matt. I went and got my paper ninety minutes ago and I could tell Fall weather has arrived."

Matt added, "Yes it has, and there's nothing we can do about it."

"You mean there's nothing you can do about it. Me, on the other hand, is another story." Richard took another sip of his coffee and said, "I think the elements outside would be a lot more tolerable if it was warmer."

Matt replied, "It's fifty-eight out now. How hot do you want it? It's supposed to be a high of sixty-six today."

Richard tilted his head to the side, closed up the newspaper, and answered, "Seventy-eight sounds right to me."

Matt responded, "I don't think it would be a good idea to be fooling around with the weather. I mean a spike of twelve degrees in temperature especially in October doesn't make sense."

A few seconds later the bedroom door opened upstairs and Sarah came down.

Richard said, "Matt when Sarah gets down here, we'll ask for her opinion."

Matt replied, "That's fine with me but I know her pretty well and she's not one for upsetting the course of things."

Sarah walked into the kitchen and said, "Good morning you two." She walked over and kissed Matt on the cheek.

Sarah opened the refrigerator and Matt said, "Go ahead and sit and relax. I'll get Thomas when he's ready."

Sarah reached for the Cran-grape juice.

Richard was still sitting in the corner and spoke up, "Sarah, your husband and I were having a brief conversation about the outside temperature. I was told today is going to be a high of sixty-six. My question is would you like it warmer?"

Sarah answered, "Richard, I don't know what you're looking to do here but I think the weather is something that should not be tampered with. We're in late October now and sixty-six is way above average. Two more months it will be winter and we'll be happy with sixty-six."

Richard responded with, "I see your point, Mrs. White. Now, to change the subject, will you be sending your husband and me out to Albertson's?"

"Yes, and I have a list started."

Richard reached in his pocket and asked, "Is this it?"

Sarah answered, "Yes, I just want to add granola bars and food for Denise's lunches."

Richard replied, "You got it, Mrs. White."

Richard never handed Sarah the list nor did he take a pen to add the two items to it. Granola bars and deli meats were added to the list in Richard's way.

Seven-Forty-Five

Matt and Richard were off to Albertson's for the weekly food shopping. On the way over Richard asked, "Do you remember me telling you we can go over details for our next show?"

Matt answered, "Yes, what do you have?"

"I'm thinking we can go through the audience scouting for more than one volunteer. This will work best with five or six volunteers. Generally, when people come to our show, they have money with them. We go through the audience and ask the volunteers one at a time if they have a dollar bill with them. We ask them to take out the dollar bill from their wallet or handbag and put it in one of their front pockets."

They pulled into Albertson's parking lot and Matt asked, "Can we finish the conversation inside?"

Richard answered, "Of course."

They went into the store and Matt asked, "As you were saying?"

Richard continued, "We get the volunteers to put the dollar bill in their front pocket. Then, I'll say to the volunteers please place a hand over the pocket that has the dollar bill. I'll count to three and then ask them to remove their dollar. When they remove it, they discover the dollar has changed to a fifty-dollar bill."

Matt asked, "Don't you think that is a little over the top? I mean we don't want too much attention drawn to ourselves."

"I've been thinking about this part. I believe it's best to have the audience leave with more money in their pocket. They'll also forget about what they just experienced. I can arrange it so the volunteers think that fifty-dollar bill was in their pocket the whole time. Therefore, we're not bringing too much attention to ourselves."

"What about at the end of the show where we announce how this concludes our show for tonight."

Richard answered, "You can still do that. Everyone in the audience will see the full show. Once they exit the theater, they will forget what they saw."

Matt said, "Okay, I like it. Let me see, I think we have everything we need. Do you agree?"

"We're all set." Matt pushed the carriage to the checkout. Ten minutes later, he was putting the groceries in the car. The two of them got back in the car and Matt drove them back to the house.

They pulled into the driveway and Matt asked Richard, "Do you know what's good about the shopping being done?"

Richard answered, "Yes, it's coffee time."

Matt responded with, "Actually, I was thinking we have the rest of the day to do what we want."

Matt took two bags of groceries and carried them into the house. Richard opened the front door for him. Matt got to the kitchen and noticed the other three bags were on the kitchen table. Richard was in the kitchen emptying the bags.

He said to Matt, "Sarah's upstairs sleeping. Try to keep the noise down."

Matt put his hand out and gave a thumbs up. He pointed to the coffeemaker and said to Richard, "See you in the dining room."

Richard nodded and poured another cup of coffee for himself.

Matt and Richard were sitting at the dining room table drinking their coffee. Richard turned slightly in his chair, pointed at the hutch, and the drawer opened. Richard's journal floated up and onto the table.

Matt sat there and asked, "Do you always have to show off?"

Richard answered, "No, I do not and Matt you've not seen me show off. Now, if I may point out the book is barely filled up halfway. The good news is I have enough ideas to fill three more journals."

"Are you serious?"

Richard answered, "I do not joke around when it comes to my favorite talents."

Matt said, "I see."

"Matthew, I predict by the beginning of next summer Mr. Turlo is going to want you to do shows on Thursday and Saturday."

"Do you mean Turco? Also, it will be us doing the shows, not just me."

"Okay, I never said I was good at remembering names and Thomas is awake, but Sarah is getting him."

Matt replied, "Okay," and asked, "Before Sarah gets down here, when are we going to put that new trick in our show?"

"November sixth we'll repeat the last show we did. That will bring us to November twentieth to put something new in. Not to worry, I have more ideas stored in the bank. Sorry, I said that wrong. I meant to say I have many more ideas stored in my head."

Sarah came downstairs holding Thomas and she said, "Good morning honey, good morning Richard."

Matt replied, "Good morning honey," and he kissed Sarah on the cheek. "Honey, go sit down and put your feet up. I'll take care of Thomas."

Sarah asked, "Are there any major plans for today?"

Matt answered, "Actually, no. We did the food shopping and we put away all the groceries. Do you have anything in mind?"

"Yes, but I think I should talk to you about it first. It's a major purchase."

Matt asked, "What's a major purchase?"

Sarah answered, "I want to get a new car. My Corolla runs okay, but it's a pain if I have to put Thomas in it to take him to a doctor's appointment."

Matt put his index finger and thumb on his chin pretending to be thinking it over. "I think we can squeeze that into the budget. Your car is paid off. You can pick out a car and we trade yours in. If I'm not mistaken, Grossinger Toyota is open on Sunday. Just a minute honey, I'll ask Richard if he remembers."

Matt went into the living room and before he could ask, Richard, answered, "They're open now. Their hours are ten to six."

Matt asked, "Did you remember that from last year?"

Richard answered, "No, I did not. I just assigned those hours and I'm sure Tim Sparks will be happy to see us. Let me make a suggestion here. I'm sure Sarah will find a car for her fancy. On the way back, stop at Toys R Us and purchase a second car seat for the other vehicle. I don't need to tell you but I'm sure there'll be a time when one of the vehicles is in the shop."

Matt replied, "That's a very good thought. Thank you. The next thing to do is have Sarah call Denise to see if she wouldn't mind watching Thomas for a few hours."

Matt walked back into the living room and said to Sarah, "Honey, do you mind getting Denise on the phone to see if she can watch Thomas for a few hours? Tell her I'll pay her extra."

Sarah answered, "Okay, I'll call her."

12

The Visit

Denise pulled in the driveway at nine forty-five. Richard opened the door and greeted her, Good morning Miss Bennett. Thank you for coming over on short notice."

Richard asked, "Would you like some coffee?"

Denise answered, "Thank you, Richard. I didn't have any coffee today." Denise reached into the cabinet and took out a mug. She saw something in the mug and it was a fifty-dollar bill. Denise took it out and said to Richard, "This was in the mug."

Richard replied, "Ah yes, that is something extra for you. Let's call it a tip or gratuity for better words."

"You know I am Sarah's friend and I don't expect to be paid for today. Sarah told me this should only take a few hours and then I can pick up a few things at Albertson's on the way home."

"Here comes Sarah now and we can talk more about the supermarket later."

Sarah walked into the kitchen and said, "Good morning Denise, and thank you for coming over on short notice. This shouldn't take us too long."

Denise took a sip of her coffee and replied, "You're welcome and I'm glad to help."

Sarah said, "Okay, Thomas is upstairs napping and we'll be leaving." Matt and Sarah went out the door, got in Sarah's car, and headed for the car dealer.

Denise sat down in the living room with her coffee and Richard sat in the seat across from her.

Denise asked Richard, "You care to explain what you meant by we'll talk about that later?"

91

Richard answered, "Yes, I suppose you have a list in mind of what you want to pick up at Albertson's."

Denise answered, "Yes, I do," and she pulled out a list with seven items written down.

Richard looked at the list and said, "This is easy enough. All of these items can be obtained at no cost from the White's kitchen. This will save you time and money."

"You're right, it will. Let me just take the orange juice with me. I'll stop at Albertson's tomorrow on the way home and I'll replace it."

"As you wish Miss Bennett but it's not necessary."

That Afternoon: One-Thirty

Matt and Sarah walked into the house and Richard asked, "How did the car shopping go?"

Matt answered, "It went great. Sarah found a car she likes and they're allowing her a fair price for her trade. I just have to go to the bank tomorrow and get a cashier's check for the balance."

Richard shook his head no and said to Matt, "Follow me please."

Matt followed Richard to his room and Richard asked, "How much does the check have to be for?"

Matt answered, "$21,395."

Richard opened his top dresser drawer and said, "Here take this." He handed Matt a cashier's check already made out to Grossinger Toyota for $21,395. The check was dated for the next day.

Matt looked at it and asked, "How did you know the amount?"

Richard replied, "I think you ask that silly question every couple of weeks. I hope I don't have to keep explaining to you how I know these things. The boss needs you."

Sarah called, "Matt, honey, do you have a minute?"

Matt answered, "Yes."

Sarah asked, "Why didn't we try to finance the car? I probably could have driven it home."

"Honey, we didn't finance it because we're better off just buying it outright. Right now, the interest rate on the loan is 6.9 percent. We can bring a cashier's check to the car dealer tomorrow after work and you can drive your new car home. Tuesday on the way home, I want to pick up another car seat so we'll have one in each car."

Denise was patiently waiting in the living room and when Sarah returned, Denise said, 'Thomas is upstairs sleeping. I fed him and he was no trouble at all. So, I'll see you tomorrow morning."

Sarah responded with, "Goodbye Denise, and thanks again."

The Next Day: Monday, October 25th

Matt walked into the house at four forty-five thirty minutes later than usual. He called in, "Richard, Denise, I'm home."

Richard was in the living room dusting the furniture and Denise was sitting in one of the wing chairs feeding Thomas. Richard greeted Matt, "Hello Matthew. Do you have a mission accomplished with the car seat?"

Matt answered, "Yes, I have and it's in my car." Matt looked at Denise and said, "Sorry, I'm late. I had to stop at Toys R Us."

Denise replied, "No problem at all. I'm just going to put Thomas back upstairs."

"Thank you, and we'll make this up to you by adding in extra to your pay."

Denise responded with, "Matt, that's not necessary."

"Okay, but you also gave up part of your Sunday afternoon."

"I gave up three and a half hours and it's not a big deal. You and Sarah are picking up her new car. I'll stick around 'til you get back."

Fifteen Minutes Later

Sarah walked into the house at five-fifteen. Matt greeted her and kissed her on the cheek.

Sarah said to Matt, "Hello honey, I just want to go upstairs, change, and then we can go."

Matt replied. "Okay, I'll get the check."

Sarah came back downstairs and Sarah drove the two of them to the Toyota dealer. Once they got in the Toyota showroom, they looked for their salesman Tim Sparks. Matt gave him the check and they signed the paperwork for the car. Sarah drove them home in her 2005 Toyota Sequoia.

13

Hypnotized

Twelve Days Later: Saturday, November 6th

Matt came downstairs to get his coffee and start the day. Richard was sitting at the table sipping his coffee.

Richard greeted Matt first, "Good morning Matt. Did you get a good night's sleep?"

Matt replied, "Good morning Richard and I slept well. Thank you for asking. I know this is our show night."

Richard added, "Yes, it is. Are you ready for it?"

"Ready as I'll ever be."

Ten Minutes Later

Sarah came downstairs and said, "Good morning Matt, Richard."

Matt returned with, "Good morning honey," and kissed Sarah on the cheek.

Richard added, "Good morning Sarah. Please have a seat and I'll bring you a hot breakfast to start your day."

Sarah waved her hand and said, "Richard, you don't have to go to all that trouble."

Sarah didn't know what was happening but she could feel herself being moved along to sit at the dining room table. It was like her legs were hypnotized. She did not feel any physical harm. The next thing she knew she was sitting at the table.

Sarah looked in Richard's direction and asked, "Richard, can you make me a Western Omelet?"

Richard answered, "I think that can be arranged."

Richard was standing on the right hand of Sarah putting a plate of food in front of her as soon as his sentence was finished.

Sarah let out, "WOW! You spoil me here. Thank you, Richard."

"It is my pleasure, Mrs. White. Now, take your time and enjoy it. If there is nothing else you require, I need to start on a couple of things."

Sarah sat at the table eating her breakfast with the baby monitor close at hand. Matt walked by and snagged the monitor off the table and said to Sarah, "You are off duty until four forty-five."

"Thank you, honey. Matt, I was thinking of calling the Firmanis later to see if they'd like to come over next Friday or Saturday"

Matt responded, "That sounds good, we've not seen them in a while. If you get a hold of them, tell Al to bring his cards. I'm sure Richard will enjoy entertaining."

Later That Day: Five Forty-Five

Matt said to Sarah, "Okay honey, Richard and I are heading out to the theater. We should be back by ten o'clock."

Sarah replied, "Okay, have a good night. I'm going to call Jeannie while Thomas is sleeping."

Sarah kissed Matt goodbye and picked up the phone. Jeannie answered the phone and Sarah invited Jeannie and Al over for the following Saturday. She asked Jeannie to tell Al to bring his cards. Richard had requested this a while ago. Jeannie told Sarah they already had plans.

Six-Forty-Five

Matt and Richard pulled into the parking garage. They waved to Tim the booth attendant as they went by. Once in the theater, they took their usual seats in the front row.

Matt said to Richard, "I just want to mention our final act does not have any audience participation. Any thoughts?"

Richard answered, "You're correct. It does not. All of the acts or illusions we do are not required to have audience participation.

However, if it bothers you, we can have two. I mean we will do this act leading it up to the grand finale."

"What grand finale?"

"Let me explain," Richard said. "Of course, once again we get a volunteer to come up on stage. When Donna comes up, you'll be introduced to her. I will be taking care of this whole thing. There'll be four circles on the stage. Two will be on the left side and two on the right. The circle will be fifteen inches in diameter.

"I'm going to have Donna stand at one end and you at the other. I'll tell Donna to relax, close her eyes, and think of where she's standing. I count to three, tell her to open her eyes and you and her will have changed places."

Matt said, "I have two questions. If we're asking for a volunteer, how do we know her name is Donna? My second question to be is that the whole thing? It doesn't sound like much."

"Yes, we're asking for a volunteer. It just so happens Donna Bowden will be our selection. To answer your second question, no, that's not the end of it. There's a lot more. After you and Donna change places, I will ask her if her sister Christine accompanied her tonight. I know she did. Donna will reply 'Yes' and I say 'Good'. I then snap my fingers and Donna is back in her seat and Christine will be occupying the circle that Donna was standing on."

"Okay, what will I be doing?"

Richard answered, "Watching and learning hopefully. Next, I thank Christine for helping out and I just point to Donna. Donna will then appear on one of the circles. I tell the audience to please give a round of applause for Christine and Donna. Next, you can tell the audience to have a good night."

Matt responded, "Okay, I'm good with that." The audience started coming in and Matt said, "We need to make ourselves scarce."

Matt and Richard went behind the curtain and waited 'til seven-thirty. The show got underway and they performed all the acts without a hitch. Around eight twenty-five Richard nodded to Matt and sent him a message saying it was time.

Matt made an announcement, "Ladies and gentlemen, we're now at the point in our show that we want to show you something new we've been working on. Sit back, relax, we hope you enjoy these."

"For this next trick, we'll need a volunteer. A woman in the seventh row quickly stood up and said, "I'll do it. I'll do it."

Matt replied, "That's great, come on up."

The volunteer walked up and Matt asked, "Can I get your name?"

She answered, "Donna, Donna Bowden."

Matt said, "Okay Donna, it's nice to meet you. This is my good friend and show partner, Richard."

Donna responded with, "It's nice to meet both of you." She shook Matt's hand and nodded to Richard.

Matt continued, "Okay, this is where Richard takes over."

Richard stepped forward and said, "Okay Donna can I have you stand on a circle here and we'll have Mr. White stand on a circle across from you. Now, Donna, I want you to close your eyes, try to relax, and think of where Mr. White is standing. I'm going to count to three. One...two...three, now you may open your eyes."

Donna opened her eyes and she was moved to the circle that Matt occupied. Matt also was moved to the circle Donna was on. Donna looked to her left and her right. She couldn't fathom how this happened. Donna never felt her body being carried, lifted, or pushed into a new location.

Richard approached Donna and asked, "Are you okay? I ask because we're not done here. Donna, did your sister Christine accompany you here tonight?"

Donna answered, "Yes, she did."

Richard replied, "Very good!"

He pointed in the direction of Christine's seat and Christine was standing in a circle next to Donna.

Next, Richard said to Christine, "Thank you for your help."

Richard pointed at the row she was sitting in and Christine was back in her seat. Next, it was Donna's turn and Richard pointed at their row a second time. Donna was reunited with her sister.

Matt announced to the audience, "Ladies and gentlemen, we have time for one more. Please sit back and enjoy it."

While Matt was talking the stagehands were moving things in place. The curtain opened and there was suspenseful music playing in the background. Matt was escorted by two assistants up a few steps. When he got to the top, he lowered himself into a wooden box in the shape of an old-fashioned coffin. The music was still playing in the background.

A few seconds later there was a small explosion on the stage just enough to set up a smokescreen and distraction. The smoke cleared and Matt could no longer be seen on the stage. Three seconds later there was a Hey sound coming from the back of the theater. Matt was standing on one of the tables.

Matt yelled out, 'Everyone please look up front!' Richard was in front of the stage.

He stretched his arms out in a welcoming motion and he floated up to the stage. Matt was making his way up front while this was going on. He walked up the stairs to the stage and stood next to Richard.

Matt made the announcement, "Ladies and gentlemen, that concludes our show for tonight. We hope you enjoyed it. My name is Matt White. This is my good friend and show partner, Richard Jenkins. Please drive safely and have a good night."

Matt then asked Richard, "Is this going to come back to haunt us? I mean, what you did there was out of the ordinary."

"Matthew, you know I don't do ordinary and in anticipation of you thinking that way, I had you say goodnight without telling the audience to tell their friends about what they saw. That makes our audience forget the trick involving you, Donna, and her sister."

"Oh, okay. Here's something we didn't do tonight. We didn't give away any free passes."

"You're right, we didn't. We can give away four at the next show to make up for it."

"Okay, are you ready to head home Mr. Jenkins?"

Richard answered, "Yes, I am. You may lead the way."

14

The Audience

Matt and Richard were in the kitchen drinking coffee. Richard asked Matt, "Were you unhappy with last night's performance?"

Matt answered, "I wouldn't say unhappy, maybe a little disappointed. I know we want to WOW the audience. I understand to do that we need to put on a show with entertaining and unique acts. I feel we also need to limit ourselves and stay away from the unbelievable. This is the second time we did a performance and you had to make the audience forget what they saw. Richard, in my opinion, we need to take it down a bit."

"Matthew, let me address your concerns. First off, I agree we need to have unique and entertaining acts. Second, we want to WOW the audience. As for limiting ourselves and staying away from the unbelievable, I cannot agree and will not agree. Let's compromise. I promise to take it down a tiny bit but we need to have something extra each time. Remember before we would perform an act that a magician has already done? We added something to it. We can do that now and then but we still need to come up with some amazing gimmicks. However, I am giving you a fair warning now, and then we're going to sneak in something unbelievable. Let's call it spectacular for a better word."

Matt walked over to the sink, rinsed out his coffee mug, and said, "Agreed."

Richard added, "One more thing, you're going to be in charge of the ordinary stuff. You get to decide which ones we do and when."

"Do I still get your help?"

Richard answered, "Of course you do. Just promise me you'll try to throw in an idea now and then." Richard pointed up and said, "Sarah will be down shortly. By shortly I mean three minutes."

Three Minutes Later

Sarah came downstairs and said, "Good morning Matt, Richard."

Matt replied, "Good morning honey," and kissed her on the cheek.

Richard added, "Good morning Mrs. White. Please have a seat at the table and I'll bring you some eggs."

Sarah responded, "Thank you, Richard. Just like always, you spoil me."

Richard added, "I don't consider this me spoiling you because I'm just doing my job. We need to keep you healthy so you can take care of Thomas."

Matt cut in and said, "You can say that again. I can't raise Thomas by myself."

Richard added, "You won't have to."

Sarah was sitting at the table eating her breakfast and then sounds could be heard coming from the baby monitor.

Matt said, "Honey, ignore that. I'm going up."

Matt went upstairs and lifted Thomas out of the crib. He came back downstairs and said, "It's changing time and then feeding."

Matt went to do an about-face and go up to the dressing table. Richard tapped Matt on the shoulder and said, "The other way," and pointed to one of the spare rooms.

He said to Matt, "I put a second table here yesterday to make it easier for Denise and you and Sarah."

"Oh great. So, the other day did you go to Babies R Us and pick out one of these?"

Richard answered, "Not exactly."

Matt asked Richard, "Did you call them and place the order over the phone for delivery?"

Richard answered the same as before, "Not exactly."

Matt replied, "Okay, we don't have to know how it got here but it was a very good idea."

Sarah got up and brought her plate to the kitchen. Sarah asked Matt, "Do you boys have any important plans for later?"

Matt answered, "As far as I know we're just making the usual run to Albertson's. I hope you have a list ready. Just to let you know every time I take Richard along; he already has the list up in his head without looking at what you wrote down"

"Okay, that's fine. I don't know if you remember this but Richard asked me a long time ago if there was anything, I thought we needed to jot it down. Then, in turn, he would make sure we have it."

Seven-Forty-Five

Matt and Richard took the ride to Albertson's. Once inside the store Matt asked Richard, "Do you care to revisit the discussion we had earlier?"

Richard answered, "Upon further review what if we do this, I promise you we'll continue to perform great illusions. Going forward, we'll discuss everything ahead of time. There'll be no more winging it or for a better word adlibbing."

Matt replied, "I can live with that."

"One more thing, let's have more of the spectacular and less of the just average, okay?"

Matt responded with, "Okay, agreed."

Around eight thirty-five, Matt pulled back into the driveway. Matt said to Richard, "I can get the bulk of this if you grab one bag." Matt got to the front door carrying two bags and Richard was standing in the kitchen folding the bags he emptied.

Matt looked at him and asked, "What are you doing?"

Richard answered, "Putting away groceries of course. I can't let you have all the fun without me."

Matt shook his head and walked back out to the van. He opened the hatch expecting to see three bags left. Matt was surprised there were none left.

He walked back into the house and said to Richard, "You could have told me you brought the rest of the bags in."

"You are right I could've told you that. The bright side of me forgetting is you got some exercise by walking. Walking is good for the heart."

Matt responded with, "So, I guess you're also an exercise expert."

"Matthew, do you remember what I told you I did before I moved into your house? I do plenty of walking during the evening hours especially on the nights I did not care to sleep in the back of the theater. I know I'm not a mortal like the rest of you but I have outlived any others that have the same powers as me."

"Okay, why are you telling me this?"

Richard answered, "I am telling you this so you might take my advice and try to stay active whenever you can. Now, if you'll excuse me, I have a little cleaning and some laundry I need to take care of." Richard walked upstairs and collected the linens for the wash.

15

Recharging

Matt came downstairs around six-fifteen and Richard was sitting in the corner at the kitchen table. Matt said, "Good morning Richard, how are you?"

Richard replied, "Good morning to you Matthew. I am doing well. There is nothing like a good night's sleep to recharge the body." Richard pointed at the cabinet and said, "Please, allow me." The cabinet door opened and a cup floated to the counter. Next, the coffee carafe tilted beside Matt's cup and filled it.

Matt said, "Nice, thanks but you know I like half-and-half in my coffee."

Richard replied, "Just look in your cup and see if that's to your liking."

Matt looked at his coffee and saw it getting lighter in color. He took a sip of the coffee and said, "I was going to put one of those sweetener envelopes in the coffee and it tastes like it's already in there."

Richard asked, "Do you mean that little empty Splenda envelope off to the side? I knew you were going to try that so I took the liberty of adding it for you."

"Thank you." Matt finished his coffee and said, "I have to go. I need to make some copies before class starts. See you around four-fifteen."

Richard replied, "Have a good day, Mr. White."

Matt walked out the door, got in his van, and headed off to work. Richard poured another coffee and thought to himself, 'This should be five minutes of peace for myself.'

Five minutes later to the second Denise pulled in the driveway. Richard opened the front door for her as she was coming up the stairs.

Denise greeted Richard, "Good morning Richard, how are you?"

Richard answered, "Just splendid Miss Bennett. I trust you had a good weekend."

Denise responded with, "Yes, I did. I did a lot of cleaning and organizing and I finished my Stephen King book. There is one thing going on outside I'm not liking. I know we're in the middle of the Fall but the temp is dropping big time. It's not only windy but it's cold as well."

"Miss Bennett the seasons are changing and there is nothing we can do about it. However, there is something I'd like to try that just may benefit you."

Denise asked, "What's that?"

Richard answered, "Sarah's on her way downstairs. After she leaves, we'll continue this conversation."

Sarah came downstairs and said, "Good morning Denise, Richard." Sarah poured herself half a glass of grapefruit juice and said, "Sorry Denise, I have to go in early. I hope you don't mind."

Denise replied, "Go ahead, I got this." Denise walked over and turned on the baby monitor. She turned around and asked Richard, "Did you say we could finish a conversation after Sarah leaves for work?"

Richard answered, "Yes, that is correct. I believe I have the remedy for you in the cold weather."

"You do? I have to hear this. Oh, wait, please don't say we should move to Nevada."

Richard replied, "You'll do nothing of the kind. You didn't hang up your jacket today."

Richard went into the kitchen, grabbed Denise's jacket, and hung it on the coat tree near the front door.

He said to Denise, "Your jacket should keep you warm enough so you won't feel the cold."

"Oh, did you give us the magic rub? asked Denise.

"Magic, I mean rub, oh no not at all. Just let me know tomorrow if this doesn't help you with going out to the car."

Denise responded with, "Okay, will do." Denise rolled her eyes when Richard walked away. She already had in mind that something was not right with Richard and she thought to herself this just sealed the deal.

Later That Day: Around Four-Twenty

Matt walked in and called out, "Hello Denise, Richard, I'm home."

Richard greeted Matt first, "Hello Matthew. I hope your day went well. Denise is upstairs putting Thomas down for a nap."

"Oh good," said Matt. "I have to remember to ask Sarah if she wants to invite her brother Sean and his wife Katelin for Thanksgiving."

Richard replied, "She can invite them but they won't be coming."

"And you know this how?" asked Matt.

"I know this because I know a lot of things. Katelin's parents live in Manchester which borders Londonderry. That's where they'll be going for Thanksgiving. It would be a good idea to have them over for Christmas."

Matt replied, "Thanks, I'll pass that along to Sarah."

Denise came downstairs and said, "Okay, I'm leaving and I'll be back tomorrow."

Matt smiled and said, "Okay, thank you." Richard gave her a friendly wave goodbye.

Denise walked out to her car, and the first thing she noticed was she was not feeling any breeze in the face or the cool temperature. She thought to herself, 'Wow, this coat is keeping me warm.' Denise planned on stopping at the Mobil station on the way home. She took a right at the end of the street and looked at her gas gauge. The needle was pointing to the letter F. 'Here is something else that's puzzling,' thought Denise.

Later On: Around Five-Forty-Five

Sarah walked in the front door and Matt was standing in the kitchen talking to Richard.

She said, "Hi honey," and kissed him on the cheek.

Matt returned the kiss and said, "Hey you."

Richard cut in and said, "Hello Mrs. White, I trust you had a good day at work. Dinner will be ready in less than twenty minutes."

Sarah replied, "Okay, I'm going upstairs to change my clothes. Be back in a few."

Seventeen Minutes Later

The three were sitting at the table eating.

Sarah asked, "Matt, do you mind if I call Sean and invite him and Katelin for Thanksgiving?"

Matt answered, "Sure, it's okay with me but does the cook mind?"

Richard responded with, "Of course not, they're your family."

He didn't mind because he already knew the answer Sean would be giving.

They finished eating and Sarah mentioned, "I'm going to call Sean before it gets too late."

Sarah went into the living room to call her brother.

Sean answered the phone right away. "Hello?"

Sarah replied, "Sean, it's me, Sarah. Are you busy?"

Sean answered, "Not so much, just watching the Nightly News. What's up?"

"Matt and I want to know if you and Katelin want to come over for Thanksgiving like last year. It'll be great seeing you two again. We can catch up and you can see my new car."

Sean cut in and said, "Sarah, I have to stop you right there. Thank you for the invite but were going over Katelin's parents this year. I'm going to have some time off after Christmas. Including Christmas, I have ten days off."

Sarah replied, "That works for us. Okay, well call me next week and we'll talk more. Make sure Katelin can get the time off."

"Okay, I will and I promise I'll call you next week. Say Hi to Matt for me."

Sarah hung up the phone and said to Matt, "Well, that was disappointing."

Matt asked, "Why what's wrong?"

Sean can't come for Thanksgiving because they're going over to Katelin's parents' house. He told me we can get together at Christmas. What do you think?"

"I think you should call them right back and tell him to make arrangements ASAP. Thanksgiving and Christmas are incredibly busy for traveling. Tell your brother to get something booked before the flights are gone." Sarah got back on the phone and called Sean to tell him what Matt said.

16

Busy and Tired

Matt came downstairs at six-twenty to get his morning coffee. Matt said, "Good morning Richard. Do I have to pour my coffee?"

Richard answered, "Good morning Matthew. If you're expecting me to spoil you? It's not going to happen."

"Don't worry about it. I was just being foolish." Matt finished his coffee and said, "I have to go. See you around four-fifteen."

Richard replied, "Have a good day Mr. White."

At six forty-five Denise's car pulled in the driveway. Richard opened the front door in anticipation of her coming up the front steps. He greeted Denise when she got to the front door, "Good morning Miss Bennett."

Denise smiled and responded with, "Good morning Richard. How are you?"

Richard answered, "Just splendid Denise and as usual help yourself to coffee. Sarah should be downstairs in five minutes."

Denise said, "Thank you." She took advantage of Richard's offer and poured herself a coffee.

Five minutes later Sarah was downstairs.

Denise quietly said to Richard, "I need to discuss something with you later after Sarah leaves."

Richard replied, "Sure thing Miss Bennett."

Sarah came in the kitchen said, "Good morning Denise, good morning Richard."

Denise answered back, "Good morning Sarah."

Richard added, "Good morning, Mrs. White. Make sure you close up your coat. It's quite windy out today."

"Okay, thank you, Richard. I'll see you tonight. Goodbye Denise." Sarah grabbed her bag and headed out the front door.

After Sarah left, Denise asked Richard, "Can we have that discussion I mentioned earlier?"

Richard sat down and said, "You go first."

"Yesterday you told me I would have no problem with the wind and cold temperature. You were correct. I did not feel it all. The second I stepped outside it felt like a Spring day. What's going on?"

Richard answered, "This is what's going on. I am trying to make things as comfortable for you here as possible. We have a way to go before Winter gets here. I don't want you to be afraid of leaving your house because of the climate."

"Okay, so you're saying you don't want me to freeze. Are you telling me that you are responsible for me not being cold yesterday?"

Richard answered, "I guess you could say that. I may as well tell you now. You're going to find out eventually."

"Find out what? asked Denise. At that moment Thomas could be heard over the baby monitor.

Richard said, "Looks like your workday is starting. We'll finish our talk after you get him settled."

Denise went upstairs, lifted Thomas out of the crib, and brought him to the changing table. She put a fresh diaper on him and then brought him downstairs for his first bottle. Denise was going to warm it up and she found out that was already taken care of. She sat in one of the wing chairs and started feeding him. Denise finished and put Thomas in the bassinet.

She went back to the kitchen and poured herself a fresh coffee. Denise could hear Richard in the laundry room. She grabbed a book from her bag and took a seat in the living room.

Richard stopped by the doorway and said to Denise, "I need about ten minutes to finish the folding and I'll join you."

"Okay, I'll be here."

Richard came into the living room less than ten minutes later. Denise closed her book and said, "I'm all ears."

Richard said, "Okay, I'm about to tell you something only two other people know and they are Matt and Sarah. I can do things that only men can dream about. I am talking about the magic and illusion show. I am the mastermind behind it. If it wasn't for me, Mr. White's show would have been terminated months ago."

Denise asked, "So, if I wish for something right here, can you do that?"

"Within reason, yes."

"Okay. I wish I had fifty-thousand dollars right here."

Richard then asked, "Can you be sworn to secrecy and not blab to anyone?"

"Yes, I promise to keep it to myself."

Richard stood up and said, "Wise decision. I'll be back in a minute. It's time for more coffee." He went into the kitchen and refilled his coffee cup.

Richard was out of sight and Denise was still in the living room. She felt pressure on her back that made it uncomfortable to lean against the chair. Denise turned in the chair and saw a black satchel. She opened the bag and saw stacks of money banded together. Denise reached inside and pulled out a couple of bundles of money and they were all one-hundred-dollar bills.

She yelled out, "Whoa, I don't think I've ever seen this much money."

Richard asked, "Are you satisfied?"

Denise answered, "More than satisfied. Do I get to keep this?"

"That depends."

"On?"

"Can you keep it to yourself and can you promise me you'll be here tomorrow?"

Denise answered, "Oh yes, I'll be here tomorrow and I'll keep it to myself."

Richard replied, "Then it's yours to take home. I'd appreciate it if you return the empty bag to me."

"I'll bring it back tomorrow."

Richard asked, "What will you do with your new-found fortune?"

"Mr. Jenkins, if there's one thing, I need very bad is a new car. My car is thirteen years old and it needs a lot of work. With this money, I won't have to take a loan. Thank you, thank you."

"You are quite welcome, Miss Bennett. Say, Denise, a splendid idea just came to mind. Tomorrow, when you come over, we can go car shopping together. We can go to Grossinger Toyota. I know one of the salesmen there."

Denise replied, "I'd love to do that except my car does not have a baby seat and it's required by law."

"How about this? You come here tomorrow with my empty bag of course. When we're ready to go shopping, there will be a baby car seat in your car. Now, you should go outside and put the bag in your car. Denise, you do not have to share the news of this with your employer."

Later On, That Day: Around Four-Twenty

Matt walked into the house and called in, "Denise, Richard, I'm home. Denise was in the living room feeding Thomas. Richard was in the kitchen cleaning the kitchen counter and table.

Matt went by the living room, waved to Denise, and stopped at the doorway. Denise smiled and said quietly, "He'll be asleep soon." Denise stood up and said, "Be right back." She went upstairs and put Thomas in the crib.

Denise came back downstairs and said to Matt, "Okay, I'm leaving and I'll be back in the morning."

Matt responded with, "Okay, have a good night and we'll see you tomorrow."

Sarah walked in at five minutes to six. Matt was standing in the kitchen doorway talking to Richard. She walked over and kissed Matt hello on the cheek.

Matt asked, "Hey, how was your day?"

Sarah answered, "Busy and tiring."

Matt replied, "Okay, why don't you go upstairs and get changed. I think dinner's going to be ready in less than fifteen minutes. Let me check with the chef first."

Richard said, "Dinner will be ready in twelve minutes Mr. White. Do you mind setting the table?"

Matt answered, "Sure, no problem."

He reached in the cabinet, grabbed three plates, and set them on the counter. He opened the drawer, removed three forks, knives, and spoons.

Matt asked, "Do you realize that every night I put spoons on the table and they're never used? The spoons would be useful if we had a pie from Albertson's."

Richard stood at the counter and said, "I agree. I hope you like Marie Callender's chocolate cream pie. Before you ask, I technically did not go there today."

Sarah came downstairs and the three of them sat down to another fine dinner by Richard. Matt commented, "This meal is incredible. I should pay you more, just for this alone."

Richard smiled and responded with, "If you paid me anything, it would be more. The arrangement we have here is all I need."

Matt asked Sarah, "Honey, is Sean supposed to call you back letting you know they're coming?"

Sarah answered, "He said he'd call next week. I told him he was invited not to wait too long to book a flight like you suggested."

They finished eating and Matt stood up and said, "Let me clear."

Richard replied, "That's nice of you Matt. Just set them in the sink and I'll take care of them in a few minutes."

Matt set the dishes in the sink and noticed something very odd. He remembered the roasting pan and two medium-sized pans were used for dinner. Where did they go? They couldn't have been cleaned that fast. Richard walked in the kitchen and said, "Thank you Matt and I already cleaned the pans my way. You can remove that mystery from your head. Come on, let's go watch the evening news."

Sarah was checking on Thomas upstairs and the phone rang. Matt said, "My prediction that'll be Sarah's brother."

Richard said, "That was a good guess, but incorrect. I believe Mr. Turco needs your attention."

Matt grabbed the phone and said, "Hello Mr. Turco. How are you?"

Steven Turco answered, "Doing great here Matt. I called with an important question."

"And that is?"

"Okay, I'm asking early to give you time to think about it. I want you to do two shows a week again."

Matt asked, "Starting when?"

"How about right after Christmas. That's plenty of time to advertise in the paper. Matt, I checked and the last ten shows were sold out."

Matt asked Mr. Turco, "Just the last ten?"

"Probably more. My record of ticket receipts only goes back that far."

"Okay, let me think about it. I promise to get back to you in a couple of days."

Matt put the phone down and it rang again less than a minute later. Matt answered it, "Hello?"

On the other end was Sean and he said, "Hey Matt, this is Sean, how are you? I know it's been a while."

Matt thought to himself not long enough. He answered, "Doing okay Sean. I'll tell Sarah you're on the phone." Matt called for Sarah and he went back and sat in the living room.

Richard asked, "Isn't that an awful thing? You were thinking it wasn't long enough for seeing your brother-in-law."

Matt shook his head and said, "Okay, I'll tell you what irks me about this situation. The guy just turned twenty-nine and he's playing video games."

"There's nothing bad about that. Everyone needs a little relaxation time. My relaxation is reading the newspaper in the morning. I'm pampering myself before doing any household chores."

Matt grimaced and said, "Yes, but in his case, he was out of work and that we had to bail him out. We got them a car. If I was out of work, I would've been searching every day for a job."

Richard put his finger up to his lips and pointed. Sarah walked in and said, "I just got off the phone with Sean and they're coming the day after Christmas for seven days."

Matt responded with, "Oh, that's great honey. It'll be nice to see them again."

116

Richard cut in and said, "I can prepare a nice Christmas dinner Sunday or Monday depending on when they get here."

Sarah added, "I think you know we all enjoy your cooking."

Richard replied, "It's my pleasure, Mrs. White."

The Next Day: Wednesday, November 10ᵗʰ

Matt came downstairs at six-twenty. He reached for a coffee mug and poured his coffee. Richard was sitting in the corner at the table. Matt greeted Richard first, "Good morning Richard, how are you?"

Richard answered, "Just splendid Matthew and good morning to you as well."

Matt asked, 'What do you think about the phone call from Mr. Turco?"

Richard answered, "There are a couple of things to consider. Number one is you'll go from not seeing your wife for three and a half hours once every two weeks to seven hours each week. If you two can tolerate that, I say go for it. Number two I know this Turco fella. Right now, we're his only cash cow for him. Do you want to do this twice a week like before? It's your decision. As for me, I'll respect whatever decision you make and I'll be right there working along beside you."

Matt replied, "Okay, I have to go. I'll think about it today at school." Matt got in his car and drove to work.

Six-Forth-Five am

Denise's car pulled in the driveway at six forty-five. Richard, as usual, went to the front door and opened it for her.

He greeted Denise first, "Good morning Miss Bennett, how are you?"

Denise answered, "Doing okay. Good morning to you also. I have your bag with me."

Richard responded with, "Excellent! Would you mind putting it right back in the same chair you discovered it in?"

"Sure."

Denise walked into the living room and put her book bag down and placed the satchel in the red chair. She bent down and took out her book for later and noticed the bag had already disappeared.

Denise thought to herself, 'this is getting spooky.'

Richard went to the living room and said, "Like always, if you want coffee, help yourself. Sarah should be down in seven minutes."

Seven Minutes Later

Sarah came downstairs as Richard predicted. She said, "Hello" to Denise and Richard. Sarah said, "Sorry, I have to make it short. I need to get to work early. I want to file some papers I left all over my desk. I have to go. Bye."

Next, Denise made sure the baby monitor was turned on. Richard asked Denise, "Did you put the money in the bank on the way home?"

Denise answered, "Actually, I just deposited a hundred dollars. I didn't want to bring too much attention to myself."

Richard responded with, "Okay, but do you realize that putting that amount once a week will take a little bit more than nine and a half years to deposit it all. I have a better solution. On the way home today deposit two hundred dollars. Then, the following Monday you'll deposit the rest. The teller working that day will think nothing of it."

Denise asked, "Are you sure about that?"

"I've been pretty much right on the mark lately. I can use bragging rights and say I've only been off-track once and it's been a long time since that happened."

Denise asked, "Do you care to tell me what you consider a long time to be?"

"I think I first noticed this when I was fifteen years old. This brings us back to the year 1698."

Denise asked, "Are you serious? You've been around that long?"

"Yes, unfortunately. The good news is Thomas is still on schedule if you want to go car shopping after."

"I want to go car shopping but as I said yesterday presently my car does not have a baby car seat."

118

"Oh, yes it does. If you want to wait after the first feeding, we can go then." Richard pointed in the direction of the stairs and said, "I think you're up."

One second later sounds were coming from the baby monitor. Denise went upstairs to tend to Thomas and Richard went out to her car and removed a detachable baby carrier. He came back into the house and placed the carrier on the dining room table. Richard went into his room and grabbed a bag similar to the one Denise took home. He sat down in one of the red chairs and said to Denise, "I'm ready when you are."

Thirty-Five Minutes Later

Denise said, "We can go now. I'll bring a spare bottle in case he starts fussing."

Denise lowered Thomas into the carrier and belted him in. She said, "This is a nice car seat."

Richard commented, "It sure does the job. It is supposed to be the top-of-the-line in baby seats."

Denise snapped the seat into the holder in the back seat of her car. Richard got in the passenger side and off they went to Grossinger Toyota. Denise pulled into the lot nice and slow. She wanted to park off to the side in the hopes that she wouldn't get pounced on by the sales staff. Richard said, "Denise, perhaps you can have a look around and I can get the attention of Mr. Sparks. He's the salesman I know."

"We can't leave Thomas unattended."

"I know that. You walk around and I will stay next to your car until I see Mr. Sparks come out of the showroom."

Denise was walking around the rows of cars and she pointed at one of the cars and thought to herself, 'That's it, this is the one.'

Tim Sparks came out of the showroom and saw Richard standing next to Denise's car. He said, "Mr. Jenkins, how are you? It's been a while."

Richard replied, "Yes, it has. Listen, I'm here with Denise and she needs a new car. Denise is the nanny to Matt and Sarah's son. There she is walking towards us."

Denise came within hearing distance of Tim and he put his hand out and said, "Hello! My name is Tim. You must be Denise. Did you see any cars that interest you?"

Denise answered, "Hello Tim, yes there is a silver Toyota 4 Runner over there. I like the looks of that one."

Tim continued, "Great, let me get the keys and you can either drive it around the property or go around the block."

Richard followed Tim into the showroom. Once they got in the doorway Richard handed Tim an envelope and asked Tim, "So, we have a deal?"

Tim answered, "Of course, thank you, Mr. Jenkins." Tim brought the keys out to Denise and said, "Here you go. If you want to go off the property with it that's okay. I just have to get a dealer plate for it."

Denise took the keys from Tim and said, "I don't think that'll be necessary." Denise drove the car in the parking lot twice and came back. She parked it back in the original spot. Denise got out of the car and asked Tim, "Can I give you a check for five hundred and bring you the rest tomorrow?"

Tim answered, "I'll take the check but there's no need to come back tomorrow. Take the car with you today. You'll leave your car here and you are now the owner of a new Toyota 4 Runner."

Denise asked, "What do you mean I'm now the owner?"

Richard looked at her, smiled, and said, "I took care of it. You need a good dependable car if you're coming to watch Thomas every day."

Tim cut in and said, "You lift the baby out of the back, and I'll put the car seat in the new car for you." Tim moved the car seat from Denise's old car to Denise's new one. Next, he went to the showroom and grabbed the paperwork. Tim brought the paperwork back outside for Denise to sign.

Denise got in her new car with Richard riding shotgun and Thomas in the back. She said to Richard along the way, "Tomorrow, I'll bring back the rest of the money and give it back to you."

Richard responded, "You'll do nothing of the kind. You just need to put that money in your bank."

"I can't let you buy the car for me. I'm giving you back the money tomorrow."

Richard replied, "Seeing as you're being so stubborn about it, do this. On the way home, deposit one hundred dollars. Bring me three hundred dollars with you on Friday and ask the teller to give you fifteen twenty-dollar bills. You bring me those three hundred and we'll be square."

They were back at the house by eleven-forty. Richard said, "Safe and sound. Denise, you get Thomas and I can prepare lunch for us."

Later On, That Day: Around Four-Twenty

Matt walked in and said, "I'm home. Richard? Denise?"

Denise was coming downstairs and said, "I just put him down. She got to the bottom of the stairs and asked Matt, "Did you see my new wheels?"

"Yes, I did. When did you get that?"

Denise answered, "Just today, and don't worry I had a car seat and Thomas was not left unattended any of the time."

"Now, Sarah's going to be jealous."

Denise asked, "Why? She just got a new car last week."

"Because your car is newer than hers."

The Next Day: Thursday, November 11ᵗʰ Veteran's Day

Matt came downstairs around six forty-five to get a coffee. Richard was sitting at the table in the corner with his newspaper in front of him.

Matt greeted Richard first, "Good morning Richard. How are you?"

Richard answered, "Just fine and good morning to you as well. Matthew, seeing as this is your day off, we can sit down later and go over some plans when you're available of course."

Matt asked, "Do you mean when Sarah's not within earshot?"

Richard answered, "You got it."

"Are you afraid Sarah will let things slip out?"

"Sarah is a female and females tend to gossip. I'm sorry I shouldn't have said that. She's a great woman who happens to be coming down the stairs in thirty seconds."

Thirty seconds later the bedroom door upstairs opened. Once again, Richard's prediction was right on the money. Sarah came into the kitchen and said, "Good morning honey," and she gave Matt a peck on the cheek. Next, she addressed Richard and said, "Good morning Richard."

Richard replied, "Good morning Sarah. May I fix you a hot breakfast?"

Sarah answered, "Richard, please I don't want you to go to all that trouble."

Richard responded with, "Nonsense, I do not know the meaning of the word trouble. Please have a seat in the dining room. Before you say anything, your husband is on monitor duty."

Sarah took her seat as instructed and said, "Thank you, Richard. You do not have to make me any fancy omelet. I can live with eggs and toast."

The swinging door to the kitchen opened again and Richard put a plate of food on the table for Sarah. Richard said, "I hope wheat toast is acceptable." Wheat toast is Sarah's preference.

After breakfast, Sarah went upstairs to check on Thomas. Matt said to Richard, "WOW! It's almost seven-thirty and Thomas hasn't stirred yet."

Richard asked, "Don't you think I had a hand in that? Sarah is going to his crib and Thomas will be waiting to come out. In four minutes, she'll be back downstairs for his bottle which you'll hand her. It just so happens that she wants to feed him upstairs in the rocking chair. Sarah and Thomas are both going to nod off in the rocker. The two of them will be dozing and that will give you and I almost an hour to discuss our upcoming plan."

Matt looked at Richard and asked, "Did you arrange all that?"

"Of course, I did. Otherwise, Thomas would have been awake before you came down this morning."

Richard put his arm out and said, 'Two hot coffees are waiting for us in the dining room. So, after you sir." He continued, "This is my plan and I believe it's a good one. We ask for a volunteer as we have done so many times in the past. You'll wheel over a cart out in front of the volunteer. The cart is going to have ten small wooden stands and seven of them will have a sharp blade sticking out of them.

122

"You're going to have the volunteer rearrange the stands on the table and then you'll cover each one of them with a brown paper bag. Each paper bag will be numbered one through ten. Next, you're going to instruct the volunteer to pick one of the numbered bags. Every time they call out a number, I will smack the corresponding bag until we are down to four. Oh, I forgot to mention I will be wearing a blindfold when the volunteer is rearranging the stands. You just need to make sure they don't see where you put the bags. Otherwise, they will know which three stands not to pick, and that will eliminate the guesswork and suspense."

Matt asked, "Okay, but what prevents the volunteer from picking one of the stands that have a blade? There are seven of them. That means there's seventy percent chance your hand will catch one of those blades."

"That's correct, but not to worry, we can counteract that two different ways. The first one is we use your hand. I am kidding. I would never hear the end of it from Sarah. I will control what number the volunteer picks."

"I have another question. If three of the stands don't have a blade underneath them, what causes these bags to remain opened and not falling over?"

Richard answered, "It's quite simple. All you need to do is put the bags over the stands. They'll stay up."

"Are you sure this will work?"

"Of course, it will work. This trick also meets your requirements. It's not too over the top. Oh, one more thing, we'll have the cameraman filming as the volunteer rearranges the stands. This way the audience can see on the monitor what's going on."

Matt nodded and said, "Good, I like it. We'll have one more to add to our collection."

Richard added, "I'm glad we had time to talk about this. We'll repeat this one in our next show. Remind me Monday when you get home and we'll talk about another show. Sarah is on her way down."

17

The Envelope

Matt came downstairs around six-twenty and poured a coffee for himself. Richard was not in his usual spot. Matt thought this was strange and then he thought to himself, 'Please, not again.' He walked by the dining room a second time and this time he noticed Richard sitting at the table.

Matt went in and asked, "What are you doing here?"

Richard answered, "Oh, good morning Mr. White. I was just making sure my journal was up to date. Come, I'll join you in the kitchen and get myself another coffee."

Matt and Richard headed into the kitchen and Richard poured his third coffee. Matt took another sip of his coffee and asked Richard, "I meant to ask you this before but I'd always forget. Aren't you nervous about the effects all the coffee you drink can do to you?"

Richard answered, "If I was worried about it; I wouldn't be doing it. Besides, do you think my body composition is like yours? Do you know anyone who's been around as long as me or even half as long as me?"

"I just don't want anything to happen to your health. Richard, I never told you this but I think of you as a very close friend." Matt started to choke up and then said, "I should be going. See you around four-fifteen."

Richard replied, "Have a good day, Mr. White."

Matt got in his van and backed out of the driveway. He passed by Denise coming in the opposite direction. Matt was not used to seeing Denise in her new car. So, it did not faze him when he didn't notice that she waved to him on the way by.

Denise pulled in the driveway right at six forty-five. Richard, as usual, opened the door for her. He greeted Denise and said, "Good morning Denise." In an almost sarcastic tone, he asked, "Are you all rested from that one long day off?"

Denise responded with, "I had a relaxing day but there's never enough time to get things done. Good morning by the way."

Richard added, "Please help yourself to coffee. Sarah should be down in a couple of minutes."

Two Minutes Later

Sarah came downstairs and went into the kitchen. She greeted Denise first, "Good morning Denise, how are you?"

Denise responded, "Doing okay, Yesterday I called my insurance company to tell them about my new car only to find out they also had the day off. Why is it that I always remember to make these important phone calls when the place I'm calling is not available?"

Sarah asked, "You have a new car?"

"Yes, it's a silver Toyota 4 Runner."

Sarah replied, "Nice, I'll have to check it out. Oh, I have to go. I'll see you on Monday."

Sarah grabbed her bag and headed out the door. She gave Denise's car a long look and thought, 'WOW! This is nice. Looks like a good car for the winter as well.'

Denise turned on the baby monitor and picked up her coffee. Richard was in the other room wiping down the table. He saw Denise go in the living room and said to her, "I'll join you in five minutes."

Five Minutes Later

Richard had a fresh coffee in hand and sat in the chair across from Denise. Richard spoke first and asked, "Are you happy with your new transportation?'

"Oh my god Mr. Jenkins, I love my new car. It is perfect for me. Thank you again." Denise stood up and said, "Before I forget, let me get you the money." She went to her bag and pulled out a twelve-inch manila envelope and handed it to Richard.

126

Richard took the envelope, looked inside, and noticed there was a lot more than three hundred dollars as he requested.

He said, "You gave back too much."

"No, really it was like I said on Wednesday I can't let you buy the car for me. I'm grateful that you gave me the money and you came with me that day. I would have ended up paying too much."

"Okay, as you wish Miss Bennett. I'll be back in a minute. I just want to put this back in my room."

Richard went into his room, put his hand inside the envelope, and put the fifteen twenty-dollar bills in his top drawer. He turned the envelope upside down and gave it a quick shake. The remaining cash would appear in Denise's bag as she was getting in her car at four-thirty.

Richard thought to himself, 'Two can play the stubborn game.'

Four-Twenty that Afternoon

Matt walked into the house and called in, "Denise, Richard, I'm home."

Denise was sitting in the living room reading. Matt waved and Denise lowered her book.

Denise said to Matt, "I just put him down for a nap a few minutes ago."

Matt replied, "Okay, I noticed you have a car seat. Can I reimburse you for that?"

Denise answered, "Oh no, really that's not necessary. Mr. Jenkins took care of that for me."

"That's how Richard is. He always wants to make sure we have what we need."

Denise asked, "Do you know he gave me a bag of money the other day? He asked me not to tell you or Sarah. Looks like I blew that secret."

"No, I didn't know that. I'm sure he wants to make sure you'll be sticking around for a while."

"I thought I was going to use it to buy the car and then I found out he also paid for that. Then he told me to put the rest in the bank.

I can't take that money from him. So, I put most of it back in an envelope and returned it to him earlier today."

Matt put his hand up and said, "You should have taken it. That means he likes you and has a lot of respect for you. Believe me, he wouldn't hand out large sums of money to anybody. He probably just wants to make sure you have everything you need."

Denise replied, "Okay, I have to go and I'll see you on Monday. Please tell Mr. Jenkins I said bye."

"Will do."

Denise went out to her car and she knew she returned most of the money to Richard. It gave her a good feeling even though she didn't follow Matt's advice. She was driving up the street and stopped at the first traffic light. When she stopped, she noticed her bag was leaning to the right. Denise didn't think anything of it because her book always makes her bag top-heavy. She pulled in her driveway at four forty-five and went into her house.

That's when she discovered the envelope back in her bag. She pulled out the envelope and looked inside. Right away, she noticed the bulk of the money was there except the three hundred dollars. Denise also saw a small handwritten note. It was from Richard and it read 'Denise, please keep this. I know you're also anxious about replacing your furniture. This is your opportunity to do just that. Perhaps you also want to get some new clothes. Either way, please accept this, Richard.'

Denise thought to herself, "That's it, I'm going to Marjen Furniture this weekend.'

Monday Morning, November 15ᵗʰ

Matt came downstairs at six twenty-five and poured himself a coffee. He noticed Richard sitting at the kitchen table in the corner. Matt greeted Richard first, "Good morning Richard, how are you?"

Richard answered, "Just splendid Matthew and good morning to you as well."

Matt asked, "Did you hear the wind howling last night?'

Richard answered, "Yes, I did. If you recall I made an offer for climate change or climate control if you want to call it that. As I remember you and Sarah did not want me interfering with the weather. You said you didn't think it would be a good idea to be fooling around with the weather."

"I said that because that's my opinion on the subject. I have to go. I'll see you around four-fifteen."

Richard replied, "Have a good day Mr. White."

Matt added, "You too," as he went out the door.

Denise was waiting to pull in the driveway as Matt was backing out. She headed up the front stairs and Richard was waiting for her with the door open.

Denise said, "Good morning Richard."

Richard responded, "Good morning to you too Denise. I trust you had a good weekend."

"Yes, I did. Saturday morning, I was at Marjen Furniture five minutes after they opened. After that, I went clothes shopping. On the way home I'm stopping at the bank and making a deposit. Do you think it will draw too much attention to myself if I deposit three hundred dollars every week?"

Richard answered, "Mrs. White is on her way down. We'll talk about this later."

Sarah came downstairs and went directly into the kitchen. She said, "Good morning Denise. How was your weekend?"

Denise answered, "It was great. I finally went and picked out a new bedroom and living room furniture. They're supposed to deliver it a week from Saturday."

Sarah replied, "Well, good for you. Uhm, I have to go. I'll see you tomorrow morning."

Denise said goodbye and turned the baby monitor on as Sarah left for work. Richard walked into the kitchen and poured two coffees for him and Denise. He motioned for Denise to join him in the living room where they both sat down. Richard said to Denise, "Now to address your question from earlier. You would not bring attention to yourself if you were to deposit three hundred dollars every week."

Denise nodded and said, "I decided that's what I'm going to do."

18

The Next Show

Matt came downstairs at six twenty-five to grab a coffee and start his day. Richard was sitting in the corner with his newspaper in front of him.

Matt greeted Richard first, "Good morning Richard. Are you ready for tonight?'

Richard answered with, "Good morning Matt. Of course, I'm ready. You know how much I like showing off my craft. We'll be doing this for the first time tonight. The audience will love it."

Matt added, "I hope so. I'm always nervous when we introduce something new to the show." The door upstairs opened and Matt said, "Looks like Sarah is up."

Sarah came downstairs and came straight to the kitchen. She said, "Good morning," and kissed him on the cheek.

Matt replied, "Good morning honey," and returned the kiss. He continued, "You are off duty until we leave for the theater this afternoon."

Richard cut in and said, "That can only mean one thing. Sarah, you are to report to the dining room for a hot breakfast."

Sarah replied, "Richard, please you don't have to."

Richard added, "I know but it's good to get your nutrients and we want to keep you healthy."

Sarah said, "Okay." She went to the dining room and took a seat at the table.

Five Minutes Later

Richard brought her in a plate with eggs, a slice of honeydew melon, and wheat toast.

Later On, That Afternoon: Around Four-Thirty

Richard said to Matt, "Perhaps it wouldn't hurt to get to the theater a little earlier. We can use the extra time to go over our new act."

Fifteen Minutes Later

Matt said goodbye to Sarah. After this, Matt and Richard left for the theater. They got to the end of the street and stopped at the stop sign as usual. Matt started forward and a pickup truck came flying up the street and almost collided with him. Matt pulled off to the side and waited for the pickup truck to go ahead of him.

Matt pulled away from the curb and when he was alongside the truck the driver put down the passenger window and screamed at Matt, "What's wrong with you? Are you blind?"

Matt countered with, "Do you have a problem?"

Richard added, "He just needs to learn a little patience and now is as good a time as any."

Matt drove forward away from the truck. The truck followed Matt for a distance of fifty yards. The truck stalled out and all kinds of smoke billowed out from under the hood. Matt looked in the mirror and saw the truck stalled out and smoking.

He asked Richard, "Did you do that?"

Richard answered, "Yes, it was time he learned about patience. I could've done a lot worse. I held back on my rage and thought it was best not to cause too much of a scene."

Matt asked, "What would you have done differently if you didn't hold back?"

"Are you familiar with the term barrel roll? Then the truck would have gone up in flames. That means two things would've been accomplished. The inpatient driver wouldn't be badgering us anymore and there would be one less hothead on the street."

They pulled into the parking garage and waved to Tim as they went by the booth. Once inside and seated, Matt said before we go over tonight's performance, I need to ask you a couple of things."

Richard replied, "Ask away."

"Okay, it seems every weekend when you're fixing breakfast you say something to Sarah like you have to eat healthily and get a good breakfast in you. My question is if she didn't eat well on the weekends is she still under the protection umbrella like you told me about a while ago?"

"Yes, she is. I don't think I ever told Sarah that and I don't know if she would understand it. I'm sure you noticed I don't let you eat junk food during the week."

Matt responded, "Okay, one more question and we'll get to the show. Could you ever take anybody's life?"

"I could but I choose not to. It would have to be for something very serious."

"Serious, how serious?"

"Let's put it this way. If anyone was ever to come after you, Sarah, Thomas, or Denise it would not be a good idea. It would be the last thing they'd want to do. It would be the last thing they'd be able to do."

"Okay, that's enough of that kind of talk. Let's go over this new act for tonight."

Richard started with, "We bring a volunteer up on stage. Now, this is somewhat dangerous so I'll be the one that slams my hand over the bags."

"I thought you told me you had control over what bag the volunteer picks."

"I will be controlling that but if they see a different number at the last second; I have to counteract it and make that bag appear on another stand. I tell you what, if all goes well you get the bags next time. Remember you have to let the volunteer move the stands around and then you ask them if they're satisfied with the mix. Next, you'll cover them with the numbered bags. Remember, seven out of ten of these will have a blade sticking up. So, all I have to do is control the pick that the volunteer chooses. That's all there is to it."

"That simple, huh? Asked Matt.

"Yes, actually it is quite simple. I will need to improvise once the volunteer has picked the first four bags."

"Can you do that?"

"Yes. I can have the blade disappear once our volunteer Sheila gets to the fifth pick."

"Oh good, I see our volunteer already has a name."

"Of course, she does. Tonight's volunteer will be Sheila Davis." Richard stood up and said, "We have less than sixty seconds until the crowd comes in."

Matt asked, "Do you have a prediction on tonight's attendance?"

"Let's put it this way sold-out and it's time to make ourselves scarce."

Fifty-five seconds later, just as Richard predicted the crowd started down the aisles. The show started right at seven-thirty. Matt and Richard performed a collection of the favorite illusions. It was eight forty-five and Richard nodded at Matt. The nod was the signal to announce to the audience.

Matt called out to the audience, "Ladies and gentlemen, we have time for just one more. Please bear with us because this is the first time that we're doing this in front of anyone. We'll need a volunteer for this one. About ten people waved their arms in the air. Matt walked out to the audience and picked the woman from the twelfth row. Matt asked the woman, "Hello, can you help us with this? I hope you're not squeamish."

The volunteer answered, "Sure" and she followed Matt up to the stage."

Matt asked, "What is your name as if he didn't already know the answer.

The volunteer answered again with, "Sheila, Sheila Davis."

Matt continued, "Okay Sheila, this is what I need you to do. Do you see this cart? You'll notice there are ten stands and seven of the ten have a sharp blade sticking up out of them. I want you to move them around a little. Before you do that, we're going to blindfold Mr. Jenkins so he can't see what's going on." Matt slipped the blindfold on

Richard's head. As soon as he was done Sheila mixed up the wooden stands on the cart. Matt said, "Sheila, just let me know when you're done."

Sheila took her hands off the wooden stands and said, "Okay."

She put her hands up as if she was being robbed. Next, Matt covered each one of the stands with a brown paper bag. Each one of the bags had a number printed on them ranging one through ten. He then instructed Richard to remove the blindfold.

Next, Matt said to Sheila, "What I want you to do now is pick a number from one through ten. Now, it's time for Mr. Jenkins to participate."

Sheila made her first pick, "Three." Richard stepped closer to the cart, smashed his hand on the number three bag and it collapsed. Sheila made her second pick, "Eight."

For a second time, Richard's swatted his hand down this time on the number eight bag. That one also collapsed. It was time for Sheila to make her third pick. At this point, the crowd was buzzing knowing two of the stands were eliminated and there were five to go without a sharp blade sticking up.

Sheila made her third pick, "Nine." For a third time, Richard slammed his hand down this time on the number nine bag and that one collapsed.

Matt cut in and said, "Sheila, you're making it too easy for Richard. There are seven more bags left here. It looks like you picked all the bags without the blade."

Richard spoke up and asked, "Or did she? Mr. White, could you please remove the remaining bags?"

Matt took the bags off the remaining seven stands and there was only one stand that had a blade. The other six just had the wooden stand. Sheila looked at the cart and said, "WOW! Where did the others go?"

Richard answered, "I'm sorry but that is part of the magic here."

Matt added, "Sheila, thank you so much for your help. We couldn't have done this without your input. I'd like to give you a couple of free passes for another show. We'll be back here in a couple of weeks and here's a little secret. We try to throw in new material every other show."

Sheila put her hand out and took the free passes. She said, "Thank you," as she went down the stairs off the stage.

Matt made the announcement, "Ladies and gentlemen, "That concludes our show for tonight. Please, if you like what you saw tell your family and friends. If you don't like what you saw, I'm sorry. Anyway, please drive safely and have a good night." Matt looked at Richard and asked, "What do you say, do we call it a night?"

Richard answered, "I'm ready when you are Mr. White."

19

Denise Over for Thanksgiving

It was very windy outside and the temperature was dropping even more. Matt came downstairs and could feel the chill and he went right to the coffee maker. Richard was sitting in the corner with the newspaper folded in front of him.

Matt greeted Richard first, "Good morning Richard. How are you?"

Richard answered, "Doing splendid Matthew, and good morning to you."

Matt took a sip of his coffee and asked, "Do you think we should have brought that cart back with us? I mean don't you think it's unsafe to leave those blades around?"

Richard again answered, "We didn't leave anything out in the open. I took care of everything while we were walking to the parking garage."

"Doing okay and feeling terrific. There's nothing like a good night's rest to recharge the body. However, there is one thing we need to discuss."

"Really, what's that?"

"Well, Thanksgiving is Thursday as you know and your wife has been toying with the idea of going out to dine. Seeing as it is only four days away, there will be a slim chance of getting into a restaurant to eat. Never mind the fact that restaurants jack up their prices for the holiday because they know they can. I have an alternate idea."

"Okay, let's hear it."

Richard replied, "We have Thanksgiving here. You and I go to Albertson's and do the shopping as we always do. Tomorrow morning, Sarah invites Denise to join us on Thursday. She'll be dining alone if she doesn't join us. Thomas is comfortable with her so what better person to help take care of Thomas?"

Matt responded, "It sounds like a plan. Wait for a second, how do you know Denise will be dining alone? I know, I know, don't answer that."

"All I ask is you think about it and either way we're going to have to visit the market. We should also ask Sarah for her thoughts. She'll be downstairs in three minutes."

Three Minutes Later

The bedroom door opened upstairs and Sarah came down. After Sarah greeted Matt and Richard the three of them took a seat at the dining room table.

Matt spoke first and asked, "What do you think about inviting Denise to have Thanksgiving dinner with us?"

Sarah answered, "I never gave it much thought. I didn't get a chance to ask her about her plans. I just assumed she'd be with her family."

Richard cut in and said, "She won't be with family because her family lives in California and that's two thousand miles away. Also, it doesn't help that she doesn't talk to her parents."

Sarah replied, "That's awful. I had no idea it was like that for her. Of course, I'll ask her when I see her tomorrow morning."

Matt took his turn in the conversation and said, "Good, now that's settled. Richard and I will go to Albertson's to stock up."

Richard added, "Please, let me fix a good breakfast for Sarah first. You, Matt, may tend to your son."

Matt looked up and then there were sounds coming from the baby monitor. He said, "I'll be right back. Sounds like someone else is hungry." Matt ran upstairs to take care of Thomas.

Matt and Richard got in Matt's car and headed out to Albertson's. Once they were in the store Matt grabbed a carriage and said, "I just want to say it looks like your idea is going to work out fine. You know inviting Denise over for Thanksgiving."

Richard responded, "Most of my ideas do work out. I think we both know that by now."

They finished shopping and went through the checkout. Matt pulled into the driveway with Richard and the groceries.

Richard said, "You carry in the bags and I'll put away the stuff."

Matt replied, "Deal."

Matt made three trips out to the van and lugged in six bags of groceries. He noticed when he made his second and third trip with the bags Richard was standing next to the counter waiting for the groceries.

He asked Richard, "How is it that when I get into the kitchen, you're waiting for me to bring in more bags?"

"It's quite simple really. Sarah is upstairs right now looking after Thomas. She is not even near the kitchen and therefore cannot see me using magic to speed things along."

Matt added, "It's probably a little late to ask, but do you feel comfortable about Thursday?"

Richard answered, "It's just one more dinner with a different main course. It will be fine. My question to you is did you give any thought to Mr. Turco's offer?"

"You mean about doing two shows a week?"

"Exactly that."

Matt responded, "I want to run it by Sarah and see how she feels about it. Would you ever want to do the whole show without me?"

Richard answered, "That's not an option at this time or any time. I know if I was doing this myself, I would be doing too much of the unbelievable. There would be too many people leaving thinking this seems impossible when they should be thinking to themselves how did he do that."

"Why don't you give me a couple of examples of what would look unbelievable."

Richard replied, "Okay, I grab a volunteer from the audience as we often do. It can't be just anyone. Say, maybe fifteen to twenty people usually volunteer. What I like to do is pick my first volunteer and then have him or her pick a person from the audience. This shows the audience the participants are not preselected."

Matt cut in and said, "Sorry to interrupt but it does not prove that. We could still have plants in the show."

"I guess you're right but it does look a little more genuine. Okay, I have the picked audience member standing beside me on the stage. I ask him if he or she has ever been hypnotized. Hopefully, they'll say 'no'. Then, I tell them there is a first for everything. I bring two chairs on stage and I pull out my hypnotizing device."

Matt interrupted again and asked, "You have a hypnotizing device?"

"Yes, it's called a pocket watch. Now, if I may continue after I have my volunteer under my spell, I tell them to imagine they're in another land, a foreign land far away. I ask them to talk to me. But first I ask them where they are. They say they are in Bologna, Italy. The volunteer talks and says, 'Ciao, came stai.'"

Matt replied, "Okay, so your volunteer could speak Italian. That's not so spectacular."

The magical part happens when I move the volunteer to seven other countries. I'll ask him or her questions and he or she will answer me in a different language each time we pick a new place to be in."

Matt added, "Now, that sounds like a very good trick but not too unbelievable. Do you have any others?"

"Yes, but maybe to be discussed at another time. Sarah is on her way downstairs."

Matt leaned his ear in toward the direction of the staircase and then looked at Richard because he didn't hear anything. Richard pointed and said, "Now!"

The door opened and Sarah started her descent down the stairs. Sarah came into the kitchen and asked, "Are you boys up to no good?"

Richard answered, "We're always up to something and it's all good. Right now, we're getting a jump start on ideas for future shows. It never hurts to be prepared."

Sarah added, "Speaking of prepared do you have everything you need for Thursday?"

"Yes, we have and it will be turkey sandwiches for lunch on Friday."

Sarah replied, "That's good to know. We can reward ourselves with a wrap sandwich and a slice of pie after we get the decorations out of the crawlspace."

Matt asked, "What decorations?"

Sarah answered, "I want to get the Christmas decorations out. It will be so much easier if we put them in one of the spare rooms for easier access."

Matt replied, "We can do that. Sarah, while I'm thinking of it, the manager asked me if I'd be interested in doing two shows each week like before."

Sarah said to Matt, "If you take advantage of this opportunity when do you start the extra nights?"

"I would be starting the day after the first of the new year. I didn't make a decision yet. I was hoping by talking to you about it first I could get your thoughts on it."

Sarah replied, "It's like this I'll miss you. We'll just have to make the best use of our Friday and Sunday nights. So, if you want to do this, go for it."

"Thank you, honey. I'll call Mr. Turco tomorrow when I get home."

Monday morning, November 22nd, Denise's car pulled in the driveway at six forty-five. Matt had already left for work.

Richard opened the front door for Denise and said, "Good morning Denise. I hope you had a good weekend."

Denise responded with, "Good morning Richard, how are you?"

"I'm having a good morning so far. Please, as always help yourself to the coffee. Sarah will be down in five minutes."

"Thank you, Mr. Jenkins."

Sarah was downstairs in the kitchen. She said, "Good morning Denise. Before I go, I want to ask, do you have plans for Thanksgiving?"

Denise answered, "I can't say that I do. My parents live on the West Coast and my sister moved there two months ago. I didn't get a chance to make travel plans."

Sarah replied, "You don't need a plan to have dinner with us. I already talked to Matt about it and we want you here for Thanksgiving. You might as well join us because this way you won't be alone. Besides, you're getting paid for it."

"Okay, thank you. I'll be here."

Sarah added, "Good, that's settled. I have to go. I'll see you tomorrow morning."

Sarah left for work a few minutes after seven. Denise turned the baby monitor on as Sarah went out the door. She took a seat in the living room and removed her book from her bag.

Richard came into the living room toting a coffee and sat in the chair across from Denise.

Denise put her book down and said, "That was very nice of Sarah to invite me for Thanksgiving. Richard, do you know if Sarah takes care of the cooking?"

Richard answered, "No, she doesn't do the cooking. You didn't hear this from me but she wouldn't be able to. She doesn't have the organizational skills for that. Don't get me wrong, she's a terrific woman and I love her like a daughter. I just wouldn't want her taking on such a daunting task."

Denise replied, "Okay, can I bring anything?"

"Yes, an appetite. Now, if you'll excuse me, I have some cleaning and laundry to take care of."

Later On, That Afternoon: Around Four-Twenty

Matt walked in the door around four-twenty. He called in the house, "Richard, Denise, I'm here."

Richard came out of the kitchen and said, "Hello Matthew. Denise is upstairs putting Thomas down for a nap. She should be down in two minutes."

Denise came downstairs and said, "Hello Matt. I just put Thomas down for a nap. Thank you very much for inviting me to Thanksgiving."

"Oh, you're welcome. Hey, we have extra rooms upstairs. What I'm saying is if you're tired and don't want to drive home your more than welcome to stay the night."

"Okay, thank you, Mr. White. I have to go and I'll see you tomorrow."

Matt said, "Bye Denise. See you tomorrow."

Matt thought to himself, 'Good, now I can call Turco.' He went to the phone and called the theater. Mr. Turco just happened to answer the phone. Matt said, "Hello Steve, this is Matt White. I thought about it and I want to take you up on the offer of picking up the extra nights. I believe you said after the first of the year."

Mr. Turco responded with, "Yes, I did. So, we'll get you scheduled for Thursdays and Saturdays starting in January. Matt, thank you for getting back to me. However, I am on the way out of here. Have a nice Thanksgiving. Tomorrow we'll get started on the advertising."

"Okay, bye Steve. You have a nice Thanksgiving as well."

Thanksgiving Morning, Thursday, November 25th

Matt came downstairs around six twenty-five. He poured himself a coffee. Richard was sitting in the corner looking at all the ads for Black Friday.

Matt said, "Good morning Richard. I see you looking at the ads. Is there anything you have in mind? You know something that'll make a good Christmas present?"

"Good morning Matthew. There is something here I have my eye on. It's an eight-quart crockpot. Best Buy will have it for forty dollars."

"That's all well and good Richard for the kitchen. Of course, we can get one of those. Is there anything you'd want for yourself?"

"Matthew, please I do not need anything. If you feel the desire to give me something, I could use a few of those Five-Star notebooks from Mead. Please, put your efforts into getting something for Denise. It's more than likely that she will not be seeing her family for Christmas either."

"How do you know this?"

Richard answered, "Here we go again. Let me show you something. You see this little piece of paper?"

Matt answered, "Yeah, what about it?"

"Okay, what time do you want dinner ready?"

"Two o'clock would be great."

Richard turned a piece of paper over and on it was the time two o'clock. Do you want to ask me that question again?"

"Fine, you got lucky. When Sarah comes down to ask her the same question and we'll see how you do."

"Good because she's on her way down. Look under the coffee mug and you'll see her time." Matt lifted the coffee mug on the counter and there was a small piece of paper. On the other side was written two-thirty.

Sarah came downstairs and headed into the kitchen.

She said, "Good morning honey," and she kissed Matt on the cheek. "Good morning Richard. Happy Thanksgiving."

Richard returned the greeting, "Good morning Sarah. I have one question for you and that is what time would you like dinner ready?"

Sarah answered, "Oh, I don't know. How about two-thirty?"

Matt cut in and said, "Oh sure, why not?"

Sarah asked, "What's wrong?"

Matt answered, "Oh nothing, it's just Richard is showing off again. Did you give Denise a time to come over?"

Richard cut in and answered, "She'll be here by nine o'clock to watch the parade with us."

Sarah said, "Oh good, that will give us a chance to have girl talk. I only get to see her five minutes every morning."

Matt spoke up and said, "I'm going to challenge my buddy Richard here that he cannot predict what time Denise wants to eat."

Sarah responded, "Wait a minute. We invited her out of the goodness of our hearts and so she wouldn't be alone on Thanksgiving. I don't think she'd want to pick a time."

Matt added, "Let's just ask her. Richard, are you up for the challenge?" Richard pulled a small piece of paper out of his pocket and handed it to Matt. Matt took the paper and looked at it. The paper had the time one-thirty."

Eight-Fifty-Five

Denise came up the front steps and knocked on the door. Sarah opened the front door and said, "Welcome, Happy Thanksgiving. You know you didn't have to knock. I never hear you knocking during the week."

Denise replied, "First off, that's because Richard is always opening the door for me. Happy Thanksgiving."

Denise had a brown bag under her arm. She asked, "Where can I put this?"

"You didn't have to bring any wine," Matt said.

Denise added, "I plan on getting a buzz so I brought three bottles of wine. Oh, should I have brought some for everybody? Just kidding."

Richard came into the living room and said, "Denise, you are a guest here today. What time would you like to eat?"

Denise answered, "Is one-thirty too early? Oh, is there anything I can do to help?"

Richard answered, "Oh no please, have a coffee and join Matt and Sarah in the living room. They're watching the parade."

Denise took her coffee and went into the living room. Sarah stood up and said, "I'll be right back. I think somebody upstairs is hungry."

Denise said, "Sarah, I can get him."

Sarah replied that quickly, "Nonsense, I want you to relax for now."

Denise thought to herself, 'I tried.' She joined Matt and took a seat in the living room. Denise said to Matt, "Thanks again for inviting me."

Matt added, "Oh, of course. No one should be alone today. Today is a day about family and giving thanks."

Sarah came back downstairs carrying Thomas. She went directly to the kitchen to get a bottle for him. Sarah took a seat in the living room to feed him.

When she was almost done, she asked Matt, "Did you get a chance to get one of those Fisher-Price floor seats at Babies R Us?"

Matt tried to think quickly because he knew he told Sarah he would stop on the way home and pick one up. Right at that moment, Sarah asked Richard who was in the kitchen sent the thought to Matt to look in the spare room.

Matt answered Sarah, "I'll be right back." Matt ran to the spare room and grabbed the floor seat and brought it into the living room.

Richard came into the living room and said, "Excuse me, dinner will be ready at one-thirty. I hope that is agreeable with everyone here."

One-Thirty That Afternoon

The four sat down to dinner. Denise spoke up and said, "Does anybody mind if I say grace?"

Matt and Sarah answered, "By all means, go ahead."

Richard stood up abruptly and said, "Sorry Denise, please start the grace without me. I need to check on something in the kitchen"

Sarah looked at Matt with a puzzled look and Matt shrugged his shoulders. Denise made the sign of the cross and started with, "Bless us, o Lord and these, thy gifts, which we are about to receive from thy bounty. Through Christ, our Lord, Amen." Denise made a sign of the cross a second time. She said, "Thank you."

Richard came into the dining room as Denise was saying thank you. He said, "Sorry, I had to check on something in the kitchen."

Matt thought to himself, 'That's strange. We'll be discussing that later.'

They finished dinner and Sarah said, "Richard, once again your cooking was the best."

Richard responded, "Thank you, Sarah. Now, I hope everyone left room for dessert. We have three pies and cheesecake."

Matt added, "Earlier, I told Denise today's a day about family and giving thanks. I have to change that to adding time for packing on the pounds."

146

Denise offered, "Hey, someone has to do it. It's too much of a temptation when I'm in the same room with cheesecake. The temptation always wins. I'll be right back."

Denise got up and brought some of the dinner dishes in the kitchen. Once in the kitchen, she noticed something strange. The kitchen looked like it was just cleaned. There were no pans soaking; there was not even a dirty coffee cup from earlier.

They finished dessert and Sarah asked. "Denise, are you up for watching a sappy movie on the Hallmark Channel?"

Denise answered, "Hey, why not." The two of them went into the living room and Sarah turned the tv on.

Sarah said, "I know it's silly but I enjoy movies. It's always the same idea where a man and woman have two hours to fall in love"

Denise agreed, "You're right. They are kind of silly. I'd rather watch those instead of some comedy wannabee."

They were halfway through the movie when Matt came to the doorway. He waited patiently for a commercial and asked, "Who's up for going to the mall tomorrow morning early?"

Sarah answered, "Wait a second. We did that last year. Does Richard need another suit?"

Matt answered, "No, no. I know we went shopping last year, but wasn't it fun?"

Sarah answered again, "Let me see. Does fun and exhausting mean the same thing?"

"Honey, I get your point. I just want to get in there and get a crockpot that's on sale. It's at *Best Buy* regularly seventy dollars and on sale for thirty."

Sarah offered, "Okay, I hope you don't mind if I sleep in. Here's an idea. Take Mr. Early bird, I mean Richard with you. I mean, isn't he the one that'll be using the crockpot?"

"Okay, okay, you sleep in. Let me know if there's anything you want. Yes, Richard is the one who'll be using it but he's using it for us so we should make things easier for him."

Sarah responded, "I know you can get us one of those alarm clocks that don't wake you up on purpose."

"Oh, that's sarcasm. You're too funny."

Denise and Sarah sat in the living room watching 'The Nine Lives of Christmas'. It was a Hallmark Christmas movie about a firefighter who was a bachelor named Zack. Zack meets Marilee who is going to school to be a veterinarian. Marilee gets evicted from her apartment and Zack lets her move to the second floor of his house that he's fixing up. Zack adopts a cat he finds outside.

Marilee develops a big crush on Zack until she sees him kissing a woman at the mayor's house. Marilee moves out of Zack's house and he realizes how much he misses her. Zack drives the fire engine on Christmas Day and finds Marilee at the local park where there is a pet adoption event. Zack explains to Marilee why they should be together.

Nine-Fifty

Both Denise and Sarah were asleep by the time the credits rolled by on the movie. Matt went into the living room and found the two of them sleeping.

He tapped Sarah on the shoulder and said softly, "Honey, it's time to go up to bed."

Denise woke up, heard Matt, and Said, "I have to get going."

Matt offered, "No, Denise, please stay here tonight. There's plenty of room upstairs. I know Richard put fresh sheets on the bed for you."

"Okay, I just don't want to impose."

Matt added, "Denise, we never would have put out the offer if we thought it was an imposition. Matt showed Denise to the guest room where she would be sleeping. Matt said, "Goodnight, we'll see you in the morning."

Friday Morning: Around Four-Ten

Matt came downstairs at four-ten all dressed and ready to go shopping. He went to the kitchen first thing to get a quick coffee. He saw Richard sitting at the table in the corner.

Matt greeted Richard first, "Good morning Richard. This sure is a lot earlier than I'm used to."

148

"Good morning Matthew. I am up every morning at four twenty-five. You find that you get so much more accomplished that way."

Matt finished his coffee and asked, "How do you get more done if all you're doing is drinking coffee and reading the newspaper?"

"Watch it, Matthew. I know I like to indulge myself in the paper in the morning. I'm also guilty of drinking plenty of coffee. However, you'll have to admit you've never seen the house cleaner. You and Sarah are always eating healthy thanks to me."

"Yes, I agree with all that."

"So, my point is I have enough time to get my chores done every day after I have my morning coffee. Now, shall we head off?"

Matt said, "Lead the way." The two of them went out the front door and got in Matt's car. Matt backed out of the driveway and they headed to the mall. Richard spoke up and said, "I realized I made an error. The crockpot is on sale at Kohl's and not Best Buy."

"That's okay. You're allowed to make a mistake now and then. We're all human"

They pulled into the Kohl's parking lot at ten minutes to six. Richard said, "This shouldn't take long. There are two more things in here I believe will be a good addition to the kitchen."

"Okay, whatever you think you need." The two of them entered Kohl's and Matt said, "I'll grab a shopping cart"

After thirty-five minutes they found the crockpot, a Caphalon cookware set, and a set of flatware. They got to the checkout register and the total for three items was $259. Matt said, "WOW! It's a good thing we're here during the sale."

Richard added, "Matthew, two things I want to say. This will not be a burden on your savings and it will make my cooking duties a lot easier."

"Okay, no problem," replied Matt.

A little after seven Matt and Richard were in the car and on the way home. Matt asked, "Should we stop on the way home and pick up some bagels and donuts?"

Richard answered, "There's no need to stop for that. They're on the kitchen counter. We can enjoy a coffee and bagel when we get back to the house. We can also tell Denise and Sarah they missed out on a good time."

Matt and Richard pulled into the driveway. They went into the house and the first thing they noticed was Denise sitting in the living room holding Thomas feeding him his first bottle of the day.

Denise smiled at Matt and said, "We're almost done. Sarah's still sleeping."

Matt smiled back and said, "Thank you."

Richard went into the kitchen and brewed a fresh pot of coffee. He placed the bagels and donuts on a serving tray and brought them into the dining room. Richard said to Matt, "Bagels, cream cheese, and donuts are on the table. Sarah will be downstairs in five minutes."

Five minutes later Sarah was downstairs.

Matt said, "Good morning honey. Did you have a good night's sleep?'

She answered, "Yes, I can't believe it's eight o'clock already. Is Denise still here?"

"She is and she just fed Thomas his bottle."

Sarah responded, "I barely heard Thomas stir and I was so tired. Next, I heard the guest room door open and it must have been Denise. Matt, she is a godsend."

"I agree. She's the right pick for us and she's here when we need her. Come to the dining room. Richard put out some bagels and donuts."

Denise stood up and walked by Sarah on her way to put Thomas in the floor seat. She said, "Good morning. I hope you don't mind me feeding Thomas."

Sarah asked, "Are you kidding me? Of course not."

Denise added, "Well, thank you very much for that delicious meal last night and for letting me stay the night. I'm going to go back to my house."

Sarah said, "You can go after you have a bagel here. Richard put bagels and donuts on the table for all. You're also more than welcome to stay."

Denise replied, "I told the card shop I'd come in for a few hours. At the time, I didn't know I was going to be here."

Richard cut in and said, "Excuse me, Denise, there are plenty of leftovers and we picked up a bag of wrap bread for sandwiches. I don't see why you can't stop by on the way home from work."

"I second that idea," Matt said.

The four of them sat at the table with a coffee and their continental breakfast. It was almost nine o'clock and Denise said, "I better get a move on. I'll be back later, hopefully by three o'clock."

Denise stood up, grabbed her bag, and said, "Bye."

Seven Hours Later

Denise came back around four o'clock and knocked on the door. Richard opened the door and said, "I'm glad you decided to take us up on the offer. I can bring you a turkey wrap if you take a seat in the dining room."

Denise smiled and said, "I can make my sandwich."

Richard countered with, "Uh, seeing as you're a guest here, you're not allowed."

Denise went into the dining room and sat down. Sarah walked in from the living room and said, "Hi! We just finished our late lunch. Join us in the living room when you're done eating."

Denise was looking at Sarah for a second. She turned forward and it was a plate with a sandwich and a glass of cider in front of her. Denise thought to herself, 'How did that happen?' I never saw Richard come into the dining room. Either I have to drink less wine or more wine on the holidays. Denise finished her sandwich and she stood up to bring the plate into the kitchen.

As soon as she put her hand forward to push the door to the kitchen Richard's hand was right there to take away the plate. Denise didn't even get a chance to go to the kitchen. She no longer had the task of bringing her plate into the kitchen so Denise decided to join Matt and Sarah in the living room. Denise plopped herself down on the loveseat and said, "This is a great feeling."

Sarah asked, "What is that?"

Denise answered, "I do not have to be at the card shop until Tuesday night."

"Well, it looks like you just have to relax, take your shoes off and put your feet up."

151

Denise removed her shoes and put her feet up. She said to Sarah, "I'm usually out of here by four-thirty so I'll stay for a while and then head home."

"Oh, you don't have to. You can stay tonight too if you like. Please stay and we can watch another Hallmark movie. This is my only chance to have my friend over."

Denise replied, "Okay, but I don't want you to get sick of me."

20

Daniel & the Tiger

Saturday morning after Thanksgiving Matt came downstairs and poured himself a coffee. He was surprised that he didn't see Richard sitting in the corner spot. Matt knocked on Richard's door to make sure he was all right. It was not like Richard not to be up and about. Matt was getting nervous when he didn't hear Richard's voice after knocking on the door.

He then opened the door to the basement and called down, "Hello! Anybody down here?"

Richard was in the basement, and answered, "Be up in a minute Matt."

He came up the stairs and said to Matt, "we have to come up with a better way."

Matt asked, "A better way for what?"

"Okay, the way I see it we need to go to Albertson's tomorrow morning. This will be a stock-up trip. There is nothing in the freezer. So, I propose this I make a list tomorrow after we come back from Albertson's of what goes in the freezer. I'll keep this list up here and every time I take something out, I'll cross it off the list."

Matt replied, "That sounds like a good plan for keeping track of the food on hand. I'll be right back. I can hear my son calling."

Matt went up the stairs as fast as he could to let Sarah sleep in. He brought Thomas down to the changing table. Sarah came downstairs around seven-fifteen. She noticed Matt was taking care of Thomas.

Sarah said, "Good morning honey," and kissed him on the cheek.

Matt replied, "Good morning. Just go sit and relax in the other room. I got Thomas."

Richard stepped out of the kitchen and into view.

He said, "Good morning Sarah. Please take a seat at the table and I'll bring you your breakfast."

Sarah offered, "Good morning Richard. You know you don't have to spoil me like this, but it's okay."

Richard asked, "How should I spoil you? Sorry, that was supposed to be a joke. Please, Sarah, it's the least I can do especially because I'm stealing your husband away for the night."

"Well, if this is your way of making up for that, you can steal him more often."

Six-Fifteen That Evening.

Matt said to Sarah, "Honey, Richard, and I are going to head off to the theater in a few minutes. Are you going to be okay?"

Sarah answered, "Of course, I'll be fine. I'm going to give Jeannie a call later to see if they want to get together."

Matt responded with, "Oh good."

Matt and Richard headed off to the theater and got there at six thirty-five. They sat in their temporary seats in the front row. Matt asked Richard, "What are we doing tonight?"

Richard answered, "We are entertaining a sold-out crowd as always. Oh, you mean what are we doing for a grand finale. Do you remember me telling you about an illusion that you found fascinating?"

Matt answered, "I think so. You hypnotize a volunteer and have him or her go off to foreign lands. Here's the thing, to me that looks like too much of a set up where the volunteer is in on it."

"Okay, let's go with plan B. We're going to use the Bengal tiger. We'll bring the cage out here. At the same time will ask for a volunteer and we assure the volunteer they will not be harmed in any way. We'll ask Daniel to pick a number from one to seven. There will be seven covered tunnels. Daniel is going to pick which tunnel the tiger is going to walk through. We'll have Daniel write his pick on a piece of paper. Then he is to fold the paper in half and put it in his pocket. He's going to write down the number two. I am going to make the tiger disappear from the cage and then come through tunnel number two. I'll make this happen before Daniel shows us his paper."

"Okay, but what prevents Whiskers from running into the audience? That would not be good."

"No, it would not Matthew. I will have this under control. Whiskers will come through the tunnel and will walk over to me. I'll rub the top of his head and lead him back to his cage."

Matt replied, "Okay, as long as you're positive no one will get hurt." It was ten minutes after seven and the crowd started in. Matt said, "We should make ourselves scarce."

The show got underway right at seven-thirty. Matt and Richard went through the show and performed the illusions perfectly. Richard was there to make sure of that. It was almost eight forty-five and Richard nodded to Matt signaling it was time for the last act.

Matt made an announcement, "Ladies and gentlemen, we have time for just one more. Richard is going to take over for a few minutes." Matt put his arm out in a gesturing motion.

Richard moved to the center and said, "I know this is everybody's favorite part. I am going to require assistance from a volunteer and not to worry you will not be harmed." Richard looked to the side and motioned for the stagehands to wield the cage. Richard continued, "Okay, please sir, what is your name?"

The volunteer answered, "Daniel Gray."

Richard replied, "Okay, Mr. Gray, please come join me up here." Dan Gray did as he was instructed and walked up on the stage. The stagehands carried out a long wooden ramp and set it in place so it was at the entrance of the cage.

Richard continued, "Okay, Mr. Gray here is a pencil and a pad of paper. I want you to jot down a number from one to seven and then tear off that piece of paper and put it in your pocket. We'll get back to that part later. Next, Richard motioned with his hand and the curtain opened. There were seven covered tunnels. Each one of these tunnels had a number hanging over them. Richard said to Dan, "I hope you remember the number you wrote down."

Richard then pointed at the cage. The tiger disappeared and made its way towards tunnel number two. The tiger stopped at Richard's side. Richard then rubbed a tag on the top of his head and led him over to the ramp to his cage.

Next, Richard said, "Dan, it's time for you to take out your piece of paper."

Dan replied, "Okay." He looked at the paper, unfolded it, and held it up.

Richard continued, "Dan please hold it a little lower and Richard gestured for the cameraman to get closer and zoom in on Dan's paper. Dan selected number two. The audience could see it on the Jumbotron.

Richard said, "How about that Dan. You predicted which tunnel the tiger was going to come through."

The audience clapped for a few minutes. Dan stood there beside Richard and Richard said, "Dan, don't go back to your seat yet. We still have a few minutes." Richard reached inside his jacket and took out a deck of cards. He instructed Dan, "Please remove the cards and look them over. Now select one card. Take care and put it anywhere else in the deck. Let me put my hand on top of the cards for a few seconds. Now please open the cards and look for the card you picked out and relocated. By the way, what was your card?"

Dan answered, "Jack of diamonds." Dan looked for his card and said, "It's not here."

Richard continued, "Your card is not here but it has to be somewhere. I think you should look in your front left pocket."

Dan reached into his pocket and found his card and gasped, "What the heck? How did it get here?"

Richard answered, "It's something I like to call magic." Matt was standing off to the side watching Richard showing off his skills.

Matt walked to the center of the stage. He shook Dan's hand and said, "Thank you for helping."

Dan asked, "Are you kidding? I enjoyed it. Thanks for picking me."

Matt said, "Have a good night." Next, Matt announced to the audience,

"Ladies and gentlemen, we hope you enjoyed the show. My name is Matt White and this is my good friend and show partner, Richard Jenkins. Please drive safely and have a good night."

Richard looked at Matt and said, "I believe we had another successful night."

"I agree. Are you ready to go home?"

The Next Morning: Sunday, November 28th

Matt came downstairs around six forty-five and poured himself a coffee. Richard was sitting in the corner sipping his third coffee. He had the newspaper in front of him. Matt greeted Richard first, "Good morning Richard. How are you?"

Richard answered, "I feel great after last night's sleep."

Matt replied, "Let me see. We were home by ten-fifteen. If you're lucky you would've been in bed by ten-twenty at the earliest. You call a measly six hours a good night's sleep?"

"Yes, I do because it's what I'm accustomed to." The bedroom door opened upstairs and Richard said, "Here comes Sarah."

Sarah came downstairs and went straight to the kitchen. She said to Matt, "Good morning honey," and she kissed him on the cheek.

Matt said, "Good morning," and he returned the kiss. "I think Richard is going to fix you breakfast and then we need to make a trip to Albertson's. Thomas hasn't stirred yet. I turned the monitor on and I'll listen for him while you eat."

Richard came into the kitchen and said, "Good morning Sarah. Please have a seat in the dining room and I can bring you a Western omelet."

One Hour Later: Almost Eight O'clock

Matt and Richard made the trip to Albertson's and stocked up. On the way back from the store Richard said to Matt, "I'm very pleased you took up the offer from Mr. Turco for the extra shows. You don't have to worry. We'll have some new material to cover the extra nights."

Matt asked, 'You'll have us covered with some new stuff?"

"Yes, I will." They pulled into Matt's driveway with nine bags of groceries. Richard continued, "I can put away all the items if you carry the bags in."

Matt responded, "You got it." Matt made his fourth trip to the house. Sarah was in the living room and had Thomas in the floor seat beside her.

Sarah said to Matt, "I called Jeannie last night."

"And?"

"They're coming over Saturday night. I told Jeannie we can get Chinese food."

Matt added, "Okay, sounds great. We haven't seen them in a while. I'm sure Al will enjoy seeing Richard."

The Next Morning: Monday, November 29th

Denise pulled in the driveway at six forty-five. Richard opened the front door for her and said, "Good morning Denise. How are you?"

Denise answered, "Tired. I need coffee."

"Please come in and help yourself as always. Sarah will be down in a few minutes."

Five Minutes Later

Sarah came downstairs. She said, "Good morning Denise."

Denise offered, "Good morning Sarah. I just want to say thank you again for having me here for Thanksgiving."

Sarah replied, "It was a pleasure having you here. I have to leave and I'll see you tomorrow."

"Okay, see you tomorrow," came from Denise.

Sarah went out of the door and left for work. Denise turned on the baby monitor. She took her coffee and sat in the living room. Richard sat in the chair across from her. Denise said, "It was very nice of Sarah to have me over for Thanksgiving. I get the feeling I was invited because they knew I was going to be by myself, but how would they know that?"

Richard answered, "You or someone else must've told her." Richard raised his eyebrows after trying to hand off that lame explanation.

Denise returned with, "I think you are someone else. How would you know I didn't have plans to see my family?"

"You didn't mention anything like that during our conversations. Something like that would've come up. I took the next thoughtful step and mentioned that I thought you would be alone on Thanksgiving. Matt told Sarah and they both agreed you shouldn't be alone. I guess that means I am guilty of telling them you had no plans to go away."

"Okay, thanks for clearing that up. I had a feeling you had something to do with it."

Four-Fifteen That Afternoon

Matt walked into the house and called in, "Richard, Denise, I'm home."

Richard emerged from the dining room, and said, "Ah, hello Matthew. I trust your day went well. Denise is upstairs putting Thomas down for a nap."

Denise came downstairs a few minutes later. Matt was standing in the doorway of the dining room and Denise said to him, "I just want to say thank you again for having me over on Thanksgiving."

Matt replied, "It was a pleasure having you here Denise. Sarah was happy to have another friend to talk to."

Denise grabbed her bag and slipped the book into it. She lifted her coat off the coat tree and put it on. Then she said, "I'll see you tomorrow Matt."

Matt replied, "Yup, I'll see you tomorrow."

Later on, Around Five-Forty

Sarah walked in the door and called in, "Matt, Richard, I'm home." Matt and Richard were standing in the kitchen talking.

Matt stepped out of the kitchen and greeted Sarah, "Het honey," and he kissed her.

"Richard said dinner will be ready in ten minutes."

Sarah responded, "Okay, I'll be right back. I just want to get changed."

159

Matt said before she could get up the stairs, "Don't change anything. I love you just the way you are."

Sarah got to the third stair, she stopped and said, "You're sweet."

The three of them sat at the table having dinner. Sarah spoke up and said to Matt, "Remember, Al and Jeannie are coming over Saturday night."

Matt offered, "Oh, I remember. We're getting Chinese food. Then. If we're lucky Richard will provide some entertainment for us."

Richard cut in and said, "Of course I will. I know Mr. Firmani enjoys seeing card tricks"

Five Days Later: Saturday, December 4th

Al and Jeannie pulled into Matt's driveway a few minutes before seven. Matt opened the door for them and said, "Hi Al, Jeannie, come in, come in."

They walked inside and Sarah said, "Hello Jeannie, it's been a while since I've seen you. Come, we'll sit in the living room and send the boys out to pick up the food."

Matt said, "I heard that. Come on Al, that's our cue. Let's go get the food." Matt and Al were in the car. On the way over Matt asked, "Al how're things?" Is work keeping you busy?"

Al answered, "Matt, I'm busier than a one-armed paper hanger."

Matt replied, "Well, it's better to be busy than not have enough work. Hey, when we get back to the house you could meet Thomas. I'm sure he'll be getting a bottle by then."

Matt and Al pulled into the driveway and went into the house. Matt said, "Honey, we're back with the food."

Sarah replied, "Good, Jeannie and I are famished. I already put plates on the table."

Sarah was sitting on the loveseat feeding Thomas while she was talking to Matt and Jeannie was sitting beside her.

"He's almost done. Richard put some big bowls on the counter and you can put the food in those. You know we can take the food from the bowls instead of the cardboard containers. We want to give the impression we're civilized. Matt, you're going to have to knock on

Richard's door. He still doesn't get it. Every time we have guests over, he thinks he shouldn't be included."

Matt replied, "Let me get us some drinks, and then I'll get Richard out here." Matt put a pitcher of iced tea on the table and five glasses. He knocked on Richard's door. Matt didn't hear any response and thought to himself, 'maybe he dozed off early.' He had to walk by the doorway to the cellar and that's when he heard footsteps coming up the stairs. Matt opened the door and there was Richard on the stairway.

He asked Richard, "What are you doing down there?"

Richard answered, "Just a little inventory of the contents in the freezer."

"That's fine but please come and join us for the food in the dining room. The Firmanis are here and Al's hoping to see some card tricks after dinner."

"Well, he will not be let down. Come, let's join the others."

The five of them sat at the dining table eating. Richard said to Al, "I hope you brought your cards with you."

Al replied, "Of course, I did. You told me before to bring them back and you would show me some new stuff."

After Dinner: A Little Before Eight

They finished eating. Sarah and Jeannie stood to clear the table. Richard also got up and took a couple of plates and the three of them went into the kitchen. Richard said, "Please leave the plates on the counter and I'll take it from here." Jeannie made one more trip in with the two large bowls. Richard was standing there and just closed the cabinet door. Jeannie was very surprised to see there were no dirty plates on the counter and she knew their kitchen did not have a dishwasher. She just shrugged it off and returned to the dining room.

Richard returned to the dining room and said to Al, "I understand you want to see some new card tricks. Al, you are in the right place. Please reach behind you. There should be a small notepad and a pen." Al reached behind him and grabbed the pad and pen.

Richard continued, "Okay, Al, I want you to think of a card from the deck as a first choice. Then, write your choice on the pad and don't show me what you wrote down. Next, write down a second choice."

Al wrote down the king of spades for the first choice and then the ace of diamonds for his second. Richard continued, "Slide the pad over to Jeannie. She and Sarah can look at your selections. Now take your cards and slide them over to Matt. Matt, please look at Al's cards and make sure they're shuffled. It would be better for you to fan the cards out on the table so everyone can see they're mixed up."

Matt fanned the cards out for everyone to see. Richard continued again, "Okay, thank you, Matt. I'll take it from here." Richard folded the cards up, tapped the deck on the table, and put them face down in front of Al. He said to Al, "Please lift the top card." Al lifted the top card and it was the king of spades. Richard continued, please turn over the second card." Al took the next one and it was the ace of diamonds.

Richard continued once more, "Jeannie, please show everyone the pad." Jeannie turned the pad over and revealed Al's choices. Of course, the cards matched what Al wrote down.

Al said, "That was great! Can you show us another one?"

Richard answered, "Yes, I can. Here is one trick that doesn't take as long. Jeannie, can you please help me with this one?"

Jeannie answered, "Sure. What do I do?"

Richard answered, "Okay, take the same cards and shuffle them a couple of times. Now cut them in half." Jeannie gave the cards a good shuffle and then cut the deck. "Next, please take the deck and fan them out face down so we cannot see their values." Jeannie spread the cards out face down as instructed. "Next, turn all the cards over so we can see them." Jeannie turned the cards over and her mouth dropped open. All the cards were blank.

Jeannie said, "WOW! That was something. I wish I knew how you did that."

Matt was sitting across from Jeannie and thought to himself, 'I think it's safe to assume everyone here wishes the same thing.'

Richard said, "Jeannie, please put the cards back together and place the deck face down. Now, with your index finger put some pressure on top of the deck but not too much." Jeannie placed the deck face down as instructed and then applied pressure with her index finger.

Richard continued, "That's great. Let's continue. Take half the cards and spread them out on the table. Your half does not have to be perfect." Jeannie took the top half and turned them over. Once again, everyone was surprised the cards had two values on them. There was a card value on top and a line in the center and a different value on the bottom half.

Jeannie spoke up and asked, "Are you going to tell me the bottom half looks like these?"

Richard hesitated and answered, "Uh, no, but you can still flip them all over." Jeannie turned the other cards over. These cards also changed. The bottom half of the cards had colored circles on them except two of the cards. The jokers were the only two cards left unchanged.

Sarah cut in and said, "WOW! Richard, you still have the magic touch with the cards."

Richard said, "Thank you, Sarah. It's almost nine-thirty and I need to retire to my room."

Al blurted out, "Oh please, just one more."

Richard looked at Al and said, "Al you're like a little kid on Christmas day wanting to open up just one more present. Okay, one more for you." Richard took the cards and asked Jeannie to shuffle them. Jeannie shuffled the cards and put them on the table. Richard then took the cards and said, "Al, I'm going to deal you five cards and I want you to pretend you're playing poker. So, if you can discard two or three cards you can get new ones to try to make your best hand."

Al replied, "Okay, I'm ready."

Richard then dealt five cards to Al. Al lifted the cards and thought to himself, 'I need a whole new hand.'

Richard asked, "How many cards do you want Al?"

Al answered, "I'll take three." Al slid over three cards he didn't want and Richard gave him three new ones. Al took the new cards and put them in his hand and thought, 'This is no better.'

Richard continued, "Okay Al, it's time to show us your cards. Do not lay them on the table. Just hold them in your hand and turn them so they're facing us." Al turned his cards around so they were facing the four people at the table. Richard leaned forward and touched one of Al's cards. Richard added, "Al, now turn the cards around so they're facing you." Al turned his cards to see them and his five cards changed.

Al raised his eyebrows. Richard asked, "Al, do you have a winning poker hand?"

Al answered, "I'll say. I have the best poker hand you can have." Al put his cards on the table. He now had a Royal straight flush that consisted of the ten through the ace of spades.

Richard stood up from the table and said, "I'm sorry. I have to call it a night."

Al and Jeannie both said, "Richard, it was great seeing you again, and thanks for the entertainment."

Richard nodded to Matt and waved to Sarah. He said, "I'll see you two in the morning." Then he walked up the hall to his bedroom.

Al spoke up and said, "Hey, I hate to ruin a good time but we need to get going. We have a busy day planned tomorrow. We have food shopping to do and mall shopping for new bed linens. Jeannie likes to get to the supermarket by nine to avoid the crowds."

Matt replied, "Don't we all. Well, thanks for coming over. It was nice visiting with you guys. We'll have to get together again sometime."

Jeannie said, "Sure, we'll do that." They put their coats on and went out the door.

As Matt was closing the door Sarah asked him, "Do you think I'm as pretty as she is?"

Matt asked, "What? Where's that coming from?"

"I noticed twice during the night you were looking right at her. You staring at her was making me feel very uncomfortable."

Matt replied, "Look, I'm sorry. I didn't mean to be staring at her. To answer your question, I don't think you're as pretty as Jeannie. In my opinion, you are far more beautiful. Yes, Jeannie is attractive in her way but she doesn't hold a candle to you. Now, can we go upstairs and go to bed?"

Sarah answered, "Okay, I just needed a little assurance."

The Next Morning: Sunday, December 5th

Matt came downstairs at six thirty-five to get coffee. Richard was sitting at the table reading the newspaper while drinking his third coffee. Matt greeted Richard first, "Good morning Richard. How are you?"

Richard answered, "Just splendid and good morning to you too. Are we be making the Albertson's trip after I fix breakfast for Sarah?"

Matt answered, "I believe we will and I just want to see if Sarah has anything to add to the list."

"Yes, of course, and I know it's not my business to talk about this but start telling Sarah you love her more often. When she gets home from work or any other time tell her she looks nice."

Matt responded with, "I understand and I will."

The bedroom opened upstairs and Richard says softly, "Here she comes now."

Matt turned on the baby monitor and went to the bottom of the stairs to greet Sarah. Sarah got to the bottom and Matt said, "Good morning honey." Sarah looked at Matt as she walked by and did not respond. Matt thought to himself, 'Oh-oh.'

Matt followed her to the kitchen and once in there she said, "Good morning Richard."

Richard replied, "Good morning Sarah. You know the drill. Please take a seat in the dining room and I'll bring you some eggs and toast."

Sarah went to the dining room and Matt followed her. Matt asked, "Honey, are you okay?"

Sarah answered, "I'm okay, I had a bad dream last night about our conversation right before bed. You were not looking good in the dream either. I'm sorry I didn't say good morning. I just needed to snap out of it."

"Honey, you have nothing to worry about. I love you and I wouldn't do anything to jeopardize our marriage."

Richard walked in with a plate of food for Sarah. He asked Matt, "Can I get you some food?"

Matt answered, "Oh no, I don't want you to go to any trouble."

Richard replied, "I understand and I'm not going to any trouble." He then took a plate of eggs and wheat toast that was behind his back and put it on the table in front of Matt. Richard said, "Enjoy you two."

Matt said, "Thank you, Richard." He then asked Sarah, "Honey we're going to Albertson's in a little bit. Do you need anything?"

Sarah answered, "Get me some granola bars and some food for Denise for next week."

"Okay, you got it." Matt finished his breakfast and he heard Thomas make a sound on the baby monitor. He said to Sarah, "Stay right there. I'll take care of him."

Sarah got up and thought to herself, 'I may as well get my book and go in the living room.'

Twenty-Five Minutes Later

Matt had Thomas fed and changed. Matt put Thomas in the floor seat near Sarah. He said to Sarah, "Okay, we're off to the store. We'll be back in about an hour."

Matt and Richard drove to Albertson's. Once in the store, Matt brought up, "I know it's six days away but this coming Saturday is show night."

"I know. Do you have any ideas? We want to show something to the audience to make them say WOW!"

"This is what I've come up with. I know it sounds risky but it's going to be great."

Matt asked, "What is it?"

Richard answered, "Okay, we'll start with the shooting range target on the stage. I'll start by telling the audience the story of William Tell shooting an apple off his son's head. Then, I'm going to have you shoot a bullet at me."

"There's one major flaw here."

"What's that?"

Matt answered, "I have never so much as held a gun never mind fired one."

Richard replied, "There's a first time for everything. Don't worry, we'll get that taken care of well before the show. I'll also have you use my gun. The idea behind this is you're going to fire the handgun at me and I'm going to catch the bullet in my hand. Do not worry over the fact you never fired a gun before. The gun is going to aim itself."

Matt asked, "What if someone in the audience yells out it's fixed?"

Richard answered, "That's simple. We'll invite him or her and let them fire the gun right after you. If the person knows anything about guns, they'll be able to tell the pistol has not been modified. We'll discuss it later when we get back to the house."

"Okay, but one quick question. Why do you have a gun?"

Richard answered, "I don't. I never said I owned one. I said you can use my gun. I don't need a gun so there's no reason to own one. I'll have one for Saturday for the performance and that'll be its only purpose."

Matt and Richard went to the checkout, loaded the groceries in the car, and then went home. They pulled in the driveway and Richard said to Matt, "We can do the usual. You carry in most of the bags and I'll put the groceries away."

Matt replied, "You're on." Matt kept up his end of the deal and carried in four bags of groceries.

On his second trip with the third and fourth bag, Richard said to him, "Grab two coffees and head to the dining room. I'll meet you there."

Matt poured a coffee for himself and one for Richard. He brought them to the dining room and Richard was already sitting at the table waiting for him. Richard had his journal open in front of him. The trick for Saturday night's performance was already in the book. Matt sat down and could see the page the book was opened to.

Matt said, "I thought the information didn't get filled in until after the performance."

"That's usually how it works. However, I am so confident this will be a success. I took the liberty and wrote the information in the journal ahead of time." Richard closed the journal and put it back in the hutch. He said to Matt, "We should go in the cellar so you can get some target practice."

Matt replied, "Wait a minute. You said you were going to have the gun aim itself."

"That's right. I did. We also have to make it look like you know what you're doing. Now, here take my pistol and aim at the target on the wall across from us. Don't worry the noise will not be enough to disturb Sarah or wake Thomas."

Matt said, "Okay," as he took the pistol and squeezed off his first shot. To Matt's surprise, he hit the paper target.

Richard watched as Matt fired the gun and he said, "Not bad, you still have five more shots. Keep practicing. You'll get the hang of it."

21

Bullet Practice

Six Days Later: Saturday, December 11ᵗʰ

Matt came downstairs at six twenty-five. He went straight into the kitchen and poured himself a coffee. Richard was sitting at the table in the corner and he greeted Matt first, "Good morning Matt. I trust you slept well."

Matt replied, "Good morning Richard. I wish I could have slept longer. We have our show tonight and I hope everything goes well."

"I'm sure everything will be fine. I know I don't have to tell you this but not a word to Sarah about tonight. It won't go over well and she's on her way downstairs."

Sarah came downstairs with Thomas in her arms. She said, "Good morning Matt. Good morning Richard."

Matt responded, "Good morning honey. You should take a seat in the dining room and I will get you some breakfast." Matt took a bottle from the refrigerator for Thomas. He said, "Honey, I'll take care of him." Matt put his hands out and took Thomas from Sarah.

Richard spoke up and said, "Yes Sarah please take a seat in the dining room and we'll I mean I'll bring you breakfast." Richard was looking at Matt while talking to Sarah.

Sarah responded, "Thank you, Richard. Once again, you're spoiling me."

Five-Forty-Five

Matt found Sarah in the living room reading. He asked her, "Do you need anything before we head out to the theater?"

Sarah answered, "No, I am all set. I'm going to call Karen Gilhooly tonight. You don't mind if I invite them over next Saturday, do you?"

Matt answered, "Not at all. That's a great idea. We can get pizza or something."

Richard interrupted and said, "Excuse me, Mrs. White, let me volunteer to make a pot roast. I'm sure they'll appreciate that more."

Sarah added, "Thank you, Richard. We just thought we'd make things easier on you."

"I am fine with cooking dinner for the four of you."

Sarah replied, "You mean the five of us and have a good night at the show."

Richard replied, "Thank you, Sarah. You have a nice night."

Matt and Richard left for the theater. They arrived around six twenty-five. The two of them took their usual seats in the front row.

Matt asked Richard, "Are you sure this will work?"

Richard answered, "I can't see it not working. I wouldn't have come up with this idea if I thought there was any room for error. Just remember the gun is going to aim itself. Go along with it and don't force it in the other direction. I plan on catching the bullet with my right hand."

The crowds started through the doorway and Matt said, "We need to get out of sight."

The show got started right at seven-thirty. Matt and Richard performed their acts flawlessly. It was eight-thirty and Richard nodded to Matt signaling it was time for their last act. Matt announced to the audience, "Ladies and gentlemen, "We have time for just one more. I'm going to let Richard take over here."

Richard walked down the stairs off the stage and said, "I need to get someone on stage with me to look at this. It has to be someone who's not nervous about holding a handgun."

A few volunteers stood up. Richard walked over and picked someone from the fourth row.

He said, "Excuse me, sir, will you come up on the stage and assist me with this? Could you give me your name, please?"

The volunteer answered, "Dave, Dave Muldoon."

Richard replied, "Okay Dave, I hope you've fired a handgun before."

Dave responded, "Yes, I have, many times."

Richard continued, "Okay Dave, I want you to take this handgun, examine it, and then you're going to take a few shots at the target."

Dave looked the gun over, removed the clip, and put it back in. He fired a shot at the paper target. Richard put his hand up and said, "Hold it, please. Richard walked to the target and said, "WOW! That was almost dead center. I can tell you've done this before. Do it one more time please."

Dave fired off another shot and this time it was a direct hit in the center. Richard said, "Excellent, one second let me put up a new target for you." Richard walked over to the line holding the target and replaced the paper. He said, "Okay Dave, take one more shot, and then I want Matt to give it a try." Dave took his third shot and that one was a little further away than the first one.

Matt walked over and Dave passed the gun to him. Richard said, "It's your turn, Matt." Richard was standing a few feet from the target.

Matt aimed and took his first shot. The first one was a half-inch from the center. Richard looked at the target and said, "Impressive, Dave might have some competition. Try again please."

Matt took his second shot and it was a quarter of an inch closer. Richard said, "Okay Matt, one more time."

Matt took his third shot and Richard stuck out his right hand simultaneously. Richard raised his right arm and opened his hand. He caught the bullet in his right hand.

Richard said, "Just a minute." He raised his right hand and held the bullet up so the cameraman could focus in on it. "Matt, you were a little off target then. Please try again." Matt fired off another shot and this time Richard caught the bullet in his left hand.

Dave had returned to his seat in the audience. He yelled out, "Hey, can I try that again?"

Richard answered, "Mr. Muldoon, please come back up here."

Dave walked back up on the stage and Matt passed the handgun back to him. Richard said, "Let me put a fresh target up there, and then you can fire away. Richard unclipped the used target and then replaced it with a new one for Dave. Richard said, "You're all set. Fire away."

Dave fired and the first shot hit the target a little outside the bull's-eye. Richard complimented Dave on his shooting, "Well done Mr. Muldoon. Please go again." Dave aimed for his next shot and this time Richard was waiting down at the end of the target. Richard put up his hand and said, "You missed that time." Richard opened his hand and he was holding the bullet between his thumb and index finger.

Dave looked at Richard's hand in disbelief. Dave shook his head and then he asked, "Can I try that once more?"

Richard answered, "Sure thing, whenever you're ready."

Dave got ready, aimed, and shot again. This time the bullet ended up in Richard's left hand. Dave said, "That's it for me." He walked across the stage to Richard and said, "Thanks for letting me be part of this. Please tell me how you did it."

"Did what?" Richard asked.

"Caught the bullets."

Richard responded with, "Oh sorry. I can't tell you that. Thanks for your help. Have a good evening."

Dave's response was, "I had a feeling you'd say that. Have a good night Mr. Jenkins and you too Mr. White."

Matt said bye to Dave and then made an announcement to the audience, "Ladies and gentlemen, that concludes our show for tonight. We hope you enjoyed it. If you liked what you saw, please tell your friends. Please drive safely and have a good night. Everyone, have a great holiday and a happy new year. We will be back Thursday, January 6th next year."

Matt said to Richard, "Well Mr. Jenkins, you ready to call it a night?"

Richard answered, "I need a few minutes to fix this." Richard showed both of his hands to Matt. His right hand had a hole through the middle of his palm. His left hand had an indentation in the middle of his palm.

Matt cried out, "Oh my god, we have to get you to the hospital."

"No, no, just give me two minutes. I can take care of this myself." Richard rubbed his hands up and down the front of his legs three times. He said, "There, that should do it." He held out his hands and

172

there was no longer any hole or indentation in his palms. Richard added, "Now, I'm ready."

On the way home Matt said to Richard, "That must have stung. Are you sure you're alright?"

Richard answered, "I'll be fine. The bullets came out faster than I anticipated. I am okay now."

Without hesitation, Matt replied, "Okay, but maybe we should eliminate that one."

The Next Day: Sunday, December 12th

The morning started like any other Sunday morning. Matt came down early for coffee. Richard was sitting in the corner at the kitchen table. He had just finished reading the newspaper. Matt began, "Good morning Richard. How are you?"

Richard answered, "Good morning Matt. Everything seems to be intact here." Richard raised both hands for Matt to see.

Matt looked closely at Richard's hands and said, "Wow, you can't even tell there was a hole there. They're all sealed up."

"I told you I'd take care of it. Speaking of taking care of it; you should turn on the baby monitor. Here comes Sarah."

Sarah came downstairs and went straight to the kitchen. Matt said, "Good morning honey," and kissed her on the cheek.

She responded, "Good morning Matt," and returned the kiss. She also said, "Good morning Richard."

Richard replied, "Good morning Sarah. Please have a seat in the dining room and I'll bring you breakfast. Matt will be taking care of Thomas when he wakes up."

"Thank you, Richard. Once again you're spoiling me." She then went to the dining room. Sarah was waiting at the table and Richard came in with a plate of scrambled eggs and wheat toast. Sarah said, "Thank you, Richard."

Richard sat at the table momentarily with Sarah. "Sarah, Matt, and I will be going to the market later if there's anything you need."

"Can you please pick me up some granola bars and some yogurt? Don't forget, the Gilhoolys are coming over Saturday night and I believe you are on cooking duty. It's not too late to change your mind."

"There's no need to change my decision about Saturday night's meal. I already have a list of what I need for that."

Less than an hour later Matt and Richard were off to the supermarket. Once in the store, Matt grabbed a carriage and they started up and down the aisles. Matt said to Richard, "I don't think we should repeat last night's performance. I am serious. I don't want anything to happen to the mastermind behind our show."

Richard replied, "I agree with mastermind but I am no longer just behind the scenes. You needn't worry about that. However, I will leave it up to you to come up with an act for our first show in January. It's on you this time."

Matt grimaced and said, "Fine, I'll come up with something. I'm not sure what though."

Richard added, "Well, let's do this. You let me know when you come up with your idea, and we'll discuss it first. We can always modify when it's time."

They finished their shopping and pushed the carriage through the checkout. Once the groceries were paid for Matt loaded the bags in the car and drove back to the house. Matt brought the groceries inside and Richard put everything away.

Sarah was in the living room with a book and her feet up. Thomas was beside her in his bouncing seat. Matt called in, "Honey, we're back."

Sarah said, "Het Matt, I was just thinking a few minutes ago."

"Oh, oh!"

"Funny. No, seriously we should invite Denise over here for Christmas. It's less than two weeks away. I know Sean and Katelin are coming over the day after but I feel bad she's going to be alone again."

"Okay, okay. You'll see her in the morning. Talk to her and see if she has any plans. If she doesn't; you can invite her over."

"Ok, thanks, I'll talk to her in the morning."

The Next Morning: Monday, December 13th

Matt came downstairs at six twenty-five and went straight to the kitchen to get coffee. Richard was at the kitchen table in his usual spot.

Richard greeted Matt first, "Good morning Matt. How are you?"

"Good morning. I feel a little tired. I need this coffee."

"That's why it's there for the pick me up."

Matt took two more sips of his coffee and said, "I have to go. See you around four-fifteen." Matt put his mug in the sink and went out the door.

Richard managed to get out, "Have a good day, Mr. White."

At six forty-five Denise pulled in the driveway and went up the front stairs. Richard opened the front door and said, "Good morning Miss Bennett. I trust you had a good weekend."

Denise walked in and said, "Yes, I did. It was nice and relaxing. How are you, Richard?"

Richard answered, "Just splendid, please help yourself to coffee. Sarah should be down in a few minutes."

Denise made sure the baby monitor was on and then poured herself a coffee. She took her coffee and sat at the kitchen table. Richard asked, "Are you still enjoying your new car? I know it's not so new at this point."

Sarah came downstairs and said, "Good morning" to Denise. She continued, "Before I forget, do you have any plans for Christmas?"

Denise replied, "Good morning Sarah and to answer your question I waited too long to book a flight. I called my mother last night and told her I will come to see her next year. However, Tom is coming over Christmas Eve."

Sarah added, "Well, you and Tom are invited over here and you can stay the night if you like. My brother Sean and his wife are coming the day after Christmas, but we have plenty of room. Please think it over and let me know. I have to go and I'll see you tomorrow."

Denise responded, "Okay, have a good day. I'll see you tomorrow."

Denise took a seat in the living room after Sarah left for work. Richard brought in a cup of coffee and put it next to her on the end table. She said, "Thank you, Richard." She took a sip from her cup and asked, "Richard, is there anything going on I should be aware of?"

"Such as?" Richard asked.

"I think it's strange that Sarah wants me here at Christmas. She said her brother and wife are coming over the next day."

Richard added, "Ah, the thing is Sarah is all about family. She feels bad your family is far away. She knew you from a long time ago. Perhaps, that is why she feels the need to be close to you. The only other acquaintances she has around here are Jeannie and Karen."

Denise took another sip of her coffee and said, "I just hope there's no trouble on the home front if you get my meaning." Five seconds later sounds were coming from the baby monitor.

Denise said, "I'm on duty."

Denise went upstairs to get Thomas out of the crib. She brought him down to the changing table and fed him his breakfast. Denise said to Richard, "This is a very nice highchair. We didn't have these when I was a baby. They were all made of wood."

Richard added, "This one was a steal from Babies R Us last week." Steal was the keyword in the sentence but Denise didn't know it and didn't need to know it. Denise finished up with Thomas and put him in his sit up seat so he could look around.

Later On: Around Four-Fifteen

Matt walked into the house and called in, "Denise, Richard, I'm home."

Denise called out, "In here in the living room." Denise was on the floor with Thomas trying to get him to roll over.

Matt walked into the living room and asked, "Are you training him to be a gymnast?"

Denise answered, "Not quite. I like it when he rolls over to look at me, he smiles like he knows he did something right" Denise started packing up her things and said, "Can you give Sarah a message for me?"

"Sure thing."

"Tell her I'll call Tom tonight and maybe we can get over here Christmas morning."

"I'll give her that message."

"Thomas had food around one-thirty so he'll probably want something in about an hour. I have to go and I'll see you tomorrow."

Matt responded with, "Okay, we'll see you tomorrow. Bye."

One Hour Later: Around Five-Thirty-Five

Sarah walked into the house and called in, "Matt, Richard, I'm home."

Matt was in the dining room when he heard Sarah. He walked over and said, "Hi Honey" and kissed her. Matt asked, "How was your day?"

"Exhausting." Sarah continued, "I just want to say hi to my angel and get changed."

Fifteen Minutes Later

They were at the dining room table having dinner. Thomas was in the floor seat where Sarah could keep an eye on him.

Matt spoke up and said, "I have a message from Denise. She told me to tell you she's going to talk to Tom tonight about coming over here on Christmas morning."

Sarah replied, "Good, maybe she'll let me know in the morning."

The Next Morning: Tuesday, December 14th

Matt came downstairs at six twenty-five and poured himself a coffee. Richard was sitting in the corner with his second cup of coffee and the newspaper. Matt greeted Richard first, "Good morning Richard. How are you?"

Richard responded with, "Good morning to you too Matt. There's nothing like a good night's rest to recharge the batteries."

Matt continued, "I wonder if Denise had a chance to speak with Tom about coming over here on Christmas."

Richard said, "Let's put it this way as of Saturday, December 25th a little after eight the morning there will be six people in the house. Denise and Tom will only be here for the day through dinnertime. Sleeping accommodations will not be necessary for those two."

Matt asked, "How do you know this?"

Richard answered, "Here we go again with the same unnecessary question."

"Let's not get into that now. I have to go and I'll see you around four- fifteen."

Matt went out the door and Richard managed to say, 'Have a good day, Mr. White."

Five Minutes Later

Denise's car pulled in the driveway. Just like routine Richard opened the door for her. She came up the front stairs and Richard greeted her, "Good morning Miss Bennett. How are you?"

Denise answered back, "Good morning Richard. I'm doing okay."

Richard continued, "Please grab yourself a coffee. Sarah should be down in five minutes."

Five Minutes Later

Sarah was downstairs just like Richard predicted. She said, "Good morning Denise. Good morning Richard."

Denise replied, "Good morning Sarah. Oh, just to let you know I spoke with Tom and he's okay with coming over here Christmas day. I can bring a couple of bottles of wine and a couple of pies for dessert. What time do you want us to come by?"

Sarah answered, 'Come anytime, and as early as you want. We're up early. I have to go. I'll see you tomorrow."

Denise replied, "Bye, see you tomorrow." Denise made sure the baby monitor was on and then sat in the living room. Richard came into the living room with a fresh coffee for Denise and himself. Denise looked up and said, "Thank you."

Richard responded, "You're welcome. I believe you were about to ask me something."

Before Denise spoke, she thought to herself, 'How does he know I have a question. I'll make it a good one and he will be ready for it. For once I'll have him stymied for an answer.' "Okay, I can't come by here empty-handed on Christmas as in the form of gifts. Do you know what I can pick up for Sarah and Matt?"

178

Richard answered, "Not only do I have an answer for you, but my suggestion for both of them will be one-stop shopping."

Denise asked, "Okay, what are you thinking of?"

Richard answered, "Sarah loves reading on the weekends. You can get her the latest Sue Grafton novel, 'S is for Silence'. As for Matt, I know he's mentioned to me how he likes the detective Sherlock Holmes. I think if you go to Barnes & Noble, you'll find what you're looking for. If you prefer to do this during the day, I can accompany you. You can stay in the car with Thomas just in case and then I can pick up the books for you."

"Thank you, Richard." Denise asked, "Is tomorrow okay with you? I only have twelve dollars with me."

Richard answered, "Tomorrow will be fine."

Later on: Around Four-Twenty

Matt walked into the house and called in, "Denise, Richard, I'm home."

Denise called out to Matt, "In the living room."

Matt went into the living room and Denise was sitting on the floor with Thomas again. Thomas was in his seat on the floor and Denise was masking a crawling motion with her hand like a spider towards Thomas. Thomas smiled every time Denise's hand got closer to him. Denise looked up at Matt and said, "I found a way of making him laugh. He loves my hand crawling towards him."

Matt replied, "Great! I'll remember that."

Denise added, "I told Sarah this morning Tom and I are coming over Christmas. Thank you for inviting me."

Matt replied, "Our pleasure. It'll be great having you here."

Denise asked Matt, "I have a question for you, and now is the time to ask it without a certain someone in the room. What can I get Richard for Christmas?"

Matt thought for a few seconds and offered, "How about a cardigan sweater. I think he'll like that versus wearing his suit coat every day. He'll appreciate it and it won't put you in the poor house."

"Okay, I'll go shopping for one of those. Thanks for the tip. I'll see you tomorrow."

179

The Next Morning: Wednesday, December 15th

Denise's car pulled in the driveway around six forty-five. Richard opened the front door for her. He always managed to be in the right place when Denise arrived. Richard greeted her first, "Good morning Miss Bennet. How are you?"

"I'm okay. Good morning Richard."

"Denise, as usual, please help yourself to coffee. I believe Sarah will be down in five minutes."

Denise went into the living room and turned the baby monitor on. Then she went back to the kitchen and poured a coffee for herself."

Five Minutes Later

Sarah was downstairs in the kitchen. Sarah said, "Good morning Denise. Good morning Richard."

Denise offered, "Good morning Sarah. Wait 'til you get outside and feel how cold it is. The temperature's gone way down. I think it's only eleven degrees out."

Sarah said, "Yeah, I heard it was supposed to start dropping. To think, it's not officially winter. Just going to have to bundle up all that more. I have to go. I'll see you tomorrow. Bye."

Denise managed to get out, "Have a nice day, Sarah."

Sarah went out the front door and the cold was a rude awakening. She hustled to her car as fast as she could. She thought to herself, 'Starting tomorrow, I need to ask Denise if she'll start my car for me in the morning.'

Sarah backed out of the driveway and headed off to work. Denise saw Sarah's car leave from where she was sitting. She just looked at the baby monitor and then sounds from Thomas came out of it. Denise thought to herself, 'Time to start earning my paycheck.'

Denise went upstairs and brought Thomas to the changing table. Next, she put him in the highchair and fed him breakfast. Denise said to Richard, "One thing is for sure this kid has a good appetite."

Richard replied, "He needs his nourishment. He's going to med school after college. After eight years of schooling, Thomas White will graduate top of his class and go on to be a cardiac surgeon."

Denise asked, "Is that all? He's not going to be the president?"

"Goodness, no, I wouldn't wish that on anyone. To change the subject, did you come today prepared to go to Barnes & Noble?"

She answered, "Yes, I did and I think we'll be ready to go in about an hour."

Ten Forty-Five: Sixty-five Minutes Later

Denise picked up Thomas and put him in the car seat. She then drove to Barnes & Noble with Richard riding shotgun. Once they got in the parking lot, Richard offered, "I think it would be better if I went to the store and you stay with Thomas. If he fusses, you'll know what to do."

"You're right. Hold on a second. Let me give you money."

Denise reached in her bag and pulled out five twenty-dollar bills. She said, "I hope that's enough."

Richard put out his hand, looked at the money, and said, "I'm sure that'll be plenty."

He went into the store and came out ten minutes later with a Barnes & Noble bag.

Richard got back in the car and said, "Mission accomplished. I have the latest Sue Grafton and a book by James Patterson. Also, I have the complete works of Sherlock Holmes by Sir Arthur Conan Doyle. You also get a free book tote bag. The receipt is in the bag."

"Thank you for doing that Richard. Did I give you enough money?"

Richard added, "You gave me too much. This is for you." Richard handed back the same money Denise gave to him.

Denise took the money and she went to put it in her bag. That's when she realized it was the same money she gave to Richard. She asked him, "What's this? Why do I have all this money back?"

"It's the strangest thing. They wouldn't take your money."

"Oh, I see. I think the reason they didn't take it is you decided not to give it to them. You know, I can pay for some things, especially gifts I'm giving."

They arrived back at the house and Richard said, "I was just being generous to show my appreciation."

"Appreciation for what?"

They went into the house and Denise put Thomas in his seat. Richard said, "Let me get us coffee." He returned to the living room with coffee for him and Denise. Denise was waiting in one of the wingchairs. Richard explained, "Before Matt and Sarah hired you, I was alone in the house with no other adult to talk to. I am so happy with the fact that you're here when they're not."

Denise asked, "Why? I don't understand."

"Okay, as you know, I can keep the house in exchange for living quarters in Mr. White's house. I also take care of the cooking, laundry, and other linens. That is not an eight-hour job. I get everything done with plenty of time to spare. Sure, I can watch the occasional talk show. I even get to plan the magic acts that Mr. White and I do together.

"Planning those takes me twenty to twenty-five minutes. What I'm trying to say is I'm grateful you're here. Because you're here, I have an adult to engage in conversation with. Without you, I'd go stir crazy. I'm also glad you and Tom decided to come over on Christmas."

Denise responded with, "Wow, that was some lengthy explanation."

"Yes, it was. I thought you should know the reason I've been generous with my finances. To tell the truth, I don't need all this money."

22

Christmas

Saturday, December 25ᵗʰ

I t was Christmas morning and Matt came downstairs at six-thirty to grab his coffee. He did not see Richard sitting at the table, which he thought was unusual. He grabbed his coffee and walked around.

That's when he heard a low voice saying, "Matthew."

Matt looked around and saw Richard standing in front of the tree. Richard said, Good morning and Merry Christmas!"

Matt replied, "Merry Christmas to you Richard,"

Richard offered, "I think we did a better job decorating the tree this year over the last year."

Matt added, 'I agree and Sarah thinks so too. Remember, she doesn't know you use a little hocus pocus to do this. I didn't tell her we didn't use any magic so technically I did not lie to her."

"You should keep it that way. Do you want some eggs before Sarah gets up? That's only ten minutes from now. Also, Denise and Tom will be here at nine o'clock."

"No, don't trouble yourself. You'll be making dinner later."

"Yes, speaking of that, I think it would be best to keep all residents out of the kitchen, and dinner will be served at two o'clock sharp."

"Okay, I'm sure that'll be fine. Hey, did you get Denise anything?'

Richard asked, "You mean as in a Christmas gift? I found a sweater for her at Macy's"

"When did you have time to go to Macy's? "

Richard answered, "Oh, I didn't have time to go there if you get my meaning. I also made sure a cash deposit was made to the nearest register to cover any missing inventory."

Matt said, "Let me ask you this. When you say missing inventory, how many things are you referring to?"

"Maybe five or six. That's not important right now. Besides, here comes Mrs. White."

Sarah came downstairs and said to Matt, "Merry Christmas honey," and she kissed him. She then said to Richard, "Good morning Richard. Merry Christmas."

Richard replied, "Merry Christmas Sarah. I was telling Matt that I think our tree decorating skills have improved since last year. This tree looks so much better than the one in the store."

Sarah offered, "That's because the tree on display in the store didn't get your magic touch." Sarah winked at Richard as she was giving him the explanation.

Sarah barely finished her sentence and Thomas was stirring upstairs. Matt said, "Looks like somebody else wants to see the tree. I'll be right back." Matt went upstairs and put Thomas in clean clothes.

He brought him downstairs and said to him, "I think you want breakfast." Matt put Thomas in the highchair and brought over a tray with little compartments in it. The tray had three compartments and each section contained a different food for Thomas's breakfast.

Sarah walked over to the highchair and said, "Merry Christmas my little angel," and she kissed him on top of his head.

Eight-Fifty-Five

Denise and Tom parked in the driveway and they went up the front stairs. Richard said, "Excuse me. I believe our guests are here." Richard opened the front door and said, "Good morning Denise. Good morning Mr. Perates. Merry Christmas to the both of you."

Denise and Tom walked in and Denise said, "Merry Christmas Richard. I hope we're not too early."

Richard added, "Of course not. Please come in and I'll make a fresh pot of coffee."

Denise and Tom walked into the living room and Denise said, "Merry Christmas Matt. Merry Christmas Sarah."

Sarah and Matt both stood up and greeted the guests. Matt asked Tom, "Can I get you coffee or eggnog? You can have it with brandy or without."

Tom answered, "No, I'll just have coffee. Thanks."

Matt said, "Follow me." Before Matt could push the door open to the kitchen, the door opened toward them and Richard was holding a tray with three cups of coffee. Matt, Tom, and Denise sat in the living room drinking their coffee.

Sarah went into the kitchen to mix up a pitcher of Brandy Alexander. Sarah reached for the pitcher in the cabinet and it wasn't there. Richard walked in and asked, "Can I help you find something?"

She answered, "Yes, I'm looking for the new pitcher I just bought from Home Goods."

Richard replied, "I am sorry. It's already in the refrigerator being used."

"Darn! I was going to mix up a pitcher of Brandy Alexander so we can offer something besides beer."

Richard responded with, "If you were to make that offer, you'll find a pitcher of it in the refrigerator. I saw that Matt picked up a bottle of brandy and crème de cacao. I assumed that's what it was for. Would you like to sample it?"

Sarah answered, "Uh, let me get Denise." Sarah went into the living room, pointed at Denise, and made a come-hither motion with her index finger.

Denise stood up, followed Sarah to the kitchen, and asked, "What's up?"

Sarah answered, "Richard made a pitcher of brandy Alexander for us. Will you test this to see if it's acceptable?"

Denise said, "Sure!" She took the glass, took a sip, and then another and two more. Denise said, "There's a problem here."

Sarah asked, "What?"

Denise answered, "This glass is empty. Richard, you did an excellent job. Reload please."

Richard acknowledged and said, "Thank you, Miss Bennett."

Sarah refilled Denise's glass and poured a small one for herself. The two of them went back to the living room and Sarah said to Denise, "This is good, but I can't drink too much of it."

Denise sat next to Tom on the loveseat and Tom asked softly, "Everything okay?"

Denise answered, "Of course, I was in the kitchen helping out." Helping to consume alcohol was Denise's idea of helping. She told Tom, "There's brandy Alexander in the kitchen if you want to try it."

Tom responded, "Thanks but that stuff is not for me. I'm just a beer guy. He leaned back in Denise's ear, "I didn't bring anything with me."

Denise added, "That's alright. Matt usually has beer in the house. Oh, you mean something else. I put your name with mine on the tags for the presents for Matt and Sarah."

Thirty Minutes Later

Sarah said, "Hey everyone, I think now is a good time to do gifts seeing as Thomas is sleeping."

Matt added, "I agree. Let me find Richard." Matt walked by the area where the tree was set up and noticed there were about twenty gifts on the floor. He did a double-take when he saw the tree and headed for the kitchen. Matt said to Richard, "We're going to do gifts and we need you. Uh, how did all that stuff get under the tree?"

Richard answered, "I took care of that. I knew you and Sarah have been very busy. Please allow me two minutes and I'll join you. I just want to prep another pot of coffee."

Five Minutes Later

Richard joined the four of them in the tree area. He had a coffee in his hand and asked, "Can I get anyone anything before we start?"

There were no requests for additional beverages and Sarah said, "Good, let's start." Sarah knelt and handed a present to Denise, one to Tom and one to Richard in that order. She then handed a present to Matt.

Denise opened her gift and it was a hooded sweatshirt with the Chicago Blackhawks logo. She said, "Thank you." She looked at Tom and said, "You know what this means. You have to take me to a hockey game."

Tom added, "Okay, if I can get the tickets."

Denise said, "Open your gift." Tom opened his gift and it was a small box that a wallet would fit in. He removed the cover and there was a leather wallet inside.

Tom said, "Thank you. The wallets I buy for myself don't last that long. This is a nice one."

Richard cut in and said, "Let's see." Tom took out the wallet and there were two tickets for a Blackhawks game the following November.

Tom added, "Thank you. Thank you so much."

Denise added, "Hey, now you have the tickets and I'll mark that on my calendar."

More gifts were exchanged and thirty minutes later it was time for dinner. Richard said to Matt, "Perhaps you can help me carry some things to the table."

"Sure thing," Matt replied.

Richard added, "There are two bottles of wine in the refrigerator thanks to Denise. Can you please open one and pour it into a carafe? Then bring the carafe and five wine glasses to the table."

Matt did as he was instructed. He went back to the kitchen and asked, "Next?"

Richard answered, "Next, you tell everyone, yourself included to have a seat at the table."

"Okay."

Five Minutes Later

The five of them were eating dinner and Sarah started the conversation, "Richard, this roast is delicious. Then again your cuisine is always top-notch."

"Thank you, Sarah. I tried to make this enjoyable for everyone. Oh, and everyone please leave room for dessert."

The desserts were put on the table. Denise said, "WOW! Everything looks great. I don't know what to take first."

Sarah added, "Take a slice of each. There are no calories on Christmas."

"If only that were true."

Matt cut in and said, "I'm getting a slice of cheesecake with strawberries. How about you, Tom?"

Tom answered, "That sounds good."

Twenty Minutes Later

Richard was the only one who didn't take dessert. He sat at one end of the table sipping a coffee. Richard said, "Let me put these pies back in the kitchen, give the table a quick wipe, and then I'd like to show everyone something I've been working on."

Denise stood up and said, "Let me gather plates up and bring them to the kitchen."

Richard stopped her and said, "Please you're a guest here. I'll take care of it."

Richard went into the kitchen; with a wave of his hand all the plates were back in the cabinets that they came from. There was no longer any proof left in the kitchen that a big meal had been cooked there.

Richard came back to the dining room, gave the table a quick wipe, and said, "Tom, would you be so kind as to grab the cards in the small cloth bag on the hutch behind you."

Tom replied, "Sure." He grabbed the cloth bag with the cards inside.

Richard asked, "Tom, I take it you want to volunteer for this?"

Tom answered, "Oh, of course. That's me alright." He asked, "What can I do?"

Richard continued, "Take the cards out of the bag. Look through the cards and make sure they're an ordinary deck."

Tom fanned through the cards and said, "They look normal to me."

Richard continued again, "Great. Tom, please take seven cards out of the deck. You can pick any cards from the deck. Then put them in the bag and close it."

Tom pulled out seven different cards and put them in the bag. He then asked, "Okay, next?"

Richard answered, "Put your right hand on the bag and I'm going to put my hand on top of yours." Richard laid his hand on top of Tom's for no more than three seconds. He removed his hand and said, Now, take the cards out of the bag and put them face up on the table."

Tom nodded and removed the cards. He asked, "How did you?"

Before Tom could finish his question, Richard put his hand out and said, "I think we're done with the bag. Tom, please fold it in half and then put it in my palm."

Tom took the bag and folded it so the opening was touching the bottom. Then he placed it in Richard's hand. Richard closed his hand and made a fist. He then held his fist up to his mouth and blew on the end of it. Richard then opened his fist and in the bag was gone.

He said, "Whoops. We were all done with that anyway." He continued, "Here Denise, you can assist me this time."

Denise said, "Sure," and asked, "What do I do?"

Richard answered, "Okay, take the cards. First, I want to explain something to everyone. When a card handler or illusionist hands you a deck of cards and asks you to examine them they're already trying to convince you everything is normal about the cards. Right away that's a red flag that tells you otherwise. With that said, Denise please look at the cards to ensure they're normal."

Denise opened the cards so they were facing her and she put a finger on a few of the cards moving them to the side. It was hard to view all of them. She was satisfied with the cards and asked, "Okay, next?"

Richard answered, "Okay, put the deck face down on the table." Denise gathered the cards and put the deck face down as instructed. Richard slowly waved his hand over the deck and instructed Denise, "Please look at the cards again."

Denise took the cards and fanned them open. She raised her eyebrows and saw the cards had changed to the jack, queen, king, and ace of spades. There were ten sets like that. Four cards changed to the jack, queen, king, and ace of hearts. Four of the cards changed to the same value but clubs and the last four changed to diamonds. Richard continued, "Now if you'll just put the deck face down again."

Denise placed the deck on the table. Richard continued, "Sarah could you please turn the cards over for all of us to see."

Sarah turned the cards over and spread them across the table. This time the deck changed to one card only. That card was the queen of hearts. The last card also had the words on it 'Property of Denise Bennett' at the top of the card. Richard reached over, closed up the cards, and said to Denise, "I believe these are yours."

Denise said, "WOW! Thank you."

Richard replied, "You're welcome and I need to take a break here. I want to save something for tomorrow's guests."

Tom spoke up and said, "That's fine. We're going to be heading out anyway. Thank you for the gifts, delicious meal, and awesome card tricks."

Matt replied, "You're welcome and we're glad you came. Hey, listen tomorrow is Sunday but unless Denise has to work, you're welcome to come by. Sarah's brother and wife are coming to visit but I think we can get together for dessert. I know we have plenty of it."

Denise responded, "Maybe, we'll take you up on that. Bye Matt, Sarah, Richard. Thanks again."

The Day After Christmas: Sunday, December 26th

Matt came downstairs at six forty-five to grab a coffee. Richard was sitting in his usual corner with the Sunday paper. Richard greeted Matt first, "Good morning Matthew. How are you?"

"Okay, just tired. I should have gone to bed earlier. We stayed up until eleven o'clock watching TV."

"That can interrupt a good night's sleep. Today is the airport run day. Are you going?"

Matt answered, "Oh no, he's not my brother. I'll be tending to Thomas."

"Matthew…"

"Okay, I'm sorry I put it that way. I know he's Sarah's family but he's just not someone I would ever look up to or want to hang around with. I guess I have to say I don't have that much respect for that individual."

Sarah came downstairs around seven-fifteen. She said, "Good morning Matt, good morning Richard. Matt, did you turn the monitor on?"

Matt answered, "No, but I will right now."

Matt turned the monitor on and Richard said, "Excuse me, Sarah, can I fix you something to eat before you head off to the airport?"

Sarah answered, "Thank you, Richard. That is so nice of you."

"You're quite welcome. Have a seat in the dining room, relax and I'll bring you your breakfast."

Eight-Fifty

Sarah went out the door and drove to Midway Airport to pick up her brother Sean and his wife Katelin. She was back at the house by ten twenty-five. She walked into the house with her brother Sean and his wife Katelin.

Sarah called in, "We're here."

Matt was in the dining room and went out to the foyer to greet them. He said, "Welcome and Merry belated Christmas by one day."

Sean put his hand out and said, "Thank you Matt, and the same to you. We haven't seen you in a long time."

Matt shook Sean's hand and while he was doing that, he thought to himself, 'Not long enough.' Matt then hugged Caitlin and said, "Merry Christmas, it's good to see you again."

Richard came out to the living room and said, "Merry Christmas Sean, Merry Christmas Katelin. Are you hungry? I can either bring you some breakfast food or a sandwich."

Katelin answered, "I can eat. We were up really early this morning and didn't have time for breakfast."

Richard added, "Breakfast it is and just to be clear the difference between this morning and other mornings is your waking time."

Sean cut in and said, "We do have coffee every morning."

"Well, we'll change that while you're here. I understand you're here until Thursday."

191

Sean waited until Sarah was alone and said, "Hi, I hope we're not making things awkward for you. We brought gifts with us. They're nothing big."

Sarah replied, "Don't worry about it. That would've made things awkward. We have things for you as well. We can go to the living room after you're done eating and exchange gifts."

Sean and Katelin finished eating and Sarah said, "Let me take your plates." Sarah scooped both plates and whisked them into the kitchen. She returned to the dining room and said to Sean, "Why don't we go in the living room and chat for a while."

Sean replied, "Sure," and the three of them went to the living room.

Richard came to the doorway of the living room and asked, "Can I bring anyone a coffee?"

Katelin spoke up and said, "Oh, thank you, Richard. We'll both have coffee."

Richard went into the kitchen. He returned carrying a tray with 4 cups of coffee and a cup of tea for Sarah. Matt started the conversation with, "Sean, Sarah told me your work has been extremely busy. It was also hard for you to get the time off."

Sean replied, "Busy is an understatement. I thought we were going to be here for the week but we have to fly back Thursday. I had a hard time getting these days off and I have to work on Friday New Year's Eve."

Sarah cut in and said, "WOW! There working you to the bone over there. If they pay you for the overtime take it when you can get it. We'll just have to make the best of your time while you're here." Sarah stood up and said, "I'll be right back."

Sarah went into the bedroom and then returned to the living room with a small plastic bag. Sarah said, "Sean, this is for you and Katelin. It's a little something from me, Matt and Richard."

Sean put out his hand, took the bag, and handed it to Katelin. Katelin reached in the bag and there was a Christmas card inside. She opened the card and it was for gift cards. There was one for the Longhorn, one for Applebee's, and two for Dunkin' Donuts.

Katelin and Sean said, "Thank you very much. We can sure use these." Katelin gave him an elbow in the side to remind him to go get the gift for Matt and Sarah. Sean spoke up and said, "Excuse me for a second." Sean ran up the stairs and opened his bag as quickly as he could. He came back downstairs with a small plastic bag.

Sean said, "Sarah, this is for you, Matt, and Richard," and he handed it back to Sarah.

Sarah opened the bag and in it was a Christmas card. She let Matt open the card. There were two gift cards inside. There was one for Maggiano's and one for the China Star restaurant.

Matt and Sarah both said, "Thank you."

Richard was coming back in from the kitchen and Matt showed Richard the card. Richard replied, "Thank you, that is very nice of you."

Sarah added, "We can have a home-cooked meal tonight as a certain someone has already promised but I don't want to mention Richard's name. OOPS! Monday and Tuesday, I'm sure we can have leftovers. Then, Wednesday night we can get Maggiano's"

Matt cut in and said, "I second that idea unless someone here does not like great Italian food." Right after that Matt asked Sarah, "Can I talk to you in the kitchen?"

Sarah followed Matt in the kitchen and Matt said to her, "I told Tom maybe he and Denise could come by for dessert. What do you want to do?"

Sarah thought for a second and answered, "Let me do this. I'll call Denise in a few minutes and I'll invite her and Tom over Friday night for Chinese food. They can ring in the new year with us."

"Good idea, let's get back to the living room."

Matt and Sarah went into the living room and Sean asked Sarah, "Is everything okay?"

Sarah answered, "Couldn't be better."

Matt was thinking otherwise. He thought to himself, 'Oh God, it's going to be a long four days.'

Richard spoke up and said, "I can have dinner ready at six o'clock if that meets your approval."

Matt replied, "What is that meets your approval. You're not the hired help here. We, meaning Sarah and I appreciate the fact you take care of the cooking here. Six o'clock is perfect as long as it works out for you. You will be dining with us. I just thought I'd get that out of the way before you try to give me a hard time about it."

Richard put his hand up and said, "As you wish Mr. White. Now, if you'll excuse me, I need to take a few things out of the freezer."

A Little Before Six O'clock.

Richard came out of the kitchen and he was wiping the sweat off of his brow. Matt just finished setting the dining table. He saw Richard using a handkerchief to wipe the perspiration on his forehead.

Matt asked, "Are you okay?"

"Yes, I just became a little overheated. Do you mind if I forgo tonight's entertainment? The guests will be here three more nights. I promise I can make it up to them."

"Richard, that's not a problem at all. You have dinner with us and we'll take care of the cleanup. Just go to bed early and get some needed rest."

The five of them were enjoying another delicious meal prepared by Richard. Sean was the first one to start a conversation. He asked Matt, "Matt, are you still doing your shows on Saturday nights?"

Matt looked up and answered, "Yes, I am, I mean we are. However, we're on a small break right now. We will return to it on Thursday, January 6th. Starting next month, we perform Thursdays and Saturdays."

Sean responded with, "WOW! You'll be going from a show every two weeks to doing two shows per week."

Matt nodded and said, "That about sums it up but we're taking a break from it in April when we go on vacation."

Katelin cut in and asked, "Vacation? Do you have anything planned?"

Sarah joined the conversation and answered, "We're going to Las Vegas for seven days."

Katelin replied, "WOW that sounds exciting. I wish we could go there."

Sarah said, "Funny you should mention that because you're going with us. It's going to be the five of us. I am telling you now so you can give your employer's plenty of notice for the time off."

Sean asked, "When did you decide this? It's such a big vacation."

Matt answered, "We've been talking about this for a couple of months. It's the vacation we've been waiting for."

Sarah added, "Well, you two think it over because you're welcome to join us. Whatever you decide is okay as long as the answer is that you're coming with us."

Sean replied, "Looks like you're trying to talk us into it."

Sarah smiled and said, "I am. It should be a lot of fun."

They finished eating and Matt asked, "Who's up for dessert? We have some good pies in the kitchen." Matt and Richard both went to the kitchen. Richard returned with some small plates and Matt carried in both pies.

It was almost seven-fifteen and Sarah said, "I think we should grab a coffee and retire to the living room."

Katelin added, "I'm up for that. Let me just get the dirty dishes in the sink first."

Richard interrupted her and said, "That's not necessary. It was too late. Katelin was already on her way into the kitchen. Once again, as she remembered this from before the kitchen showed no signs a meal had been cooked there. She thought to herself, 'Everything can't get cleaned up this fast. Hmmm.'

Richard said to Katelin, "Thank you for your help. As I told Matt earlier, I'll be retiring to my quarters after dinner and everyone please have a good night."

Three Days Later: Wednesday, December 29th

Matt came downstairs around six forty-five to have coffee. Richard was in his corner spot with his newspaper in front of him. Matt greeted Richard first and said, "Good morning Richard."

Richard responded, 'Good morning Mr. White. Are you up for breakfast when the others come downstairs? It won't be a problem. Please try to keep the others out of the kitchen after they get their coffee. It's easier for me to get it ready with no one else around."

Matt said, "I understand."

Matt knew exactly what Richard meant. He knew it was easy to zap up meals all prepped without anyone seeing him at his handiwork.

Katelin and Sean came downstairs around seven twenty. Sarah's door opened and she came downstairs right after them.

Matt heard the door and said, "I better turn on the monitor."

Richard prepared breakfast for the four of them. He saw Matt in the living room and gave a motion for him to help carry the food to the dining room. Matt put the plates on the table and then heard Thomas from the monitor.

"I'll get him," Sarah said.

Matt fired back, "Incorrect, please sit and eat. I'm sure my food can be warmed up later."

Matt ran up the stairs as fast as he could. He brought Thomas to the changing table and carried him down and put him in his highchair. Matt gave Thomas some spoons of mushy oatmeal. After Matt was done feeding Thomas, he put him in the floor seat. The others were already in the living room talking.

Matt looked at Sarah as he was putting Thomas down and whispered, "Be back in a few minutes." He went into the kitchen thinking he would microwave his food. Matt noticed it was on a different plate.

Richard was pouring a coffee for himself and said, "I thought you'd like it better fresh. Enjoy.". Richard put his hand out motioning for Matt to sit at the table.

Katelin, Sean, and Sarah were still in the living room and Katelin asked, "How far is the supermarket from here?"

Sarah answered, "It's just four or five blocks, not far at all. Why?"

"I want to pick up some snacks like granola bars for the plane trip back tomorrow."

Sarah said, "I guess we can take a quick ride over there. They're open twenty-four hours during the week. I'll get our coats. Sean, do you want to come with us?"

Sarah went to the closet to get her and Katelin's coat. Richard was walking by holding a small plastic bag. Richard said to Sarah, "I'll trade you." He handed Sarah the bag and pushed the closet door closed before she could get the coats out.

Sarah asked, "What's this?"

He answered, "Nourishment for Katelin and Sean tomorrow there is no reason to go out this afternoon. The temperature dropped to 8 degrees. You want to be feeling that."

Sarah replied, "Very well, let me give this to Katelin." Sarah turned around, and Katelin was close behind her. Sarah said, "This is from Richard. He doesn't want us leaving the house because of how cold it is."

Katelin took the bag and there were four granola bars and four candy bars inside. She looked at Sarah and asked, "How does he know?"

"What do you mean?" Sarah asked.

"These are my favorite and I know Sean likes Snickers bars."

Sarah answered, "I'm sorry. I don't have an answer for that. I don't know what to tell you. Richard knows a lot and it's almost as if he has a sixth sense to just know everything."

Later On, That Day: Around Five-Thirty

Sarah asked Matt, "Are you going to pick up the food for Maggiano's?"

Matt answered, "Sure, I'll take Sean with me."

Matt and Sean took the ride to Maggiano's. On the way over Sean asked Matt, "How did you pick Las Vegas for a vacation?"

Matt answered, "Truth be told, it was Richard's idea. I want, I mean we want to see if we can go see a magic show out there. We'll get a chance to be on the audience side of it for a change."

Sean responded with, "That sounds like you're using the vacation to get some ideas for your shows."

"I didn't say that. We want to see the quality of the shows that are out there. My grandfather did this for a living and my dad took me to one of the shows when I was nine years old. Needless to say, I didn't get a full grasp of what was happening."

Sean added, "Thank you for inviting us. I am sure we'll have a good time and I'm looking forward to it."

Matt and Sean were back at the house with the food.

Less than ten minutes later the five were at the dining room table having dinner. Matt started the conversation and said to Sarah, "Honey, Sean agrees with me on our vacation."

Sarah asked, "What do you mean he agrees with you?"

"Sean told me he's looking forward to the vacation and it should be a great time."

Sarah replied, "So, he agrees with all of us. I am looking forward to seeing the shows. They have some good Cirque du Soleil shows there."

Matt added, "We can do all that."

Katelin cut in and said, "I'd like to go to the old part of Las Vegas one night. It's called Fremont Street. There's a free light show there every night."

Fifteen Minutes Later

They finished their dinner and then had dessert. Richard stood up and said, "Let me clear and wipe down the table. After which, I can show everyone some card tricks I've been practicing."

Katelin said, "That sounds great. Please, let me help you." Katelin followed Richard to the kitchen with the two leftover pies.

Once in the kitchen, Richard instructed Katelin to leave the pies on the kitchen table. Katelin caught sight of what happened the previous Saturday evening. She noticed or couldn't help noticing there weren't any plates soaking. This was the same scenario that Denise witnessed when she was over there Christmas night. Katelin thought at the very least she would see empty food containers from Maggiano's. Those weren't there either. She was back in the dining room and she was having flashbacks of last year.

Katelin remembered they flew home the Sunday after Thanksgiving and when she and Sean got home the packages were leaning against their apartment door. Ever since then Katelin thought there was something not right here. Something was going on that she couldn't explain. She took a seat at the dining room table next to Sean.

He looked at her and asked, "Are you alright?"

Katelin answered, "Yes, I'm fine. Why?"

"You look like you saw a ghost."

Richard came back to the dining room and asked, "Everyone ready? Where's Sarah?"

Matt answered, "She's taking care of Thomas."

Richard added, "We'll just give her a few minutes then."

Sean cut in and said, "Excuse me, Mr. Jenkins, I saw a tv show once where the magician threw his cards at a window. He threw the cards from a hospital bed. The cards hit the glass and one of the cards stayed there but it was on the opposite side stuck to the glass. Do you know how he could have done that?"

Richard looked up for a second giving the impression he was contemplating the situation and answered, "Yes, but that's not something I can show you tonight. Secondly, you do not need to address me as Mr. Jenkins. However, I just thought of a way I might be able to perform that tonight. My concern is the lack of daylight but we can turn on the outdoor lighting in the garage. Sean, it's cold outside. I'll do this for you but I'll need you to go outside and retrieve my card."

Sean responded, "Sure, I'll go out and get it."

Sarah came downstairs and said, "Thomas is sleeping."

Richard started with, "Sarah, Sean told me about a card trick he saw on tv and he wants to know if I can demonstrate it." Richard's attention turned towards Sean, "Sean, I'm going to show you this and I'll add something to it. Please reach behind you and on the hutch, there should be a deck of cards. There will be a pad and pen if you'll grab that as well."

Sean reached behind him for the cards. There was no pad but he didn't say anything. He looked at Matt. Matt said softly to Sean. "Look again." Sean reached behind him a second time and the pad and pen were there.

Richard said, "Good, we can begin. Sean, I want you to shuffle the cards as much as you want. Next, you're going to think of a card in the deck, write your choice down on the pad, and do not show me your selection." Sean wrote the king of hearts on the paper and then turned the pad upside down. Richard took off his suit jacket and said, "I hope this works. My throwing arm is not as good as it used to be." He took the cards, threw them at the dining room window. Richard said, "I was afraid of that. There's not sufficient lighting out there to get the full effect."

Matt cut in and said, "Wait a second. I'll get a flashlight."

He went into the kitchen and returned with a heavy-duty halogen flashlight. Matt turned it on and pointed it at the window. There was Sean's card the king of hearts.

Richard continued, "Sean, please turn the pad over so we can see your selection."

Sean turned the pad over so the others could see he wrote the king of hearts. Sean said, "That was impressive. In the version, I saw the magician didn't let the spectator pick a card before the throw."

Richard added, "I didn't think so. You'll be needing your coat and take the flashlight with you."

Sean replied, "Oh right. I forgot."

Sean went outside to retrieve the card. While Sean was doing that, Richard said, "Excuse me, I need a fresh coffee. Can I get anything for anyone?"

There were no requests and Richard went into the kitchen with Matt following. Matt said to Richard, "Hey, I have to agree with Sean on this one. Your version of that last card trick is very impressive. Maybe we should add that to the show provided you can teach me how it's done."

Richard put two fingers on his chin, tapped his chin, and said, "It would make a good addition to the show. It's just not something I can show you, not now anyway. Here comes your brother-in-law."

Sean came to the front door and said, "WOW! It is cold out there."

Richard offered, "At least it won't be so bad for your trip back tomorrow."

Sean added, "Oh, it's going to be a heatwave alright. The high in the morning is supposed to be thirty-one degrees and not twenty-six."

Matt interrupted and said, "Let's go back to the dining room. I'm sure Richard has more for us up his sleeve."

Richard offered, "Before we can go back in the other room let me make two things clear to you right now. First, for you Sean when I said at least it won't be so bad for your trip back I was referring to a forty-two-degree climb in temperature. Matt, as for your comment up his sleeve all of my illusions or tricks come from up here." Richard pointed at his temple.

Matt replied, "Sorry, I wasn't thinking."

They were back in the dining room and Katelin asked, "Can you do any magic without using cards? I know we're not in a big theater."

Richard answered, "I believe there's something I can show you. How about mind-reading?"

Katelin asked, "You can read my mind?"

Matt jumped in and said, "Might not be a good idea."

Richard said, "Oh, please just this once. It's all in fun. Katelin, think of anything you want. It can be something that happened earlier today or happened years ago. It can also be of something you want to happen or just think about an object in this room."

Katelin responded, "Okay, go ahead."

Richard replied, "You were thinking about the boy that you wanted to ask you to the Junior Snowball dance and he didn't ask you. That upset you at the time. I believe his name was Brad, Brad Lidden."

Katelin said, "Oh my God, you got it right."

Richard added, "I can also tell you the reason he didn't ask you. I believe you found out the reason why a week and a half later."

Sarah cut in and said, "Spill it, I have to hear this."

Richard said, "Katelin found out Brad did not ask her because he was so nervous, you'd say no and he'd feel bad. That's the reason why when Deborah Convey asked him, he accepted."

Katelin said, "WOW! This guy knows everything."

Richard acknowledged Katelin and said, "Thank you for the compliment but I only know everything about the individuals in this room. Now, if you'll allow me to continue."

Sarah cut in and said, "Richard, I remember when I was only nine years old, we had a cat for a pet. I'm not telling you the name of the cat."

Richard offered, "You don't have to. I know you were devastated when Fluffy got sick and he had to be put down. But, please let's not dwell on sad times. I save the best entertainment I have for last."

Sean interrupted Richard and asked, "Excuse me, Richard, can you do that trick again where you throw the cards at the window? I'm not positive but I think I know how you did it."

Richard knew Sean had something else in mind but he figured why not. Richard started, "Okay Sean, just like before, shuffle the cards thoroughly. Write down on the pad your selected card." Sean shuffled the cards a few times. While Sean was shuffling the cards, he conveniently let one card drop on his lap. He looked at the card and it was the jack of diamonds. Richard continued, "Okay, here goes."

Richard threw the deck of cards at the window and all but one card fell to the floor. Richard said to Matt, "We're going to have to borrow that flashlight again."

Matt replied, "Sure. Here you go." Matt aimed the light at the window and others could see the jack of diamonds stuck in place on the outside of the glass.

Sean jumped out of his seat and said, "That couldn't have happened."

Richard asked, "Why is that, Sean?"

"Because when I was shuffling the cards a card fell in my lap and I tucked it under my leg. It was the jack of diamonds"

Richard fired back, "I see. That card is either stuck to your leg or under your chair. I think you should show us the card."

I took the card off the chair without looking at it. Katelin spoke up, "Sean, that's not the jack of diamonds."

Sean asked, "What?"

Katelin grabbed Sean's hand and turned it so the card was facing him. She said, "See? It's not the jack." Sean looked at the card and it was the ten of clubs. Sean's jaw dropped.

Richard tried to explain, "Sean, let me clear something up for you. I am the entertainment here tonight. It's not in your best interest to make me look bad. One, because it won't happen and reason number two, please don't take this the wrong way but I am way smarter than you. As soon as you asked me to do the trick a second time, I knew you wanted to try to debunk me. How did that go, Sean? Okay, we have time for one more but now I think we should dispense with the cards. Matthew, I'll need your help one more time."

Matt asked, "Yes?"

Richard asked, "Can you please get me one of those salad bowls?"

Matt answered, "Sure." He went into the kitchen, opened the cabinet door, and took out a bowl. He returned to the dining room and set it on the table.

Richard said, "Thank you, Matt." Richard continued and he reached in his pocket and pulled out a small spongy red ball. He handed the ball to Katelin and told her, "Please check this over. You'll see it's just a small spongy ball."

Katelin rolled the ball around in her hand and said, "It feels ordinary to me" and she handed the ball back to Richard. Richard pointed down to indicate just leave it there.

He continued, "Okay, Sean, place the bowl over the ball and we'll see what happens."

Sean took the bowl, turned it upside down, and covered the red ball as instructed. "Okay, I'm going to count to three and point at the bowl. One...two...three." Richard pointed at the bowl. He then told Sean, "Please lift the bowl and turn it over."

Sean turned the bowl over and everyone saw that the ball was gone. Katelin offered, "WOW! That was impressive, but can you put it back?"

"I'll give it a whirl. Here, Katelin, take this bowl and set it on the hutch behind you. May I borrow your glass? It will serve better here because it is see-through. Sarah, I also need yours." Richard took both drinking glasses and turned them upside down on the table in front of him. Both glasses still had a small amount of liquid inside them. When he turned the glasses over, the liquid was gone.

Matt was sitting next to Sarah while this was going on. He was cringing and thinking to himself, 'Whoa, how am I going to explain this?'

Richard continued, "Katelin, Sean, you see both glasses here. Please keep an eye on them and watch what happens after I count to three. One...two...three." Richard pointed to the glasses and each one had some of the sponge balls falling from inside of the glass to the table while the glasses were inverted.

Sean said, "Mr. Jenkins, I promise never to try to pull one over on you again. You are some great magician."

Richard replied, "Thank you, Sean. I appreciate you saying that. It's getting to be almost ten o'clock and I hope you'll excuse me. It was nice seeing the two of you again but I need to retire for the evening. I'll see you in the morning."

The group said goodnight to Richard. Matt asked Sarah, "What do you think? It's getting late."

Sarah answered, "I'm ready for bed myself." She said to Sean and Katelin, "You're welcome to stay up and watch TV if you want."

Katelin responded with, "We'll be heading up also. We have to be at the airport early tomorrow."

The Next Morning: December 30th

Matt came downstairs at six-thirty and made a beeline for the coffee maker. Richard was sitting in the corner and he just finished reading the newspaper.

Matt greeted Richard first, "Good morning Richard." Matt turned on the baby monitor.

"Good morning Matt. What time does the airport shuttle set sail?"

"Sarah told me they want to leave by seven-ten. They should be coming down shortly…" Matt stopped before he could finish his sentence.

The bedroom door opened upstairs and Richard said, "That will be Sean and Katelin. Sarah will be three seconds behind them."

Sean and Katelin were downstairs first. Sean asked, "Is there coffee?"

Richard answered him, "Of course there is. Help yourself, Sean. Good morning Sean and good morning Katelin."

Sarah went into Thomas's room and was downstairs a few minutes later. She met Matt in the kitchen and said, "Good morning honey." Sarah kissed Matt on the cheek.

Matt returned, "Good morning. Do you want me to take him?"

"No, can you just slide the highchair over?" Matt pushed the highchair closer to the kitchen table and Sarah put Thomas in. She fed Thomas his breakfast. Then Sarah asked Matt, "Can you do me a huge favor?"

Matt answered, "Yes, I'll bring Sean and Katelin to the airport."

"Thank you, honey. Did Richard show you how to do that, how to read minds?"

"No, he did not. When you said favor, I knew you'd want to stay home and relax. Of course, I'll take them. You work hard all week."

It was almost seven o'clock and Matt said, "I'm going to warm up the van. Sean, we'll be leaving in fifteen minutes. Where are your bags? I'll put them in the van while you and Katelin finish your coffees."

The three of them left for the airport at ten minutes after seven. Matt pulled the van up to the drop-off and helped get the bags out of the car. He shook Sean's hand and said, "Hey, call us when you get home. Katelin, it was nice seeing you again," and he hugged her.

Matt was back home a little before eight-thirty.

*New Year's Eve: Friday, December 31*st

Denise and Tom pulled into Matt's driveway at six-thirty. They went up the front stairs and Matt opened the door for them and said, "Welcome and Happy New Year's Eve. Sarah's upstairs and will be down in a few minutes."

Sarah came downstairs and said, "Hello Denise, hello Tom. Did Matt offer you a drink? If not, can I get you something?"

Denise answered, "I'll take a glass of wine I put a bottle of wine and champagne in the refrigerator for later."

Tom spoke up and said, "Nothing for me yet thanks. I'll wait 'til we get the food."

Matt said, "Speaking of which, "Are you ready to ride shotgun, we can go pick up the Chinese food."

Tom answered, "Sure, but I think we need to stop at the liquor store."

Matt asked, "For?"

"I didn't bring any beer with me."

"I didn't ask you to. Don't worry about it, I have plenty. Tom, tonight our goal is to have a good time."

They got back to the house a little before seven-thirty. Matt brought the food directly to the kitchen. Richard was in the kitchen and he said, "Here, we can use these bowls for the food. I'll put the plates on the table." Matt carried the bowl to the dining room and grabbed two beers for him and Tom.

The five of them were at the table eating and Tom spoke up and said, "This is good stuff, especially the crab Rangoon. I'm just saying you think because the restaurant is pushing out so much food tonight that it wouldn't be as great of a quality."

Matt replied, "We've been going to this place for years. I never found the food to be off."

They finished eating and Richard offered, "Let me clear the table and give it a quick wipe down. If our guests don't mind, I would like to show you a few new card tricks I've been working on."

Ten Minutes Later

Richard was back in the dining room and ready to show off his skills. Richard said, "Sorry for the delay. Let's begin. Tom, can you please reach behind you and grab the deck of playing cards."

Tom took the deck off the hutch and said, "Here you go."

Richard took the cards, slid them out of the box, and handed them to Denise. He said, "Denise, I'm a firm believer in ladies first. I need you to fan through the cards and shuffle thoroughly. Oh, and just to let you know this trick has never been seen by anyone."

Denise shuffled the cards three times and she said, "I think we're good here."

Richard said, "Okay, Denise I'm going to rifle through the cards and I want you to say stop when you want."

Richard rifled through the cards and Denise said, "Stop!"

He then told Denise, "Take the next card and take this Sharpie and put your initials on it and then hand it back to me." Denise took the card and wrote DB on the top of the card and then handed it to Richard. He took the card, folded it in half, folded it a second and a third time. Richard put his right hand out and placed the folded card in his hand.

He closed his hand so the card was not visible. He knocked on the table twice and then he opened his hand and the card was gone. After he opened his hand Tom coughed twice and made a face as if he just ate something unpleasant. Tom opened his mouth and pulled out the folded-up card.

Matt, Sarah, and Denise said, "WHOA! Bravo, that was AWESOME!"

Tom had a puzzled look not understanding how the card ended up in the back of his mouth. Denise asked him, "Were you in on this?"

Tom answered, "I didn't think so, but it looks like I was drafted as a helper."

Richard said, "Wait, Denise, you did open the cards to make sure it's the right one." Denise took a napkin, wiped the card off, and unfolded it. Of course, it was the one that was in Richard's hand.

Tom said, "Richard, that was nothing short of incredible. I wish I knew how you did that."

Richard came back with, "Tom, I'm sorry I like to keep those things to myself. Now. I have good news."

"Good news?" Tom asked.

"It's your turn to help."

Tom replied, "I thought that was my turn."

"Oh no, we're just getting started."

"With permission from everyone here I'd like to show you a few more card tricks. After all, it's New Year's Eve and the ball doesn't drop until about twenty seconds before midnight."

Matt interrupted and asked, "Hold on a second. Are you telling us you're going to be awake for that?"

Richard answered, "I believe I will. So, please let us continue. I have a lot to show you. Tom, if you'd be so kind as to assist me and not to worry you will not be coughing up any cards."

Tom replied, "Okay, what do you want me to do?"

Richard said, "Good, we'll begin. Tom, please take the cards and remove two of the jacks and two kings. It doesn't matter which suits you pick just as long as we have four cards. Next, place them face down on the table."

Tom removed the Jack of hearts and Jack of spades. He also removed the King of clubs and King of diamonds.

Richard asked, "Are you ready?"

"Yes, I am. I have four cards here."

Richard took the remainder of the deck (forty-eight cards) and he tapped the pile with the four cards twice. He then instructed Tom, "Tom, please turn over your four cards."

Tom turned over the pile of four cards. The rest of the group was stymied. The four cards changed to the four aces. Matt spoke up and said, "Very good, I'm getting another beer. Tom, can I get you one?"

Tom answered, "Sure, you don't have to ask me twice."

Matt got up from the table and as he did, he made a tight lips smirk. With his head, he gave a come here signal to Richard. Richard started the conversation as Matt took two beers from the fridge. He said to Matt, "I know what you're thinking and not to worry I'm not going over the top. I'm just trying to entertain the guests."

Matt and Richard both returned to the dining room. Matt gave Tom his beer. Richard sat and said, "We will continue if anyone wants to see some new card tricks and these are new to everyone."

Denise spoke up and said, "I'm up for that."

Richard continued with, "Great, Denise you and Sarah can help with this one."

Sarah asked, "What do you want us to do?"

Richard went on, "Pick twelve cards out of the deck. Out of these twelve cards, I want Denise to write down on the pad one of the cards, and then she is to conceal her selection."

Sarah took out twelve cards and showed them to Denise. Denise wrote down the queen of hearts for her choice. Denise said to Richard, "Okay, we're ready." Sarah slid the twelve cards in Richard's direction.

Richard stood up and said, "I hope this works." He took the twelve cards and threw them up to the ceiling. Eleven of the twelve cards stuck to the ceiling. One of the cards came right back and that was the queen of hearts. Richard said to Denise, "I believe this is your card. Is that what you wrote on the pad?"

Denise answered, "I think you already know the answer is yes. I wish I could do that."

"You know, Denise, you've probably seen me do maybe fifteen different card tricks since you started coming to the White household. I want you to think about this. Can you ever recall seeing me do the same trick twice?"

Denise sat there and said, "Hmmm I don't think I have."

"Exactly, so it's always my job to make sure it's fresh and keep it new. I guess you could say my skill always keeps me on my guard or my toes for a lack of better words. So, we'll continue right after I grab a hot coffee."

Richard went into the kitchen and poured himself more coffee. He returned to the dining room. Matt spoke up and said, "Hey, we still have about ninety minutes to go. Take a few minutes for yourself and drink your coffee. We can wait."

Richard took the last sip of his coffee and said, "I find my coffee perks me up and recharges me any time of the day. But let's continue before I lose my train of thought. I always save the best for last. I have two more to show you and I consider both of these a couple of my personal favorites. Sarah, please take half the cards. You can deal out half or just guess at the half."

Sarah counted out half the cards and put them to the side. Richard continued, "Okay, Sarah look at the half you picked out and ensure they're not all the same. We also want them to be a good mix."

Sarah fanned through her half of the cards and made sure they were all different. Sarah said, "These are all good."

"Splendid! Now, Tom will you give us a card value but not the suit."

Tom offered, "Ten."

"Denise, I need you to choose a suit, and please don't say pinstriped or double-breasted."

Denise started to chuckle and said, "Diamonds, besides diamonds are a girl's best friend. She looked at Tom when she said that.

Richard said, "Okay, we'll continue. Tom chose ten and Denise chose diamonds. Sarah, please count down until you get to the tenth card and then turn it over." Sarah moved the first nine cards to the right of the pile and flipped the tenth one over. The tenth card was the ten of diamonds.

Tom said, "Wait for a second and asked, "What if I called out the Jack instead of a ten?"

"Then I would've had Sarah count down to the eleventh card but you didn't do that. Just like if you said queen that would represent the twelfth card. The king would represent the thirteenth. We can try it again if you like. Let me just slide these ten cards to the bottom of the pile. Richard continued, "Please pick a card value."

Matt was the first to reply and called out, "Seven."

"Sarah, will you please choose a suit."

Sarah called out, "Clubs."

Richard instructed Tom, "Tom will you please count down 'til you get to the seventh card."

Tom moved the first six cards to the right of the pile and flipped the seventh one over. The seventh card was the seven of clubs.

Richard said, "Please don't say I wish I could do that. If you liked what you saw just nod and then I can squeeze in the last trick. This is the last one and I need help from everyone. Matt, please reach behind you in on the hutch you'll find a small bowl with the various coins. Next, take the bowl and pour the coins onto the table."

Matt reached behind him for the bowl and grabbed it. There were eight coins in the bowl. Four of them were quarters and the other four were half dollars. Richard added, "I need everyone here to put a quarter in one hand and a half dollar in your other hand."

The four of them took a quarter and put that in one hand and put the half dollar in the other. Richard then took a black Sharpie out of his jacket pocket. He then said, "Okay, now everyone put your hands forward and maintain a tight fist around each coin." Richard then took the Sharpie and tapped each hand at the table. Next, Richard said, "I'm going to count to three and you should feel something happen. One...two...three."

Matt said, "I felt it."

Sarah jumped in and said, "I felt something."

Tom added, "Me too."

Denise jumped in and said, "I just felt something."

Richard continued, "Everyone can now open their fists." Sarah opened her hands first. She no longer had a coin in either hand. Matt was next to open his fists. He also no longer had a coin in either hand. Tom was the third one to open his fists. Both of his hands were also empty.

Denise was the last one to open her fists. She opened her fists and four coins fell out of each hand.

Denise said, "WOW! I'm three dollars richer than when I first walked in here. But how do coins vanish out of someone's hand and reappear in someone else's?"

Matt spoke up and said, "I can give you Richard's answer. It's what he calls magic and I hope you don't think he's going to give you the secret. I can't tell you how he does this and I work with him during the shows. Sorry, Richard for speaking for you."

Richard offered, "That's quite alright." Richard looked at his watch. It was eleven forty-five. He said to Matt, "I need to say goodnight to everyone."

Matt said, "Don't worry about it. Go hit the bed. I'm sure you're exhausted. I'll tell everyone you said goodnight. Oh, and Richard, see you next year."

Matt said, "Look, everyone, Richard asked me to tell you all to have a good night. He's not used to staying up this late."

Sarah spoke up and said, "Matt, it's five minutes to midnight. I'll turn on the TV. Can you get the champagne and glasses?"

"Sure." Matt went to the kitchen and there was a tray on the counter with four champagne glasses. There was a note next to the tray on the counter. The note said: *Matt just pick up the corkscrew with your right hand and the cork will come off the bottle very easily.*

Matt brought the tray of poured glasses of champagne in the living room and offered one to Denise, Sarah, and Tom. Dick Clark was on the TV in the background. The ball was dropping 10...9...8...7...6...5...4...3...2...1. The year 2005 was on the TV screen. Matt and Sarah were kissing as well as Tom and Denise.

Sarah picked up the remote and lowered the volume on the TV. She sat back down in one of the wing chairs and Matt was already in the other one. Denise and Tom were sitting in the loveseat. Sarah spoke up and said, "Looks like another year has gone by."

Denise replied, "True. Last year went by fast for me."

Two Minutes Later

Tom spoke up and said, "I'm not trying to put a damper on things but I think we need to go. What do you say, Denise?"

211

Matt said, "Hold on a second there. I know you had a few because I had seven beers and you kept up with me. I want you to stay here tonight. There are two extra bedrooms upstairs."

Sarah said, "They don't need two. Oops, sorry. I shouldn't have said that, but Matt's right. Stay here tonight."

Denise came back with, "Okay, you talked us into it, but we'll leave early in the morning."

23

A New Year of Shows

It was the first show of the year. Matt came home from work at four fifteen. He went through the front door like he was on a mission. He didn't call into the house this time and that was so unlike him. Tonight, is their first show in two and a half weeks and he was very nervous about it. Most of the day he was thinking he hoped he didn't make a mistake about doubling his workload.

Denise was sitting in the living room and she had her bag all packed and ready to go.

Matt went into the living room and asked, "Hey, how'd it go today?"

She answered, "Everything went fine. Thomas is snoozing upstairs right now." Denise noticed something odd and asked him, "Why are you all jittery?"

Matt asked, "Does it show? It's the first show in two and a half weeks for us. I hope everything goes okay."

Denise stepped closer to Matt and rubbed his arms up and down to try to get him to relax. She said, "Look, I'm sure everything's going to be fine. Richard is in his room. You should go talk to him about tonight. I bet he can reassure you and I'll stay here as long as you need me."

Matt put his hand up and said, "Thank you."

He knocked on Richard's door. Richard opened the door and stepped out. Richard said, "Matthew about tonight, you don't have to worry. Tonight, will be smooth sailing. We have new material to perform and I have it all worked out."

"We have new material?"

213

"We most certainly do. We'll go over it when we get to the theater. By the way, it's a sold-out show tonight, Matt."

"Okay, Richard. Give me a minute here. I have to ask Denise something."

Matt asked Denise, "Do you mind staying until Sarah gets here?" She answered, "Of course not."

Richard nudged Matt and asked Denise, "Can we interest you having dinner early with us? It's been a long time since we've done a show on a weeknight. I don't think it would be a good idea for our stomachs to be growling on the stage."

Denise answered, "I was just going to grab a cheeseburger on the way home."

Richard cut in and said, "What a coincidence, it just so happens that's what I'm preparing for us."

"So, I guess you talked me into it." Right after Denise finished answering sounds were coming from the monitor. Denise looked at Matt and said, "I'll get him."

Denise went upstairs and lifted Thomas out of the crib. She put a fresh diaper on him and then brought him downstairs. Denise slid the highchair next to the kitchen table and put Thomas in it. She went to open the refrigerator and Richard stopped her. Richard pointed to a tray on the counter and said, "You're all set."

She said, "Thank you. There you go again making things easier for me."

"I try," was the reply from Richard.

Denise was all done feeding Thomas and she put him in his toddler chair. Then Richard brought three cheeseburgers to the table. Matt made a trip from the kitchen and brought in some ketchup, mustard, and relish. Denise said, "Thank you very much for dinner. It saves me from making a stop on the way home."

Matt offered, "It's the least we can do. Think of it as our way of saying thanks for sticking around. We'll be leaving shortly after we're done eating."

Matt and Richard left for the theater. Matt drove them into the parking garage and waved to Tim, the parking attendant in the booth as they went by. Once in the theater, they took their temporary seats in the front row as they have done so many times in the past.

Richard asked, "Doesn't it feel great to be back, Matt?"

"Once I'm on that stage the feeling will be great. Right now, it feels weird."

"Trust me, it'll go away. Now, let's go over what I have planned for tonight." Richard spent a little more than fifteen minutes explaining to Matt his plans for the grand finale. The audience started coming in and Richard said, "We better get out of sight."

The show started promptly at seven-thirty. Matt and Richard went through the acts flawlessly. They had not performed together for more than two weeks and there were no signs of hesitation or mishaps during their performance. The time got to be eight- forty and Richard gave Matt the nod as a signal to get the final act going.

Matt called out to the audience, "Ladies and gentlemen, we have time for one more. We'll also need the help of a volunteer and not to worry you will not be harmed in any way." Matt thought to himself, 'I hope the same goes for me.'

About fifteen people raised their hands to volunteer. Matt picked the woman from the twelfth row in the middle. He said to the woman, "Excuse me, Miss, can you come up here and help us?"

The volunteer made her way up to the front. Matt put his hand out and said, "Hello, my name is Matt and this is Richard. And you are?"

The volunteer answered, "Debby, Debby Kroft." She shook Matt's hand and then went and did the same to Richard. She then said, "Nice to meet you."

The curtain opened behind them and there was an oversized bed frame with the top hovering above it being supported by lengths of rope. The top portion of the frame had forty-eight knives sticking out of it. One of the assistants helped Matt onto the frame and then tied one of Matt's wrists to the left corner of the frame and the other wrist to the right corner of the frame.

215

Richard walked Debbie over to a small table. This table had twelve ropes anchored down to it. Richard said to Debbie, "Okay, Debby what I need you to do is pick a number from one through twelve. I will then untie the numbered rope you pick. Seven of these ropes are tied to the top part of the frame. If I untie that rope the frame will come slamming down and it won't be a pretty picture for Mr. White. So, you must choose wisely."

Debbie replied, "Okay, I'll try." Debbie made her first choice, "Number six." Richard untied rope number six and nothing happened.

Richard continued, "Okay, Debbie, next?"

Debbie responded with, "Nine." Richard untied rope number nine and again nothing happened.

Richard once again said to Debbie, "Please choose again."

Debbie made her third selection, "Eleven." Richard untied rope number eleven and just like before nothing happened.

Again, Richard told Debbie to make another choice. He said, "Okay, Debbie, there are nine more ropes to choose from. Only two of them have a safe choice. What is your next choice?"

Debbie spoke up and said, "Number ten." Richard untied the tenth rope and for a fourth time, nothing happened. Matt was laying on the bed and was looking more nervous every time Debbie made another selection.

Richard said, "Debbie, either you have ESP or you have the knack of making the right pick all the time. There are eight more ropes to choose from and only one of them is the safe choice. Debbie, please make your fifth selection and remember if you make the wrong one, my partner will have a very early retirement."

Debbie said, "I know, I know" She put her hand on her forehead with a worried look and said, "Number twelve." Richard untied the twelfth rope and miraculously nothing happened.

Richard said to Debbie, "You made some excellent choices. Next, will you untie one side of the frame where Matt is tied down and I'll free up his other side?"

Matthew was freed from the bedframe of knives. He sat up on the edge and jumped off. Richard said to him, "Matthew, I think it's only fitting after what you just endured that you untie the next rope."

Matt untied one of the ropes and the top frame came slamming down at lightning speed. He said, "I'm glad that one wasn't picked earlier. Thank you, Debbie. This could've turned into a solo act had you made the wrong pick. We have to say goodnight to the audience but please don't go back to your seat yet."

Matt called out to the audience, "Ladies and gentlemen, that concludes our show for tonight. Please tell your friends if you liked what you saw. My name is Matt White and this is my good friend and show partner, Richard Jenkins. Please drive safely and have a good night."

Matt turned to Debbie and said, "Okay Debbie, thank you for helping. Because you were such a good sport, I want to give you a couple of free passes for another show. We are here on Thursday and Saturday evenings."

Debbie took the envelope with the two passes inside and said, "Thank you." She then went down the stairs off the stage and left the theater.

Matt asked Richard, "Well Mr. Jenkins, are you ready to call it a night?"

Richard answered, "Lead the way, Mr. White."

The Next Morning: Friday, January 7th

Matt came downstairs at six twenty-five and poured himself a coffee. Richard was sitting in the usual corner. He just finished reading his newspaper.

Matt greeted Richard in between sipping his coffee, "Good morning Richard. I don't know about you but I can still feel the effects of last night. I don't mean the excitement of being on stage. I'm talking about not getting in bed till ten-thirty. I can't just put my head on the pillow and doze off."

Richard asked, "How much coffee do you have in your cup?"

"It's about half. Why?"

"Top it off and bring it over here."

Matt poured more coffee in his cup and walked over to where Richard was sitting. Richard put his hand around Matt's cup and he said, "Drink that before you leave. Your energy level will be up and you'll feel a lot better. Your fatigue will be gone."

Matt gave Richard the thumbs up and took some more sips of his coffee. Richard made like a wave of motion with his hand to signal Matt to keep drinking his coffee. Matt took a couple more sips and emptied the cup. He then said to Richard, "I have to go, I'll see you around four-fifteen."

Matt went out the door, got in his car, and by the time he got to the end of the street he felt a burst of energy come upon him. He felt as if he just drank an energy drink without half the crash. Matt thought to himself, 'I'll have to get Richard to do that more often. He was right. The fatigue is gone.'

Denise pulled in the driveway and went up the front stairs. Richard was waiting at the front door and opened it for her. Richard said, "Good morning Miss Bennett. How are you?"

Denise answered, "A little tired, actually very tired. For whatever reason, I had trouble falling asleep last night."

Richard added, "As always, please help yourself to the coffee. Sarah will be down in a few minutes."

Four Minutes Later

Sarah was downstairs. She said, "Good morning Denise, good morning Richard. Denise thank you for staying later yesterday so the guys could go to the theater."

Denise responded, "Good morning Sarah, and please don't think anything of it. I'm glad I could help."

Richard said, "Good morning Sarah, I have your bag ready for you." Sarah took a quick look in the bag and noticed a couple of Dannon yogurts that were her favorite flavors. She remembered there weren't any of those in the refrigerator last night. Sarah closed the bag and attributed that she's been working so hard was the reason she didn't see the yogurt in the refrigerator last night. She went out the front door and headed off to work.

Matt walked into the house and called in, "Denise, Richard, I'm here."

Matt went into the kitchen and Richard was prepping dinner. Richard greeted Matt, "Hello Matt, I trust your day went well. Do you still have that feeling of exhaustion?"

"Actually no, that was gone by the time I got to the end of the street this morning. But I think you pretty much knew that."

"Oh, Denise is upstairs with Thomas putting him down for a nap. She'll be down momentarily."

Matt came back with, "Good, I want to talk to her about yesterday." Minutes later Denise was downstairs and Matt said, "Hey, about yesterday thanks again for sticking around."

Denise offered, "Don't worry about it. I spoke with Sarah this morning and told her the same thing."

Matt asked, "Do you think we can impose upon you to stick around later on Thursdays? I can make it up to you moneywise."

She answered, "Of course I'll do it and just leave my salary the way it is. You guys have done enough for me already. Thomas is upstairs sleeping and I'll see you on Monday. Have a good weekend."

Late Afternoon, Saturday, January 8th

It was almost 6:15 and Matt said, "Honey, we're going to be leaving soon. Are you going to be, okay? You can call one of your friends and invite them over."

Sarah added, "I'll be fine. I have my latest Sue Grafton novel. I will call Jeannie later and invite them over next Friday for pizza."

Matt added, "That'll be great. See you tonight. We should be back by ten-thirty."

Matt and Richard got in Matt's van and made their way to the theater. They drove into the parking garage and waved to Tim as usual. Once in the theater, they took their temporary seats in the front row. Matt asked, "Should we be going over something right now? Or are we going to repeat Thursday night's show?"

Richard answered, "I think it will be all right if we repeat Thursday night's show next Thursday. I have something special for tonight. This is what we'll do…"

Five Minutes After Seven

The audience started coming in. Matt said to Richard, "We need to make ourselves scarce."

The show got underway at seven-thirty on the dot. The two of them performed their acts as a well-oiled machine. It was almost eight-forty and Richard nodded to Matt signaling it was time to start their final act. Matt called out to the audience, "Ladies and gentlemen, we have time for one more. We are also in need of a volunteer and as always there is nothing to be nervous about. You will not be harmed or injured in any way."

Matt looked out to the left and then to the right for a volunteer. He picked the gentleman on the end from the ninth row. Matt said, "Excuse me, sir, can you come up here and give us a hand?"

The volunteer went up on stage and Matt asked, "Your name is?"

The volunteer answered, "James, James Savio."

Matt said, "Okay, nice to meet you, James." Matt put his hand out to shake his hand. Matt added, "My name is Matt and this is my partner, Richard."

The curtain in the background went up and two of the assistants brought out a large wooden box the size of a large hope chest. Matt said, "James, we need you up here to assist Richard. He is going to take over and I am going to step into this box and Richard will lock it. Then you will be helping him."

Matt stepped in the box. Richard closed the door and handed James a Master padlock and said to James, "Please secure the box and then give me the key." James snapped the padlock closed and handed the key to Richard. Richard continued, "James, I need you to help me turn the box two rotations. We want the audience to see the back of this is perfectly flat."

Richard and James turned the box around twice and stopped. Richard continued, "Okay I just need to check the lock one more time." Richard gave a tug on the lock and said, "That's secure. So, I guess we won't need this anymore." Richard took the key and threw it behind him. Then they heard pounding and muffled noises coming from inside the box. Richard yelled, "Oh no, that's Matt, he needs to get out. There is a very limited supply of oxygen in there. James, please give me the key."

James replied quickly, "I gave it to you about five minutes ago after I closed the lock."

"You didn't give me the right key. That key is in your pocket."

James reached in his pocket and said, "I don't know why I would still have it." After fishing around, he found the key in his pocket. James said, "I got it" and handed the key to Richard.

The audience started laughing when they saw Matt walking out from beside the curtain. He walked over to James and Richard. He asked, "What are you guys doing?"

James did a double-take when he saw Matt. He said, "I don't understand. You were locked in there. How did you get out?"

Matt answered, "I had to get out." Richard finally got the door opened and Matt said, "See? There's no room in there." When the doors were opened the audience could see the wardrobe was filled with woodchips. Matt never explained to James how he got out. Mostly because he couldn't tell James that Richard is a wizard and can make anything happen.

Matt said to James, "Thank you very much for your help. We have to say goodnight to the audience but please do not go back to your seat yet."

Matt called out to the audience and made the announcement, "Ladies and gentlemen, that concludes our show for tonight. Please if you liked what you saw tell your friends. My name is Matt White and this is my good friend and show partner, Richard Jenkins. Drive safely and have a good night."

Matt looked at James and said, "Thanks again for being a good sport and helping out. I want to give you a couple of free passes for another show."

James put his hand out and said, "Thank you, I had a good time." James put the envelope in his pocket, said goodnight and then he left.

Matt asked Richard, "Well, Mr. Jenkins, are you ready to call it a night?"

"Ready when you are Mr. White," replied Richard.

The Next Morning: Sunday, January 9th

Richard was sitting in his usual corner reading his newspaper. Matt came downstairs at six forty and poured a coffee for himself.

Richard greeted Matt first, "Good morning Matthew. I thought last night's show went well."

Matt came back with, "I agree, and good morning by the way." Matt put his coffee down briefly to turn on the baby monitor.

Richard replied, "I want you to hear this before Sarah gets down here. It's good news and nothing to panic about. I have approximately thirty more ideas we can incorporate into the shows."

"Really?"

"Yes, now it'll be a while before we have to repeat something in the show. It will be received so much better when it has a fresh look."

Right after Richard got out the last word the bedroom door opened upstairs. Richard pointed and said, "Sarah's coming, so ex nay on this secret stuff."

Matt nodded and poured himself a second cup of coffee. Sarah walked over to Matt and said, "Good morning honey," and she kissed Matt on the cheek. She then said, "Good morning Richard."

Richard replied, "Good morning Sarah. Whenever you're ready have a seat in the dining room and I can bring you a western omelet."

Sarah responded, "Thank you, Richard."

She then said to Matt, "Matt, Richard is spoiling me again."

Matt asked, "Are you not happy with that? You see how we ate during the week. I think he spoils the both of us. He also makes Denise's work a lot easier."

"Okay, I can live with that. Join me in the dining room for a few minutes."

Matt followed Sarah in the dining room and as soon as he sat down, Thomas decided he needed attention. Matt said, "I'll be right back."

Matt went up the stairs two at a time. He lifted Thomas out of the crib and put a fresh Pamper on him. He came back downstairs carrying Thomas and went into the kitchen to grab the highchair.

Richard pointed, and said, "It's in the dining room and his food is on the table waiting."

Matt went into the dining room and put Thomas in the highchair. Richard was in the dining room right behind him with breakfast for Sarah. Richard asked, "Matt, can I get you any breakfast?"

Matt answered, "More coffee."

Sarah said, "This is nice. I get to have my breakfast in the same room with my son and husband. Matt just to let you know I invited Jeannie and Al over for Friday night."

Matt responded, "Oh, that's right. You told me you were going to do that. Richard and I are going to Albertson's if you can think of anything."

Sarah added, "Yes, please pick me up some Dannon yogurts and Quaker Oats granola bars. Oh, and make sure there's enough food for Thomas for the week."

Matt offered, "Okay, I can take care of that."

Matt and Richard left for Albertson's a little after eight-fifteen. Once in the store Matt started in on Richard and said, "Earlier this morning you said you had about thirty more ideas. Is that true?"

Richard answered, "More or less."

"What do you mean more or less?"

Richard answered, "Okay, the number thirty is an understatement. I have about ten times that. I'll admit some border on the unbelievable but I have to say about three-quarters of them will suit us just fine. We need to wrap up the food shopping here and speed things along."

Matt said, "Sarah asked me to grab a few things."

Richard asked, "Were they Dannon yogurts, Quaker Oats granola bars and make sure Thomas has enough food for the week?"

"Yes, that's it."

"Okay, all those things are in the carriage already. We should also grab a couple of bottles of diet Pepsi. You said Al and Jeannie are coming over Friday night."

Matt replied, "That's right. Thanks for remembering." They went through the checkout and Matt put the bags in the back of the van.

On the way back to the house Richard said, "How about the same as always you carry the bags in and I'll put the items away."

24

In Training

Four Days Later: Thursday, January 13th

Matt came home around four-fifteen. Just like last Thursday he went into the house without announcing his arrival. Denise was in the living room sitting on the floor next to Thomas.

Denise waved to Matt and said, "I'm training him to be an expert crawler."

Matt responded with, "Good, that means he can start crawling to the highchair."

"Matt, before you say anything, I know you and Richard are going to the theater tonight. I'll be here and besides; I was invited to free lasagna."

"Richard sure makes a mean lasagna. Since he's moved in here, I haven't had a bad meal yet."

Matt and Richard headed off to the theater at six-fifteen. Just like the routine, they waved to Tim the parking garage attendant. They entered the theater and took the temporary seats in the front row.

Matt asked Richard, "Are we repeating the grand finale from last Thursday?"

Richard answered, "I know I said we'd do that but we don't have to repeat anything yet. This is what I think we should do..."

The show started at exactly seven-thirty. Matt and Richard went through their acts and made it look so easy. It was eight-forty and Richard gave Matt a nod indicating it was time to get the last act going.

Matt called out to the audience, "Ladies and gentlemen, we have time for one more. We'll require assistance from a volunteer, please. I need someone to work with Richard for a few minutes. Matt looked at all the hands that went up. He picked the woman from the fifteenth row.

Matt asked, "Will you come up here and help us? It's perfectly safe."

The volunteer walked up to the stage and Matt asked her, "And your name is?"

She answered, "Theresa, Theresa Sharkey. You can call me Terry."

Matt replied, "Okay Terry, it's nice to meet you. My name is Matt and this is Richard."

Terry shook Matt's and then Richard's hand. The curtain opened as soon as they were done shaking hands. "Now, Terry, you see what we have here is a set of doorways. If you open each door, you'll see the back of the stage. What I want you to do is examine each door, step inside for a second, and then you're going to pick which door you want me to step into."

Terry opened the doors, stepped inside, and then came back as instructed. Matt said, "Very good, now if you'll help us turn the whole frame one-half turn. It's on wheels so it should move easily."

Matt pulled on one end while Richard and Terry pushed on the other. The audience now had a view of the door frame and could see the left side and right side.

It was Richard's turn to give the next set of directions. "Okay Terry, the decision is yours. Which door do you want Matt to go in?"

Terry answered, "The middle one."

"Excellent choice! Now, Matt will open the middle door and as he does, please go to the other side to greet him coming through."

Matt opened the middle door and Terry went to the side of the frame. Matt was not on the other side. Terry looked back to the left. She knew she saw him open the door. Terry also witnessed Matt starting to go through. She finally said to Richard, "He's not there."

Richard thought for a second, "Hmmm seems like we have a problem here." Richard opened the middle door, stepped in briefly, and then back out."

Terry was puzzled and sounded off to Richard, "I don't understand. You didn't have a problem going through the doorway and coming back. When Matt did it, he wasn't so successful."

226

Richard continued, "Now would be a good time to check the other doors. He opened the first door, opened it, went through, and came back. Richard then went through the third doorway and closed the door behind him.

Terry yelled, "WAIT!" She ran over, opened the door, and Richard already vanished.

Terry mumbled to herself, "Where'd they go, where'd they go." She tried to open the third door and that was stuck. Terry then tried the other two and the other two wouldn't budge. Then she heard a knock on the middle door. Terry tried that door again and this time it opened. Matt was on the other side of the door.

Matt offered, "Hey, I hope we didn't scare you. Where's Richard?"

She answered, "I don't know. He went through the third door. After that, I tried to open all three doors and they were stuck."

"That's Richard to a tee. He likes to show off whenever possible."

Next, Matt and Terry heard Richard's voice saying, "No more than anyone else. I'm down here you two." Richard was sitting in the front row. He stood and said, "Thank you" to the audience member who briefly gave up their seat. Richard walked up to the stage and gave Matt a nod for another act well executed.

Matt said to Terry, "Thank you. We have to say goodnight to the audience but don't go back to your seat yet. Matt called out to the audience, "Ladies and gentlemen, that concludes our show for tonight. If you liked what you saw please tell your friends. My name is Matt White and this is my good friend and show partner, Richard Jenkins. Please drive safely and have a good night."

Matt then looked at Terry and said, "Thank you for being such a good sport and helping us. I'd like to give you a couple of free tickets for another show."

Terry took the envelope from Matt. She said, "Thank you, and thank you for letting me help. I had a good time. Goodnight." Terry walked off the stage and left the theater.

Matt asked Richard, "Well Mr. Jenkins, are you ready to call it a night?"

Richard answered, "Lead the way, Mr. White."

The Next Day: Friday, January 14ᵗʰ

Matt pulled in the driveway a little before four-fifteen. Denise was coming down the stairs carrying Thomas. She greeted Matt, "Hi! He just woke up. I'll take care of him."

Matt offered, "Hello Denise. Thank you."

Matt found Richard in the kitchen and offered, "I hope you remembered Al and Jeannie are coming over tonight. So, no cooking for you."

Richard responded with, "Of course I remembered. I'm just making a fresh garden salad to go with the pizza."

Later On: Around Six

Sarah pulled in the driveway, walked into the house, and called in, "Matt, Richard, I'm home."

Matt was in the living room sitting on the floor next to Thomas. He yelled, "Hey honey, we're in here."

Sarah went into the living room, bent down, and kissed Matt. She kissed Thomas on top of his head. She said, "I'm going to change out of my work clothes. Al and Jeannie are coming and they'll be here by six-thirty."

Al and Jeannie pulled in Matt's driveway at six-thirty on the dot. They went up the front stairs and Sarah opened the door for them. Sarah greeted them, "Welcome! Come in, come in."

The two of them walked in and Matt said, "Hey Al, hey Jeannie. Let me take your coats. Al, I'm putting yours on the back of the chair. We'll be going to get the pizza soon. There's no sense putting it in the closet."

Sarah jumped in and said, "Speaking of which, shouldn't you be getting a move on?"

Matt came back with, "Right, let's go, Al." Al and Matt got in Matt's van and drove to Maggiano's.

On the way over Al said to Matt, "Matt, I want to take care of the pizza tonight. You guys are always treating us."

"Al, that won't be necessary. I tell you what. You can get it next time."

"You said that the last time. You said I can get it the next time."

Matt asked, "So, I said I can get it the next time? There, the problem is solved. NO, Al, really let me treat. You guys are coming over and I know Sarah gets lonely and now I'm at the theater a lot more."

They went inside Maggiano's and Matt paid for the pizzas. The two of them got back in Matt's van and Al asked, "Okay, you didn't let me treat for the pizza. Now, I feel guilty about asking this."

"Ask me anything you want Al."

"Do you think Richard will do a couple of card tricks after we eat?"

Matt answered, "Richard loves showing off his craft. He eats it up when he has an audience. All we have to do is ask him."

They got back to the house and sat down to dinner. Thomas was bouncing in his busy chair. Jeannie was the first to open the conversation. "How's your work going Sarah?"

"It's keeping me busy. I have to tell you it was not fun for the first two weeks going back. For the first two weeks, I had to drop Thomas off at daycare on the way to work. Thanks to Denise, I don't have to do that anymore. She comes to the house every day and she's excellent with Thomas."

Jeannie responded with, "Well it's important that you have someone you trust to watch him."

Sarah asked Jeannie, "How about you? How's your work going?"

Jeannie answered, "It's very busy now. I'm glad I had a couple of extra days off near Christmas."

They finished eating and Jeannie said, "Here, let me help clean up the table."

Richard tried to stop her by saying, "That's not necessary. Please sit and relax. He was too late. Jeannie was already at the door to the kitchen holding the salad bowls and two glasses.

Al leaned across the table and quietly asked Matt, "Did you ask him?"

Matt answered, "Oh, no, sorry. Richard, I forgot to ask you. Will you show us a couple of card tricks after the table is cleaned?' Al put his hands over his face out of embarrassment.

Richard came back with, 'Of course, I will. Anything for Mr. Firmani."

Al groveled, "Sorry Mr. Jenkins that I didn't ask you myself."

"Al, not to worry, and seeing as you two are here now, I will show you some new things I've been working on. Jeannie, please reach behind you and get the deck of cards on the hutch.

Jeannie reached behind her, grabbed the deck, and put it on the table. Before she let go of them, Richard said, "You have the deck. How about we start with you helping. Please look at the cards and then give them a quick shuffle." Jeannie fanned the deck open as much as she could, closed the deck, and then shuffled them. Richard continued, "Please give Al the top four cards, and then I want Al to show you his four cards."

Richard asked, "Al, do you know the cards in your hand?"

Al answered, "Yes."

Richard proceeded, "Al please concentrate on the highest card in your hand and then lay the four of them face down on the table." Al laid his cards down and he had the ace of hearts in mind. Richard continued, "Okay Al, I'm just going to take the remaining deck and lightly touch the top card of your pile." Richard tapped Al's pile with the corner of the deck. He continued, "Ok Al, please reveal your four cards."

Al turned over his cards and the four people watching said, "WHOA!" Al's four cards transformed into the four aces.

Richard continued, "Now Jeannie, you saw Al's cards in the beginning. Are those cards different?"

She answered, "One of the cards is the same and that is the ace of hearts. The other three are different. I don't suppose you want to tell us how you did that."

Richard responded to Jeannie's comment, "You are supposing correct. I do not want to tell you. Now, I can either explain to you why I don't want to tell you how I did the trick or we can advance to the next one."

Jeannie and Al both agreed, "It's understandable if you don't want to tell us. It's your secret."

Matt jumped in and yelled, "ADVANCE, continue."

Richard said, "Okay, let's move the cards off to the side for a few minutes. We'll give them a chance to recuperate. They've been working hard."

"Now Al, I want you to clear your head and think of only one thought."

Al said, "Okay, ready."

Richard started, "Okay Al, you were just thinking you hope you have a slow day next week so you can leave an hour early and stop at Jiffy Lube."

Al smiled and said, "He's right."

Sarah jumped in and said, "Okay, I'm sorry Richard but you have to convince me. Now, try to read my mind."

Richard thought for a few seconds, "Al, please grab the pad and pen on the hutch and put it in front of Sarah." Al turned and grabbed the pad and pen. Richard continued, "Sarah, this time I want you to write down one thought and then slide the pad over to Matt. Keep the information covered."

Sarah picked up the pen. She wrote down, 'I wonder what time Thomas will wake in the morning. She put her hand over the writing and slid the pad over to Matt. Sarah said, "Okay, I'm ready."

Richard added, "Good, do not reveal the pad yet. You were thinking about what time is Thomas going to wake in the morning. You may now uncover the pad."

Sarah took her hands off the pad and announced, "As usual, Richard is correct."

Richard offered, "Okay, if everyone will excuse me for a minute. I want to get a refill on my coffee. Does anyone else require anything?"

While Richard was gone Al asked, "Is there anything he can't do?"

Matt took that one, "Richard will tell you he can't drive. He can drive me crazy though."

The door pushed open and Richard said to Matt, "Stick with teaching Math. Comedy is not one of your attributes."

Matt shot back, "I was just being silly. You don't drive me crazy. I have Sarah for that."

Sarah said to Matt, "Your hole just keeps getting deeper Matt."

Richard was at the end of the table and asked, "Shall we continue?" Richard took the deck of cards and said, "I'm going to deal two cards face up on the left side of the table and two cards face up on the right side. Now, I'm going to lay one handkerchief over each pile." Richard laid out the two handkerchiefs. He continued, "Al, I want you to uncover one pile, and Jeannie will remove the handkerchief from the other one after I count to three. One...two...three." Both handkerchiefs were removed. The two cards disappeared that Al uncovered. The two cards that Jeannie covered changed altogether.

Al asked, "What is going on here?"

Matt spoke up and answered, "I can answer that. It's what Richard calls magic. You can ask Richard how he did that but he can't tell you. On that note, I'm getting a soda. Does anyone need anything?" There were no takers on Matt's offer. Matt went into the kitchen and returned with a can of Diet Pepsi.

Richard said, "Okay, we'll do one more, and then we need to stop. One of us and I am referring to myself, needs to retire to their room for the evening." Richard proceeded again, "Okay Al, how about taking the cards and deal me thirteen cards." Al dealt out thirteen cards to Richard. Next, Richard picked up the cards and held them up so everyone could see them but him. "Okay Al, I want you to take one of these cards and tell me which one you're picking."

Al reached for a card and said, "Okay, I'm taking the three of spades." Al put the card face down to the left of him.

"Okay Al, now I want you to take two cards but do not reveal them to me and then put the two cards on top of the three of spades." Al took out two cards and laid them on top of the three of spades as he was instructed. Richard continued, "Al, this time I want you to take away three cards out of my hand. Again, do not show them to me."

Al took three cards and laid them on top of the other three. Richard continued, "Okay, very good Al. I know this is getting repetitive and you should have six cards face down there. This time I want you to take four cards from my hand and then put them on top of the six." Al chose four cards from Richard's hand and laid them on top of his pile. Richard again continued, "Al, I have three cards left.

So, please put these on top of your pile. Al took the last three cards from Richard's hand and put them on the pile.

Richard for the last time said, "Okay Al, you have all of my cards. I'm going to count to three and when I point at you, I want you to turn your cards over. One…two…three." Richard took the top card from the remaining deck. He lightly tapped Al's pile with that card and then pointed at Al.

Al turned the cards over and said, "NICE!" All of Al's cards turned to spades.

Matt bellowed, "WOW!!!" I've never seen that done before. Well played Richard."

Richard added, "Thank you, Matt. Now, if everyone will excuse me, I need to get some sleep. Al, you can keep those cards. Jeannie, very nice seeing you again. Goodnight Matt, goodnight Sarah. I will see you in the morning."

Everyone said goodnight to Richard and then Matt confirmed to Al, "You see I told you all we have to do is ask him. He loves to show off his stuff."

Al replied, "I find it fascinating. You can probably take it or leave it because you see it all the time. Either way, we have to get going. I'm getting tired and I saw Jeannie trying to suppress a yawn earlier."

Matt responded with, "I understand. Next time we get together we can make it on a Sunday and you guys can come over earlier in the day."

The Next Day: Saturday, January 15th

It was late in the afternoon close to four-forty-five and Matt was sitting on the living room floor with Thomas trying to get him to crawl. Thomas already knew how to make himself move forward by pulling himself on his hands and then he drops on his stomach.

Sarah walked by the doorway of the living room and said to Matt, "He's not ready for that yet but he's getting there. Richard told me the pasta and meatballs will be ready in three minutes."

Matt sounded back, "Score, we haven't had Richard's Italian cooking in a while."

233

Matt and Richard left for the theater at six-fifteen. Just like clockwork they drove by Tim the parking attendant and waved. Once in the theater, they sat in their temporary seats in the front row. Matt said to Richard, "Now, this is our fourth show since the beginning of the year. Are we repeating anything?"

Richard's retorted, "It's still not necessary. This is what I think we should do…"

Richard finished explaining his idea. Matt said, "The audience is coming in. We need to get out of sight."

The show started right at seven-thirty. Matt and Richard went through their acts and every illusion and every trick was perfectly executed. It was eight-forty and Richard gave Matt the nod to get the final act going.

Matt called out to the audience, "Ladies and gentlemen, we have time for one more and as always we'll require assistance from a volunteer. I usually say you're not to worry. You will not be harmed or injured in any way. I say that every time because my partner tells me to. I wasn't given those directions for tonight. Hmmm."

Matt looked at the batch of volunteers and picked a gentleman from the tenth row. Matt asked the volunteer, "Sir, will you come up here and help us?"

The volunteer nodded and went up on the stage. Matt asked, "Your name is?"

The volunteer answered, "Jeff Pelliot."

Matt responded, "Okay Jeff, it's nice to meet you. My name is Matt and this is Richard." Matt shook Jeff's hand and then Richard did the same. The curtain opened and Matt said, "Okay Jeff, we have a trunk here and this is where Richard takes over."

Richard opened the trunk and pulled out the extra-large burlap bag. He said to Matt, "It's time for you to step into the bag." Matt stepped in the bag and Richard said, "Okay Jeff, cinch up the bag tie a knot at the top but don't make it too tight." Matt crouched down in the trunk. Richard closed the lid and then said, "Jeff please fasten the padlock and I'll hold onto the key."

Jeff snapped the lock shut and gave Richard the key. "Here you go."

Richard looked at the key and said, "We don't need this anymore." He took the key and threw it across the floor.

Jeff put his one hand on his left temple and his right hand on the other side, and asked, "How are we going to get him out of there?"

Richard asked, "What do you mean? Oh right. Matt said to count to seven, then turn the trunk around and unlock it." Jeff and Richard both turned the trunk around. Then they felt pounding coming from the inside. Richard said, "Hold on a second, I have a spare key." Richard was so nervous about not getting Matt out fast enough he handed Jeff the key. Jeff opened the lock and took it out of the hasp. He flipped the hasp up and it opened the trunk only to find an empty bag.

Jeff asked, "What the. How did?"

Then Jeff and Richard heard Matt's voice saying, "You guys were taking way too long to get me out of that hotbox." They started looking around. Matt said, "I'm down here." Matt was standing on the floor in front of the first row. He walked back up to the stage and smiled at Jeff. Matt said, "Thanks for your help, Jeff. We have to say goodnight to the audience but don't go back to your seat yet."

Matt called out to the audience, "Ladies and gentlemen. That concludes our show for tonight. If you liked what you saw, please tell your friends. My name is Matt White and this is my good friend and show partner, Richard Jenkins. Please drive safely and have a good night."

Matt then said to Jeff, "Jeff, thank you again for your help up here. As a way of appreciation, I want to give you two free passes to a later show."

Jeff put his hand out, took the passes, and said, "Thank you, I had a good time tonight. Have a good night." Jeff went down the stairs off the stage and left the theater.

Richard asked Matt, "Well Mr. White, are you ready to call it a night?"

Matt answered, "Ready as I'll ever be. Let's go."

235

The Next Morning: Sunday, January 16th

Matt was downstairs getting coffee at six-thirty. Richard was sitting in the corner drinking his coffee. He had the Sunday paper in front of him on the table.

Matt greeted Richard first, "Good morning! How are you?"

"I feel fully energized from my coffee. Good morning to you too Matt. Let me see, the first prediction is Sarah will be down at seven twenty. Then, she's going to tell you she needs about seven things from Albertson's."

"And you know this how? Okay, what seven things is she going to put on the list or ask for?"

"Okay, assorted jars of baby food, granola bars, grapes, one pound of low-salt turkey from the deli, pita bread, Sleepy Time tea, and two containers of Crystal Light. She'll be down in a few minutes. You can see if she has a list ready."

Seven-Twenty

Sarah came downstairs and found Matt and Richard in the kitchen. She said, "Good morning Matt," and then kissed him on the cheek. She next said, "Good morning Richard."

Matt went into the living room and turned on the baby monitor. He started to say something to Sarah. "Honey." That was all he could get out when sounds from Thomas came out of the monitor. Matt said, "Be right back."

Matt ran up the stairs and went into Thomas's room. He took him out of the crib and brought him to the changing table. After Matt brought Thomas downstairs he said, "I found someone who wants to be fed."

Matt slid the highchair next to the table. Sarah said, "Honey, wait I'll take care of him. I'm sure you boys are itching to get to Albertson's before the crowd does. That reminds me I started a small list with a few things on it."

Matt thought to himself, 'Should I ask this.' I think I already know the answer. "Honey, please define a few."

"Seven."

"Of course, I mean no problem. We'll be heading out in a few minutes. Matt took Sarah's list off the kitchen counter.

Matt opened the back door intending to warm up his car. It was only twenty-four degrees out. Matt expressed, "Whoa! I wasn't expecting that."

Richard asked, "What's wrong?"

"The wrong is it feels like we live in Antarctica."

"It's time to bundle up and hope for the best. The frigid temps will be around only a few more weeks. However, the bad news is tomorrow there will be a drop in temperature."

Five Minutes Later

They were out the door on the way to Albertson's. Matt asked, "Did you say we have a drop in temperature coming?"

Richard answered, "Unfortunately, yes. Right now, it's twenty-four out. Tomorrow morning you'll be braving a high of fifteen. Wednesday there'll be another drop of three more degrees and Friday the temperature will go down another four degrees. That's not the worst of it either."

"How can it get any worse?"

"Okay, the air temperature will be down to zero by Tuesday, January 25th. Unfortunately, it will teeter back and forth from zero to minus two for about three weeks. Now, aren't you glad you didn't want me fooling around with the weather? I believe you thought it was a bad idea."

"That was Sarah's response. I know there's a point at how much you should interfere. Sometimes it's a good idea to let mother nature take its toll."

They pulled into the parking lot of Albertson's. For the first time, Matt skipped grabbing a carriage from the outside carriage corral. He knew the handle on the carriages would be freezing to the touch. Once in the store Matt pulled out a carriage and said, "Whoa, these are no better."

Richard asked, "Is there a problem?"

"Yes, the handle of the carriage is freezing. It's like putting your tongue on a popsicle and it sticks."

237

"Let me have a look at this." Richard rubbed his right arm over the handle of the carriage from left to right. He then said, "Try it now."

Matt placed his hand on the carriage slowly one at a time expecting the worst. He said, "That's a lot better."

They went through the aisles filling the carriage with their weekly needs and the request from Sarah's list. In the third aisle, Richard spoke up and said, "I want to tell you something about Denise."

"What about Denise?"

"Okay, maybe about six weeks ago Denise came over in the morning. After you left for work, we had a chat as we so often do. Denise told me how the cold affects her and every winter she has a hard time getting used to it."

They were still going through the aisles and Matt said, "Please hold that thought. I want to make sure we have everything from Sarah's list." Matt looked in the carriage and said to Richard, "Okay, you were saying."

"I thought it would be best that I do something for Denise. I asked her where her jacket was. She told me she left it on the back of the chair. I said to her let me hang it in the closet for you. I didn't hang it in the closet right away. I intervened when I picked it up. She still doesn't know it. Maybe, it was wrong what I did but I had to act quickly. I knew she'd be good with Thomas and we couldn't have her backing out."

"Okay, but how did you intervene?"

Richard answered, "You know that combination sweater jacket that she wears here every day?"

"I know the one you mean."

"I picked up her jacket and hung it on the coat tree. I put both of my hands on the shoulders of the garment. I made sure every time she had it on, she'd be feeling warm instead of cold."

"Better hope she doesn't change jackets."

They pushed the carriage out of the store over to Matt's van. Matt loaded the groceries into the back. Richard pushed the carriage to the corral and then got in the van. Before they left the parking lot, he said to Matt, "I'll take care of putting the groceries away when we get back to the house."

Matt went into the house at five minutes after four. Denise was sitting on the living room floor with Thomas. She waved to Matt and said, "Hello! Is there a fire I don't know about?"

Matt retorted, "Sorry, I just get so nervous about these Thursday night shows. It's like I have an uneasy feeling we're not ready for it. All that worrying is unnecessary because Richard always has it under control. I'll be right back. I want to get changed."

Before Matt got up the stairs, Richard stepped out of the kitchen and said, "Good afternoon Matt. Food will be ready in seven minutes."

Denise brought in the highchair, entered the dining room, and placed it on the corner so Thomas would have a view of her and Matt. The three of them sat at the table eating. Denise spoke up and said, "You know Matt, I never mind staying. You don't have to feed me dinner on Thursdays."

Matt took another bite of his chicken and said, "Denise, I tried to bribe you by adding to your check and you said I didn't have to. Now, you're staying late so Richard and I can get to the theater by six-thirty. Feeding you is the least we can do."

They finished dinner and Matt got up to clear the table. Richard said, "You can leave the plates on the counter and I'll tend to them in a minute."

Richard took a plate of food and put a layer of Glad Wrap over it. He set it on the counter and put a sticky note on it with Sarah's name. Matt made a second trip to the kitchen and said, "Here are the glasses, and the table's cleared."

"Good, maybe you can ask Denise to tell Sarah about the plate I left on the counter, and then we'll head off to the theater."

"Got it." Matt went out to Denise, "Denise, we're heading out. Thanks again for sticking around and I'll see you tomorrow."

Denise replied, "Okay. Goodbye Matt. Bye Richard."

Five-Thirty-Five

Matt and Richard were on their way to the theater. Matt said in the van, "We're leaving earlier than usual. Why?"

Richard answered, "You'll see. It's because of the future event."

"What?"

"Be patient. You'll find out."

Matt got to Main Street. The traffic was at a standstill. There was a police officer in the middle of the street making the traffic wait. After sitting there for ten minutes, Matt saw a big tow truck approaching in his rearview mirror. The stationary line of nine cars was waved over to yield for the tow truck. They were held in the line for almost twenty-five minutes.

Traffic was rolling again and Richard offered, "Now, you know why we left early."

Matt and Richard were in the theater by six thirty-five. They took their temporary seats in the front row.

Matt asked, "What are the plans for tonight? I don't know what we're doing."

Richard nodded halfway, put his hand up, and said, "Not to worry, I have it covered. We have something new for tonight. I don't think we need to repeat our performances yet. We'll go over it in a minute."

Matt was sitting there listening. He asked, "WOW! Can you hear the wind out there? It's only fifteen degrees. I'm not looking forward to the walk to the car tonight."

"That's a simple fix. We won't walk to the car. Problem is solved."

"Okay, what about not walking by the booth where Tim stands? He always waves to us when we walk by."

"That's true. He does recognize us when his eyes are open if you get my meaning. I don't blame him for falling asleep. He has a boring job and he's there late. Anyway, this is what we'll do tonight..."

A few minutes later the crowd started in and Matt let out, "It's time to make ourselves scarce." The two of them got up and went backstage.

The show got underway right at seven-thirty. Matt and Richard went through their routine like a well-oiled machine. It was almost eight-thirty and Richard looked at Matt and gave him the nod indicating it was time for the announcement.

Matt called out to the audience, "Ladies and gentlemen, we have time for one more. We're looking for a few volunteers, maybe three or four. We also want two members from the audience to come up here." Two people from the front row stood up and walked closer to the stage. Matt continued, "You two will pick the volunteers for tonight."

The two picked four volunteers for the act.

Matt called out, "Okay, you four come on up."

The chosen volunteers went up on the stage. Matt handed each one a scribble pad and pen. He instructed them, "Okay, now I'm putting you in the hands of my partner Richard."

Richard approached the four individuals and started, "First of all, thank you for donating your time. I want to give you a little background. A few weeks ago, a woman asked me if I could read her mind. I told her I'd give it a whirl."

Richard continued, "Okay, Mr. White gave each one of you a pad and pen. I want each of you to think of anything you want. Then write it down and keep the pad hidden. I will then tell each one of you what you wrote down. Please begin now."

The four participants took a minute and wrote down their thoughts. Richard pointed at the screen above while they were doing this and there were the words, PLEASE BE PATIENT. The screen went blank and Richard asked, "Are you ready?"

All four of them said, "Yes."

Richard continued, "Good, we'll start with you, young lady. I believe your name is, wait don't tell me. Does it start with a B?"

She answered, "Yes, it does."

Richard again continued, "Okay Barbara, I'm going to tell you what you wrote on your pad. You wrote down Disappointed that you didn't get to Macy's to pick up the espresso combo cappuccino maker when it was on sale. Please turn your pad around so the cameraman can see it."

Richard motioned for the cameraman to get closer and focus on Barbara's pad. Barbara's selection appeared on the screen above. The audience had a clear view of what she wrote down. It proved Richard's prediction was accurate.

Barbara stood there in disbelief and asked Richard, "Can you tell us how you did that?"

Richard quickly answered, "No, I cannot. Sorry, but please do not leave the stage yet. We're not done." Richard continued, "Okay, how about volunteer number two. Sir, please step forward so we can get your name."

The man stepped forward and shook Richard's hand. "Hello, my name is Dave, Dave Hegan."

Richard returned the greeting, "Okay, Mr. Hegan, I'm going to tell you what you have on your pad. You wrote down Sunday Chicago Black Hawks will play the New York Rangers. You're rooting for the Black Hawks. Could you please do as Barbara did and let the cameraman see your pad? The cameraman moved in closer and the screen above was showing Dave's pad. Once again, Richard was right on the money with his prediction.

Dave looked at Richard while his pad was visible on the screen and then he let out, "I'm impressed."

Richard replied, "Splendid, but please do not leave the stage yet. We're not quite finished." Richard again continued, "Let's move on to volunteer number three. Miss, could you please step forward."

The volunteer stood across from Richard and he asked, "Can I get your name?"

She answered, "Doreen Cullen."

Richard added, "Okay, Miss Cullen, as you know my name is Richard and that is my show partner and very good friend Matt. Now, I'm going to tell you what's on your pad. Keep the pad hidden for now. You put on the pad remember to make an appointment next week for new tires. Doreen, please let the cameraman come in and get a look at your pad." The cameraman moved in close and zoomed in on Doreen's pad. The audience saw that for a third time Richard's prediction was correct.

Doreen smiled, put her hands over her face in shock, and yelled, "WOW!"

Richard added, "Let me save you some time here. I cannot show you how that's done. However, please do not leave the stage. We have one more to go. Please go stand next to Barbara and Dave."

For the last volunteer, Richard asked him to step forward. The volunteer stood across from Richard. Richard said, "Okay, it's time to get your name."

The volunteer responded, "Mark Joley."

Richard proceeded, "Okay Mark, as you know my name is Richard, and Matt is standing off to the side behind the other volunteers. At this time, I'm going to tell you what you wrote on your pad. I also see you took the liberty of writing on the second piece of paper. You hid the first one in your pocket. Those were not the instructions. Therefore, this is what I'm going to do. I'm going to tell you what you have on the pad now and then I'll tell you what you have on the paper in your pocket. On the pad you put It's a shame you gave up watching the Bulls game for this."

The audience let out, "AWWWW"

Richard added, "So now, let's have the cameraman come in closer." The cameraman moved in close and aimed right at Mark's pad. Once again, for a fourth time, Richard's prediction was spot on.

"Now Mark, let's have a look at the paper you stashed in your pocket. Before you unfold it, you have on there you think you might have parked too close to the car next to you. You hid that in your pocket because you wanted to come up with something better. Did you come up with something better? I apologize if you did not enjoy tonight's performance. Mark, Mr. White, and I are dedicated to trying to entertain everyone here. So, you would have had a better time if you just concentrated on what's going on around you, Steve. Mark is not your name, is it?"

He answered, "No, it's Steve. Sorry, I thought I could fool you, and sorry about what I wrote. I realize now you're the real deal."

"Apology accepted. Maybe you can tell a couple of your friends. Okay, now, everyone here gets a couple of free passes to a show for another night. You may return to your seats."

The four volunteers left the stage and returned to their seats. Richard half smiled, looked at Matt, and Matt knew it was time to say good night. "Ladies and gentlemen that concludes our show for tonight. If you like what you saw, please tell your friends. My name is Matt White, and this is my good friend and show partner, Richard Jenkins. Please drive safely and have a good night."

Matt looked to Richard and asked, "Well Mr. Jenkins, are you ready to call it a night?"

He answered, "Yes, I am. I just want to add I am not pleased with the performance tonight."

"You mean you're not happy with the last volunteer. It's quite commendable acting the way you did."

Richard continued, "It was a disappointment and I wish to rectify it a week from Saturday."

Two Days Later: Saturday, January 22nd

Matt was downstairs at six thirty-five pouring himself a coffee. Richard was sitting at the kitchen table in the corner. His newspaper was folded in front of him. Matt greeted Richard first, "Good morning Richard. Are you still licking your wounds from Thursday night or are you over it?"

Richard responded, "Good morning Matt. I'm not letting Thursday night's fool upset me. I know we try and one of our main goals is to keep it authentic."

"I agree. I'd like to see Mark or Steve or whatever he wants to call himself do that. I can't believe he tried to fool you with a different name."

"Uh, not going to happen. Listen, Sarah is on her way downstairs."

The bedroom door opened upstairs and Matt moved the highchair into the dining room. "Might as well get ready."

Sarah was downstairs. "Good morning Matt, Richard."

She leaned in and kissed Matt on the cheek. Matt returned the kiss and Sarah asked him, "Is it possible I heard some words of disappointment while I was still upstairs?"

"Last night's final act did not go as well as we hoped for."

Richard jumped in the conversation. "There was a non-believer or for a better word a heckler there last night. He was determined to ruin the good time for everyone else."

"That's awful! I'm sorry," Sarah said.

Matt chimed in, "Richard figured out the volunteer tried to pull one over on him by saying his name was Mark. Richard saw right through that. He finally softened up when Richard corrected him."

Just as Matt finished his statement sounds were coming from the baby monitor. Matt raised one eyebrow and said, "Looks like someone wants breakfast. I'll be back in a few."

Matt hustled up the stairs to get Thomas.

Sarah was standing in the kitchen doorway and Richard offered his culinary skills. Sarah, Matt is taking care of Thomas. Why don't you have a seat in the dining room, and I'll bring you a hot breakfast. How does a western omelet sound?"

Ten Minutes Later

Richard brought a serving tray with Sarah's omelet, juice, and a fresh hot coffee for himself. Richard put the food in front of Sarah.

"Thank you, Richard." She took a bite of food.

"As usual this is delicious. I thought about what happened at the show Thursday night. I think you can rectify the dilemma by switching the Saturday night show to an afternoon show. You would draw in a different crowd with a younger audience. Kids like to see magic more so than adults."

"Perhaps you're on to something here. I will talk it over with Matt later on. After all, he deserves a say in this. It's his show."

"Oh yeah, it's his show. Only you're the saving grace for the show and the brains behind it."

Matt came downstairs, put Thomas in his highchair, and fed him his breakfast. While Matt was sitting there Sarah started, "Honey, I was talking to Richard and made a suggestion. I think this will help prevent a repeat of unappreciative guests in the future."

Matt asked, "What's your suggestion?"

"You switch your showtime from Saturday night to afternoon. Make it a matinee. There's a better chance of drawing in a younger crowd. Kids like magic more than adults. Richard told me he would talk it over with you. If you did that, we'd have our Saturday nights back. Matt, I see the people I work with more than I see you."

"Okay, okay, I get it. I will call Mr. Turco Monday after work. Honey, you're right we should see each other more often."

Richard came into the dining room and asked, "Matt, can I get you some breakfast?"

Matt answered, "How about just a coffee refill?"

"You got it."

Matt and Richard left in Matt's van for the theater. They were in their temporary seats in the front row by ten minutes to seven.

"Now's a good time as any to get it out in the open, Matt. It seems that Sarah would prefer an afternoon show versus an evening show."

"It doesn't seem it, Richard. It is it. She laid out a couple of good reasons to switch. I told her I'd call Mr. Turco after work. I hope that's agreeable with you."

"You mean you want me to subject myself to getting a better night's sleep by sleeping later on Saturdays? I am more than on board with that idea. As for tonight, I told you earlier I wanted to do the show over from last week."

"Okay, but what will I be doing?"

"You can pick the volunteers tonight. Let's get three this time. This will speed things up. Oh look, here comes the crowd. We need to get out of sight."

The show started right at seven-thirty. Matt and Richard went through the first half of the show performing their acts flawlessly. At eight forty-five Richard nodded to Matt indicating it was time to start their last act. Richard knew things were going to go better tonight. He was not happy with what happened on that Thursday night.

Matt made the announcement and called out to the audience, "Ladies and gentlemen, we have just enough time for one more. We'll be needing a few volunteers. Oh, and not to worry you will not be harmed in any way."

Matt walked off the stage down to the floor. He said to the audience, "Okay, I need three volunteers."

Matt picked the woman from the sixth row in the center. Then he picked a man from the fourth row in the left section. Lastly, he selected another woman in the eleventh row from the right section. "Can you three come to join us up on stage?"

The three volunteers followed Matt up. Matt handed each one of them a pad and a Sharpie fine tip marker.

"I am leaving you in the hands of my friend Richard," Matt said.

Richard stepped to the center of the stage. "Ladies and gentlemen about four weeks ago a woman asked me if I knew how to do mind-reading. I told her I'd give it a whirl. I think you'll like what you're about to see."

He focused on the three volunteers. "Okay!" Richard said, "When you came up here Mr. White handed you a pad and a Sharpie marker. This is what I need you to do. Write down on the pad what you're thinking about at this moment. I am then going to talk with you one at a time and I'll predict what you wrote down. You can begin now."

Richard waited two minutes and continued, "Okay, can we start with you, Miss? Can I get your name?"

The volunteer answered, "Grace Cooke."

"Okay, Grace, it's nice to meet you. My name is Richard and that handsome fellow over there is my show partner Matt. Please, for now, keep your pad hidden. I'm going to tell you what you wrote down. You wished that you picked up the Keurig coffee maker that was on sale last week. Grace, will you please hold the pad so the cameraman can zoom in on it."

Grace lowered her pad and the cameraman got up close to it. The pad was now showing on the Jumbotron screen above. The audience could see Richard's prediction was correct.

Grace was smiling as Richard cited what was on her pad word for word. She gasped, "WOW! That was impressive."

"Thank you, Grace. Please wait next to Matt over there. We're not finished."

"Okay, sir, please step forward." The next volunteer stood across from Richard. Richard asked him, "Can I get your name?"

The volunteer answered, "Ryan Sullivan."

"Okay, Ryan please keep your pad hidden. I'm going to tell everyone what was on your pad. You wrote down I hope my snowblower lasts the rest of the Winter without breaking. Ryan looked down at his pad and smiled.

"Ryan, please hold your pad so the cameraman can get a shot of it." Ryan let the cameraman in close and once again the large screen above showed Richard's prediction was dead on. Richard said to Ryan,

"Please stand next to Grace over there. We're almost done." Ryan walked over and stood next to Grace.

Richard continued with the last volunteer, "Excuse me, Miss, could you please step forward." The last volunteer stood across from Richard and he asked, "Can I get your name?"

The volunteer answered, "Colleen Shanahan."

Richard continued, "It's nice to meet you, Colleen. As you know by now my name is Richard and over there is my good friend and show partner Matt. For now, please keep your pad concealed. I'm going to tell you what you wrote down. You wrote down I'm so nervous I hope I do this right. Colleen, first off, there's nothing to be nervous about." Colleen was turning red. Richard continued, "Do you want to try again?"

Colleen answered, "Okay."

"Please think of something and write it down right away. Again, keep your pad hidden. I'm going to tell you what's on the pad. You wrote down, my next car's going to be a Ford Mustang."

Colleen wearing a huge smile replied, "You nailed it."

"That's great. Can you please let the cameraman zoom in on your pad?" The cameraman focused in on Colleen's pad and the screen above proved Richard to be correct for the third time. The audience enjoyed this and applauded for a few minutes. "Thank you for your help, Colleen. Please stand next to Ryan over there. I believe Mr. White has an announcement to make."

Matt called out to the audience, "Ladies and gentlemen, that concludes our show for tonight. We hope you like what you saw. My name is Matt White and this is my show partner and good friend Richard Jenkins. If you liked what you saw, please tell your friends. Please drive safely and have a good night."

Next, Matt took three envelopes out of his pocket. He said to the volunteers, "Thank you for being good sports. We want to give you a couple of free tickets to another show later on." Matt handed the envelopes to Grace, Ryan, and Colleen. They all said thank you and headed off the stage.

Once they were gone Matt asked Richard, "Mr. Jenkins, are you ready to call it a night?"

Richard answered, "Lead the way, Mr. White."

Matt walked into the house right at four-fifteen. He called, "Denise, Richard, I'm here."

Denise was sitting on the floor in the living room keeping an eye on Thomas. She waved to Matt. Matt stopped and asked, "Can you give me just ten minutes or so? I need to make a phone call before I forget."

Denise offered, "Sure. Take your time."

Matt went to the phone and called Steve Turco. The call went to his voicemail. Matt left this for a message: Hello Mr. Turco, this is Matt White. 'Can you please call me back when you can? I want to run something by you concerning my schedule.' Matt put the phone down and went into the living room.

"Is everything okay, Matt?"

"Oh sure, Denise. I'm trying to get my Saturday nights back by switching the evening show to the afternoon."

As soon as Matt finished his sentence, the phone rang. Matt grabbed the phone and said, "Hello!"

Steve Turco was on the other end and he asked, "What can I do for you, Matt?"

"I want to know if we can switch our Saturday nights to the afternoons like a matinee thing."

"Uh, let me think about this for a minute; okay if you can do Saturday nights through the end of February. My dilemma is I already have something booked in the afternoons. Their engagement expires the last Saturday in February. I have no problem with you doing afternoons starting March 5th. This will also give me time to run an ad in the paper and change the poster outside."

Matt responded, "That works for me. Thank you, I appreciate your help."

"Oh, one more thing Matt. My name is not Mr. Turco. It's Steve."

"Right, sorry. Bye."

Matt put the phone down, went into the living room, and said to Denise, "Glad I got that out of the way. Thanks for sticking around."

Denise said, "No problem. That's why I'm here. Denise put her coat on and said, "I'll see you tomorrow."

Five-Forty

Sarah walked into the house. She called in, "Matt, Richard, I'm home."

Matt was in the living room sitting next to Thomas. Sarah greeted Matt, "There are my two favorite men."

Matt smiled and offered, "Richard said dinner will be ready at six."

She knelt, kissed Matt, and kissed Thomas on the top of his head. Sarah added, "I'll be back. I want to change out of these work clothes."

The three of them were at the dining room table having dinner. Matt broke the ice and told Richard and Sarah.

"I have news. I spoke to Mr. Turco at the theater and I told him I'd rather do a matinee show on Saturday instead of Saturday night. The good news is he said okay. However, the new schedule can't start until March 5th. Currently, there's another show booked in the afternoon through the end of February. That leaves us with six more Saturday evening shows."

Sarah came back, "I can deal with that seeing as we'll have our weekend nights back."

Three Days Later: Thursday, January 27th

Matt walked into the house at four- fifteen. He called in, "Denise, Richard, I'm here." Denise was sitting on the living room floor next to Thomas. Matt went directly to the kitchen and saw Richard preparing dinner. He gave Richard a quick "Hey."

Matt walked back into the living room and sat in one of the wing chairs near where Denise was sitting. He asked her, "How did it go today?"

Denise answered, "There were no problems. I found out we're having Richard's meatball sandwiches tonight. Matt, Richard is an excellent cook."

"I agree with you there. I get to enjoy it almost every night."

Matt and Richard left for the theater at ten minutes after six. They drove the usual route and waved to Tim as they went by his booth in the parking garage. They were sitting in the front row of the theater by six thirty-five. Matt asked, "What's the plan for tonight?"

Richard answered, "The plan is for us to entertain and to win the audience over. They'll love this. This is what we're going to do…"

After going over details of what Richard calls his super illusion; they could tell the door to the theater was open and Matt said, "We need to get out of sight."

The show started right at seven-thirty. Matt and Richard performed some of the acts together. Then Matt showed the audience a couple of card tricks. Richard was waiting behind the curtain off to one side. He was getting impatient and this was so unlike him. Matt spent approximately ten minutes in front of the audience by himself. He finished his part and signaled for Richard to come back and join him.

Matt called out to the audience, "Ladies and gentlemen, we have just enough time for one more. I'll now turn the show over to my partner Richard."

Richard walked to the center of the stage and called out, "Ladies and gentlemen I find that when I do these shows I can't help but think I find nothing more entertaining than transformation. If you are interested in volunteering to help with this please raise your hand. Mr. White will come down and select a few volunteers. He may even select a few people who don't have a hand raised. Just kidding. Oh, and something I need to mention no harm will come to me I mean you while you're on stage."

Matt walked off the stage down to the audience. First, he turned to Richard and asked very quietly, "How many?"

Richard answered, "Four will suffice."

Matt hand-picked four volunteers from various locations of the audience. He said, "Okay, you four follow me."

The four volunteers were on the stage and Richard was standing next to them. Richard pointed to the side and the curtain went up behind them. There were three makeshift screens behind them and all positioned so the audience could see the ends of them. Richard started with the volunteers and gave instructions, "My partner Matt will show you what we need you to do."

Matt stepped over to the screens. The three screens each had a different color to them. The darkest one was gray. The second darkest was a dim gray and the lightest one was translucent almost see-through. Matt stepped through the curtains one at a time and motioned for one of the volunteers to do the same.

Richard put up his hand and said, "Just a second, we need to get the participants' names just in case."

"Just in case of what? asked Matt.

"Oh, nothing."

"Good." Matt continued and asked the first volunteer her name. She answered, "Cheryl McDonough."

Matt whispered to Richard, "She's ready."

Richard came and took over, "Okay Cheryl would you mind stepping through the curtains? It does not matter the order you pick."

Cheryl walked through the openings of each curtain in the same order as Matt did. She asked, "What's next?"

Richard continued and answered, "Ah, patience. Please stand next to Mr. White while the others have a turn. Will the next volunteer please step forward?"

The volunteer stepped forward and Matt asked, "Can I get your name, sir?"

The volunteer answered, "Roger LeBlanc."

Richard walked over to Roger and introduced himself, "So nice to meet you, Roger. Would you mind stepping through the curtains as Cheryl did?"

He answered, "Sure." Roger went through the first curtain and proceeded to number two. The second curtain was lighter in color than the first one. Roger found the opening and encountered a wall preventing him from stepping through. With a puzzled look, he uttered.

"Something's not right here. Something's blocking me. There's a wall here."

"Hmm, let's have a look." Richard walked over to Roger, spread the curtain, and offered, "You're all set now."

Roger stepped to the opening mumbling, "There was a wall here." He made it through the third curtain without any issues.

Richard put his hand up and said, "Well done, please go stand over there next to Matt and Cheryl. We have one more willing participant brave enough to take this on."

Matt put his hand out and said, "I believe you're next. Step forward and give Richard your name."

The volunteer stepped next to Richard and Richard asked, "Can we get your name please?"

"Shayna Brennan," She said.

"Okay, Shayna, it's nice to meet you. I am Richard and the fellow over there in the dark suit is my good friend and show partner, Matt. Are you ready to brave the passageways unaware of what lies ahead?"

Shayna answered, "Yeah, I guess so." This might not have been her best answer as she's about to discover just that.

Richard continued, "Very well. You may proceed."

Shayna walked over to the first curtain and decided to step through it. As she was putting her left leg through, she felt something soft touching it. Shayna looked at the long soft drape and it appeared to have two entrances. Richard called out to Shayna, "Shayna, keep going." Richard knew there was more fun to come.

Shayna made it through the curtain and proceeded to the second one. She remembered Roger encountered a temporary block and she was ready for it. Shayna put her left leg through with ease. As she made it through, she noticed the flow was different. The floor had changed to cobblestone. Shayna knew right away something was not right. She looked to the left and a policeman was standing there dressed like a London bobby. He started walking towards her very quickly. Shayna put her hands up, all nervous not knowing what to do. She tried to turn around and the curtain was gone. She faintly heard Richard, "Keep going, Shayna."

Shayna hurried over to the next curtain and stepped through it without a problem. Richard was on the other side and those clapping and laughter from the audience at the same time. Shayna looked down and she had a different outfit on.

Matt, Richard, Roger, and Cheryl were waiting for Shayna to make it through. Richard put his hands together and said, "Welcome back."

Shayna responded, "Thank you" and then she asked, "How did I get this?"

Richard explained, "It appears you went back in time to the mid-1800s in London. That explains the bobby you saw and the outfit you're wearing. I hope you don't mind, It's all-in fun."

Matt asked Shayna, "What did you think of that?"

Shayna answered, "I thought it was great but I have to admit I got nervous when I stepped through the second curtain and I didn't recognize my surroundings."

"We appreciate you being a good sport. We need to say good night to the audience. Please, do not go back to your seat yet."

Matt made the announcement, "Ladies and gentlemen, that concludes our show for tonight. We hope you enjoyed it. My name is Matt White and this is my good friend and show partner, Richard Jenkins. Drive safely and have a good night."

Matt reached into his coat pocket and took out three envelopes. He said to the volunteers, "Please take these passes to a later show for helping out."

Next, Matt asked Richard, "Well Mr. Jenkins, are you ready to call it a night?"

"Lead the way, Mr. White."

Two Days Later: Saturday, January 29th

Matt came downstairs at six thirty-five and Richard was sitting in his usual corner. His newspaper was folded in front of him. Richard greeted Matt, "Good morning Matt. I hope you slept well."

Matt poured his coffee and returned, "I slept great. Good morning by the way."

"I've been mulling this over and this is bothering me. I wanted last night's act to be great and it wasn't. It was too long and looked as if we were just trying to pull a prank on somebody."

Matt pulled out the other kitchen chair and sat down. "You know, not everything is going to be mind-blowing. You don't think there are some shows that people see where a tenth of the audience is thinking boring. It even happens at the shows the professionals put on."

"Perhaps you are right. Your words do not sway me from the promise I made to you a long time ago. I told you to let me help you and the audience will say WOW! They'll tell their friends and get them to come to see the show."

Matt sipped from his coffee again and returned, "We have a show tonight and we can revert to something from before. A show that was a big hit like the water tank trick. That was a big hit."

"Agreed. I want to go over something with you later today. It's nothing bad just an idea I've come up with. Speaking of up Sarah's about to open the bedroom door upstairs."

Sarah came downstairs and went straight into the kitchen and said, "Good morning Matt, Richard." She gave Matt a peck on the cheek.

Matt returned the kiss and said, "Good morning honey."

"Good morning Sarah. If you two are ready I can bring you breakfast."

"Thank you, Richard. You know you don't have to do this every weekend."

"I understand and I'm just trying to show my appreciation for you, and Matt making me feel welcome. Besides, during the week you don't come down early enough for breakfast. Let's take advantage of this."

Sounds were coming from the monitor and Matt spoke up, "That's my cue." Matt hustled up the stairs and took Thomas out of the crib. He put a fresh Pamper on him and brought him downstairs.

Matt went into the kitchen and Richard was on his way out carrying a tray with breakfast for Sarah. Richard informed Matt, "The food and highchair are waiting for you in the dining room."

"Thank you." Matt went into the dining room, put Thomas in his chair, and began feeding him.

Sarah was sitting at one end of the table with her food in front of her. She asked Matt, "How did it go last night?"

"I think it was okay but Richard was not satisfied with the outcome. He thought it was too long and it should have been better."

Sarah took another bite of her food and offered, "It sounds like Richard's too hard on himself. Not everything you two do is going to bring the audience to their feet. There's going to be some acts that are ho-hum."

"Are you kidding me? Don't let Richard hear you say that. That's not satisfactory for Richard."

"He needs to lower his expectations. You two already have quite a collection of illusions. Before I forget, I'm going to call Jeannie and invite them over for Friday."

Matt nodded and offered, "Chinese food, it is."

Five-Forty-Five

Matt and Richard were on their way to the theater and Richard spoke up, "I have an idea that's going to help us with the acts we're doing. I'll tell you more when we get in the theater."

The two of them were sitting in the front row and Matt asked, "What's your idea?"

"Okay, you know how you and Sarah have guests over on Friday nights. Sometimes it's the Gilhoolys and other times the Firmanis. On a rare occasion, we see Denise and Tom Perates. After we have dinner, we can have a preview showing of the next planned illusion. We can get an opinion from our mini audience."

Matt added, "Sounds good except for one problem. The dining room is only so big. The table is perfect for card tricks and illusions that don't require any large props."

'That's only a problem if we let it be. I know how to shrink large down to small. Don't worry. I don't mean make you and I the size of a mouse."

As soon as Richard finished his sentence the crowd started in. Matt let out, "We should make ourselves scarce."

The show got underway right at seven-thirty. Matt and Richard went through their usual acts. They were an hour and fifteen minutes into the show when Richard gave Matt the look indicating it was time for their last act. Matt made an announcement, "Ladies and gentlemen, we have just enough time for one more."

Richard took over and motioned to the monitor, "Everyone please look at the monitor playing above. It's a film clip of Harry

Houdini performing his famous Water Torture cell trick. Tonight, we're going to show you our version. We hope you enjoy it."

The stagehands set everything in place and Matt came out to the center wearing a tight swimsuit. Matt walked up the ladder on the side of the water tank. An assistant was waiting for Matt on the side of the tank and another one in the back of the tank. His hands were shackled and then he was lowered upside down into the tank.

"Ladies and gentlemen, keep an eye on the timer above the tank, and let's hope Mr. White makes it out in time," Richard said.

The timer counted the seconds. One…two…three…four, the audience was watching as Matt was hanging upside down in the tank. Matt was struggling to free himself of the handcuffs.

The timer was ticking away nine…ten…eleven…twelve…thirteen. The audience looked on as Matt moved his arms with the little freedom he had. The timer continued seventeen…eighteen…nineteen…twenty…twenty-one.

The noise coming from the audience was down to a low mumbling sound. Matt wiggled his wrists just enough he felt the handcuffs open and fall off. From there he rolled himself over so he was no longer inverted in the tank. Matt pulled himself to the top of the tank and waved to the audience.

The audience clapped in their seats. An assistant brought a robe out to Matt as he walked down the ladder out of the tank. Matt took a bow and then pointed to Richard who did the same. He put his hand up to stop the cheering from the audience.

Matt quickly went off the stage to put on some dry clothing.

He waved to the audience a second time, and made his goodnight announcement, "Ladies and gentlemen, that concludes our show. We hope you like what you saw. If you did, please tell your friends. My name is Matt White and this is my good friend and show partner, Richard Jenkins. Please drive safely and have a good night."

Matt asked Richard, "What do you think? Any better?"

"Yes, much better, let's go home, Mr. White."

Five Days Later: Thursday, February 3rd

Matt walked into the house a little before four-fifteen. He called in, "Denise, Richard, I'm home. Matt walked into the kitchen; Richard was sitting at the table. Matt said, "Hey!"

"How are you? Dinner will be ready in ten minutes. We're having pork chops tonight. I hope you don't mind."

"I think I can force those down. I'll go wash up."

Ten Minutes Later

The three were at the table eating. Denise opened the conversation. "This food is perfect. I wish I could cook like this."

Richard added, "Thanks for the kind words. I think the success of a good meal is a lot of experience in front of the stove." Richard should have said, 'The secret to a good meal is being able to conjure up what you want when there's no one around to see what you're doing.' He was not about to tell Denise that.

Denise looked at Matt, put up her index finger, "Sarah asked me to remind you the Firmanis are coming over tomorrow night."

Matt's response was, "Oh yes, I remember." Nothing could be further from the truth.

Five-Forty-Five

Matt and Richard left for the theater and they were in their front row seats by six-twenty.

Richard offered to Matt, "All is good and we can do one of our favorites from before. I'm thinking about Metamorphosis."

"Okay, sounds good. Now, my question to you is do you see how difficult it is to come up with new ideas for the shows? Especially ones that we think are great. If you want to stay with some of our better shows for a while, I'm all for it."

Richard smirked, 'We can talk more about this later. I see people are starting to come in. We should get out of sight."

Their show started right at seven-thirty. Matt performed some of his tricks by himself. Twenty minutes later in the show, Richard joined him. They were an hour and fifteen minutes into the show when Richard nodded to Matt indicating that it was time for their last act.

Matt called out to the audience, "Ladies and gentlemen, we have just enough time for one more."

Richard walked away to get out of sight momentarily and he pointed to the monitor to get the video playing.

Richard came back out to the stage and Matt addressed the audience a second time, "Ladies and gentlemen, please look at the screen above. The illusion being performed is called the Metamorphosis. Tonight, we're going to show you our version of this. Sit, back, relax and you're sure to enjoy our version."

The video finished playing and Richard called out to the audience, "Ladies and gentlemen, we need two volunteers to come up here and examine this crate."

Matt picked two members from the audience to come up and help. Richard started, "Please sir, can I get your name?"

The volunteer answered, "John Savio."

Richard continued, "Okay, it's nice to meet you, John. I am Richard and that is Matt over there. John, can you please walk around the crate to ensure it's sturdy? Also, check to make sure there are no false hidden doors."

The volunteer checked all around the crate and offered, "It looks good to me."

Richard replied, "Okay, thank you for your help, John. You may return to your seat."

Richard continued and addressed the other volunteer, "Please be patient Miss. We'll need your help in a minute. But can I get your name first?"

The volunteer responded, "Susan Wall."

Richard opened the crate and stepped into a full-size cloth bag. He said to Susan, "Susan when I crouch down, please close the lid and lock the crate. Hold onto the key and do not lose it."

Susan nodded after she received Richard's instructions. She locked the crate and held the key in her left hand. That's when Matt walked over and said, "Excuse me, Susan, can I see that key?" Before she could say anything, Matt took the key from her and threw it behind them. Matt looked at Susan and said, "We won't be needing that."

Matt continued, "Are you ready? I'm going to stand on top of the crate and you're going to count to three."

Matt stood on top of the crate and Susan counted, "One…two…three." Just then a small puff of smoke a little larger than a football appeared. Matt disappeared and Richard was in his place in a standing position hovering over the crate. Richard's body lowered slowly on top of the crate. He stepped off so he was standing beside Susan.

Richard said to Susan, "I hope you have that key."

Susan replied, "Mr. White took it out of my hand and threw it back there."

"I think you should look in your pocket. Maybe Matt didn't throw it back there like you said he did. Are you sure it's not in there?"

"Here it is. I don't know how that happened. I didn't put it in my pocket."

"Let's try the key. If he's in there, we have to get him out."

Richard and Susan were kneeling in front of the crate. Susan was trying to unlock the crate. That's when Matt walked over and asked, "What are you two doing?"

The audience broke into laughter. Susan opened the crate and six balloons came out of the crate. The balloons had faces on them. The faces were Matt, Susan, and Richard. Susan cried out, "WOW! That was amazing."

Matt looked at Susan and said, "Thank you very much for your help. Please don't go back to your seat yet. Just stay there while we say goodnight to the audience." Matt then called out to the audience, "Ladies and gentlemen, that concludes our show for tonight. We hope you enjoyed tonight's performance. My name is Matt White and this is my good friend and show partner, Richard Jenkins. Please drive safely and have a good night. Matt then said to Susan, "Because you were such a good sport, we want to give you a couple of free passes to another show."

Susan took the passes and said, "Thank you."

Matt spotted John standing, waiting to get out of his row. Matt put up a finger gesturing for John to hold up. He approached John and gave him a couple of free passes.

Matt went back up on the stage and asked Richard, 'Well Mr. Jenkins are you ready to call it a night?"

Richard answered, "Lead the way, Mr. White."

Friday Afternoon

Matt walked into the house a little before four-fifteen. Richard was sitting in the living room. Denise was sitting on the floor with Thomas.

"Hey! What's going on?" Matt asked.

Denise answered, "You're here and that means I get to start my weekend. So, go ahead and get changed if you want so I can start my food shopping."

Matt offered, "Be right back." He went upstairs, took his sport coat off, and changed into some more casual clothing.

Matt came back downstairs a few minutes later and Denise said, "Okay, see you Monday. Oh, and good luck tonight Richard."

Denise left and Matt asked, "Did you tell her about the plan of a mini audience to see your material?"

Richard answered, "Yes, I mentioned that. I hope that's okay."

"Sure, it's fine,"

Five-Fifty

Sarah walked in the door a little before six. Matt greeted her with a kiss and said, "Hey honey."

She returned the kiss to Matt and said, "I have to get upstairs. Al and Jeannie are coming over at six-thirty."

Six-Thirty

Al and Jeannie pulled into Matt's driveway. They went up the front stairs and Richard opened the door for them. Richard said, "Ah, the Firmanis have arrived. Please come in."

Matt walked over and said, "Al, Hi, do not bother taking your coat off. We're going to pick up the food."

Al responded, 'Okay, Matt, do you want me to drive?"

261

"Sure. I want to talk to you about something on the way." Once in the car, Matt brought up, "You know how Richard always provides the entertainment after we're done eating. There will be no card tricks tonight. You're going to see firsthand a new trick that Richard wants to work into the show. Just remember all we want from you is an honest opinion."

"We can give you that, Matt."

Sixty Minutes Later That Evening.

They finished eating their Chinese food and Jeannie said, "Here, let me help clear the table."

Richard added, "Thank you, Jeannie. Please just leave the plates on the kitchen counter. I'll return to the dining room in a minute."

Richard returned to the dining room to give the table a quick wipe. Next, he went into his room and returned carrying a box the size of four pizza boxes stacked on top of each other.

He got Al's attention, "I know you were hoping to see card tricks tonight. That's not going to happen this evening. Tonight, we want you and Jeannie to sit, and listen to what we have planned for a week from Saturday. Please, both of you let me know if you like or dislike the idea."

Jeannie spoke up, "We'll give you an honest opinion."

Richard offered, "Thank you. Now, if you look inside the box, you'll see a couple of toy figures and that's supposed to represent me and Matt. There are also a couple of miniature cages with a tiger inside one of them. My idea is I'm going to have Matt point at the tiger, count to three and then Matt magically changes places with the tiger. Then, I'm going to have a volunteer come up and this time I'll count to three. Then the volunteer changes places with Matt. What do you think?"

Al answered, "I like it."

Jeannie added, "There's just one thing that concerns me. Can the tiger get loose?"

Richard answered, "Of course not."

Jeannie replied, "Then I think this illusion is worthy of being in the show."

262

Richard smiled a little and responded, "Thank you, Jeannie, and thank you, Al. I'll be back in a few minutes."

Richard returned to the dining room. He brought a hot cup of coffee with him and he set his cup down on the table. He said to Al, "I did not plan on this." Richard reached into his coat pocket and pulled out a deck of cards. "Do the four of you mind indulging me?"

Sarah spoke first and answered, "Please make it you three. I need to check on Thomas." Sarah then went upstairs.

Richard continued, "Al, why don't you go first seeing as you're a guest here. Just remove the cards and shuffle them."

Al picked up the box, opened the flap, and let the cards slide out. He started shuffling when Richard spoke up and asked, "Are you forgetting something?"

Richard tapped the box with the cards. Al already emptied the box or so he thought. Al let out, "What the? I took the cards out of here."

Jeannie spoke up, "You did. He's goofing you."

Richard continued, "Okay Al, take the cards and divide them into two even piles. Remove the top card from each pile and show them to us." Al turned over the top card on the left pile and it was the five of diamonds. He then lifted the card off the right pile and it was the eight of clubs.

Richard continued, "Take those two cards and start another pile and put them face down. Then, take the pile on the left and put it face up. Then do the same to the pile on the right. Next, remove the fourth card from the pile on the left and the fifth card down from the pile on the right. Now, show the two cards to everyone here."

Al pulled out the card from the left pile and one from the pile on the right and showed them to the others at the table. The two cards were the five of diamonds and the eight of clubs.

Al gasped, "WHOA! That means the first two cards changed." Al turned over the other two cards which somehow changed into three cards. The new card on the bottom was a little bit smaller than the other cards. The little card had a message with the words, 'NO IT DOESN'T' Al said, "That was good, really good. Someone else should get a turn now."

Richard put his hand up and said, "Jeannie, it looks like you're the volunteer. Don't worry. It will be painless and fun. Are you ready?"

Jeannie answered, "I'm always ready."

"Splendid! Take the same cards your husband was using and give them a good shuffle. Try to do a better job than Al. He had trouble getting the cards out of the box." Richard winked at Al.

Jeannie scooped up the cards and gave them a good shuffle. Richard continued, "Take a card out of the middle; look at it but don't show it to me. Now, put it facedown underneath the napkin. Next, write down on scrap paper the card you put under the napkin. Turn the paper over to make sure I can't see it. I'm just going to pass my hand over the napkin once. Then, I want you to lift the napkin and turn your paper over."

Richard made a pass over the napkin with his right hand. Jeannie turned the paper over and in a surprised tone, she said, "That's not what I wrote down. I wrote down the ten of diamonds. That's the card I placed under the napkin."

Richard added, "Then let's have a look under the napkin." He took away the napkin and the card changed to the seven of hearts. The paper had the seven of hearts written on it.

Jeannie's mouth opened and she yelled, "Whoa! How does a card change that's trapped under a napkin?"

Richard answered, "The solution is simple. It's a fine example of magic. Thank you for letting me show you these card tricks. Unfortunately, it's late and almost my bedtime. It was great seeing both of you. Matt, I will see you in the morning."

Al and Jeannie said good night to Richard. Then Jeannie said to Al, "We should go also. I want to do a couple of errands in the morning and I want to get an early start."

Al responded, "Ready when you are. Matt, thanks for having us, and please tell Sarah we said good night. I hope we can do this again."

Saturday Morning, February 5th

Matt was downstairs at six-thirty-five pouring himself a coffee. Richard was sitting at the table in the corner with his newspaper folded in front of him. Matt greeted Richard first, "Good morning Richard. How are you?"

Richard answered, "Just splendid. There's nothing like a good night's sleep to get your energy level back."

"What are we doing tonight?"

"Matt, you get the same answer I gave you last time you asked me that. Tonight, we're entertaining and we'll be doing it to a sold-out theater. Don't worry. We'll go over the details later. Now is a good time to turn the baby monitor on. Sarah is on her way downstairs."

Matt went into the living room and turned on the monitor. Sarah came downstairs and went straight to the kitchen. She said, "Good morning Matt, good morning Richard."

Matt returned the good morning and gave Sarah a peck on the cheek.

Richard offered, "Good morning Sarah, if you would take a seat in the dining room, I can bring you breakfast."

Sarah responded, "Thank you, Richard. That's so nice of you."

Later On: Around Six-Fifteen

Matt and Richard left for the theater. They parked the van in the garage and they were in their front row seats by six-fifty-five. Matt asked Richard, "What's the plan? You said we had to go over it."

"Correct, I did say that and that is what we'll do. This is what I have planned…"

Ten Minutes Later

The door to the theater opened and the crowd started coming in. "We better get out of sight," came from Richard.

Their show started at exactly seven-thirty. Matt and Richard did some of their best illusions together. It was eight-thirty-five and Richard pointed to Matt letting him know it was time for the announcement. Matt called out to the audience, "Ladies and gentlemen, we have time for just one more. We need assistance from one volunteer. Richard walked down the stairs off the stage and picked the volunteer. He asked a woman, "What is your name?"

The volunteer answered, "Donna Walton."

Richard continued, "Okay Donna, I need you to verify that Matt is in the straitjacket and it is nice and snug." Donna walked around Matt and checked all the buckles in the back. Next, a cable was lowered from the ceiling and attached to the back of Matt's jacket. Another cable was tied around his feet. The cables from the ceiling started pulling and created tension. Richard pointed to the right and two assistants brought out a trampoline.

The cable became tauter and started pulling Matt up in the air. Richard addressed the audience, "Ladies and gentlemen, you are about to witness my partner dangle upside down while in the straitjacket. It is Matt's job to escape and free himself in under twenty seconds." A digital timer was lowered from the ceiling and hung six feet to the left of Matt. The clock started counting, One...two...three. Matt hung there and tried to free himself from the jacket. He remembered what Richard told him to do for the water tank trick. This was not an option.

Then, he heard Richard's voice in his head saying, 'Matt, try to stiffen your fingers on both of your hands. Then, you'll be able to pull the jacket over your head.' Matt stiffened his fingers and pulled out his arms as fast as he could. He let himself fall on the trampoline and then crawled to the edge. Matt lowered himself off the trampoline and onto the stage. The audience clapped for almost five minutes. Matt took a bow and then pointed to Richard who did the same.

Matt walked over to Donna and said, "Don't go back to your seat yet. We need to say good night to the audience."

Matt called out to the audience, "Ladies and gentlemen, that concludes our show for tonight. We hope you liked what you saw. My name is Matt White and this is my good friend and show partner, Richard Jenkins. Please drive safely and have a good night."

Next, Matt motioned for Donna to come back over. He said to her, "Donna, thank you for helping us. I want to give you a couple of free passes to another show."

Donna put her hand out, took the passes, and replied, "Thank you." Then she walked off the stage.

Matt asked Richard, "Mr. Jenkins, are you ready to call it a night?"

"Just lead the way, Mr. White."

Sunday Morning, February 6th

Matt came downstairs at six-thirty-five and poured himself a coffee. Richard was not in the kitchen and that was so unlike him. Matt walked into the living room and there was Richard just looking out the window.

Matt said, "Hey! Good morning. I didn't expect to see you here."

Richard offered, "Good morning Matthew. Just looking out the window here and thinking about the warm weather coming. Of course, it's still a couple of months away."

"Yeah before you know it, we'll be on a plane on our way to Las Vegas. That's going to be a good time."

Richard added, "Yes, it will be. Turn on the baby monitor. The door is about to open upstairs."

Just as Richard predicted the door opened upstairs as Matt was turning on the monitor. Sarah came down and went straight to the kitchen. She called in, "Hello?"

Matt went into the kitchen and said, "Good morning honey. You walked right by us. We were in the living room." Matt leaned in and kissed her on the cheek.

Sarah returned the kiss and said, "Good morning honey."

Richard was right behind Matt and asked Sarah, "Are you ready for breakfast to start your day?"

She answered, "Thank you, Richard. Sarah went into the dining room and sat down at the table.

Matt followed Sarah and sat at the end of the table next to her. He set down his coffee, got up, and went to get the baby monitor. Matt was one step from the doorway when the door opened and Richard was handing him the monitor. Richard said, "Don't sit yet. I'll pass you the highchair."

A few minutes later Richard brought in a plate of eggs and toast for Sarah. Matt stood up to get himself more coffee. Before he got to the kitchen sounds from Thomas came from the monitor. Matt said, "I'll be back in a few."

Richard came back to the dining room and left a glass of grapefruit juice at Sarah's plate. He grabbed Matt's coffee mug from the table.

Matt came downstairs carrying Thomas and placed him in the highchair. Richard carried in Thomas's food tray and Matt said, "Thank you."

Richard replied, "You're welcome. Matt, can I get you more coffee?"

Matt was feeding Thomas his breakfast, looked at Richard, and answered, "That'll be great, thanks."

Richard brought in a cup of coffee for Matt. Matt was still feeding Thomas and Sarah asked, "How did it go last night?"

Matt answered, "It went very well. We tried something new and the audience loved it."

"Something new?" Do you mind sharing?"

"Oh, I was put in a straitjacket, hung upside down and I had to get out of it."

"You were hanging upside down?" asked Sarah.

"Yeah, but there was a trampoline below for me to land on when I freed myself from the straitjacket."

"I'm thinking about this. I think that sounds dangerous. Do I need to have another discussion with Richard?"

Just then the dining-room door opened and Richard said to Sarah, "It's perfectly safe. Please believe me, I'm not going to let anything happen to your husband."

Richard pulled out a chair and sat down as he was talking. He continued, "You have my word on this. Now, I believe you were about to tell Matt about the list you have started for Albertson's."

"Yes, that's right." As soon as the words left Sarah's lips, she thought to herself, 'How did he know that?"

Matt and Richard were off to Albertson's by eight-forty-five. Once in the store, Matt grabbed a carriage and they navigated their way through the aisles. Matt asked Richard, "Do you think you put Sarah's mind at ease? She seemed nervous when I told her what we did last night."

Richard answered, "I hope I gave her some reassurance. Sarah needs to understand I just can't have you on stage pulling a rabbit out of your hat. Well, you can do that, but that's not going to achieve our goal. Our goal is to entertain and get the audience to tell friends and family about the show."

"I agree with you there. She just gets nervous and overprotective of me."

They finished their food shopping and, on the way back Richard said, "I tried to tell Sarah before I would never let anything happen to you. If I thought there was a chance something bad was going to happen, I'd be sure to intervene." They were home a few minutes later. Matt carried the groceries inside and Richard put the items away."

Four Days Later: Thursday, February 10th

Matt walked into the house at four-twenty. Denise was sitting on the living room floor with her back against one of the wing chairs. She had Thomas beside her.

Matt saw her and said, "Hey!"

Denise responded, "Hey yourself. I think we're having cheeseburgers tonight."

"Oh good. How was Thomas today?"

"He was great. I put him down a little after twelve and he napped for two hours. This job is getting easier by the day."

Matt was taking off his jacket while Denise was talking and he replied, "Don't say that too often. We'll pay you less. Just kidding."

Matt and Richard left for the theater a little after six-twenty. They were in the front row talking. Richard asked Matt, "Are you satisfied with the way things are progressing?"

Matt returned with a question to Richard, "How do you mean?"

"Do you ever wish you had a bigger theater to perform? Do you ever wish you weren't teaching and doing the magic full time?"

"Oh sure, I would love it if the theater was bigger. As for doing magic full time, that's not something I want. I'm sorry if that answer disappoints you."

"It's not so disappointing. It would have been better if the answer was different. I was hoping you'd say not give up teaching which you did but maybe teach less and then squeeze in more performances."

"What's the plan for tonight?"

"We're entertaining tonight. This is what we're going to do…"

Richard took a few minutes and gave Matt the lowdown. He looked over his shoulder and saw the door open in the back. He said, "We need to get out of sight."

The show started right at seven-thirty. Matt performed a couple of simple card tricks with the cameraman right at his side. Next, Richard joined Matt and they presented some of their illusions together. An hour and fifteen minutes went by and Richard signaled to Matt by giving him the nod. It was time for the grand finale. Matt called out to the audience and made the announcement, "Ladies and gentlemen, we have time for just one more. We also need help from one individual."

About a dozen people in the audience raised a hand. Matt continued, "I forgot to mention our volunteer cannot be afraid of knives." Half of the hands in the audience went down. Matt walked back and forth. He selected a gentleman from the ninth row on the left side of the audience.

Matt called out, "Please, sir can you join us up on stage?"

The volunteer made his way out to the center and went up the stairs onto the stage. Matt asked the volunteer, "Can we get your name, sir?"

The volunteer answered, "Jason Reynolds."

"Okay, Jason, it's nice to meet you. My name is Matt and over there is my partner, Richard. You'll be working with him."

Jason walked over to Richard. Richard said, "Jason you'll see we have a table here with six very sharp knives. They're so sharp, they're dangerous. Here, you can hold one of them for a second. Now take the knife and strike the paper with it." Jason made a striking down motion with the knife and it split like it was cutting through the air.

Richard continued, "Next we'll have Mr. White stand up against the target, I mean the wall over there."

Richard escorted Matt to the spot. Matt asked quietly, "Are you sure this will work?"

Richard whispered, "I think so but don't worry about it. I'm not."

Richard continued, "Next Jason I'm going to throw a knife at the wall where Matt is standing. Then, you'll throw one." Richard took the biggest knife there and threw it in Matt's direction. The knife stuck in the wall just half an inch to Matt's left side.

Richard continued, "Okay, Jason, it's your turn."

Jason nervously spoke up, "Maybe I shouldn't have come up. My arm is not that great for throwing. What if I miss and hit Matt?"

"Good point, good point, let me see, Matt, do you have health insurance?"

Matt answered loud enough for the audience to hear, "Yes, I do through my work."

Richard continued, "Okay, Jason, you see there is nothing to worry about. Go ahead and fire away."

Jason reached down and his hand was still trembling. Richard put his hand on the underside of Jason's forearm. He said, "Relax, you'll do fine."

Jason threw the knife as hard as he could. The knife left Jason's hand and ended up in the curtain.

Richard asked, "Do we have a seamstress in the audience? I see the problem here, Jason. It's the inadequate lighting we have. Let's try this. Try these glasses on and things should clear up."

Jason took the glasses, put them on, and said "WOW! You're right. These make everything more visible."

Next, Richard took one of the remaining four knives and threw it as hard as he could at the wall. This time the knife landed an inch away from Matt's shoulder.

Richard said to Jason, "Okay Jason, you're up" Jason looked down at the knives, picked one up, and aimed it at the wall. This time Jason's knife landed right between Matt's legs.

Matt looked down and thought to himself, 'It's a good thing I don't wear baggy pants.'

Richard continued, "Okay Jason it looks like you have the hang of it. Why don't you take your next throw and I will throw the last knife?"

Jason said, "Okay, he grabbed a third knife, aimed at the wall, and threw it as hard as he could. The knife landed a half-inch from Matt's right ear. Matt gulped and closed his eyes.

It was Richard's turn for the last throw. "I will throw the last knife. Let's see how good my aim is. Richard threw the knife and the four knives in the wall reacted like they were being drawn in the opposite direction. Jason panicked and moved twelve inches to the right and Richard moved to the opposite side. All four knives landed on the table where they started. Jason stood there with his mouth open in disbelief.

Matt stepped away from the wall. The audience was clapping. Matt thought to himself, 'This was too over the top. We talked about this.' Matt put his hands up to recognize the audience and walked towards Jason. He shook Jason's hand and said, "Thank you for your help. Your aim is right on target. Please stay up here while we say goodnight to the audience."

Matt called out to the audience, "Ladies and gentlemen that concludes our show for tonight. We hope you enjoyed the show. My name is Matt White. This is my good friend and show partner, Richard Jenkins. Please drive safely and have a good night."

Next Matt walked over to Jason and said, "Thank you for being a good sport. I want to give you a couple of free passes to another show. Oh, and Richard needs his glasses back."

Jason took the passes, handed Matt back the glasses, and replied, "Thank you." He then walked off the stage and left.

Matt looked at Richard and asked, "Well Mr. Jenkins, are you ready to call it a night?"

"I most certainly am. Lead the way, Mr. White."

Two Days Later: Saturday, February 12th

Matt was in the kitchen by six-thirty-five drinking coffee with Richard. Richard was talking to Matt.

He mentioned, "We're all set for tonight. As I recall tonight's finale has already been approved by Al and Jeannie. This should, I mean will be a good night."

Matt was holding his coffee and nodded in agreement. He went into the living room and turned on the baby monitor. Matt returned to the kitchen and acknowledged Richard's statement, "You had a great idea by having someone listen to your plan ahead of time,"

"This will work to our advantage. For example, we can do it when the Gilhoolys come over on Friday."

"The Gilhoolys, Friday?"

"Yes. Richard pointed in the direction of upstairs. You'll see."

The bedroom door opened upstairs and Sarah came down. She went straight to the kitchen. Matt and Richard were both standing there and Matt said, "Good morning honey," and he kissed her on the cheek.

Sarah added, "Good morning Matt," and she returned the kiss to her husband. "Good morning Richard."

"Good morning Sarah. You should have a seat in the other room and I'll bring you breakfast."

Sarah went into the dining room. Matt brought in the highchair and monitor.

He said, "Just getting ready."

Matt heard sounds coming from the baby monitor and knew that was his cue to fetch Thomas. He went upstairs and took him out of the crib, changed his diaper, and then brought him down to the dining room. Matt started feeding Thomas.

Sarah was sitting beside Matt and spoke up, "I think I'll call Karen tonight and invite her and Jim over for next Friday. What do you think?"

"Oh yeah, that sounds great." Matt suddenly had a flashback of part of the conversation he had with Richard earlier. He added, "We haven't seen them in a while. It'll be good to get together."

Later On, that Evening: Six-Fifteen

Matt said to Sarah, "Honey, we're going to head out now. We should be home by ten-fifteen."

Sarah offered, "Okay honey, good luck."

273

Matt and Richard were in the theater by six-thirty-five. They were sitting in the front row. Richard spoke first, "Just think only two more Saturday evening shows after this one."

Matt added, "I'm just looking forward to the warmer weather. It can't get here fast enough for me."

"As I recall, I made an offer to make things more comfortable or tolerable. But I was told to let Mother Nature take its course."

"Yes, and it was so nice of you to listen. That's sarcasm by the way. Oh, here comes the crowd. Let's get out of here."

The show started right at seven-thirty. Matt and Richard performed together for the first twenty minutes. Then Matt came down to the floor and showed the audience a few card tricks with the cameraman close behind him. Next, Richard came out to the center of the stage and showed the audience a couple of small illusions.

One of the illusions he made a vase of flowers disappear and then reappear in a different location. In another one of his illusions, he brought out a wooden table and then addressed the audience, "Ladies and gentlemen, this is no ordinary table. It's been used in numerous seances. At times there is no controlling it." Richard waved his finger; the table went in the air almost two feet and turned around.

It continued rotating five times and then stopped. Spectators from the audience tried as hard as they could to see any fishing lines or wires for controlling the table. They were unsuccessful and the reason is there wasn't any. The audience clapped after the table was lowered back down. Richard put his arm out and Matt came out to join him.

Matt made an announcement, "Ladies and gentlemen we have just enough time for one more. We're going to need help from one volunteer." Matt walked down the stairs and selected a woman from the tenth row. Matt asked, "Miss, do you want to come up and help us?"

The woman answered, "Sure!" and followed Matt on to the stage.

Once on the stage, Matt asked, "Can I get your name?"

The volunteer answered, "Michelle O'Neil."

Matt continued, "Okay Michelle, it's nice to meet you. That is my partner Richard over there. Both of us must follow his instructions to the letter."

274

The curtain opened and there were two large animal cages on the stage. One of the cages was empty and the other one contained a tiger pacing back and forth. Richard started, "Okay Michelle first I'm going to have Mr. White escort you up the stairs of the cage so you can see it's empty." Matt put out his arm, Michelle went up the stairs first and Matt was right behind her.

At the top of the stairs, Michelle turned and said, "It's empty."

Both of them came back down the stairs. Richard called out to the audience, "Ladies and gentlemen, you're about to witness what I refer to as a double transformation. Please keep your eyes on the tiger." Richard pointed at the tiger with his left hand. The tiger disappeared and reappeared in the other cage. Matt also disappeared and reappeared in the cage the tiger was originally in. Richard said, "One more time." He pointed again and this time the tiger went back to his original cage. Matt vanished and reappeared along with Michelle in the other cage.

Michelle was in the cage next to Matt and she screamed, "OMG! What's happening?"

Matt answered quietly, "Don't worry. It's almost over." One of the stagehands came over to the cage and pulled the door open for them. Matt helped Michelle down the stairs.

Matt asked Michelle, "Are you alright?"

She answered, "A little shaken up but I'll survive. That was scary. I didn't know that was going to happen."

Matt added, "That makes two of us. But, wait here a minute while we say goodnight to the audience."

Matt once again called out to the audience, "Ladies and gentlemen, that concludes our show for tonight. We hope you liked what you saw. My name is Matt White. This is my good friend and show partner, Richard Jenkins. Please drive safely and have a good night."

Next, Matt turned to Michelle and said, "Thank you for your help and being such a good sport. We want to give you a couple of free passes to another show."

Michelle took the envelope with the passes and said, "Thank you, it was fun but a little scary. She went down the stairs and left the theater."

Matt asked, "Well Mr. Jenkins, are you ready to call it a night?"

"Absolutely! Lead the way, Mr. White."

Five Days Later: Thursday, February 17th

Matt was home by four-fifteen. He went past the living room and went straight to the kitchen. Matt did not announce he was home. That was totally out of his routine. He was oblivious to Denise waving to him. She was sitting on the living room floor playing with Thomas.

Matt did not see Richard in the kitchen. He walked back towards the living room and he heard Richard saying, "In here Matt." Richard was sitting at the dining room table with his journal open in front of him.

Matt said to him, "There you are. What's going on?"

Richard answered, "Just making sure my book is up to date. I'll be done in a minute. Then, I'll start on dinner."

Six-Fifteen

Matt and Richard left for the theater. They put the van in the garage and were sitting in the front row by six-forty. Matt asked, "What do you have planned for tonight?"

Richard answered, "This is what we're doing…"

Richard finished explaining the details of the grand finale. He looked up and saw the theater door open and said, "We need to make ourselves scarce."

The show started right at seven-thirty. Matt and Richard performed their illusions perfectly. It was almost eight-forty and Richard nodded to Matt. He used this signal to let Matt know it was time to start the last act.

Matt announced to the audience, "Ladies and gentlemen, we have just enough time for one more. We're going to need the help from one volunteer."

About fifteen people raised their hands to come up. Matt walked off the stage and picked a woman from the tenth row in the middle.

Matt asked the volunteer, "Okay, Miss can you come up and give us a hand? The volunteer followed Matt onto the stage. Matt asked her, "Can I get your name?"

She answered, "Wendy Lewis."

Matt responded, "Okay, Wendy, I'm putting you in the charge of my partner Richard. He will be giving the instructions."

Richard spoke up and said, "Okay Wendy, I want you to look directly at the front row. Take note there are twelve people there, six men and six women. I need you to take this pen and paper and write down three different seat numbers. Do not show me what your choices are. I am going to close my eyes. Also, please let the cameraman get a view of your paper so the audience can see it on the monitor."

Richard had his eyes closed while Wendy put her selections on the pad. Richard continued, "Wendy, I hope you're ready. You wrote down 5,8, and 11."

Wendy smiled and said, "That's right."

Richard again continued, "Now we need the people from seats five, eight, and eleven to join us on stage."

A woman from seat five stood and asked Richard, "What are we going to do?"

He answered, "You three are going to help entertain the audience. You have nothing to worry about. That is, I don't think anything will go wrong."

Matt jumped in and explained, "Please that's Richard's weak attempt at humor. Come on up. It'll be fun."

The three volunteers were on stage and Matt said, "Okay, one at a time, can we get your names?"

The first volunteer spoke up and said, "Sharon Davenport."

Matt replied, "Okay Sharon, I am Matt and that is Richard over there. It's nice to meet you. Could you go stand next to Wendy over there? Richard will be telling you what to do."

Matt pointed to the second volunteer and asked, "Can we get your name, sir?"

The man answered, "Mike Dupont."

Matt nodded and said, "Okay Mike I am Matt and that is Richard over there. Could you go stand next to Sharon and Wendy over there?"

Matt continued, "Okay we have a third volunteer and your name is?"

The volunteer answered, "Denise Tremblay."

Matt added, "Okay Denise, it's nice to meet you. Could you please stand next to the other three over there? I'll be leaving you four in the hands of Richard."

Richard took over and said, "Wendy could you please wait next to Matt. Okay Denise, Mike, and Sharon, I have a question for the three of you. Have any of you been to Las Vegas?"

Denise and Sharon both said, "No."

Mike answered, "The same goes for me."

Richard continued, "That can all change tonight."

Matt was getting nervous and he was thinking to himself, 'Please not so over the top.'

Then Richard's voice came into Matt's head, 'Matthew, relax, I have this under control."

Richard again continued with the three volunteers. "Okay, I have in my coat pocket six index cards. Each one of them has written on the back the names of different areas on the Las Vegas Strip. I'm going to take the cards out of my pocket and I want each of you to select a card. Please do not show me the information on the card."

Denise, Mike, and Sharon each picked a card from Richard's hand. At his request, they kept the information to themselves. Richard again continued, "Okay, we'll start with Denise. Denise, I believe you picked seeing the water fountains in front of the Bellagio."

Denise smiled and said, "WOW! That's right."

Richard again continued, "I hope you're ready. Please bring back a souvenir."

Denise tried to ask, "Ready for what?" Richard was already swinging his arm upward and extending his hand. Denise vanished and she was gone. A low rumbling sound could be heard from the audience.

Richard looked in Mike's direction and started, "Mike, I believe your card had to stand in front of the Statue of Liberty on the corner of West Tropicana Ave and Las Vegas Boulevard South."

Mike smiled and responded, "You got it!"

Richard asked, "Are you ready? Just like I told Denise to bring back a souvenir." Richard waved his arm and Mike disappeared.

There was one more person on the stage. Richard looked at Sharon and said, "Sharon, you picked the card that says standing in front of the Mirage Volcano."

Sharon smiled and replied, "That's right."

Richard nodded and said, "Get ready. Just like I mentioned to Denise and Mike, please bring back a souvenir." Richard waved his arm and swished his hand to the right. Sharon disappeared.

Next, Richard took this quiet opportunity to address the audience. "Ladies and gentlemen, you just witnessed something that has never been done before. Three individuals have been sent out to another location seventeen hundred miles away. I am going to bring back our three volunteers in five minutes. This illusion is not something with smoke and mirrors. I assure you tonight you have not been bamboozled. Now, I'm going to count to three and our travelers will return in the order they left. One...two...three."

Denise appeared on the stage. She was holding a travel coffee mug with Bellagio's name on it. Next, Mike returned to the stage and he was holding a dark blue t-shirt with the letters NYFD on it. Last but not least Sharon appeared on stage and she was holding a wine glass with the Mirage name on it.

The audience stood up and started clapping after Sharon appeared on the stage. Richard took a half bow and put his hand out gesturing for Matt to return to the stage. Matt stood beside Richard and said quietly, "You stole the show."

Richard responded, "I don't see it that way and I didn't steal anything. I just helped us. It's time to say goodnight to the audience."

Matt focused his attention on the four volunteers, "Could you please wait here a minute? We need to say goodnight to the audience." He then called out to the audience, "Ladies and gentlemen, that concludes our show for tonight. My name is Matt White and this is my very good friend and show partner, Richard Jenkins. Please drive safely and have a good night."

Matt then walked over to the four helpers and said to them, "Thank you very much for helping. I want to give each of you a couple of free passes to another show.

Matt reached into his pocket and pulled out four envelopes and handed one to Denise, Mike, Sharon, and Wendy. They took the envelopes and said, "Thank you," and then walked off the stage.

Matt looked at Richard and asked, "Mr. Jenkins, are you ready to call it a night?"

"Lead the way, Mr. White."

Two Days Later: Saturday, February 19th

Saturday morning started like any other. Matt came downstairs around six-thirty to get coffee. Richard was in his usual spot reading his newspaper. Matt greeted Richard first, "Good morning Richard. How are you?"

Richard replied, "Good morning Matt. I am well this morning. I already know what you're going to comment on. Please, at no time last night did I consider things going over the top. I believe the audience liked what they saw last night. Isn't that the subject of importance and our goal?"

"Yes, you're right about that."

"I know I am and here's something else I know Sarah will open the door in one…two…three." The bedroom door opened upstairs.

Matt heard the doorknob when it clicked and spouted, "Of course!"

Sarah came downstairs at seven o'clock. She said, "Good morning honey" to Matt and kissed him on the cheek. She then greeted Richard with, "Good morning Richard."

Richard returned, "Good morning Sarah. Please take a seat in the dining room when you're ready. Matt is on his way to retrieve Thomas. I'll bring in the highchair."

Matt quipped, "I am?" Soon as Matt let that out Thomas was crying upstairs. He went upstairs, took Thomas out of the crib, and put a fresh diaper on him. Then, he brought him downstairs and sat him in the highchair next to Sarah.

Next, Matt went into the kitchen to get food for Thomas. Richard was in there putting food on a plate for Sarah. He asked Matt, "Can I get something for you? The stove is still hot."

Matt answered, "No thank you. I'll be good with just more coffee."

"Very well," came from Richard.

Matt went into the dining room, sat at the end, and started feeding Thomas. Richard came in right behind him and put a plate down in front of Sarah and a coffee for Matt.

Matt replied, "Thank you for the coffee."

Sarah was eating and started the conversation, "So, am I thinking this right? You only have two more Saturday evening shows to go including tonight."

Matt commented, "That's right."

Richard walked in and he said, "If there's nothing else, I'm going to tidy up in the kitchen."

"All set here," came from Matt.

Sarah asked Matt, "Are you getting tired from doing these shows?"

"It's hard to describe the feeling. I'm wiped out at the end of the night. There's no denying that. But when I'm on stage with Richard I can feel a surge of energy going through my body."

"Do you think that is Richard's doing?"

"Why would you think that?" Matt knew she was right but was not going to admit it.

"Because he likes doing this more than you do. You told me before he said he can't do this without you. I think he can. He just doesn't want to."

"I know one thing for sure. I'm looking forward to warmer weather. I was freezing walking from the theater to the garage. That is not a long walk."

"Well, here's something to look forward to. We have eight more weeks and we'll be on our way to Las Vegas. The time will go by before you know it."

Later That Evening: Around Six-Fifteen

Matt found Sarah in the living room and asked, "Are you going to be okay tonight?"

Sarah answered, "Of course, I only have two more Saturday nights without you. I think I'll give Denise a call after you leave to catch up and see what she's up to."

"Okay, we're going to head out. We should be back by ten-thirty." Matt leaned into the chair and kissed Sarah goodbye.

Matt and Richard left for the theater at six-twenty. They were sitting in the front row by six-forty. Matt asked Richard, "So, what's the plan for tonight?"

Richard answered, "The plan is the same as always. We're here to entertain and give the audience a good show. That's what we're going to do. This is the plan…"

Richard just finished his explanation and the theater door opened. The audience started coming in. Matt said, "We should get out of sight."

The show started promptly at seven-thirty. Matt performed a couple of small illusions by himself. Richard joined him on stage twenty minutes into the show. They worked on a couple of illusions together. It was almost eight-forty-five and Richard nodded to Matt. That was Richard's way of letting him know it was time for the last act.

Matt announced to the audience, "Ladies and gentlemen we have just enough time for one more. We're going to need help from two volunteers. Oh, and please not to worry, It's perfectly safe up here."

Matt walked down to the floor and looked around for volunteers. He chose someone from the fourth row in the middle section and then someone from the seventeenth row on the left-hand side. Matt had the two volunteers follow him up on stage.

Once the three of them were up there, Matt asked the first volunteer, "Can I get your name, sir?"

The volunteer answered, "Dave LeBlanc."

Matt responded, "Okay Dave, please stand right here for a minute. We need to get the other volunteer's name."

Matt pointed at the woman and said, "You're next."

She replied, "Linda Costigan. What are we doing up here?"

Matt pointed at Richard and answered, "Whatever he tells us to do. He's in charge."

Richard started and said to the audience, "Ladies and gentlemen, "I call this my rendition of the Transformation. Sit back, relax, and get ready to be WOWED."

Richard proceeded, "Okay, I need Dave to examine these two wooden crates. You can step inside and bang on the walls."

Dave walked inside the crates and banged on the walls just as he was invited to. He said, "They appear to be sound and sturdy to me."

Richard continued, "Now, I need Mr. White to step in one of the crates. Linda, you decide which crate you want Matt to go in."

Linda looked at both of them and decided, "Matt should go in the left one."

Richard added, "Matt, you heard Linda., Please step inside the left crate."

Matt stepped inside the crate on the left. Richard had Dave closed the door and then a net was lowered over the crate. Richard reached into his coat pocket and pulled out his black telescoping wand and said, "I'm just going to tap the side of the crate and we'll see what happens." Richard tapped the crate with the wand making sure he was striking through the holes in the net.

Richard again continued, "Can you two help me lift the net off the crate?"

The three of them lifted the net off the crate and Richard had Linda open the door. Matt was not inside. Linda said, "He's not in here. Where did he go?"

Dave was standing in the doorway of the crate looking in. Linda was right behind him and Richard was standing beside her. Just then, the door to the other crate opened and Matt stepped out. He walked over to where the other three were standing and asked, "What are you looking for?"

Linda answered quickly, "You!"

The audience laughed. Richard put his hand up in an attempt to control the crowd. Richard continued, "Please, let's try this again. Matt, I need you and Dave to step in the crate on the right. Linda, I want you to go step in the crate on the left. I will close the door for you. Okay, just like before I'm going to tap on the crate so Linda does not be alarmed from the knocking sounds." Richard tapped on the crate and said, "Oh sorry, I forgot something, the mystery smoke."

Richard pointed with his left index finger and a small amount of smoke appeared.

Richard continued, "Okay, let's check the crates." Richard opened the crate on the left and Dave stepped out. Next, he opened the door to the other crate and Linda stepped out. Richard said, "Ah, that's the switch we were looking for. Wait a minute. Dave, didn't Matt go in the same crate as you?"

Dave answered, "Yes, he did."

Richard continued, "This is not good. It appears we lost a show partner."

Then a voice was heard from the center aisle. "No, you didn't. I'm right here." Matt started walking up towards the stage and the audience was clapping.

Once on the stage, he said to Dave and Linda, "We have to say goodnight to the audience but stick around. I have something for you."

Matt called out to the audience, "Ladies and gentlemen, that concludes our show for tonight. We hope you enjoyed the show. My name is Matt White. This is my very good friend and show partner, Richard Jenkins. Please drive safely and have a good night."

Matt then addressed Dave and Linda, "Thank you for your help tonight. I want to give you a couple of free passes to another show for being good sports and helping out."

Dave put his hand out and took both envelopes and handed one to Linda. The two of them said thank you and left the theater.

Matt asked Richard, "Mr. Jenkins, are you ready to call it a night?'

Richard answered, 'Ready when you are Matt."

The Next Morning: Sunday, February 20th

Matt came downstairs at six-forty-five to grab a coffee and start his day. Richard was sitting at the table in the corner with his newspaper folded in front of him.

Richard greeted Matt first, "Good morning Matthew, I hope you slept well."

"Oh yes, I sure did. Okay, what's the first prediction of the day? I bet you can't give me three."

"First of all, that is not a challenge for me. Number one: Sarah will be downstairs at 7:05. Number two: Sarah will bring up us going to Albertson's. Number three: She'll have nine things written on a list. As a bonus, number four: Sarah is going to tell you she invited Denise over for Friday night. She will bring Tom. By the way that works for me. We can have them give us an opinion on a private showing."

"Oh, good, you have something new you want to show them?"

"I'm working on it and I'll have it ready for them."

Seven-O-Three

The bedroom door opened upstairs and Sarah came down. She said, "Good morning Matt. Good morning Richard." Sarah kissed Matt on the cheek.

Matt replied, "Good morning honey," and returned the kiss.

Richard pointed at the kitchen clock. Matt said, "I know, I know."

Richard once again suggested, "Sarah, please have a seat in the dining room and I'll bring breakfast to you."

Sarah responded, "Thank you, Richard." Then she asked, "Oh, do you two have a trip planned to Albertson's? I have a list of nine things that I know we need."

Richard answered, "I believe that's part of the morning agenda."

Just then, there were sounds coming from the baby monitor. Matt spoke and said, "I'll get him."

Richard looked at Matt as he was walking away. He caught Matt's attention and held up two fingers and then three fingers. Matt gave Richard a thumbs up on his way up the stairs. He went into Thomas's room and took him out of the crib.

Matt came back downstairs and put Thomas in the highchair. The highchair was already placed beside Sarah. Matt started feeding Thomas and Sarah brought up, "Matt, before I forget, Denise is coming over Friday night. She's going to ask Tom so the four of us can get together."

"Of course!"

"What's wrong? Do you not want them to come over?"

"No, it's fine. Sorry, my mind was somewhere else."

The dining-room door opened and Richard asked, "Matt, can I get you a refill on your coffee? Oh, and are we good with number four?"

"Yes, and yes, Mr. Smarty-pants."

Sarah asked, "What's that about? "

"It appears we have a descendant of Nostradamus living with us. I asked Richard to make three predictions this morning. That wasn't good enough for him. He made four."

Eight-Fifty-Five

Matt and Richard took Matt's van to the supermarket. Once in the store, Matt grabbed a carriage from the coral. The two of them started the task of filling the carriage with necessary items. Matt asked Richard, "Did Sarah give you the list?"

"Yes, she did, and by the way that list is unnecessary writing on Sarah's part. You can tell her I said that. Uh, maybe better not. That will open up a floodgate of questions if you know what I mean."

They went through the checkout and then Matt loaded the bags in the back of the van. Matt pulled into the driveway and Richard suggested, "If you carry the bags in, I'll put away the groceries."

Matt replied, "Okay, let me get my key out."

Richard pointed at the door and it opened. He asked, "Key for what?"

Four Days Later: Thursday, February 24th

Matt arrived home at ten minutes after four. He called in, "Denise, Richard, I'm home."

Denise was sitting on the floor keeping Thomas entertained. Matt found Richard in the kitchen. Richard greeted Matt, "Hello Mr. White, I trust you had a good day at school. I have lasagna made up for us. It will be ready in ten minutes."

Matt looked around as if conducting a quick inspection. He found no traces of what he was looking for. Matt said to Richard, "I'll be back in a few minutes. I want to get cleaned up."

"Got it."

On the way upstairs Matt thought to himself, 'Is Richard conjuring up meals? It wouldn't be a good idea with Denise here.'

Matt was back downstairs a few minutes later. He went into the kitchen and Richard said, "You're just in time."

Richard handed Matt a large bowl with a garden salad in it. Matt placed the bowl on the table and returned to the kitchen. Richard then handed him three salad bowls and two bottles of salad dressing. On the last trip to the kitchen, Matt carried in the lasagna and set it on an oversized trivet on the table.

Three Minutes Later

Denise, Matt, and Richard were at the table eating dinner. Matt started the conversation, "Denise, Sarah told me you and possibly Tom will be joining us tomorrow night. Just to let you know, you're in for a treat."

"A treat?"

Richard hopped in the conversation, 'Yes, Denise, I have this idea for when the Whites have friends over, we can show them a sample of what we have in the works. This is just to get an opinion. We might not use it if it's not well received."

Denise asked, "So, what are you going to show us?"

"I can't reveal that to you now. I don't want you to form an opinion before you see the whole thing. You'll just have to be patient."

"Okay," replied Denise.

Six-Fifteen

Matt and Richard left for the theater. They pulled in the garage and they were both seated in the front row by six-forty. Matt started the conversation off and asked, "What are we doing tonight?"

Richard answered, "I'm glad you asked that Matt. Tonight is going to be big. I want to show this to Denise and Tom tomorrow. I know that's the opposite of my idea. But I'm sure this will be a big hit. This is what we're going to do…"

287

Their show began at exactly seven-thirty. Matt did some small illusions including card tricks. He had Richard join him twenty minutes later. The two of them performed some acts together. It was almost eight-forty-five and Richard gave Matt a nod signaling it was time to start the grand finale.

Matt called out to the audience and made the announcement, "Ladies and gentlemen, we have just enough time for one more. We need help from five and it would make things a lot easier if we could get four people seated side by side. "

Matt walked down to the floor and selected a woman from the sixth row. He asked her, "Miss, would you like to come up here on the stage and lend a hand?" The volunteer stepped out of the row. Matt asked her, "Can I get your name?"

She answered, "Debbie Mahoney."

Matt said, "Debbie, it's nice to meet you. I am Matt and this is my partner, Richard. I need you to pick the other four volunteers."

Debbie scanned the audience and she saw a group of four in different sections. Debbie picked four people from the tenth row on the left side of the audience. Matt said, "Thank you, Debbie. Okay, Richard will now be giving the instructions."

Debbie looked at Richard, smiled, and said, "Okay."

Richard proceeded, "First off, it's a pleasure to meet you, Debbie." He then called out to the audience. "Ladies and gentlemen, what you're about to see tonight is nothing short of amazing. Oh, and thank you to our four volunteers out there. Excuse me, are you all related?" Richard already knew they were. He thought by playing dumb to not knowing makes the act look more authentic.

The oldest of the group yelled out, "Yes. My name is John; this is my wife Cindy, and these are our two sons, Rob and Mike."

Richard called out, "Very good. Can we get your last name?" This was more information Richard asked needlessly.

The father answered, "O'Donnell."

"Splendid! We have the O'Donnell family in the audience. You might be sorry you raised your hands."

"What?"

"Oh, nothing." Richard continued, "Okay Debbie, I need you to pick a different row number and it can be from any section. You're

288

also going to pick four-seat numbers. They should be in a consecutive sequence."

Debbie asked, "What does consecutive sequence mean?"

Matt hopped in and answered, "It just means when you list numbers, they should be in a series one after another. Don't mind Richard; he's just trying to show off his vocabulary."

Debbie replied, "I got it, thanks."

Richard put his hand up before Debbie revealed her numbers. He said, "Please don't tell me. Write your selections on this pad. This will make things a little more interesting."

Debbie took the pad. She wrote down Row G from the center, seats twelve through fifteen. She said, "I'm ready."

She did not have to show Richard the pad. He knew exactly where to go. Richard continued, "That's wonderful. I hope the O'Donnell family is ready." Richard walked down the stairs and made his way over to where the O'Donnells were sitting. He pulled out his black wand; gave it a wave and the O'Donnell family and Richard were gone.

There was a low rumbling noise from the audience. Richard reappeared on the stage. He asked, Debbie, "Can you hold the pad so the cameraman can get a close look at it?" There was a light going back and forth on the audience. It stopped when it spotted the O'Donnells. They were sitting in new seats and waving. The O'Donnells ended up in Row G in the center in seats twelve through fifteen.

The audience was clapping. Richard put up his hand to settle the crowd down. Debbie asked Richard, "What happened to the four people that were sitting in row G?"

Richard answered, "Funny you should mention that. Let me see. Richard was tapping his index finger on his chin. "Ah, yes, now I remember. They're right here in the front row." Richard pointed to the front row at the four seats that weren't there earlier.

Again, the audience was clapping. Richard nodded to the audience to say thank you. He put his arm out and pointed to Matt. Matt waved to the audience. He stood right next to Richard and whispered, "Passes?"

Richard returned, "You have three envelopes in your jacket. One has the O'Donnell name on it. One is for Debbie and the other has Murphy on it the group who were displaced."

"Good!" Matt addressed Debbie, "We have to say good night to the audience but please wait here. I have something for you."

Matt called out to the audience, "Ladies and gentlemen, that concludes our show for tonight. We hope you enjoyed what you saw. My name is Matt White and this is my show partner and very good friend, Richard Jenkins. Please drive safely and have a good night." Matt walked forward to the edge of the stage to get Mr. O'Donnell's attention. Matt said, "Excuse me, John, I have this for you. This is our way of saying thanks for helping with the show." Matt handed John an envelope with four passes inside.

John took the envelope from Matt; he peeked inside and said, "Thank you." Then John and his family left the theater.

Next, Matt approached Debbie and said, "Debbie, we want to give you these two free passes for a later show. Thanks for being a good sport and helping out up here."

Debbie took the passes from Matt and said, "Thank you. I had a good time tonight." Debbie then went down the stairs and left the theater.

Matt said to Richard, "Everyone's gone and I didn't get to give the Murphy family this envelope."

"Here, let me see that." Richard took the envelope from Matt. He squeezed it a little and it was gone.

Matt asked, "What good did that do?"

"The problem is solved. The envelope is now in Mr. Murphy's jacket pocket. He will make the discovery when he gets home. Now, I have one question for you. Mr. White, are you ready to call it a night?"

"Stick with me, Mr. Jenkins."

The Next Day: Friday, February 25th

Matt walked into the house by four-fifteen. He called in, "Hello Denise, Richard, I'm home."

Denise was sitting in one of the wing chairs with her book. She closed her book and put it back in the bag. Matt saw her getting out of the chair and said, "Hey! How are you?"

Denise answered, "Good! Thomas went down for a late nap. I only got him down about twenty minutes ago. So, we can do this in two different ways. I was going to leave when you got here. Or I can stay here and not go home. Tom can just come here."

Matt replied, "Oh, go home and then freshen up. I can handle my son from here. I'm not all that helpless."

"Okay." She asked, "What time do you want us to come over?"

"6:30 will be good. I'll take Tom with me to pick up Chinese food."

"Okay, I'll be back later with Tom and a bottle of wine."

Matt responded, "Great, see you in a while."

Six-Thirty That Night

Denise and Tom went up the front stairs and knocked on the front door. Richard opened the door and greeted the guests, "Hello Miss Bennett, long time no see. Hello Mr. Perates, how are you?"

Tom answered, "Good, thank you for asking. How are you, Mr. Jenkins?"

"Splendid Tom, just taking it one day at a time."

Matt came out of the kitchen, greeted the guests, and said, "Tom, do not take your coat off. We're going for a ride."

Sarah was coming downstairs while Matt was talking to Tom. She saw Denise and said, "Hey!"

Denise replied, "Hi! I brought us a bottle of wine."

"Oh, you mean business."

"No, this is for a good time."

Seven O'clock

Matt and Tom were back at the house with the food. Matt asked Tom, "Do you want a beer? Follow me into the kitchen."

Matt pushed the kitchen door open and Richard was in the kitchen getting some napkins out of the drawers. Richard said, "There are two cans of Michelob Ultra with two Solo plastic cups next to them. I believe that's what you're looking for."

Matt handed a beer and a cup to Tom. Tom offered, "Thanks, are you sure I can't give you something for the food?"

"I'm sure. Besides, Denise brought a bottle of wine. Tell you what, later on, you'll be giving Richard your full attention in the dining room. He'll appreciate that."

They finished eating. Sarah stood and started clearing plates off the table. Richard took the plates from Sarah's hand and said, "I don't think so and besides…" Richard pointed to the monitor. Thomas woke up.

Sarah said, "If you'll excuse me." Sarah went and checked on Thomas.

Matt followed her and said, "Honey, I'll take care of him."

Sarah offered, "No, no, go back in the dining room and socialize with Denise and Tom."

"Okay, but we'll wait for you for the entertainment."

Matt went back into the dining room. Denise was wiping down the table. Matt asked her, "Where's Richard?"

Denise answered, "He said he had to get something out of his room and he'd only be a few minutes."

Matt decided to check on Richard. Just as Matt got within six feet of Richard's room the door opened abruptly. Matt asked, "Everything okay?"

Richard answered, "Couldn't be better."

"Okay, Sarah went upstairs and I told her we'd wait for her to come down for the entertainment."

"That means less than fifteen minutes. That gives me enough time to impress your school colleague. Follow me."

Matt and Richard both returned to the dining room. Matt asked, "Want another beer, Tom?"

Tom answered, "Okay," and he got up from his chair."

Richard put his hand up and said, "Please remain seated Tom; the fun's about to start. Mr. White will get your beer. First, a question for you. Do you believe in magic? Better, I should ask do you think things can happen that can't be explained?"

Tom answered, "I like watching magic such as card tricks and things disappearing. But I am sure there's always something the magician did to make it look real."

Richard continued, "Okay, I like that answer. I can tell you're being honest. So, let me show you something here. The dress shirt you're wearing I believe the name on the collar is Van Heusen. Is that correct?"

"Yes, it is. How did you know that?"

Matt joined the conversation and said, "I've known this guy longer than anyone here and I don't know how he knows all these things."

Richard continued, "Tom, would you mind removing your shirt? It will only be for a moment and you'll get it back in one piece."

Tom replied, "Okay. I don't mind. I'll take it off." Tom unbuttoned his shirt, took it off, and placed it on the table.

Richard reached across the table, took Tom's shirt, and held it in a way if there was anything in the shirt pocket it would fall out. He handed it back to Tom and said, "Thank you. You may put this back on."

Tom put his shirt back on and buttoned it. Richard said, "Now, the fun begins." Richard took a deck of cards out of his pocket and said to Tom, "Please pick out any card you want out of the deck. Do not show me the card."

Tom said, "Okay, I got one."

"Next, place your card under this pile of napkins."

Tom put the card under the napkins. Richard asked, "Are you ready?" Richard snapped his fingers, then said to Tom, "Look under the napkins."

Tom lifted the napkins. His card was gone. He lifted the napkins a second time thinking maybe the card stuck to the bottom of the pile. The card was not there. Tom asked, "Okay, where'd it go?"

Richard answered, "You may want to check your pocket."

Tom looked in his pocket just as Richard suggested. "Here it is. How did you do that?"

"We can address that question later, Besides, here comes Sarah. I want her to see what we have next."

Sarah walked into the dining room and asked, "What did I miss, anything good?"

Tom spoke up and answered, "This guy's amazing. He had me take my shirt off to show everyone my pocket was empty. Seconds later there was a card inside."

Sarah offered, "Richard is something alright. He's good for being around Matt. I never have to cook a thing, and on weekend mornings I get a hot breakfast."

Richard had excused himself when Sarah walked into the dining room. He returned just to the doorway and said, "Oh, what Sarah said is true. Oh, and Mr. White a private word please."

Matt said, "Excuse me. I'll be right back."

Matt followed Richard to the kitchen. Richard turned and said, "I have something to show Denise and Tom."

Matt replied, "Good!" He asked, "Is it what we talked about the other night?"

"Actually no, look in here." Richard opened the refrigerator and there was a chocolate cream pie. I remembered you told me Denise was looking a little gaunt."

"I did not say that. Let me bring this in. We'll have dessert and then you can go back to the entertaining."

"Sounds ideal."

Just then Denise walked into the kitchen and said, "Excuse me." She asked, "Didn't you tell me you were going to show something to me and Tom?"

"Yes, I did and you are just in time."

"For?"

"Would you mind putting both your hands' palms up and close together. Now, stay still for a few seconds." Richard put five dessert plates in Denise's hands. "There, you may now have the privilege of carrying these to the dining room. I'll bring some forks and an appetite."

The three of them returned to the dining room with the dessert. Matt offered, "This is the plan. We take a little break and have dessert. Then Richard continues with the entertainment."

Tom spoke up and said, "Okay, I guess I'll have to force myself to have a piece of the pie. I usually don't care for sweets. Just ask Denise."

After Denise put her pie on her plate she said, "Tom be careful; your nose is getting longer."

They finished their dessert and Richard said, "Okay, let's get the table cleared. Denise stood up to help and Richard put his hand up and said, "Please, sit and relax."

Richard looked in Matt's direction as he was getting up to carry the dirty plates to the kitchen. Matt followed him to the kitchen and asked, "What's up?"

Richard answered, "Okay, I have my display ready. There's a change in plans. I have something new put together. I'll do the talking. Just follow my lead."

"Okay." Matt went back into the dining room and announced, "Richard will be out in a minute."

Richard emerged from his room carrying a cardboard box large enough to hold a microwave. He explained to Denise and the others at the table, "You see there is a platform on the right side. On top of the platform, there is going to be a wooden box. We're going to bring out a volunteer and have them stand on the left side facing the audience. I am going to wave my right hand. The volunteer disappears and ends up in the wooden box on top of the platform."

Tom commented, "I like it, but I already figured out your secret."

Richard replied, "Please tell us what you figured out Tom."

Tom added, "Once you make the volunteer disappear, he or she makes their way to the platform and climbs into the wooden box from the bottom."

Richard continued, "That's one way to look at it, but impossible. You see, I didn't mention this but the platform is merely going to be some uncovered staging. Why would I have a volunteer walk in full view to get into a wooden box that is locked by the way? And, you figured out how I make the volunteer disappear?"

"No, I haven't. Sorry, I should've kept my comments to myself."

"Apology accepted Tom."

Denise spoke up and asked, "Can I give you my opinion and then ask you something about it?"

Richard answered, "By all means, proceed."

"Okay, I like the part where the volunteer disappears. My question is how do you do it"

Richard tilted his head for a second and said, "Please don't hold your breath waiting for the answer. The old saying is a good magician never reveals his secrets. I think I'm better than no wait I know I'm better than a good magician. Therefore, I cannot reveal this information. However, what I can do is show you a couple more card tricks. I think I have about forty-five minutes of life left in me before I have to retire for the evening."

Richard looked around the room and asked, "Are there any takers? It's all-new tonight and has never been seen before."

Sarah spoke out and replied, "Let's go for it."

Richard started in, "I knew there would be someone here that appreciates this. Sarah, because you spoke up you get to be the first guinea pig. I mean my helper. Let's start by taking the deck of cards from under the napkin." Sarah saw one lone napkin on the table and she noticed it was flush on the table. She reached for the napkin, pulled it away and the deck of cards was right where Richard said they would be.

Richard continued, "Sarah please think of one of the cards but do not reveal it to anyone here. Next, take the cards and give them a good mixing while they're still flat on the table." Sarah took both hands and moved the cards around so they were all mixed. Richard continued, "One thing I forgot to mention please jot down the card value on the pad and then flip the pad over to keep your selection hidden." Sarah took the pen and wrote the ten of diamonds on the pad and then turned it over.

Richard continued, "Okay, Sarah, because you only thought about a card means that you didn't see the card. I want you to touch the card you thought of. Remember, it is also the same as what you wrote on the pad."

Sarah asked, "How am I supposed to know where it is in this mess?"

Richard answered, "Think about that card. I know you can do this. I have faith in you."

Sarah looked the pile over carefully and then she touched a card with her right index finger. "I think that's it."

Matt spoke up and said, "Turn it over, let's see."

Sarah turned the card over and it was the ten of diamonds. She gasped, "I don't know how I did that. I just thought about the card and then picked one."

296

Richard smiled and said, "Looks like you made the right choice." He continued, "I think we can do one more. Denise, would you mind helping me out here?"

She answered, "Sure!"

Richard added, "Okay, gather up the cards and give them a good shuffle."

Denise gathered up the cards in one pile and shuffled them three times. Richard called out, "Wait! It appears Sarah thought she could keep a souvenir from the last trick." Richard pointed and a card (the ten of diamonds) was stuck to the underside of her forearm.

Sarah looked at the card stuck to her arm and said, "I don't know how that got there."

Denise replied, "Yeah, I bet. You had your turn in the spotlight. Just sit there patiently and observe how it's done." Then Denise asked, "Mr. Jenkins, how's it done?"

Richard continued, "I will show you. First, we'll add the card from Sarah's arm to the deck. Denise, put that card in the deck anywhere you like. Then split the deck in half and fan the cards out face up one pile at a time so Matt, Sarah, and Tom can see no two cards are alike."

Denise took the two piles and fanned them open so the others could see. Richard continued, "Okay, close up the cards and turn the two plies over so they're face down. I want you to turn over the top card from the pile on the left place it beside the pile face up." Denise flipped over the top card and as she was doing so Richard snapped his fingers. Richard continued, "Now, from the pile on the right take the top card and put it face down beside the pile. Take the next card and place it face up."

Denise put the top card face down and the next one face-up as instructed.

Richard continued, "Both of these cards are important and you'll see why in about twenty seconds. The card you placed face-up was the five of clubs. The one you put face down is the king of hearts. You may verify that or take my word for it. I would choose the latter." Denise lifted the face-down card and peeked at it.

Richard questioned, "Have you lost faith in me, Miss Bennett? Seeing as the card showing is a five, count down until you get to the fifth card and turn that one over."

Denise moved the cards and counted down to the fifth one. She turned the fifth one over and it was the king of hearts. Denise said, "WOW! All these cards were different when we started."

Matt cut in and commented, "Denise you have to remember who's running the show here. This guy can make anything happen."

Richard put his hand up and said, "Matthew, enough you're making me out to be like one of the gods from Greek Mythology. However, you were accurate in what you said about me. Let us continue with this card trick. Remember we have to get back to the pile on the left. Going back to this pile you flipped over the top card and it was the jack of diamonds. Please take the jack and lightly touch the rest of the deck and then put it back down. Next, turn the pile over and see if there's anything different."

Denise turned the pile over and what happened was nothing short of amazing. All the cards changed to the jack of diamonds. Denise's mouth dropped open as she was at a loss for words.

Tom reached forward and said, "That was AWESOME!" Tom reached for the pile of cards that had the king of hearts and asked, "May I look at these?" Tom didn't wait for a response. He fanned the cards open and all but three of them also changed to the jack of diamonds. Tom tilted his head and said, "Of course."

Richard then said, "I hope you enjoyed that little bit of entertainment. However, it is getting late and I need to turn in for the night." After saying that Richard stood and said, "Good night all. Tom, it was good seeing you again. Denise, I'll see you Monday morning. Matt and Sarah, I'll see you in the morning." Richard then left the dining room and the guests said good night to him.

Denise spoke up and said, "We should get going. I'm getting tired and I'm sure you two are."

Matt smiled and replied, "Before you go you can come to the show tomorrow night if you want. It's going to be our last Saturday night show."

Denise spoke quickly, "Oh gee, uh Tom volunteered to take me shopping tomorrow late afternoon for a few things."

Tom asked, "I did? When did I do that?"

Denise elbowed Tom lightly and said, "Pay attention silly."

Sounds were coming from the baby monitor. Sarah stood up and said, "I have to take care of Thomas. Thanks for coming by. It was nice seeing you Tom and I'll see you Monday morning Denise." Denise and Tom said good night to Sarah and then Matt.

The Next Day: Saturday, February 26th

It was almost six-fifteen Saturday evening. Matt went into the living room where Sarah was sitting and said to Sarah, "Well honey, this is our last Saturday night show."

Sarah's response was, "I thought this day would never come. After tonight, I have my husband on Saturday nights."

"That's right and that is something for both of us to look forward to. Well, we're going to head out now. We should be home by ten-thirty."

Matt drove to the theater and they were sitting in the front row by six forty-five. Matt brought up, "You know I thought I was doing a nice thing last night when I invited Denise and Tom to the show. They would've had free passes. Denise made up something about her and Tom going shopping."

Richard nodded and said, "Row three, seats one and two in the center section."

"What does that mean?"

"It means Denise called Sarah while you were in the shower and asked if your offer was still good for the show. Sarah called the theater and asked them to hold two seats. Denise and Tom will be there. Because they're going to be there, we're going to do something new tonight."

"Great! What are we doing?"

"I'll let you know as soon as I think of it. Give me a second. Okay, make it five. I got it. This is what we're going to do…"

The show started at exactly seven-thirty. Matt performed a couple of illusions by himself. He then invited Richard to join him on stage and they did a couple of acts together. Matt left Richard on his own. Richard walked to center stage and addressed the audience, "Ladies and gentlemen, I'm sure most of you don't know me. My name is Richard Jenkins and I am Matt White's partner. I love showing off the card tricks I can do and now I want to show all of you some of my work. Please, can I have a volunteer up here with me?"

More than a dozen people raised their hands to volunteer. Richard continued, "Let me see, who should I pick." Richard walked over to the left section and picked a gentleman from the ninth row. Richard said, "Now, sir, can we have you come up here and you can help me impress the audience."

The volunteer joined Richard on stage. Richard asked the volunteer, "Sir, can you honestly say we have never met before?"

The volunteer answered, "That's true. We have never met before."

"Then, how do you explain the fact I know your first name is Ken and your last name is Martin? Sorry, I probably shouldn't have revealed that. Anyway, let's get started." Richard took a deck of cards from the inside of his jacket. He said, "Ken, take these cards and give them a good mix."

Ken took the cards and shuffled them a few times. He was about to hand the cards back to Richard when Richard put his hand up and said, "Wait, please take one of the cards for yourself. I'm going to turn around so I don't see your selection. Also, let the cameraman who's coming up behind you see your card. Finally, slip the card into your coat pocket." Ken took his card and let the cameraman see it. It was the ten of diamonds.

Richard continued, "Okay, Ken I did not see your card. So, what I'm going to do is I'm going to guess the card you picked and put in your pocket. Let me see you selected the king of spades."

Ken tilted his head a little to the right and said, "Sorry, that, wasn't it? It was the ten of diamonds."

"Very well then, please take the card out of your pocket and show everyone." Ken took out his card, looked at it and his eyes opened wide. Richard continued, "Please let the cameraman see your card." The cameraman focused on Ken's card and it was the king of spades as Richard predicted.

Richard finished up, "Ken, thank you for your help. You may keep the cards as a souvenir and don't forget this." Richard leaned forward and took the ten of diamonds out of Ken's pocket.

Ken took the cards from Richard and left the stage. Richard addressed the audience, "Ladies and gentlemen, thank you for being here tonight. As you can tell, I like showing off simple illusions or tricks I can do. But it's only fitting that Mr. White comes and joins us on the stage."

Matt walked out from behind the curtain. The audience gave him a warm welcome with applause. Matt addressed the audience, "Ladies and gentlemen, how about a little round of appreciation for my friend Richard." The audience clapped again. "Okay, we have time for just one more and we're going to need a volunteer." Matt walked down the stairs off the stage and found a woman from the right-hand section of the audience.

Matt asked her name and she answered, "Paula."

Matt said, "Pleased to meet you, Paula." As Matt was talking, he could see Richard flashing two fingers indicating that he wanted two additional volunteers on the stage with him. Matt said to the audience, "Please whoever wanted to volunteer don't sit down yet." Matt asked Paula to select two people from the audience. Paula picked a man and a woman for volunteers. Matt had Paula and the other two volunteers follow him up on stage.

As soon as Matt got on the stage, he addressed the two volunteers and said, "Hello my name is Matt this is my friend Richard. I am going to leave you in the hands of Richard." Matt walked off to the side and stood beside Paula.

Paula asked Matt, "What's he going to do?"

Matt answered, "Good question, Sorry, I don't know. Oh, he mentioned something about mind reading."

Richard took over and with his right hand, he motioned with two fingers to the female volunteer to step forward. Richard started, "Hello! My name is Richard. You don't have to tell me your name. It's Ellen. Am I correct?"

Ellen nodded and answered, "Yes!"

Richard continued, "Okay, Ellen you are thirty-three years old. You work for an investment firm in Chicago. You're married and you have a ten-year-old son Devon. Oh, one more thing you drive a Nissan Maxima. How much did I get right?"

Ellen answered, "You were one hundred percent accurate."

"Thank you for confirming that Ellen. If you wouldn't mind waiting next to Matt and Paula, I have one more person to take care of."

Richard continued, "Okay, George, front and center please."

George stood next to Richard and George asked, "Hey, how did you know my…?"

Richard answered, "You mean name? I understand how you want to know how I did that but sorry it would take too long to explain. Okay, George, you see this collar I have?" Richard took what looked like a see-through garden hose in the shape of a large horseshoe. He put it around his neck and said to George, "Watch what happens." Richard said to George, "My name is Richard. I just turned twenty-three years old." The collar turned bright red. Richard continued, "Now, George, I want you to put the collar around your neck to test it. Tell a whopper to make it light up."

George put the collar around his neck. He didn't know it but Richard used a little of his powers to prevent George from telling a lie. George started by saying, "My name is George Petersen. I am forty-three years old. I live in a suburb in Chicago and I work in an office building on the third floor." The collar never lit up.

Richard took the collar back from George and said, "I think you're having trouble with this. Here, let me show you again."

Richard placed the collar around his neck and spoke, "My name is Richard Ashbury and I was born in Montpelier, Vermont." As soon as Richard got to the second name the collar flashed red a few times. It stayed a solid red when he finished his sentence. Richard continued, "George let's try without the collar and we'll let my hand take place of the collar.

Richard took the collar and he walked towards Matt. He asked Matt, "Matthew, would you mind holding this?"

Matt took it and answered, "Not at all." Before Matt finished his sentence, the collar was glowing bright red in his hand. The audience broke into laughter for a few seconds.

Richard continued, "Here George just touch my elbow with your right hand for a few seconds. Now, watch, I'm going to raise my right hand. Now, please try again."

George started, "My name is George Petersen and I am twenty-nine years old. I am married to a beautiful woman named Sharon and we live in Illinois. We are on vacation this week." Richard's hand turned red as soon as George said the phrase twenty-nine years old and his hand remained solid red.

George smiled and said, "It worked that time."

"Yes, it did George and I hope you enjoyed this. Don't go back to your seat yet. Would you mind waiting next to Ellen and Paula? I believe it's time for Mr. White to say good night to the audience."

Matt walked to the center of the stage and addressed the audience, "Ladies and gentlemen, that concludes our show for tonight. I want to thank everyone for coming out tonight. This was our last Saturday night show. Our time is getting moved to a matinee's timeslot on Saturdays. My name is Matt White and this is my good friend and partner Richard Jenkins. Please drive safely and have a good night."

Next Matt addressed the three volunteers and said to them, "Thank you very much for your help. We want to give you some free passes to another show. For those of you with kids, we start our matinees next Saturday." Matt handed each one of them an envelope with four passes in each one. They took the passes, said thank you, and left the theater.

Then Matt asked Richard, "Well, Mr. Jenkins, are you ready to call it a night?"

"Lead the way, Mr. White."

Sunday Morning, February 27th

Matt came downstairs at six-thirty-five and poured himself a coffee. Richard was sitting at the table with the newspaper folded in front of him.

Matt greeted Richard first, "Good morning Richard. How are you?"

Richard answered, "Just splendid Matthew. How are you?"

"Doing okay. Last night the show went an extra twenty minutes. Was that because you made up the final act at the last minute?"

"That and because I crammed in that card trick right before the final act."

"Does this mean our show is going to suffer quality-wise because the Saturday evening is moving to a matinee time slot?"

"Uhm first bite your tongue. Second, that's not going to happen as long as I have something to say about it. Now, how about six predictions to start the day?"

"You're on!"

"Okay, number one, Sarah will be down here by 7:12. Two, she will ask in the dining room if we plan on a trip to Albertson's. Three, Sarah will mention she has a list started with a few things but she won't remember where she left it. Four, Denise will call and ask if she left her Stephen King book here. By the way, it's under one of the chairs in the living room. Five, Mr. Firmani will call and ask to speak to you. He doesn't tell Sarah the reason he's calling. Finally, number six, some rude person is going to drive through the parking lot fast. He thinks he's going to splash us. Boy, he is sadly mistaken."

Seven-Ten

Matt pointed to the clock on the kitchen wall. Richard nodded and pointed to his right ear indicating to Matt to listen. They listened, heard the bedroom door open and close upstairs, and then heard the bathroom door close. Matt looked at Richard and smiled. He was certain Sarah wouldn't have time to spend in the bathroom and then be downstairs in two minutes. He was wrong, so wrong.

Sarah was downstairs at Richard's predicted time. Matt walked over right away and turned on the baby monitor. Sarah was holding an empty shampoo bottle when she said, "Good morning honey." She then kissed Matt on the cheek.

Matt replied, "Good morning," and returned the kiss.

Sarah greeted Richard with, "Good morning Richard."

Richard returned, "Good morning Sarah. If you'll take a seat in the dining room, I'll bring you breakfast."

"Thank you, Richard. As always, you spoil me." Sarah walked into the dining room. Richard went into the room behind her and set a placemat on the table. Sarah said, "I could have done that. Oh, are you and Matt planning on going to Albertson's?"

Richard answered, "I believe we are. I'll tell Matt you want to know and it's in my job description to spoil you."

"No, it's not and I have a list started with a few things on it but I can't remember where I left it."

"Perhaps you left it in your coat pocket. Richard already knew where the list was. He just thought it would look better that he didn't let Sarah know he knew everything.

Sarah got up from the table, she went to the closet and fished in her coat pocket. Just as Richard suggested Sarah's partial shopping list was in her coat pocket. She went back to the dining room and sat. Richard brought her food in and Sarah said, "Thank you," and handed Richard the list.

Richard went back to the kitchen with the list in his hand. The phone rang and Matt asked, "Is this one of the predictions coming true?"

Matt answered the phone, "Hello?"

Denise was on the other end. "Good morning, Matt. It's Denise. I hope I didn't wake you guys."

Matt responded, "Good morning Denise. You would have had to call way before six to wake us. What can I do for you?"

Denise asked, "Did I leave my Stephen King book over there?"

"Just a second, I'll look." Matt went into the living room and the book was under one of the chairs as Richard said it would be. Matt went back to the phone and said, "Hi! I got it. Richard and I are going to Albertson's within the hour. We can drop it off on the way."

"Thank you, Matt. Tell Sarah I said Hi!"

"I'll do that. Goodbye Denise."

Matt brought the highchair in the dining room and said to Sarah, "That was Denise. She left her book here. I told her we'd drop it off on the way to Albertson's."

Matt continued, "I'll be right back. I'll get Thomas." Matt hustled up the stairs and returned with Thomas.

Richard went into the dining room and was carrying a plate with Thomas's food already on it. He handed it to Matt and Matt said, "Thank you."

While Matt was feeding Thomas Sarah asked, "How did it go last night? You came home later than usual."

"It went very well. You know, I don't know how to do this without Richard. From week to week, he amazes the audience. I think the audience just tolerates me. These last maybe ten shows or more I don't know what I'm doing 'til I get to the theater and that makes me nervous. The saving grace here is when Richard makes things up that evening, they're all good."

Sarah replied, "Talk to Richard. Tell him how you feel."

Richard came into the dining room and asked, "Sarah, may I take your plate?"

Sarah nodded and said, "Thank you."

As Richard was picking up Sarah's plate, he said to Matt, "You can tell me how you feel on the way to Denise's house."

Matt and Richard left for Albertson's at eight-forty intending to stop at Denise's house on the way. After they left Denise's house Richard started the conversation, "I thought you were going to bring it up, but you didn't. If it bothers you not knowing what we're going to do we can make a change. From now on, I will go over it with you the night before. If you don't agree with the plan, I am always open to discussion. Please, I prefer you to say something if you have a problem with my plan."

Matt replied, "Agreed!" The next stop was Albertson's. Once in the store, Matt grabbed a carriage and they started up and down the aisles. They loaded items from Sarah's list and other various needed items. They went through the checkout and then loaded the groceries in the van. Then they headed home. Matt pulled in the driveway, carried in the groceries, and Richard put them away.

Once in the house, Sarah called out, "Matt, I'm in the living room. Before I forget, Al Firmani called. He didn't say what he wanted. I told him you'd call him back."

"Yeah, he probably wants to get together."

Three Days Later: Wednesday, March 2nd

They just finished dinner. Richard grabbed a couple of plates and carried them into the kitchen. Matt was right behind him carrying his plate with the dirty silverware. Richard was rinsing off the plates. He motioned for Matt to leave the stuff on the counter.

Richard quietly said to Matt, "Tomorrow this is what we're doing…Okay? Are we good?"

"Yes, very good."

The Next Day: Thursday, March 3rd

Matt walked into the house at four-fifteen. Denise was sitting on the living room floor next to Thomas. She had her hands behind him just in case he fell backward. Matt stopped and waved, smiled, and said, "If he takes his first step it would not be advisable to tell Sarah you saw it."

Denise smiled and replied, "I understand."

Matt went into the kitchen to find Richard. Richard was in front of the stove turning over some hamburger patties on a broiler pan. Matt said, "Hey! Whoa! You're cooking the mortal way. I'm impressed."

Richard cracked a small smile and said, "There's a pair of spying eyes in the house if you know what I mean. This will be ready in less than fifteen minutes if you want to get cleaned up."

Six-Twenty-Five

Matt and Richard left for the theater and were in their seats by six-forty -five. Richard's head was tilted back. It was obvious he was in deep thought.

Matt said, "You're thinking about something. I think I know what it is but I'll ask anyway."

Richard answered, "Only six more weeks and we're on our way."

"Yeah, it will be good to kick back, relax, and see some entertainment instead of providing it."

"Also, wait 'til you experience the weather out there. We'll be there when it's just right and not stifling hot."

"That'll suit me just fine. I'm tired of going out first thing in the morning and feeling the cold air slapping me in the face."

Richard replied, "I have the perfect solution for that. Bring a hanger to school and leave your sport jacket in the closet. This will allow you to bundle up easier with a winter coat and a scarf around your neck. You won't feel so bulky and we're probably looking at another three to four weeks of nasty temps." Just then the door at the top of the theater opened and Richard said, "We should go wait out back."

The show started at exactly seven-thirty. Tonight's show started differently with Richard starting the lineup. He sprang this idea on Matt at the last second. Richard used up most of the time and packed in two great illusions. Matt stood patiently behind the curtain waiting to be invited out to join Richard.

In the first illusion, Richard invited a volunteer to help him on stage. The volunteer stood across from Richard and Richard gave him instructions, "Please take this red cloth and I want you to drape it over this flower vase. Next, I am going to count to three. Right after I get to three, I want you to pull on the corner of the red cloth. Ready? The volunteer nodded. Richard continued, "One…two…three." Dave pulled on the red cloth and the vase was gone.

Dave said, "Whoa! I've only seen that done on TV but never this close up in person. I want to know how you did that."

"Oh, that won't be happening tonight. However, I do have two more acts to do and you can have a close-up view on the stage if you wait off to the side."

Dave nodded and went to the side of the stage.

Richard continued and invited another volunteer up on the stage. As the volunteer was walking up Richard briefly touched the left side of his temple. By doing so he sent a message to Matt and reassured him he'd be just a few more minutes. Then Matt would be joining him.

A woman came up on the stage and Richard said, "Welcome! Can I get your name?"

She replied, "Shelly, Shelly Hogan."

Richard continued, "Nice to meet you, Shelly, I have a question for you. Do you believe objects can float?"

Shelly answered, "Yes, in space where there's no gravity."

Richard continued, "Good answer Shelly but I want to show you there's a little more to it than that." Richard motioned to the stagehand and he brought out an object resembling a thick frisbee. He continued, "Now, Shelly please take the frisbee and you'll notice the frisbee has a little extra weight on it and then take twelve steps back. Now, throw the frisbee to me." Shelly threw the frisbee. It went almost six feet and fell to the floor not reaching Richard. Richard walked over and picked up the frisbee. As he was bent over, he said, "That was not the result I was looking for."

Richard handed Shelly the frisbee and said, "Please try again but give me a second to get back to my spot. Maybe, you should lean forward a little as you throw the frisbee."

Shelly said, "Okay."

Shelly leaned forward and threw the frisbee. It went almost seven feet and then went straight up in the air out of sight. The audience burst into laughter.

Richard commented, "Oops!" Then he asked, "Can we get another one of those?"

Matt stepped out from behind the curtain. He handed Shelly a frisbee and said softly, "Try not to lose this one."

Shelly smiled and nodded. Richard continued, "Okay, once more." Shelly threw the frisbee and once again the frisbee went way up in the air. Richard threw his arms in the air and said to Shelly, "That's enough of that. We're going to run out of frisbees.

He walked over to Shelly, put a hand on her shoulder, and said, "Thanks for helping" Richard took his hand away and he was clutching one of the frisbees. Richard said, "Just looking for one more."

Richard asked, "Mr. White, could you please join us on stage?"

Matt walked out and stood next to Richard. Richard asked Matt, "May I examine your jacket?"

Matt took off his jacket and handed it to Richard. Richard gave Matt's jacket a good shake. Two frisbees fell out, followed by a baseball, a catcher's mitt, a football, and a basketball. The audience was laughing again. Richard smiled and said, "Got the frisbees back."

Richard handed one of the frisbees to Shelly and said, "Here you may keep this as a souvenir. Thanks for your help. You can take your seat or stand next to Dave for a close view of our next illusion. We have one more to go."

Richard asked Matt, "Are you ready to go to work? Sorry, I was stealing the show."

Matt nodded and said, "Let me address the audience. Ladies and gentlemen, we have just enough time for one more. Please look at the monitor above me. You're going to see a quick clip of Houdini performing his Water Torture trick. Tonight, we're going to do our rendition of the same. Sit back, relax, and we hope you enjoy it."

Matt went backstage to change while the video was playing. He came back out wearing a swimsuit designed from the 1920s. The curtain opened and there was a seven-foot-high tank on the stage filled with water. Matt walked to the side of the tank.

Richard said, "Just a second, I have some nice wrist bands for you."

Matt walked over to Richard and put his arms out in front of him. Richard fastened the handcuffs one on each wrist. Matt then walked up the stairs on the side of the tank. Two assistants were waiting for him at the top of the platform.

Richard addressed the audience, "Ladies and gentlemen before Mr. White is lowered in the tank, I just want to point out there will not be a curtain dropping in front of the tank just like in the video clip. Please watch carefully."

Two assistants lowered Matt into the tank headfirst. A second's counter lowered from above and the seconds counter started counting. 1...2...3...Matt was moving his head back and forth. The clock continued counting 9...10...11...The audience was buzzing and a low mumbling could be heard. The clock continued counting 15...16...17...As soon as the 17 displayed the cuffs popped off of Matt's wrists. Matt inverted himself in the tank, rose to the top, and grabbed the outside edges. He held himself in place with one hand and waved to the audience. Matt put his arm on the other side and allowed the assistants to help him out. One of the assistants handed Matt a towel. Matt gave a quick wave to the audience and ran backstage to get changed.

The audience was clapping. Matt came back out and as he was walking out Richard put his arm out signaling the audience to show their appreciation. The audience continued with applause and Matt pointed at Richard.

Matt walked over to where Dave and Shelly were standing and said, "Don't go back to your seats yet. I have to say goodnight to the audience."

"Ladies and gentlemen, that concludes our show for tonight. We hope you liked what you saw. My name is Matt White and this is my good friend and show partner, Richard Jenkins. Please drive safely and have a good night."

Next, Matt approached Dave and Shelly and said, "Hey, we appreciate your help tonight. We want to give you some free passes to a later show. Just to let you know until further notice we will not be doing anymore Saturday evening shows. That's being moved to a matinee time slot. There are four tickets in each envelope so you can bring your kids. It'll be fun."

Matt handed Dave and Shelly an envelope. They both said, "Thank you," and left the theater.

After they left, Matt asked Richard, "Well, Mr. Jenkins, are you ready to call it a night?"

"Lead the way, Mr. White."

Saturday Morning, March 5th

Matt came downstairs at six-forty-five. He went straight to the kitchen and poured himself a coffee. Richard was sitting at the kitchen table. He addressed Matt first, "Good morning Matt. I already know what you're going to say and I'm sorry. I didn't brief you on Thursday night's show. The tiger will be there this afternoon. There's going to be a lot of kids in the audience."

Seven-Fifteen

Sarah came downstairs and went into the kitchen. She found Matt and Richard there talking. Sarah said, "Good morning honey. I hope I'm not interrupting a secret meeting," and she kissed Matt on the cheek.

Matt returned the kiss and said, "Good morning honey. I'll be back; I'm going to turn the monitor on. Matt went and picked up the baby monitor in one hand and the highchair in the other.

Richard spoke up and said, "Good morning Sarah. I trust you slept well last night. I can bring you breakfast if you grab a seat in the dining room.

Sarah replied, "Thank you, Richard," as she made her way into the dining room.

Matt went up the stairs and then returned to the dining room. He then placed Thomas in the highchair. Richard walked into the dining room right after Matt. He carried in a tray holding a plate of food for Sarah and food for Thomas. Richard said, "Here you go Sarah, here you are Matt. I'll be back with juice. Matt, can I get you coffee?"

Matt answered, "That'll be great, thanks."

Richard returned with a coffee and a glass of juice. He put the coffee in front of Matt and the juice in front of Sarah.

Matt looked up and said, "Thank you."

Eleven-Forty-Five

Matt drove him and Richard to the theater. They were sitting in the front row by twelve-twenty-five. Richard asked Matt, "So, are we all set for today? Do you know what we're doing?"

"Yes, I do. Something is puzzling me though."

"And that is?"

"I can't hear him. You'd think by now we'd hear Whiskers."

Richard pointed and asked, "You mean?'

"As soon as Richard pointed there were two roars from behind the curtain. Richard said, "We should go say hi. He's probably getting hungry."

They got up and went backstage to see the tiger. There was Whiskers in the cage pacing back and forth. Richard said, "Hey buddy." Richard reached in his pocket and took out a small piece of raw meat for the tiger. He took out a second one and held it as close to the cage as possible. Whiskers moved his head right against the bars and with his tongue took the treat from Richard's hand.

Matt said, "You're a lot braver than I am. I'd never do that."

"I did that to calm him down. He'll be content and a little sleepy until we need him."

The show started at one o'clock. Matt started with some illusions by himself. After doing this for about forty-five minutes he invited Richard to join him on stage. Richard joined him on stage and Matt said, "It's all you for a few minutes."

Richard called out to the audience, "Ladies and gentlemen, boys and girls welcome to the show. My name is Richard and I am Mr. White's assistant. I want to take this time to show the kids something interesting. Can I have two helpers come up and help me, please? Parents, not to worry, this will be fun."

About twenty-five kids raised their hands eager to get picked. Richard went down the stairs, picked a girl from the seventh row, and then a boy from the eleventh row on the left side. Richard had the two kids follow him up on stage. Richard addressed the girl first and asked, "What is your name?"

She answered, "Becky."

"Okay Becky, hang tight for a second. I want to talk to another volunteer. Richard asked the boy, "What is your name, sir?"

The boy answered, "Ken."

Richard continued, "Okay, I have something for each of you." Richard signaled to the stagehand and he brought out two hula hoops. He continued, "Becky, you get to pick your color."

Becky pointed and said, "I'll take the purple one."

Richard handed her the purple hoop and gave Ken the red one. Richard asked, "Do you kids know what to do with these? Please don't make me show you."

Becky and Ken put the hula hoops around themselves. "Okay, this is what's going to happen. A song is going to play and when the song stops you stop gyrating and let the hula hoop fall to the floor. Okay, begin."

The theme song from the Lone Ranger started playing and went for almost two minutes. The music stopped and the kids stopped moving so the hoops would fall. Richard said, "Very good. We'll call that a practice run. Okay, one more time." The music started back up and the kids resumed spinning their hoops around.

This went on for almost three minutes. The music stopped and both kids stopped moving. Becky expected her hoop to fall to the floor when she stopped moving her hips. That was not the case. Becky looked down and the hoop was still circling her. Needless to say, Becky had a puzzled look on her face.

Ken was having a different problem with his hula hoop. He stopped moving around and his hoop kept spinning. It picked up speed and started spinning faster and then lifted off his torso. It went up in the air and about seven feet and then landed on the floor.

Richard walked over and touched the hula hoop around Becky's waist. It stopped spinning and fell to the floor. Richard said, "Hmmm, it looks like these hula hoops have a mind of their own. I hope you didn't mind me having fun with you. I tell you what you can keep these as a souvenir but I will hold them up until the show's over. Then, you come and collect them. You may return to your seats. Thank you for your help." Becky and Ken left the stage and went back to their seats.

Richard walked past the closest hula hoop and then picked up the one the furthest away from him. He waved to the audience to get their attention and then put both hoops on end. He let go of them and walked away. The hoops rolled behind him and followed him off the stage. Part of the audience was laughing and the others were clapping.

Richard went back out to the audience and said, "I'm looking for another victim; I mean volunteer. Perhaps someone a little older this time, for instance, how about you Miss?"

Richard pointed at a woman who was in the seventh row. He said, "Miss, thank you so much for volunteering. Come, join me up here and we'll have some fun."

The drafted volunteer followed Richard on the stage. Richard turned and asked her, "Can I get your name?"

She answered, "Linda Davis."

Richard continued, "Okay, Linda, I have a brand-new deck of cards here." Richard handed Linda the box and instructed her, "Please take off the plastic wrapper, remove the cards and examine them. You'll notice the cards are in suit order. This doesn't have anything to do with what we're doing here." As Richard was talking, he motioned for the cameraman to come in close. Richard continued, "Okay, Linda, I want you to look through the cards and select one. Do not show me your pick. Let the cameraman see so it'll show up on the monitor above. Oh, I forgot. Take this pad and pen and write down your selection. Then put the card in your pocket. Let me know when you're done."

Linda wrote down her card on the pad. She tore the paper from the pad, folded it in half, and then slipped it into her pocket. Then Linda said, "Okay, I'm done."

Richard replied, "Okay, great Linda. I am going to guess the card you took. Are you ready?"

"Yes, I am."

"Okay, you took the queen of diamonds."

Linda made a face and responded, "Not quite."

Richard asked, "I didn't get it right? Well, take the card out of your pocket and show everyone."

Linda took her card out and she expected to see the ten of hearts. Instead, she saw the queen of diamonds. She said, "I know I had the ten of hearts. See? I even wrote it down." Linda opened her hand, unfolded the paper, and it was the queen.

Richard smiled and added, "That's okay Linda. I understand. You're putting in a lot of hours at work. You must be tired."

Linda asked, "Okay, the cameraman he zoomed in on the card. Can you replay what was shown on the monitor?"

Richard motioned to Jeff and Jeff nodded, and replied, "Sure thing."

The monitor played Linda removing a card and then holding it for three seconds. It was the queen of diamonds. Linda said, "I don't understand. How did you do that?"

Richard put his right index finger in front of his lips. Then he whispered, "I'll tell you later."

"Later?"

"Yes, when pigs fly. Thank you for your help. Here, take these cards as a souvenir. You may go back to your seat."

Linda took the cards and said, "Thank you," and then returned to her seat.

The audience was clapping. Richard put his hand up and said, "Thank you, it's time for Mr. White to come join us."

Matt walked back out to the stage and made an announcement, "Ladies and gentlemen, boys and girls, we have time for just one more."

315

Richard started to walk away and Matt asked, "Where are you going?"

Richard answered, "Back there; this is your gig. Don't worry, nothing will go wrong. I'm adding a little twist to this. You'll see."

The curtain opened and there was a cage with a Bengal tiger inside. The tiger was pacing back and forth just itching to get out. Matt announced, "Okay, ladies and gentlemen, boys and girls, I'm going to make this tiger disappear."

Richard was behind the curtain thinking to himself 'You're going to make the tiger disappear?'

Matt pulled a large grey curtain down in front of the cage. Matt called out, "Okay 1...2...3." He let the curtain back up and the tiger was gone. Sounds were coming from the audience. Matt continued, "Okay, time for the tiger to come back."

The curtain was still down in front of the cage. Richard, backstage waved his finger and the curtain went up inside the brackets like a window shade out of control. The tiger appeared in full view for the audience to see. The audience cheered.

Richard came out from behind the curtain and walked to the side of the cage. He waved his finger and the tiger pushed the door open. The tiger came downstairs and rubbed his head against Richard's leg. Richard reached in his pocket and took out a couple of treats for the tiger. Richard made a noise with his tongue hitting the roof of his mouth. The tiger followed Richard over to the side and went back up the ramp into the cage. The audience was clapping.

Matt called out to the audience, "Ladies and gentlemen, boys and girls, that concludes our show for today. My name is Matt White and this is my good friend and show partner, Richard Jenkins. Please drive safely and enjoy the rest of your weekend."

Richard said to Matt, "I have a couple of souvenirs to hand out before we go." Richard whistled and the two hula hoops rolled out to him. Richard then took the hula hoops and brought them to the stage. Becky and Ken were waiting for them as promised.

Matt asked Richard, "Mr. Jenkins, are you all set?"

"Lead the way, Mr. White."

Matt drove them home and they were in the driveway by four o'clock. They went into the house and Matt purposely kept his voice low in case Thomas was down for an afternoon nap.

Sarah was sitting in the living room and she said, "Hi, how did it go?"

Matt answered, "It was great and the bonus is, I don't feel like I have to lay down. I could use a coffee though."

"I was hoping you weren't going to say that."

"Why?"

"I had a slight mishap in the kitchen. I used the toaster and when I pushed down the plunger without realizing I accidentally moved the toaster up against the cord to the coffeemaker and the cord melted."

"Are you okay? You didn't burn yourself, did you? We can replace the coffeemaker. That's nothing."

As soon as Matt said nothing Richard entered the living room and handed Matt a cup of coffee.

Matt said, "Thank you and where did you get this?"

Richard answered, "The kitchen, oh you thought the coffeemaker was out of commission. I gave the cord a quick fix. The unit should be replaced though."

Matt walked into the kitchen and noticed the coffeemaker light was on but not plugged in. Matt thought to himself, 'He calls this a quick fix'

Richard went into the kitchen less than a minute after Matt. Matt turned his head quickly and asked Richard, "You call this a quick fix.' There's no electricity going to the appliance."

"I know; take it easy. I couldn't say in front of Sarah Oh no problem. I just used some hocus pocus to make the coffee. That wouldn't have gone over well."

Matt replied, "I understand, I mean we need coffee in the morning and I very well can't banish my wife from the kitchen until we replace the coffeemaker. I have an idea."

Matt asked Sarah, "Honey, I just had an idea. Would you like to take a break and go shopping? Is there anything you need at the mall? I know we need a new coffeemaker. I can stay here."

Sarah answered, "Hmmm, let me call Denise. Maybe she'll come with me."

Matt responded, "Good idea. Just don't forget the coffeemaker."

Ten Minutes Later

Sarah left to pick up Denise to go shopping with her. Matt was given a sense of relief knowing she wouldn't be alone.

Matt said to Richard, "I'm glad she's out of the house. I mean she needs to get a break now and then."

Richard looked over and Thomas was in the living room holding himself up about to push a small statue off the end table. Richard said, "Speaking of break and he pointed with a finger and made the statue float to the fireplace mantle.

Matt asked, "Are you in the mood to sit in the living room and we can plan some things for our upcoming shows. We have eleven more performances before our vacation."

"Great idea. I have a few ideas I want to run by you. Here's another thought. Why don't you give Mr. Firmani a call? Invite him and Jeannie over tomorrow afternoon for a late lunch. We can show them something and get their feedback."

"I'll give him a call. Wait, before I do, what's a good time?"

"That's up to you and Sarah. You know me I don't need much notice about putting dinner together. As long as we can keep any prying females out of the kitchen, I can whip up anything."

"Okay, I'll be right back. Matt went into the kitchen and called Al.

"Hello!" came from Al.

Matt answered back, "Hey Al, this is Matt. If you and Jeannie aren't busy tomorrow, we'd love to have you over for a mid-afternoon lunch."

Al replied, "Thanks Matt, as far as I know, we're not busy." Al asked, "What time?"

"Is one-thirty okay with you?"

"Sure, we'll see you tomorrow."

Seven-Twenty That Evening

318

Sarah pulled into the driveway. She came into the house and said, "Hello!"

Matt was in the living room walking Thomas around. Thomas smiled when he saw Sarah. Matt said, "Hey, I purposely kept him up so you could say goodnight to him."

"Thanks, I appreciate that."

"Sure, did you find the same one coffeemaker I mean?

Sarah's mouth dropped open and she said, "I did but I left it in the car."

"Okay, why don't you bring Thomas upstairs and I'll get it out of the car. By the way, I invited Al and Jeannie over tomorrow for a late lunch."

"Oh, okay, great," Sarah said as she was walking upstairs with Thomas.

25

Best Vacation Ever

Six Weeks Later: Sunday, April 17th

Denise pulled in the driveway at twelve-thirty. She had a large duffel bag with her. She went up the front stairs and Matt opened the door.

Matt said, "Hey! Denise, I just want to say how much we appreciate this. Do you have a bag in the car? I'll get it."

One-Fifteen

The Flight Van pulled up and picked up Matt, Sarah and Richard, and their bags. They were at the airport and checked in by one-fifty. The three of them walked over to their departure gate.

Sarah recognized her brother and his wife and said, "Look there's Sean and Katelin."

They went and joined Sean and Katelin. Katelin spoke up and said, "Hey, you guys. How are you?" Sarah moved off to the side and hugged Sean.

Sean said, "Our flight is supposed to board at two-thirty. It's a three-and-a-half-hour flight. We should be there at ten minutes after four with the time change."

It was Monday the first full day of their vacation. The five of them met downstairs at the food court. Sarah asked, "Does anybody want to get a coffee and a bagel or pastry here? We can sit and talk about what we're going to do."

The group sat at a table with coffee and pastries. Richard spoke up and asked, "Would anybody care to see a magic show? There is an incredible show here at the Tropicana and the beauty of this is it's an afternoon show. If any of us feel tired later we can always go back to the room and take a nap. Remember we're two hours ahead in Chicago."

Sean spoke up and said, "We gained three hours."

Matt cut in and said, "That's the main reason we're here. Richard, what's the name of the show?"

Richard answered, "It's called Xtreme Magic starring Dirk Arthur. I have not seen this show myself, but I've heard this is the best afternoon show in Las Vegas."

Sarah spoke up and said, "Okay, let's see if we can get five tickets."

They went down to the Tropicana and bought tickets for the 2:00 show. The group had lunch at the Calypso buffet before the show. They finished their lunch and Richard said to Matt, "Looks like these tickets we bought include a libation."

Sean said, "Pardon me for being ignorant, but what is a libation?"

Katelin answered, "Sean, it's just a fancy word used for a drink or a toast. Sean, is this your magazine?"

Sean answered, "Well, I took it off the table from the coffee shop. There's a page here that is a tribute to Dirk Arthur.

It says: *'For five years Michelle Thibodeaux co-starred with magician Dirk Arthur at the Tropicana Hotel in what became the most successful afternoon family magic show in the history of Las Vegas! The show featured complicated choreography, large illusions, and tigers, and leopards. Dirk has long been a leading advocate for the preservation of endangered species, and his shows raise funds for various animal care and conservation programs! Thank you, Dirk, for your friendship and for helping to make our show magical!! Love, Michelle.'*

Sarah stood up and said, "It's almost one-thirty. Maybe we should head over to the theater." Once in the theater Matt was looking around and said, "This place is pretty nice. The theater in Chicago is not like this."

Richard replied, "That's because that theater has a lot of history to it. What I'm trying to say is it's old."

The theater got dark and there was an announcement, "Ladies and gentlemen, boys and girls welcome to the Tropicana. Sit back, relax because it's time to be amazed by Xtreme Magic starring Dirk Arthur." It was still somewhat dark in the theater. There was a large object being lowered from the ceiling above the stage. Then a spotlight went on the side of the large object and Dirk Arthur stepped out from behind the object and waved to the audience.

The object was lifted back up and another prop was brought out to the center of the stage. This object resembled an extra-large version of a basket that snake charmers used. There were also two beautiful showgirls on the stage with Dirk Arthur. Dirk tilted the object a little to show the audience it was empty. Two of the girls were turning the basket around with Dirk. They stopped after making three revolutions. Dirk opened the lid and a small leopard crawled out of the basket.

Matt whispered to Richard and asked, "Does our show need some of those girls?" Richard did not answer but Matt received an elbow from Sarah who was sitting to the left of him. Sarah looked at Matt and gave him a mean stare.

Next, there was a chamber with glass walls lowered. The walls of the chamber were covered with a sheet. Dirk walked over to the chamber carrying a long pole with a flame on the end of it. He put the pole inside the chamber for a few seconds and set the floor of the chamber on fire. A sheet dropped and there was a Bengal tiger inside the box.

Matt asked Richard softly, "What do you think so far?"

Richard answered with one word, "Phenomenal."

Matt added, "We should go talk to him after the show. Please promise you won't show off."

The show continued and again there was a glass wall chamber hanging from the ceiling. Dirk went over to the chamber and walked around it and snapped his fingers. A sheet dropped down blocking the view of the chamber from the audience. Dirk waved his hand and the sheet dropped down allowing the audience to see a tiger inside.

Dirk then walked over to a six-foot rectangular box that one of his assistants was sitting on. The girl got off the box and Dirk opened it, tilted it forward, and then closed it again. He walked a little to the right and waved both arms in the direction of the suspended chamber holding the tiger. There was a small explosion and the tiger was transferred to the box.

Sean was watching intently and enjoying the show. He couldn't help but want to find out how this magic was being done. Sean took a pen and wrote on his drink napkin, 'Do you know how he does this?' He then slid the napkin over to Richard.

Richard looked at the napkin, turned it over, and slid it back to Sean. Sean took the napkin and all that was on it was the word Later.

The show continued and there was some staging upfront set up covered with a red sheet. Dirk Arthur walked over and tapped his hand on one of the supports of the staging and the red sheet fell and there was a helicopter. The audience was clapping again.

Sarah was clapping and she whispered in Matt's ear, "I wish Denise was here to see this."

Matt leaned over and asked, "Do you want me to tell Richard you said that?"

Sarah shook her head back and forth to indicate 'no'

Next, Dirk Arthur announced that he was going to show a film about the care of the animals. The film played and showed a black panther and a snow leopard playing together. Dirk was narrating in the background explaining how some of the animals are an endangered species. He continued with the narration showing a trainer and him running around with the cats.

Right across the film were the words 'DIRK ARTHUR HAS LONG BEEN AN ADVOCATE FOR THE PRESERVATION OF WILDLIFE.' The film ended a few minutes later.

The film stopped playing and Dirk Arthur came down the stairs off the stage and said to the audience, "At this time, I'd like to pick out someone from the audience to assist me." Dirk walked over and picked a little girl named Becky. Dirk reached behind him and took a small bucket off the stage that had a lid. Dirk said to Becky, "Please put your hand inside and make sure the bucket is empty." Dirk lifted the lid and Becky put her hand inside and fished around to prove it was empty.

Dirk then handed Becky a black wand and asked her to tap the bucket on top. Becky tapped the lid and then gave the wand back to Dirk. Dirk said, "Becky, please look inside one more time." Becky lifted the lid, looked inside, and smiled. Dirk asked Becky, "Is it still empty?"

Becky smiled and answered, "No, there's a bunny in there."

Dirk replied, "Ah, see what you did with the magic wand? Just because you were such a great helper, I want to give you this magic coloring book."

Becky took the coloring book and said, "Thank you." Then she returned to her seat.

Dirk asked the audience, "Are you ready for more?"

Before the audience could answer he ran over to the center of the stage and there was another glass chamber. One of his assistants brought over a straitjacket and two of the girls fastened it on him. He then ducked down and got into the glass chamber.

A red sheet dropped down blocking the audience's view to the chamber. A few seconds later a lion was sitting in the chamber that Dirk ducked into. Dirk escaped from the straitjacket and he was out of the box. He came out to the center and escorted the lion off the stage.

A few minutes later the curtain opened and there was a white Lamborghini on the stage. Dirk went over to it and raised his arms a little with his palms face down. The car rose a few feet. Dirk went up the steps to the car. He opened the driver's side door and got in. The car was floating with Dirk inside. Dirk was inside the car and it went higher. He waved bye to the audience as it went out of sight.

The house lights came on indicating the show was over. There was an announcement from the theater, "We hope you enjoyed Xtreme Magic. Dirk Arthur will be in the lobby if you want to say Hello on the way out."

Matt asked Sarah, "Do you mind if we say 'Hi' on the way out?"

Sarah answered, "Oh no, you guys go ahead. I have to find the ladies' room and then Katelin and I want to look around in the casino."

They got to the lobby and Dirk Arthur was sitting on a stool greeting people as they were coming out.

Matt, Richard, and Sean stopped when they got to Dirk Arthur. Sean was the first to speak and he said, "I just want to let you know that was some great show."

Dirk replied, "Thank you. I'm glad you enjoyed it."

Matt was next to talk to Dirk. Matt added, "That was spectacular. Oh, Mr. Arthur, this is my good friend and show partner, Richard Jenkins."

Dirk put out his hand and said, "Nice to meet you. Did you like the show?"

Richard replied, "So much so if I had to describe it in one word it would be phenomenal."

Sean spoke up and said, "Hey Matt, I'm going to see if I can find the girls."

Matt replied, "Sure, we'll be along in ten minutes or so." Matt continued, "Mr. Arthur, Richard, and I have a magic and illusions show back home in Chicago."

"Really? Do you want to tell me about it?"

Richard answered, "We try to keep most of it simple. You know believable but once a month we'll introduce new fascinating material. Currently, our shows are Thursday nights and Saturday afternoons."

Dirk asked, "New material?"

Richard answered, "Well, new acts if you want to call it that. Say, if you can spare fifteen to twenty minutes, we'll be glad to give you a quick demonstration. May we borrow your stage?"

Dirk answered, "Well, actually it's the property of the Tropicana. However, I don't think they'll mind."

"Thank you so much." Richard then whispered in Matt's ear. Matt nodded and left the lobby. Richard said, "He'll be right back. Please, let's take a walk down the aisle. For you to get the full effect you need to view it from upfront here." Dirk and Richard were standing up front and Richard said, 'Let me see, one…two…three."

Matt was back and there was a minimum of sixty people following him. Richard said, "Great work Matthew. Sorry, Dirk, we require an audience. Okay, picture this I walk over to the audience and we pick out six volunteers from different locations of the theater." Matt and Richard picked six individuals. Richard then asked the volunteers, "Please, could you take out a dollar bill and hold it up in the air. Okay, now put the dollar in your front left or right pocket. Next, I want the six of you to put your hand over the pocket that has the dollar. I'm going to count to three and then you'll remove your hand and then the dollar. One…two…three, everyone please take out their dollar."

The six volunteers took their dollars out and they let out gasps of excitement. One of them said, "I'm glad I came here."

One of the other volunteers said, "Nice! My dollar just turned into a fifty."

The others let out, "Mine too."

Richard said to Dirk, "We do things like that. There's a spot of magic involved and the audience leaves happy."

Dirk said, "I see. Well, that was a bit of a surprise. Let me ask you this. Would you consider coming back tomorrow and I can have you come up here on the stage? You can do one of your acts."

Richard answered, "We'd love to."

Matt cut in and said, "Hold on a second there. Have you forgotten there are three other people with us?"

Richard answered again, "No, I have not. It seems that Katelin and Sarah have already taken a fancy to the slot machines at Bellagio. They'll be occupied for quite some time."

Matt asked Dirk, "What time do you want us here?"

Dirk answered, "How about one-fifteen. That will give us a chance to go over some things."

Matt replied, "Okay, we'll see you tomorrow."

Matt said to Richard, "So, now we have to find the others."

Richard replied, "Correction, Matthew, we have to go join the others. We know where they are. Well, I do anyway. Matt and Richard walked over to the Bellagio. Once inside they went right into the casino. Richard spotted the others first. Richard said, "There they are."

Matt and Richard arrived at where the three of them were sitting at the slot machines. He said to Sarah, "Hi honey. I have good news, actually great news."

Sarah asked, "What's your great news?"

"Dirk Arthur invited me and Richard back to his show tomorrow to perform on his stage."

Sarah said, "So what you're telling us is you're here to work. Okay, look this is our vacation too. I can understand you two want to go back to see Dirk Arthur. I'll make a deal with you. You guys go back there tomorrow but Katelin, Sean, and I want to see some other shows."

"Sure, we can do that. Which ones do you have in mind?"

"We want to see Mystere' at Treasure Island, Danny Gans at the Mirage, and Jubilee. Jubilee's right at Bally's. If you promise to behave, we can go to the later show. Some of the girls are topless in the later show."

Matt said, "I'm not much of a gambler. You three enjoy yourselves at the machines and Richard and I can go get tickets for the shows."

"Okay honey, sounds good."

While Matt and Sarah were talking Richard walked over and looked at the slot machine Sean was playing. Richard asked Sean, "Are you winning anything?"

"No, I am doing lousy. I just put in my fourth twenty."

"Oh, that's not good." Richard put his hand on the side of the machine as Sean was talking. He said to Sean, "I hope your luck changes."

Matt asked Richard, "Feel like going for another walk? We need to go buy tickets."

"Ready when you are friend."

Matt and Richard left the casino. Matt said, "Let's see we need to go to the Mirage first. That's where Danny Gans is performing."

As soon as they got to the doorway to the Bellagio Mall Sean won a thousand credits on his slot machine. Sean screamed, "Oh my God!" and he put his hand on Katelin's arm. He said, "Honey, check it out."

Katelin looked and asked, "Did you see that message flash by on the machine? It said Sean is buying dinner for the five of us."

Richard said to Matt, "We do not have to go all the way over to the Mirage. We need five tickets to see Danny Gans." Richard reached inside his coat pocket and pulled out an envelope. The envelope had the Mirage logo on the top left corner.

Richard continued, "We need four tickets for Mystere'. I will not be attending that one. Can you hold this envelope?" Richard handed Matt an envelope that had the Treasure Island logo in the upper left-hand corner. One more time Richard said, "We also need four tickets to Don Arden's Jubilee the evening version. I will not be attending that one either." Richard reached in his pocket a third time and this time pulled out an envelope that had Jubilee Theater in the upper left-hand corner. Richard added, "I think our work is done here."

"So, what do we do now?"

"What else? We go to the food court and sit down with a coffee. We can talk about what we're going to do tomorrow."

The two of them were sitting at a table having coffee. Matt asked Richard, "Can you believe it? These two coffees were almost six dollars."

Richard answered, 'That's a good way to put a damper on a vacation. Our coffees are almost gone. Let me get us another one." Richard walked up to the counter.

An employee asked, "Can I help you?"

Richard answered, "Yes, can I get two large coffees, one regular and one black."

The girl behind the register replied, "You sure can. That'll be $5.94"

Richard asked, "How much?" When he asked the girl, he was staring directly at her eyes."

She said, "Oh, that'll be a dollar-fifteen."

Richard responded with, "That's what I thought you said." He handed the girl two dollars and told her to keep the change. Richard took the coffees and went back to the table where Matt was waiting.

Richard sat down and said, "I got us a discount on the coffee. You still owe me a dollar. Let's see, what are we going to do tomorrow at Dirk's show? Matthew, once again, I saved the day."

"Why, because you got us a discount on the coffee?"

"No, because I just thought of what we'll do tomorrow at the show. We did this together some time ago. You made the whole front row disappear for a few minutes."

"You mean you made the front row disappear. I was there taking the credit. I wouldn't have been able to do that if you weren't there."

Matthew, that part doesn't matter. I noticed the way the audience is set up. The front is different from the theater in Chicago. In this theater, there are small tables that seat four people. This allows us to impress Dirk Arthur. He's going to ask us what we want to do. I'll tell him it's going to be a surprise. All we ask of him is that he shakes the hands of the individuals sitting at the front tables. This will prove to him that the people up front are real and it's just not some hologram the audience is seeing."

329

The five of them left for the Mirage Theater to see Danny Gans at 7:30. The show went on for almost two hours. The show featured Danny singing while doing impressions. He was very good. The five of them were outside the Mirage by nine-forty.

Matt asked, "What's next?"

Katelin jumped in and asked, "Can we go to the Botanical Gardens? It's in the Bellagio."

Matt, Sarah, and Sean all agreed, "Sure. Why not."

Matt asked Richard, "Are you up for a stroll to see the flower works?"

Richard answered, "Sure, I can grab a coffee at the pastry shop. It's right outside the Gardens. The group walked through the gardens and Richard said, "I'll be right back. Don't wait for me."

Richard walked over to the Jean-Philippe Patisserie pastry shop. He was only in the mood for a coffee. Richard saw the price of coffee on a board in the shop and he thought to himself, 'This is worse than the other place.' He knew exactly what to do.

Richard approached the counter and an employee with the name badge Raphael stepped forward and asked, "Can I help you?"

Richard answered, "Yes, I want a large black coffee. I tell you what I will show you two different card tricks right here and then you decide what you want to charge me for the coffee."

Raphael's manager was in the background and said, "Excuse me, sir, if you want to show us some card tricks, that's all well and good but someone is paying for the coffee."

Richard heard this and he thought to himself, 'Looks like we have to use the plan from earlier.' He asked the manager, "How much are the coffees?"

The manager was wearing an apron with a name badge pinned to it. The badge had Heather on it. Heather answered, "It'll be a dollar-fifteen for the two coffees, sir."

Richard placed two dollars on the counter and said, "Thank you, Heather. Keep the change." Richard went and caught up with the others and said, "Sorry, there was a difference of opinion over there.

But everything is good now. Look, I hate to be a party bomb but it's a little after ten and a bed and pillow are calling my name."

Sarah replied to Richard, "Go back to the hotel. We won't be that far behind you."

The Next Day: Wednesday, April 20th

Matt and Richard went to the Tropicana and arrived there a little before one-fifteen. Matt said to Richard, "I hope Mr. Arthur didn't change his mind."

Richard asked, "Why would he do that? All we're doing is showing him we're capable of putting on a good performance. Hopefully, he'll be waiting for us near the entrance so we don't have to go looking for him."

Matt said, "There he is."

Dirk said, "Hello. You're right on time. So why don't we just go down to the front of the theater and you can describe what you want to do."

Matt and Richard followed Dirk down to the front and Richard did the talking. He said, "Okay, we want you to help us with this. We want you to take a couple of minutes before you introduce us and shake hands with the audience sitting at the tables up front."

Dirk asked, "Okay, aside from being friendly, what is that for?"

Matt cut in and said, "That's going to prove to you and the rest of the audience that the sixteen people in the front are genuine and just not some hologram. At first, we thought we would surprise you. We plan to make the four tables disappear audience members included."

Dirk responded with, "Sounds great. How does it work?"

Richard added, "Sorry, we keep that to ourselves."

Dirk added, "I can respect that. I didn't let you two in on any of my secrets yesterday. Will the others be stopping by today?"

Matt answered, "I think they're still in the hotel."

Dirk offered, "You can call the hotel and talk to your wife. Tell her they're more than welcome to see the show on me. They just need to go to the box office and tell them Dirk said to say, 'Code name, Willie.' That'll get them in for free."

Matt asked, "How did you come up with Willie?"

Dirk answered, "Willie is the name of my Bengal tiger. He is three years old now."

Twenty-Five Minutes Later

Extreme Magic got underway as Dirk Arthur made a grand entrance. A prop was brought out to the center of the stage. The object was approximately four feet high and resembled an extra-large vase. There were also two showgirls on each side of the vase. Dirk tilted the vase to one side and gave the audience proof the vase was empty.

The two girls and Dirk turned the vase around a few times. They stopped after they made three revolutions. Dirk opened the lid and a leopard crawled out to the top and jumped off the edge of the vase. The audience clapped for a few minutes until Dirk ran over to the side of the stage.

Forty-five minutes into the show Dirk announced that he was going to show a film about the care of the animals. The film played and showed a black panther and a snow leopard playing together. Dirk was narrating in the background explaining how some of the animals are an endangered species. He continued with the narration showing a trainer and him running around with the cats.

Right across the film were the words: DIRK ARTHUR HAS LONG BEEN AN ADVOCATE FOR THE PRESERVATION OF WILDLIFE.' The film stopped a couple of minutes later.

Fifteen minutes after the film was done playing Dirk said to the audience, "Ladies and gentlemen, right now I want to bring out two gentlemen I met yesterday. This is Matt White and Richard Jenkins. They told me they wanted the opportunity to show you some magic.

Dirk went off the stage down to the audience and shook hands with the people at the four tables in front. Then he went off to the side out of sight.

Matt and Richard moved to the center and Matt said, "Ladies and gentlemen thank you for bearing with us and allowing us the time to show you this."

Richard cut in and said, "At this time we'll be needing participation from the audience. We want to send the group of people from the tables in the front on a small journey. Please you're not to worry. We'll get you back safely, I think. So please if the sixteen of you will just close your eyes momentarily."

As soon as Richard finished talking Matt waved his right arm above the two tables on the right and then Richard did the same on the left. They stopped waving their arms the sixteen people and tables were gone. There was a buzzing coming from the crowd.

Matt picked out someone from the audience in the third row and asked them. "Can you join us up here?"

The man said, "Okay, but I don't want to disappear."

Matt added, "You don't have to. I just want you to walk up towards Richard." The volunteer walked in the direction of Matt and then over to Richard. Matt continued, "You do realize you just walked through where the tables were. Thank you for your help, sir. You may return to your seat."

It was Richard's turn to chime in. "I think it's time they come back." Richard waved his arm down by his side and Matt did the same on the right side. The four tables and sixteen people from the audience were back where they started. The audience clapped for almost five minutes.

Matt and Richard both took a small bow and waved to the audience. Dirk came back and yelled out, "How about that? Please give it up one more time for Matt White and Richard Jenkins." Dirk added, "Okay, let's continue."

Dirk performed an illusion involving a lion. After that, Dirk said, "Ladies and gentlemen we have time for just one more, so let's do it." The curtain opened and there was a box on the stage in the shape of an old-fashioned coffin. There was suspenseful music playing in the background. One of Dirk's assistants escorted him up a few steps alongside the wooden box. Dirk got to the top step and lowered himself inside.

The suspenseful music was still playing.

Ten Seconds Later

There was an explosion on the stage and a smokescreen as a result of the explosion. The smoke cleared and Dirk was nowhere in sight.

There was a 'Hey' noise coming from the back and Dirk was standing on one of the tables. Dirk stepped down from the table and shook hands with a member of the audience. The crowd went wild with applause.

A few minutes later the house lights came on indicating the show was over. There was an announcement from the theater, "We hope you enjoyed Xtreme Magic. Dirk Arthur will be in the lobby if you want to say Hello on the way out."

The audience filed out and some of them stopped and said Hi to Dirk. Matt and Richard were waiting near the front of the theater. Matt said to Richard, "We should go over there to say thanks for letting us be part of the show."

Richard replied, "Okay, get ready for him to tell us he wants to see more."

"What do you mean? More of what?"

They took their time to get to the line heading out to the lobby. They were in the back of the line and there was Dirk on the stool. Dirk said, "Hey, thanks again for coming by. I thought you guys were great. I want to see more."

Matt and Richard both looked at each other. Matt said, "Here's the thing. This is the vacation that my wife and I waited to take."

Dirk replied, "I see. Have you ever been to Hoover Dam?"

"No, I haven't. I'm sure Sarah and the others would love to do that."

Dirk continued, "This is what you do. Go back and tell them about the idea and I can give you five free tickets to get into Hoover Dam. Would you at least consider coming back tomorrow? You have to give me a chance to figure out how you made those people disappear."

Richard cut in and said, "Excuse me, Mr. Arthur. I would love to come back and work with you again. However, I'm afraid you're not going to figure out how we did our act today."

Matt added, "Dirk, if Richard comes by tomorrow, you're getting the best and I mean that. I have to tell you something." Matt looked at Richard and Richard nodded, "If it wasn't for Richard, I'd have no show back home."

Dirk responded, "Hmmm, I think I understand."

Richard added, "Here, Mr. Arthur, let me show you this, and then we'll leave." Richard pulled a deck of cards out of his coat pocket. He told Dirk, "Take the cards, look at them, and then give them a good shuffle." Dirk took the cards, looked at them, and then shuffled them a few times. Richard continued, "I'm going to hold the cards fanned out so you can see them. You're going to pick out a card and put it face down on the table. I'm going to guess the card you pick."

Dirk took out a card and put it face down as instructed. He thought he took the jack of hearts but he was in for a surprise.

Richard continued, "I hope you're ready. You picked the king of spades."

"Sorry, that's not right."

"Then please turn the card over so I can see where I went wrong." Dirk turned the card over and it was the king of spades."

"See. What did I tell you? He can do anything."

Dirk replied, "That card trick was impressive. Matt, Richard, I have to go back and take care of some things before the four o'clock show. I hope you'll consider coming back tomorrow. Even if you want to do some card tricks, I'm assuming you can do others."

Richard shot back, "Your assumption is quite accurate, to say the least. Mr. Arthur, I accept your invitation. With your permission, I can help you make your show even better than it is now."

Dirk responded by saying, "Mr. Jenkins, you sound like a man with conviction and great determination."

Matt cut in and said, "We have to go, oh, and at least one of us will see you tomorrow."

Three-Forty-Five That Afternoon

On the way out of the Tropicana, Matt said to Richard, "I hope Sarah's not upset about me being gone so long."

Richard offered, "Nonsense, they're in the casino right now having a grand old time. It seems Sarah has just won sixteen hundred credits on the slots. I believe that's four hundred dollars. Am I right?"

"Oh yes, you're right. Do you think she has a lucky machine today?"

"No, it's her turn today."

Matt asked, "What do you mean it's her turn?"

Richard answered, "I fixed it so one day Sean would win big on one of the machines, then Sarah, and then Katelin. This keeps the three of them in a good mood. I also thought it out and the day that Sarah is winning big, Katelin and Sean are breaking even. Tonight, the four of you are going to Treasure Island to see Mystere'. That is one of the Cirque du Soleil shows. You'll enjoy that."

Matt replied, "I wish you were coming with us."

"It is not necessary to worry about me. I can keep myself occupied. So, if you don't mind, I would like to return to my room and close my eyes for a few minutes. Matt, please go join the others, I'll be fine."

Within a few minutes, Richard changed the plan of going back to the room to rest his eyes. He was walking on the south side of Las Vegas Boulevard. The sidewalk was loaded with possible spectators.

He thought to himself, 'This is a smorgasbord. It's time to start showing off.'

Richard stopped when he reached a good spot to lean against. He pulled out a deck of cards, removed them from the box and put the box back in his pocket. Richard took five of the cards and threw them up in the air. The cards went up in the air about ten feet and stayed there for a few seconds.

A couple was walking by and they witnessed Richard throwing the cards. The cards came back down and Richard caught them. The couple stopped and the man asked Richard, "Excuse me, how did you do that?"

Richard answered, "Oh, I was just testing my cards. I love doing card tricks and every deck I use contains five or six lucky cards. I caught all those before they hit the ground so I know they must be my lucky cards."

The man asked Richard, "Can you show us a card trick? Oh, my name is Eric by the way and this is my wife Ellen."

Richard came back, "It's a pleasure to meet you. My name is Richard. Here Eric, take my cards and give them a good shuffle. Then place seven cards in Ellen's hand face down. Ellen, do not look at the cards yet." Richard pulled out a folded-up piece of paper from his coat pocket. He continued, "I am going to write down the seven cards you put in Ellen's hand. One more thing, Eric I am not using a marked deck."

Eric shuffled the cards a few times and then dealt seven cards in Ellen's waiting hand. Eric said, "Okay, I did my part."

Richard replied, "Very good, here are my guesses. Please compare them to the cards in your wife's hand."

Eric opened Richard's paper. Richard wrote these card values on the paper: two of diamonds, ace of diamonds, six of clubs, nine of clubs, eight of spades, seven of hearts, and ten of hearts. Eric was looking at Richard's paper and comparing it to Ellen's cards. Not only did Richard's guesses match but they lined up in the order that was in Ellen's hand.

Ellen said, "That was incredible. How could you do that?"

Eric jumped in and said, "Richard, we're here this week because our fifteen-year-old son is at a video game convention. He is at the Paris Convention Center and he would love to see this kind of stuff."

Richard responded, "Eric it is almost four-thirty. What time does your son finish up at the convention?"

"I believe he said he'd be done by five-thirty today."

"Very well, the other members of my party are going to a show at Treasure Island. I am not going with them. I can meet you at the food court at Bally's around six-fifteen."

Ellen jumped in and said, "That's perfect. We'll treat you at the food court."

"Thank you, but that won't be necessary. Just bring your son."

Six-Ten

Richard was sitting at a high-top table with a coffee in front of him. It was six-fifteen and he spotted Eric, Ellen, and their son walking toward him. Richard stood up and put his empty coffee cup in the barrel.

Eric said to Richard, "Thank you for meeting us here. This is our son."

Richard put out his hand before Eric could say, Daniel. Richard said, "It's nice to meet you, Dan. Your parents told me earlier you like seeing card tricks."

Dan replied, "That's true. I saw someone on tv doing some card tricks. I don't remember his name and I thought to myself, 'I wish I could do that."

Richard replied, "Let's do this, I can spend roughly forty-five minutes here. So, the first thirty minutes will be for showing you and the last fifteen will be instructional."

Ellen jumped in and asked, "Can you show us that one again that you did earlier?"

Richard answered, "I don't think so. You already saw that. That won't be entertaining for you. So, let's do this. Wait, wait, sorry."

Richard pulled a fifty-dollar bill out of his pocket and he asked Eric, "Did you tell me you were itching to go over to Sbarro's and pick up a couple of pizzas?"

Eric answered, "Say no more but please put that back in your pocket. It's on me."

Richard continued, "Okay Dan, take these cards and look them over. Give them a good shuffle. Let me know when you're ready."

Dan shuffled the cards a few times and said, "Okay."

Richard continued, "Now, go through the deck and take out any card you want. Do not show it to me. Put that card face down on the table and to make things more interesting take this pad and pen and write your card on it."

Dan took out one card as instructed and he wrote it down on the pad. He placed his card and the pad face down on the table. Dan said, "Okay, all set."

Richard continued, "Okay Dan, I'm going to tell you the card you picked. You pulled out the jack of hearts."

Dan came back, "Sorry, that wasn't it."

Richard put up a finger and said, "Usually I get that on the first guess. Please turn your card over so I can see where I went wrong."

Dan turned his card over and he had a puzzled look on his face. The card he turned over was the jack of hearts. Dan said, "I swear I had a different card. I wrote the ten of clubs on the pad. Let's check that." Dan turned the pad over it had the jack of hearts on it.

Richard said, "Hmmm, you think maybe you're playing too many video games? Just kidding. Here let me show you one more and then I'll show you something you can take with you." Richard took another deck of cards out of his pocket. He took them out of the box and put less than half of them to the side.

Richard continued, "We won't be needing those. Okay, Dan, I'm going to deal you out some cards face down in front of you. Don't look at them until I tell you to. Now, I'm going to lay some out face up in front of me. I want you to look at my cards and think of one but don't tell me the card. Let me know when you're ready."

Dan responded. "Okay, got one."

Richard scooped up the cards that we're in front of him and he laid them back out. Richard continued, "Okay Dan, what card were you thinking of?"

Dan answered, "The Ace of spades and it's not there."

"Okay Dan, look at the cards that are face down in front of you."

Dan turned the cards over and there was the ace of spades. Dan said, "WOW! That was pretty good."

Richard continued, "Let me show you this one and you can take this with you." Richard took out a different deck of cards. He riffled through the cards and said, "Dan, you see the cards going by and you can see they're all different."

"Okay."

"Now, I want you to cut the deck in half and when you lift off the half, I need you to show me the bottom card of your cut and then hand me the top half." Dan cut the cards and held the top half so Richard could see the bottom card. He then handed that portion of cards to Richard. Richard continued, "Dan now look at the top card of the bottom pile. Do not show it to me. Now I'm going to put the top half back on and just push down with my finger. Now, look at the top card."

Dan looked at the top card and said, "Hey, that's the card that was in the middle. That was pretty neat too."

Richard added, "Dan, you can keep these cards. It's the least I can do. Your dad brought pizza over here for us. We'll have a slice and then I'll teach you how to do the trick."

The group left the hotel at nine-forty-five and went to Madame Tussaud's Wax Museum. Sean spoke up and asked, "Time for the big question, how are we getting there?"

Sarah answered, "I don't see why we can't walk. It's not that far and the walk will be good exercise."

Katelin jumped in, "I'm for that. Can we stop at the coffee station?"

Richard volunteered, "I'll go ahead and get us five coffees."

Katelin offered, "I'll go with you. I have some money." They both got on the elevator and went down to the lobby. Once in the elevator, Katelin said, "I am so glad it's not super-hot out here."

Richard replied, "I think we picked the right month. When we get to the coffee station let me place the order and do not open your bag."

"Why don't you want me to open my bag?"

"Because then you'd proceed to extract money from it and that's not necessary. Besides, the girl at the coffee station knows me."

"So, what does that mean?"

They got to the coffee station and Richard asked, "Hello! Can we get four medium and one large black coffee?"

Maria from behind the counter answered, "Sure thing. That'll be two dollars."

Richard handed Maria three dollars and said, "Thank you." He looked at Katelin and said, "That's what it means."

Twenty Minutes Later

The group spent an hour in the wax museum and then Sarah asked Matt if they could go in the Grand Canal Shoppes and go for a ride on the gondolas. The five of them walked into the front entrance of the Venetian and walked into the Canal Shops.

They found the entrance to the gondola rides. Richard said to Matt, "I just paid for the tickets for four. You have a good time. I believe I just spotted a goldmine playground for me in the mall. The Houdini Magic Shop is over there. I will visit them first and then go to see Mr. Arthur."

Matt responded, "Okay, have a good time. I'm sure we'll see you later in the room, maybe?"

Matt, Sarah, Sean, and Katelin were in the line to get on the gondolas. Richard went to the Houdini Magic Shop he started looking around. The wall on the left side of the store was loaded with card tricks and other novelty items on peg hooks. There was a woman behind the counter and she asked, "Can I help you, sir?"

Richard answered, "Yes, I am looking for some playing cards."

"Okay, we have the Blank Deck, Locked Deck, Wonder Deck, and we have this new one called the Mind Control Deck."

"WOW! You have a nice selection of trick cards and other novelty items. I'll take one of these Blank Decks, the Mind Control Deck, and a couple of ordinary playing cards. I find those just as useful."

The clerk went to ring up the order and she asked, "How do you want to pay?"

Richard answered, "I prefer to use this." He pulled out a few twenty-dollar bills.

She said, "That works; that'll be $46.75 with the tax. Can I ask you a question?"

"Of course, ask anything you want."

"Why do you think the regular playing cards are just as good or as you put it as useful?"

"Okay, let me show you." Richard put three more dollars on the counter from his coat pocket and said, "I'll need another deck of cards."

Sharon put the cards on the counter and Richard continued, "With a new deck of regular cards I have the option of asking the spectator in this case you to examine the cards taking note they should be in suit order. I can't do that with the other cards that are all set up. Here let me show you something. We'll use my new cards. Take any two cards you want out of the deck. Now, put one card back in the box and put the other card in your pocket. Here you can take my receipt and write on the back of it the card you put in the box."

Sharon put one of the cards in her pocket; put one in the box and wrote on the back of the receipt as instructed. She left the receipt on the counter face down. She asked, "Okay, next?"

"I'm going to tell you the card you put in your pocket and the one you put in the box. Are you ready?"

"I'm ready."

"Okay, jack of hearts in the box and you put the king of spades in your pocket."

Sharon made a sad face and said, "Nice try, but not the right ones."

Richard said, "Okay, sorry you got me. How about taking that card out of the box and your pocket and show me your cards?"

Sharon took the card from her pocket and it was the king of spades. She opened the box and let her card fall out. It was the jack of hearts. She turned the receipt over and it had the jack of hearts written on it. Sharon's mouth was hanging open as if she saw a ghost.

Richard said, "It looks like my guesses were correct."

Sharon responded, "I'll say. You have to teach me how to do that."

"Ummm, no I don't Have a nice day. Thank you for your time. "

Richard left the Grand Canal Shoppes and headed back in the direction of the hotel room. Once in the room he sat down for a few minutes and closed his eyes. What Richard thought would be a few minutes turned out to be a little more than an hour. He looked at the clock on the nightstand and it was already twelve-forty.

Richard knew Extreme Magic was at two o'clock. He stood up and put his coat back on. Richard wrote Matt a note and stepped out of the room. One minute later he was at the doorway of the Tropicana. Richard opened the door and made his way over to the theater. He walked into the theater from the doors at the top. There was an usher in the theater moving seats around the table.

The usher said, "Excuse me, sir, if you're here for the show we start seating at one-thirty."

Richard replied, "I am looking for Mr. Arthur. I believe he is expecting me."

Dirk Arthur came around from the stage and said, "Hey! I thought I heard voices. How are you?"

"I am doing well. Thank you for asking. I have something you can add to the show today and I think it will impress the audience."

"Good, what do you have?"

"Okay, first thing, you know the pause in your show where the screen comes down and there's a film playing about the cats?"

"Yes."

"Okay, after the film is done, you're going to walk through the audience with one of the cats, a leopard perhaps."

Dirk replied, "One question," and then asked, "Have you been drinking? You must have seen how the cats are always pulling on the lead."

"Then I suggest you bring me out back and show me the cat you wouldn't mind bringing out."

"Okay, come on. I hope you're not squeamish with things like this."

Dirk and Richard walked out back to where Dirk had the cats. Dirk pointed to two leopards, a white snow and a black one. "I always get the big lion in there too. He shows up in one of the cages. I'll be right back."

Dirk went to put water in some bowls and when he came back Richard had one of the gates open and he was patting the white snow leopard on the head. Dirk got nervous and without getting too loud he asked, "What are you doing?"

"I am just talking to one of the co-stars of the show. She already assured me she'll be on her best behavior when you walk her through the audience."

"Okay. Please be careful over there. I don't want you to get bitten." Dirk walked over got the cat to back up into the cage. He closed the door. "Okay, let me ask you, are you one hundred percent sure I can bring the cat through the audience?"

"I am so sure of it. If anything, even starts to go wrong I will be there. Also, as a gesture of goodwill, I will donate my services to you free for the next three weeks."

"Okay, are you joining me today?"

"Today, I'm here to observe. Maybe tomorrow, I can be up there with you."

Two O'clock

Extreme Magic started right at two o'clock. A prop was brought out that was about four feet high and resembled an extra tall vase. Dirk Arthur had an assistant up there with him standing behind the vase. Dirk lowered the vase to a forty-five-degree angle to show the audience the vase was empty. Dirk then put the lid back on and then Dirk and his assistant turned the vase around three times. Dirk opened the lid and a leopard crawled out to the top and jumped off the edge of the vase. Dirk grabbed an end of the leash and escorted the leopard off the stage. The audience clapped for a few minutes.

Next, there was a glass box lowered onto the floor. Dirk walked over to the glass box holding a long pole. He tapped the pole on the floor and a flame came out of the top. Dirk put the pole in the box and took it out three times to set the floor of it on fire. An off-white sheet fell and blocked the view of the box. A few seconds later the sheet fell to the floor. The flames were no longer there and there was a Bengal tiger inside. The audience gave a resounding applause.

The show continued and again there was a cage hanging from the ceiling. Dirk walked over to where the cage was hanging. He pointed up at the cage. Dirk waved his arm and a sheet dropped down blocking the audience's view of the cage. Dirk waved his arm and the sheet dropped again and there was a tiger in the cage.

Dirk walked over to the left side of the stage. There was an eight-foot rectangular box and Dirk lifted the lid. Dirk and his assistant tilted the box forward so the audience could see it was empty. Dirk then put the lid down. Dirk turned and went a little to the right where the suspended cage was. He pointed at the suspended cage. One second later there was a small explosion and the tiger disappeared from the cage and reappeared in the box. The audience loved it.

Forty-five minutes into the show Dirk announced he was going to show a film about the care of the animals. The film started and a black panther and a snow leopard were playing together. Dirk was narrating in the background and explained how some of the animals are an endangered species. He continued with the narration and it showed Dirk and a trainer running around with the cats.

Across the film were the words: DIRK ARTHUR HAS LONG BEEN AN ADVOCATE FOR THE PRESERVATION OF WILDLIFE.

Dirk walked off to the side where Richard was watching and Dirk asked him, "What do you think so far?"

Richard answered, "Looks good so far. I'm going to stay here while you escort the leopard through the audience. Then. I'm going to head out. I think you need to take something out of the show and put something different in there. This way you won't lengthen the show but you'll mix things up a little so all your shows are not the same. This works for me and Mr. White back in Chicago."

Dirk came back with, "Okay, I'll consider that. I have to get a cat."

Dirk went and took the leopard out of the back. He said to the audience, "Ladies and gentlemen, this is Priscilla. She is three years old. I'm going to bring her through the audience. Please, no sudden outbursts." Dirk walked Priscilla through and then brought her out to the cages in the back.

Dirk passed by Richard on the way to the cage. On the way back Richard said to Dirk, "I see that went off without any problems. I'll be back tomorrow at noon."

"Sounds great," came from Dirk.

The Next Day: Friday, April 22nd

Katelin, Matt, Richard, Sarah, and Sean gathered at the food court around nine-forty-five. Matt asked, "So what's the plan for today?"

Sean spoke up and asked, "Is anybody here interested in going to Fremont Street? It's supposed to be the original Las Vegas. There's a light show above Fremont Street that is in sync with the music."

Matt added, "That sounds like fun. We can see what some of the older casinos look like."

Sarah joined in and said, "We should check out Tony Roma's. It says here, they have dinners for $8.95."

Katelin asked, "Would anybody mind if we walk around the Miracle Mile Shops?"

Matt jumped in and answered, "I'm game. I might need to get a second coffee while I'm in there."

The five of them left the food court and cut through the Paris Casino to go to the Miracle Mile Shops. As soon as they opened the door to the mall an employee tried to approach them about buying timesharing. Richard said, "Please, I'll take care of this. Excuse me miss; nobody is interested in time-sharing today. I hope you understand."

The woman replied, "Yes, I do. Then she put her clipboard and brochures down.

The group ventured further into the mall. Matt saw the Nestle Toll House Shop in the corner and asked, "Anyone else?" Matt ended up getting three coffees for him, Richard, and Sean.

There was a store on the left called Swarovski's. Sarah said, "I have to go in here."

Matt thought to himself, 'Oh boy.'

Sean spoke up and said, "These people aren't stupid. This store is one of the first ones you get to. This way you didn't have a chance to spend your money yet."

Matt came back, "Well put Sean."

They spent about fifteen minutes in Swarovski's and ventured further on. They came upon an intersection and there were a couple of food places and a small theater. Richard took Matt by the arm and said, "They're calling me."

Matt asked, "Who?" Then he looked over and there was another Houdini Magic Shop.

Richard said, "I have to go in. Come on."

Matt said to Sarah, "Richard and I are going to the Houdini store. We'll catch up to you."

Sarah replied, "Oh no. We'll come with you."

The group of them walked into the shop and Richard was looking around. He said, "Excuse me," and asked, "Do you have any playing cards? However, I prefer the ones that are regular ordinary cards."

The clerk from behind the counter asked, "You don't like these?"

"No, because when you take say the Wonder Deck you are limited to what you can do. Okay, first off, I want four decks of cards."

The clerk put them on a counter and Richard placed a twenty-dollar bill beside them. Then Richard said to Sean, "Do me a favor, open one of these decks, and then hand the cards to Scott."

Richard continued, "Okay Scott, these are new cards. You saw Sean open them. Now, I want you to give them a good shuffle. Then, take any card out of there you want, look at it, and put it back in the deck, but turn it over first. Don't show me your card."

Scott said, "Okay." He pulled a card from the middle of the deck. Scott asked, "Next?"

"Okay, just leave the deck right here. Now, I'm assuming you turned the card over before putting it back. I'm just going to touch the edge of the cards with my index finger." Richard touched the cards and said, "Okay, Scott, find your card."

Scott took the deck, fanned the cards open. His card was not there. Scott asked, "Alright, where did it go?"

"I think my buddy got involved again. Sean, what's in your wallet? I always wanted to ask that by the way."

Sean took out his wallet and answered, "Not much, the slots weren't that nice to me yesterday. Let me see, I have seven twenties, one five-dollar bill, and one folded up a playing card." Sean handed Richard the card.

Richard asked, "Scott, is this your card?"

"Yes. I wish I could do that."

"A lot of people do. Let me see, I just opened these cards. Let me get a new deck." Richard took more money out of his pocket.

Scott put his hand up and said, 'Take it, thanks for the entertainment."

The five of them left the store and Richard said to Matt, "I told Mr. Arthur I would be there at noon and that I'd help him today."

Matt responded, "Okay, well, we plan on going to Fremont Street. We didn't finalize a leaving time yet but I'm thinking of five- forty-five."

Richard came back. "I'll be back before then."

It was almost eleven-thirty and Richard headed towards the exit of the mall. Richard saw a long hallway on the way out. He walked down the hallway, turned around with no one in sight. Richard made himself disappear and then reappear at the back of the theater of the Tropicana.

Richard walked to the front of the theater and looked up at the ceiling. He pointed with three of his fingers causing the hanging cage to be moved to the left. Richard then pointed a second time and the hanging cage was duplicated on the right. Richard thought to himself, 'That's taken care of.'

Dirk came around from backstage and said, "I thought I heard someone walking around out here."

Richard replied, "I hope this meets your approval. There are now two suspended cages one on the left and right."

Dirk looked up and asked, "What's the purpose of that?"

"Okay, you know how a cage is lowered down slowly and then the sheet drops down?"

"Yes."

"Okay, I thought you could have two cages come down one right after another. One cage will have a tiger in it when the sheet gets dropped and the other cage will be empty. We pull the covering back up and that cage goes back up in the air. You escort the tiger out of the first cage and when you come back out the second cage comes back down and there are two tigers in it. You get them out of the cage with the help of the trainer. What do you think? It's just one different thing you can throw in. You know just like walking the leopard through the audience."

"Okay, I get it. Did you say you were leaving Saturday?'

"Yes, we are. Why?"

"Because I do not feel comfortable walking the cat through the audience if you're not here."

"Then you don't have to. It's just a suggestion. Now, today I think you should bring me out right before you run the film. I will entertain the audience with some impressive card tricks. Then. I will stick around while you bring the cat through the audience."

Two-O'clock

Extreme Magic started at two o'clock. Dirk Arthur came out and a large prop was brought to the left side of the stage. The prop was approximately four feet high and looked like an extra-large vase. One of Dirk's assistants was standing behind the vase. Dirk leaned the vase over and allowed the audience to see the vase was empty.

Dirk and his assistant turned the vase around a few times. They stopped after three revolutions. Dirk opened the lid and a leopard crawled out to the top and jumped off the edge of the vase. Dirk escorted the leopard off the stage. The audience clapped for a few minutes.

Next, Dirk ran to the center and with both hands pointed above to the left and then to the right. A cage was lowered on the left side and then another one was lowered on the right. They both had a covering around them. The covering fell on the left cage and there was a tiger inside. Dirk opened the cage and escorted the tiger off the stage. He ran by Richard and on his way back Richard said, "Don't put the cage up."

Dirk asked, "Why?"

"Just trust me, please. Just point at it like you're trying to get the audience to look in that direction."

Dirk ran back to the center and he pointed at the empty cage on the left and then the one on the right. The one on the right went up. There was a small bang and a puff of smoke the size of a basketball in front of the cage. The smoke cleared and there was a tiger in the cage. Dirk again escorted the tiger off the stage. He ran by Richard and said, "Hey, that was a great idea."

"I thought so. Get back out there." The cage on the right started coming back down. Dirk waved his arm, pointed at the cage and the covering fell and there were two tigers in it. A trainer ran out to help. Dirk opened the door. The trainer took one leash and escorted the tiger off the stage and Dirk did the same to the other one.

Five-Thirty That Evening

The five of them took two cabs to get to Fremont Street. After they got out of the cab, Sarah started, "We should go put our name in Tony Roma's." There was a ten-minute wait for a table.

The hostess had to step away from her station. Richard was going to ask her about the facilities. He asked Matt and the others. "Is everyone getting hungry?"

Katelin answered, "Yes, we didn't take time for lunch."

Sean jumped in, "In hindsight that probably wasn't a good idea."

Five minutes later, they were called to the table. They were out of Tony Roma's by six -twenty. Matt commented, "That food was very good and a great deal too."

Katelin added, "I agree with that. Does anybody know when the overhead light show starts?"

They were walking by someone operating a kiosk selling sweatshirts and light jackets. The person said, "Excuse me, the next show should be at seven."

"Thank you,' came back from Sean. Sean was looking at the sweatshirts and said, "WOW! These feel like good quality."

The woman replied, "They're a good deal but it's cash only. The sizes go up to 2XL." Sean paid for a grey hooded sweatshirt with Las Vegas lettering on it.

The light show started at seven o'clock. There were songs from Green Day, Queen, and the Who. They stayed there until almost ten-thirty and they headed back to the hotel. They got back to the hotel by ten minutes after eleven. The five of them were in the elevator and Matt said, "Okay, we'll meet downstairs at ten. We have to be at the airport by twelve."

26

Will He or Won't He?

Saturday morning at nine-forty-five

There was a rapping on Matt's hotel room door. Matt opened the door and Richard was standing there. Richard said, "Good morning Matthew. Something has come up and I'm afraid I'm not able to make that trip in the van with you. Matthew, I am sorry. I promised to help Mr. Arthur during the next three weeks. It wouldn't hurt to contact Mr. Firmani to fill in when you return home."

Matt replied, "Be careful. I want to see you in three weeks. Our flight leaves at three-ten if you change your mind."

Five Hours Later at Two-Forty-Five

Katelin, Matt, Sarah, and Sean were at the gate at McCarren International Airport. Sarah asked Matt, "Didn't Richard say he'd meet us here?"

Matt answered, "No, he didn't say that. He delivered the bad news this morning that we won't be seeing him for three weeks."

Nine-Twenty

The cab pulled up in the driveway of Matt's house. Matt paid the driver. They went to the front door with their bags and the front door opened for them. Denise was walking away from the door and said, "Hey! Welcome back." Denise was at the entrance to the living room folding a blanket she had on the couch,

Sarah replied, "Thank you. Denise you don't have to run out now. You can stay again tonight. I was looking forward to breakfast with you in the morning but one of us didn't make the flight back. However, if you don't mind me cooking, I would love for you to stay and you can fill me in on what Thomas did this past week."

The Next Morning: Sunday, April 24th

Matt came downstairs at six-thirty-five knowing he was going to have to make the coffee. He was hoping he was mistaken and he was going to see Richard in his usual spot. But he wasn't there. Matt poured his coffee and sat at the table. He thought to himself, 'I hope Richard comes back in three weeks and I know this is selfish of me but I hope he is not thrilled with working with Mr. Arthur. I miss him already. Our show isn't as good without him. Richard. Please come back home. I miss you already.'

To be continued….

Author Larry Cashman lives in Londonderry, New Hampshire. He has a son, Sean, and a daughter-in-law, Katelin. He also has two grandchildren, James and Julia, and a loving companion Lynne. This is his second attempt at writing with the Richard series.

CPSIA information can be obtained
at www.ICGtesting.com
Printed in the USA
BVHW090717150621
609530BV00009B/1687

9 781954 868335